THE GIRL IN THE CORN

JASON OFFUTT

CamCat Books

CamCat Publishing, LLC
Brentwood, Tennessee 37027
camcatpublishing.com

Hardcover ISBN 9780744304992
Paperback ISBN 9780744304473
Large-Print Paperback ISBN 9780744304480
eBook ISBN 9780744304510
Audiobook ISBN 9780744304589

Library of Congress Control Number: 2021947067

Cover and book design by Maryann Appel

5   3   1   2   4

For my sister Jodie,
whose love of spooky things equaled my own.
Miss you, sis.

Chapter One  1986

[1]

A WHISPER OF COOL MORNING air rippled the curtains of
six-year-old Thomas Cavanaugh's bedroom window, bringing with it
the sweet breath of the lilacs planted outside. The hint of cow manure lingered even after the breeze died, but the boy barely noticed;
he was used to it. He sat up in bed, his mom's soft singing drifting
into the room from the garden outside. Thomas liked it when his
mom sang, the voice somehow as sweet as the flowers' scent. He
dressed, pulling on a *He-Man and the Masters of the Universe* T-shirt
and black shorts before he bounded down the stairs and outside to
a long rectangle of a vegetable garden his dad had cut in the yard

with his tractor and field plow. Sweet corn rose in straight green stalks in that garden, as did peas, cabbages, onions, and other vegetables he pushed around his plate until his mom got tired of waiting for him to eat and took them away. Strawberries were Thomas's favorite, but his mom had yet to work her way to the berry patch at the end of the garden.

She knelt in the rows of green beans that grew closest to the house, her floppy straw hat hiding her short blonde hair, some song from the radio on her lips as she pulled weeds with hands covered with big leather gloves.

Thomas knelt in the garden, just like his mom, but he didn't pull weeds. "Sometimes it's hard to tell the good plants from the bad plants, Tommy," his dad had explained when Thomas asked to help. Yesterday, the day before, last week? Thomas didn't remember. He liked to help, and if his mom had to pull those awful weeds (they must be awful if she wanted them gone), Thomas wanted to do that too. Today, though, Thomas simply waited quietly for his mom to work her way from the green beans through the sweet corn and to the strawberries.

Sunlight shone through drops of dew hanging from the corn leaves—tiny, fragile diamonds. Thomas held his face close enough to the drops he could see their light split into colors. To him, they were magic.

"I call you on the phone, but you're not there . . ." His mom's singing came softly through the sweet corn. She was closer now. "I sit at home alone and wonder where." A smile slid across Thomas's face. She always sang in the garden. If she sang, she was happy, and if she was happy, she might let him eat a few strawberries without even washing them.

"Can't eat or sleep, I miss your touch . . ."

Clouds gathered over the garden from seemingly nowhere, swelling like an enormous bag of burnt microwave popcorn. The cool morning breeze was stifled, and a burst of hot air pushed against Thomas's cheek as if someone blew across his face.

The air popped, pushing against his eardrums.

"Huh?" Thomas grunted, his voice too soft for his mother to hear over her Leesa Loman song.

She didn't react to the pop, or the clouds, or the hot burst of furnace air.

"Mom?" he whispered, the word muffled as if he'd said it through a pillow.

A corn leaf to his right shook and he turned toward it; the long, blade-like leaf dipped; the sudden movement broke the dewdrop's hold on the plant, and the dew fell to the ground. Thomas froze and stared at the cornstalk, twice as tall as his six-year-old body but still too young to grow corn. His mom's song dropped into the hum she used whenever she forgot the words, but Thomas couldn't hear her anymore, not really; the world became quiet and out of focus—everything except the cornstalk.

A tiny foot stepped from behind the stalk about halfway up the plant, and settled on a leaf. The foot had no shoes; the lithe leg attached to it had no pants. His throat grew tight as a woman, a tiny woman, slowly stepped from behind the stalk, stood on the leaf, and smiled, her face radiating joy. Her smile was the only thing that kept Thomas from running.

"You've brought me pain . . ." His mom sang, but the words sounded as if she were underwater. "Why do you mean so much?"

The tiny woman—only as tall as the He-Man toys in his room—wore a shiny white dress, her hair red as a crayon. He leaned closer to look at her like he had at the dewdrop, but she stepped back to hide behind the cornstalk. He stopped and squinted. Her face was delicate and pretty. Pretty, like his mom's.

"Who are you?" Thomas whispered.

The little person pressed her fingers to her lips and shook her head.

Thomas gasped. "You're a fairy."

Gloved hands pushed through the stalks about six feet away, and his mom stepped through. Her song stopped and something popped next to Thomas; for a brief moment pressure pushed against his ears.

"Oh, Thomas," his mom said, a grin pulling at her lips as she squatted at his eye level. "When did you sneak out here? Are you ready for some strawberries?"

His gaze shot from his mom to the stalk of corn, but the little woman was no longer there.

"She's gone," he whispered.

"Who's gone, Bubby?"

He reached for the corn. Maybe she's still there. Maybe the corn is enchanted. Thomas liked that word, *enchanted*. He knew it meant magic, but it sounded even more mysterious. He touched the leaf. It was a deep green blade, streaked with parallel veins, surprisingly firm, but nonetheless just a leaf.

"Never mind," Thomas said, his voice trailing off. "Yes, I'd like some strawberries, please."

When he looked up at the sky, the clouds were gone.

[2]

The smell of hot fried chicken drifted across the table as Thomas's mom placed a platter shrouded in grease-stained paper towels in front of her husband. Mashed potatoes heaped in a Pyrex bowl decorated with orange and brown flowers sat in the middle of the table; a smaller bowl of lima beans was closer to Thomas.

"Honey, this looks wonderful," his dad said. He always said that because he was always right, and Thomas knew it. His mom's food was the best.

His dad lifted a paper towel and stuck a piece of chicken with his fork. "And I'm guessing Tommy wants a . . ."

"Thigh," Thomas said.

His dad grinned and dropped a steaming thigh on Thomas's plate. "When I was a kid, I always went for the leg, Tommy."

"There's more meat on a thigh," Thomas said, spooning lima beans onto his plate. "And it doesn't have that pointy bone thingy."

His dad laughed. Thomas loved hearing him laugh; it made the whole house sound as happy as his mom's garden singing.

His mom scooped a spoonful of mashed potatoes next to Thomas's beans, then put some on her own plate and handed the bowl to his dad. "Tommy helped me in the garden this morning," she said, then smiled. "So, we don't have any strawberries for dessert."

His dad leaned across the table toward Thomas, his elbows on either side of his plate.

"Well, it's a good thing your mother made fried chicken. I won't be hungry for dessert."

Thomas forced a smile as he stabbed beans with a fork. He'd seen something today, something that didn't exist, and his dad was talking about dessert. The little woman didn't have wings, but Thomas thought of everything she could be, and he knew what she was. He knew it, he knew it, he knew it. But he couldn't tell his mom or dad, could he? The little woman didn't want him to.

A knot began to form in his stomach. No, Thomas Cavanaugh, he scolded himself. No tummy aches today. Not with fried chicken.

He looked up from his plate at his mom and dad sitting at the short ends of the rectangular kitchen table. His dad bit a piece off a chicken breast; the golden, flaky crust pulled off most of the skin, revealing the white meat beneath. His mom took a drink of water and set her glass down.

Thomas breathed in deeply and said, "I saw a fairy in the garden today."

The clanking of forks on china died, the kitchen grew quiet. Thomas suddenly felt warm. His mom and dad's eyes were on him. He could feel them staring.

"You saw a what?" his dad asked.

Thomas's throat felt tight, and he had to pee.

"A fairy," he whispered. "In the garden."

His mom's hand gently patted Thomas's right forearm. "A fairy, honey?" she said, her voice calm, soothing. "In the garden? What did it look like?"

He looked at his mom; she was smiling. Thomas's throat relaxed, the ball in his stomach grew smaller. "Like a woman. A little woman."

"Was it a girl?" his dad asked, the chicken still in his hands. "Maybe she was lost."

Thomas shook his heads. "No. It wasn't a girl," he said, his voice stronger. "She looked like a grown-up woman. She was just little, like a doll."

"Tommy, that's just—" his dad started, then stopped. Thomas looked at his mom. Just like the fairy, he knew she'd just told his dad to be quiet.

She turned back toward Thomas. "What did she do, honey?"

Thomas's tummy felt better now. His mom believed him, maybe. It didn't matter that his dad didn't. Mom did, and she was the boss.

"She stood on a cornstalk. She made the dew drop."

His dad snorted. His mom flashed his dad a hard glance, then turned back to Thomas. "Did she say anything?"

Thomas shrugged. "No. She didn't say anything, but she told me to be quiet, like this." He put a finger over his mouth and shook his head.

His mom leaned her elbows on the table. "Why did she want you to be quiet, honey?"

It was because of his mom, but why didn't she like his mom? "She didn't want you to know she was there."

His dad opened his mouth to talk, then paused and took a bite of chicken instead.

His mom's face tensed. "Why didn't she want me to know about her?"

Thomas shrugged again. "Maybe because she thinks you're scary, I guess."

A "ha" shot from his dad's mouth; his mom turned toward him. "You're not helping, Kyle." When she looked back at Thomas, he was eating potatoes. "Then what happened, honey?"

Thomas swallowed, took another forkful of potatoes, mashing it into his lima beans.

"She was just gone. I looked at you, then when I looked back, the fairy wasn't there anymore." He pushed the food into his mouth, put his fork down, and grabbed the chicken thigh with both small hands.

"Have you ever seen the fairy before?"

Thomas shook his head and bit into the thigh; the crust crunched as his teeth sank in. His mom glanced at his dad and smiled.

"Well, a fairy," she said. "You don't see one of those every day, do you?"

She turned to Thomas, the smile never leaving her face.

[3]

His mom clicked the switch next to the door from the hallway and Thomas's bedroom became dark as charcoal. The clock on the night-stand, its digital numbers red, showed 9:00. The golden hour of early summer had gone; the sun was just dropping past the horizon out one window as the white half-moon rose in the other.

Soon the stars would shine like pinpricks on black velvet. The milking barn stood in the east window. Once bright red with a black roof, the sun-faded paint had turned pink and begun to peel, the bleached barn wood beneath exposed. An owl hooted nearby; coy-otes yipped far away.

"Can you close the window?" Thomas asked, a pull of fear com-ing from somewhere deep inside. He didn't know why it was there; the open window had never bothered him before.

His mom brushed his bangs across his forehead and smiled down at Thomas. "Don't be silly, honey. It'll get hot in here. Just leave it open, the night air will help you sleep."

"But—"

His mom bent to kiss his forehead. "Good night, baby," she whispered.

Thomas wrapped his arms around her neck and held fast. "Do you believe me?" he asked.

She smiled and brushed her hair from her eyes. "About what, baby?"

She had to believe him. Moms always believe, dads don't. "About the fairy," he said, his voice soft.

Her smile faded slightly, but she forced it to remain. Then she touched Thomas's face, her hands gentle on his skin. "I believe you believe you saw it," she said. "And that's good enough for me."

She paused, studying her son's face in the faint light. "Did it frighten you?"

Thomas shook his head. "No. She looked nice. She was pretty, like you."

His mom laughed, then kissed him again. "I'm glad she wasn't scary, but remember, not every pretty face is nice."

He thought about that before answering. "I know. Carly in my class is pretty, but she wipes boogers on my desk when Mrs. Beltram isn't looking."

His mom slowly stood. "I think Carly just likes you, but we're not talking about that yet. Good night, Tommy."

"Good night, Mom."

"Good night, champ," his dad said from the bedroom door, leaning on the door frame with his large, calloused hands shoved into his jeans pockets. His dad still had to milk the two Guernseys in the barn. Thomas liked the barn; he liked to search the loft for rusty treasures hidden under the old, dusty straw.

Thomas knew his dad didn't believe in fairies. He believed in work, sweat, and cow poop that smelled like money. His dad crossed the room to stand next to his mom, slipping his arm around her waist.

"I'm with your mother on this one," he said. "I believe you believe. Now get some sleep, you're going with me to John Deere in the morning."

Thomas's eyes opened wide. "Do I get to sit on your lap and drive?"

His dad glanced nervously at his mom and stood up straight.

"Only down our driveway," he said. "I think you've gotten me into enough trouble for one night. Now get to sleep. Love you, kiddo."

"Love you too," Thomas said, his voice trailing as sleep began to crawl over him. His parents left the room and shut off the hall light.

———⊱✷⊰———

Thomas's eyes grew accustomed to the dark, and shapes formed; some as the light had left them, others shifting in the moonlight.

Come on, Thomas thought. It's just the dark, and Mom said darkness can't hurt me.

A cloud quickly passed over the moon and a figure, tall and thin, loomed over him beside his bed.

It's the lamp, it's only the lamp, tapped through his thoughts. But the lamp looked like a man. A night bird called, and a yelp was caught in Thomas's throat. A fox yipped in the distance. Thomas kicked his feet until his blanket and sheet were balled up at the foot of his bed, his eyes on the figure that must be a lamp. It *must* be. The curtains hung motionless. The screech of the old barn's tall, heavy, sliding door came through Thomas's open window. His dad was heading inside to milk the cows, but the moos Thomas expected never came.

The cows always mooed. His dad said it felt good for them to get rid of all that milk. To them, milking was—

A light, no brighter than a toy's, shone outside his second-floor window. His neck muscles strained as he tried to look toward that light, but a feeling, like huge fingers wrapped around his head, wouldn't let him move it. He tried to pull his legs up toward him, but they wouldn't listen either. Outside, the night animals had all stopped talking.

"Hello, Thomas," a voice said, the words soft and melodic, almost as if they weren't spoken aloud. The dim room grew darker; the bright, friendly moon no longer hung in his window. The light was gone; an empty feeling dropped into his chest.

Thomas's pajamas grew wet.

I peed. No. I'm not a baby. I didn't pee in my bed. Only babies pee in their bed.

A fleeting image of his dad frowning flew through his head.

"Aren't you going to say hello back?"

"H-hello?" The word came out almost too soft to hear.

"Shh," the voice hushed. "Don't talk so loud. I can hear you. I can always hear you."

The air closed in around Thomas, squeezing. His breath came in bursts, his heart thumped with the beat of a drum. A stranger was in his room.

"Who—who are you?" A scream waited inside.

Silence commanded the night.

"You saw me today, in the garden," the voice finally said.

"I want my mom. I want my dad." A tear leaked from one eye and mingled with the sweat that crawled down his face.

A giggle echoed around the room, coming from nowhere and everywhere. The fairy. The fairy was in *his room*. The strange grip on his muscles relaxed and he sat up in bed, scanning his dresser, his shelves, his Superman poster, looking for the fairy. The knot in his stomach was back.

"Go away," he wanted to say, but the words never made it past his thoughts.

"You're special, Thomas," the fairy said, the giggle tainting each word. "So special I want to show you to everyone. Will you come with me? There's something you need to help me find."

The air weighed on his chest, compacting the scream waiting deep inside into nothing more than a squeak.

"Go away."

"You don't want me to go away, Thomas," she said. "You want to follow me."

He'd wanted to go with her today in the garden. To grab the enchanted cornstalk and follow her to Fairyland, but that was in the light of morning, with his mom singing a Leesa Loman song, not in the dark when Thomas was alone and soaked with pee.

He shook his head. "No."

The fairy laughed this time, the sound harsh. Despite the heat, Thomas's body shivered.

"I need you, Thomas."

"I'm just a kid," Thomas whispered, his eyes searching the room for the fairy that belonged to the voice.

"I'm by the window," the voice said. "When you leave a window open, you never know what may come in."

Then he saw her. The tiny woman stood on Thomas's toy shelf, next to Skeletor's Snake Mountain hideout. She didn't look bad, but his mom was right—not every pretty face was nice. At the fairy's feet, a pastry layered like a cake sat atop one of his mom's good plates. Something curled at the top of the pastry; Thomas thought it might be chocolate. His stomach rumbled.

"Yes, it is chocolate, Thomas." She paused, though her voice sounded urgent, like when his mom tried to hurry his dad for church. When she spoke again, the softness had returned, the weight of the air lifted. "I know you like chocolate. Just take a bite. One bite, then you will understand everything."

No. No. No. Something inside told Thomas this was wrong.

"No thank you," Thomas said, his words louder, trying hard to gain control. He breathed deeply and then exhaled slowly, like his mom did when she was frustrated. His mouth was dry, so dry. The little woman stood next to the plastic mountain, hands on hips. Thomas knew what that look meant, but he was not going to eat the chocolate.

"All right," she said. "I'll come back to see you someday, Thomas, and we'll talk about this again."

The fairy's hands moved in circles and a wave of purple light poured from the little person to Thomas. A yawn grabbed him.

"I have to go to sleep now," he said.

Thomas curled into a ball around his pillow, pulled his covers up high, and fell asleep.

[4]

The scent of flowers again drifted in from the open window. The moon was long gone, the morning sun already poking above the line of trees that separated their farm from the county highway. The heat that had drenched his body in sweat was replaced by the cool air of spring. But there was something else in the air. Thomas sniffed.

He slid a hand beneath the covers; the sheets and his pajama pants were wet.

I peed the bed?

"When you leave a window open, you never know what may come in," repeated in his mind.

The fairy.

He sat up. The little woman was gone, but the plate with the blue flowers still sat on the toy shelf. Thomas pulled himself out of his wet sheets to stand on the hardwood floor.

He stepped forward slowly; he scrunched his nose as an unpleasant smell invaded his nostrils. Something was on the plate, but it wasn't cake.

A fat, fresh turd sat on his mom's good plate.

He grabbed the lip of the plate and shook the turd out the window. It fell into the flower bed below.

"She tried to get me to eat poop," came out in a whisper.

The blue-and-white plate clanked as he set it on the floor, a brown streak down its middle; he pushed it under the bed with his foot before walking to each window in his room and pulling it shut.

Chapter Two  1990

[1]

THOMAS PULLED HIS ARM BACK and threw as hard as he could, shifting his weight forward like his dad had shown him. His throwing arm snapped forward directly over his right shoulder. "None of that sidearm stuff, Tommy," his dad said after Thomas caught a high fly ball and tossed it back with a flick. "You don't have as much control over the ball that way." So, Thomas threw overhand, and he threw straight—mostly.

His dad pulled off his Pioneer Seed cap and wiped the late-July sweat from his forehead with the sleeve of his once-white T-shirt. "Take five. I'm beat, Tommy," he said as he walked over and sat hard on a metal lawn chair. "I gotta get back to work. If your mom comes home and finds me playing baseball, she's going to think that's all I do all summer when she's in the salt mines." He smiled at his son. "Go get yourself a soda, Tommy, and bring me a beer, will you?"

Thomas nodded, tucked his glove and the ball under his left arm, and jogged toward the steps of the wide, wraparound porch. It was two in the afternoon, and his dad wanted a beer. When Danny McGinty's dad started drinking beer in the morning, things went bad. His dad didn't do that, not yet, but he didn't used to drink beer in the afternoon.

Thomas approached the porch steps and stopped. Muddy footprints formed a line moving up the steps and across the chipped white paint, one after the other.

Somebody's in our house.

The knot, that familiar knot of panic in his stomach, tightened like a fist.

Dad. I should get Dad, he thought. But he didn't get his dad. I'm ten years old. I can do it myself.

Thomas's hand shook as he grabbed the handle and slowly opened the wooden screen door to the kitchen, the rusting spring creaking in the quiet air. He slipped inside and shut the door softly behind him. The kitchen of the old farmhouse was huge, designed when homes had tall ceilings and big windows, when people cooked and baked all day.

He stood in the familiar room, his heart pounding in his ears because right then, the kitchen seemed like an alien place populated by monsters.

The kitchen was empty and quiet; the only sound was the ticking of Great-grandma Donally's antique clock in the corner. The door leading to the downstairs office was shut and the wide archway into the living room revealed nothing. His mom's painting of the farm hung on the wall behind the dinner table: the house, the barn, the machine shed, and Bessie and Doofus standing in the lot, all as if she'd taken a photo of them.

The footprints walked beneath the painting. Goose bumps rose on Thomas's forearms. Did the intruder stop? Did they pause to look at his mom's artwork?

The ticking followed as he padded on worn tennis shoes through the kitchen, careful not to smudge any of the still-wet prints. Then the clock's ticking became muffled, and the kitchen turned hazy and distorted, as if he were looking through an empty soda bottle.

Thomas stepped toward the archway into the living room.

Brrrring.

He jumped.

Brrrring.

It's the phone. It's just the phone.

Brrrring.

Maybe it's Mom. I should get it.

Brrrring.

But fear wouldn't let his feet move him closer to the telephone.

Brrrring.

It rang again, and the answering machine clicked to life.

"Hello. This is Kyle," his dad's voice said.

"Deborah," said his mother.

"And Tommy," said his own.

"We're not home right now," they all said.

"If you'll leave a message after the beep . . ." Kyle continued.

"We'll get back to you soon," Deborah said.

Thomas giggled on the tape as the answering machine beeped. Now he stood, nerves taut.

"Hello, Thomas," a familiar voice said on the answering machine. It wasn't his mom. It was—

"The fairy," he whispered.

His stomach wasn't just a knot anymore. It had been doused in gasoline and lit with a match. The muddy footprints continued into the living room and up the stairs to the second story, the prints growing smaller with each step. Thomas's baseball glove slipped from his armpit and landed with a loud slap, and the ball rolled out of the glove, across the hardwood floor, and disappeared beneath the couch.

Dad, rushed into his head. Get Dad.

Getdad.

GetdadGetdadGetdadGetdadGetdad.

"I'm upstairs in your room," the fairy girl said on the tape recording. "Come play with me."

A thud sounded upstairs, but a scrape from the living room swung his head back. The baseball, grass-stained and scarred, came rolling from beneath the couch, rolling toward Thomas, dipping and curving over every imperfection in the old floor.

From behind the couch, a giggle.

A scream tore from Thomas's throat and the giggle turned into a laugh. He sprinted through the kitchen and out the door, the screen slamming shut behind him.

His dad was on his feet the second Thomas bolted from the house, his eyes swollen in fear, his mouth in a silent scream.

"Tommy?"

Thomas tried to stop but ran straight into his dad. It was like running into a tree. His dad gripped his arms gently in his big hands and bent to see his face.

"What's wrong?"

Thomas's hands shook; tears painted his cheeks. "There's some-body in the house," he said, his voice wavering, unsure.

His dad knelt, tilting his head to look up at his son. "How do you know, buddy? What did you see?"

Thomas took in a deep breath and brushed the tears from his face with his forearm. "Footprints," he said, steadier now. "Muddy footprints. And a voice. A giggle. It talked to me."

His dad's mouth hardened into a grimace. "Get Dad. Always get Dad," he said.

"I did," he said.

His dad jogged to his rusty Ford F-150, pushed up the front seat, and pulled his deer rifle from behind it. He chambered a round and motioned Thomas toward the house. "Stay behind me and keep quiet."

Thomas followed. The once-friendly two-story house loomed over them as they closed the twenty yards from the truck. The sec-ond-story windows leered at him; the curtains in his bedroom win-dow fluttered, then flapped shut. Something lurked there, hiding in his room.

Something with muddy feet.

His dad stopped, throwing a hand behind him to slow Thomas down. "Shhhh," he whispered, nodding at the footprints. "Goddam-mit. There *is* somebody in the house."

His boot ascended the first step; the old plank creaked beneath him.

Sweat dripped into Thomas's eyes, but he didn't wipe it away. He couldn't; the thing inside the house might move at any second, and he didn't want to miss it. He kept his eyes open as long as he could between blinks.

His dad held up his right palm and Thomas froze in mid-stride.

His dad waved his fingers, motioning Thomas to the hinge side of the screen door.

"Open it," he mouthed.

Thomas nodded and moved on tiptoes, his back pressing against the wall. His eyelids slammed shut and he inhaled slowly. You're too old to be this scared, he thought.

His eyes crept open, and he grabbed the handle of the screen door, the ancient hinges shrieking as Thomas pulled it toward him. His dad stepped into the kitchen; the smell of this morning's sausage and pancakes still hung in the air, along with another new and unpleasant scent. Thomas inhaled deeply and a cough scratched his throat, trying to escape. The stench of rotting animal carcass clung to everything. His dad waved him forward, and he crept in.

His dad strode through the kitchen and into the living room, swinging the rifle toward the couch, the curtains, the easy chair. Thomas paused long enough to look at the answering machine on the kitchen counter. The red light didn't blink. There was no message.

"Tommy," his dad hissed, beckoning him closer. "Focus."

Thomas trudged through the air that grew thick around his ankles, his every step labored as if the floor were mud. His dad didn't seem to notice as he stopped in the center of the room.

A *thunk*, like someone had dropped a big, fat dictionary, came from upstairs. Thomas's breath stuck in his chest. His dad swept the rifle toward the staircase. Thomas's baseball hit the second step, then the third, before it bounced down two at a time and skittered across the living-room floor.

"Shit," his dad whispered, the rifle butt buried in his shoulder, his aim centered on the top of the stairs.

The ball stopped at Thomas's feet.

[2]

Sheriff Boyd Donally tossed an empty Miller Lite can out the pa-
trol-car window, making sure it made the ditch. He couldn't care less
about littering. It gave the convicts in county lockup something to
pick up. He steered the Crown Vic onto the gravel lane that led to
the Cavanaugh place. He figured it could probably get there by itself
if he gave it the chance. Deputies were out of the question for the
Cavanaughs; the sheriff was family.

Kyle and Tommy stood outside the house. Boyd slapped the
gearshift into park and eyeballed his brother-in-law.

"What you doing with that rifle, Kyle?" Boyd asked. "Deer season isn't for four months."

"Thanks for coming, Boyd," Kyle said.

Boyd stepped from the tan cruiser and slapped Kyle's shoulder.

"Glad to do it." He grabbed Tommy in a bear hug and lifted him
from the ground. "How you holding up, big man?"

"Okay," Tommy said. "It's kinda creepy."

Boyd put him down and mussed the boy's hair. "Always is." His
eyes swung toward the driveway, then back to Kyle. "Debbie here?"

Kyle shook his head.

"I wouldn't tell her if I was you," he said. "Little sis has always
been a bit excitable."

A soft smile crossed Kyle's face as he nodded. "Tell me about it."

"Hey, Tommy," Boyd said before pointing at the house. "You all
want to show me these footprints before she does get home."

Kyle led Boyd into the house and through the living room,
Thomas following behind them.

"This is strange." Boyd stood at the bottom of the stairs, eyeing
the muddy footprints. "It looks like there were two people here," he

said, pointing to the bottom of the steps, "because the footprints that enter the house are adult, and by the time they get here, they're the size of a kid's. Doesn't make sense."

"Feet sizes can't change," Kyle said. "And people can't just vanish."

Boyd tipped his felt Stratton hat back on his head and knelt on the stairs. He pulled an ink pen from his pocket, and he wiped it through the mud.

"It's just as wet as it looks," he said. "Damnedest thing." He turned to Kyle. "You been upstairs?"

Kyle shook his head. "No. That's where—"

"The baseball came from," Boyd finished. His hand dropped to his gun belt and unbuttoned the strap over his service revolver. "I'm going up. You boys are welcome to join me. It's your house."

Boyd had been sheriff of Buchanan County eleven years, deputy five before that. He'd been involved in a shootout and a high-speed car chase, and he'd taken a statement from a guy who swore he saw a bigfoot sitting on playground equipment at an abandoned elementary school, but he'd seen nothing like this.

His heavy feet moved as silently as they could as he made his way up the steps, his weight on the outsides of each stair where it was still strong and wouldn't moan. Sweat soaked into his hatband as he neared the top. Boyd breathed as if he were the patient in one of those hospital shows right before the doctor broke out the defibrillator.

The footprints led to Thomas's room, disappearing below the closed door. Boyd held an open hand behind him, and his brother-in-law and nephew stopped.

"Dad," Thomas whispered, but Kyle didn't answer.

Boyd's hand formed a fist, and he hoped like hell his nephew knew to shut the hell up.

His fingers deftly lifted the unhooked leather strap as he slid his weapon from the holster. Boyd had fired at a suspect before, hit him in the shoulder too. But that bastard was on meth and didn't feel a thing. He never wanted to shoot anyone again. Boyd pulled his shirtsleeve across his sweaty mustache before gripping the weapon in both hands. He sucked in a deep breath and wrapped a hand around the door handle, flinching as the old mechanism clicked. He pushed the door open and raised his weapon.

The hot, coppery scent of blood engulfed him as he stepped over the threshold. A girl, about six years old, with dirty red hair stood in the center of the bedroom, smiling at him. Her once-white dress was yellowed with age, smudged with dirt. A red splotch dotted one cheek, like she was ill.

She smiled.

"Who—" Boyd began before her smile widened to her ears; her teeth were needles. Boyd's arms dropped slowly in air that felt as thick as water and he inhaled sharply.

The girl waved bye-bye. Boyd's knees shook, the service weapon forgotten in his hands. The air pressure in the room changed, pushing against his eardrums. Then a pop, and the little girl with all those teeth vanished.

Poof. Gone.

"Fuck me," Boyd whispered, leaning his shoulder against the door frame to keep his shaking knees from dropping him to the floor.

[3]

The old lawn chair sagged under Boyd's weight, which was fine, because he didn't plan on moving for a while, the late-afternoon sun nearing the treetops. The porch was clean now—Tommy had mopped it just like his daddy said. Tommy's a good boy. The screen door protested as Kyle pushed through it. He slid a beer can into Boyd's hand.

"Thanks for coming out," Kyle said. "You could have sent a deputy, but you came yourself. That means a lot, Boyd. I mean that."

Kyle opened his beer can; the crack was so sudden and loud, Boyd flinched.

"Yeah," he said, then cleared his throat. "No problem. I cleared the house. I guess someone's just messing with you."

Someone with lizard teeth who can disappear like a goddamn stage magician. Boyd's thick fingers fumbled with the tab before his can finally opened.

"Yeah," Kyle said. "But I don't know who would want to."

"Stupid teenagers, I suspect," Boyd said, his gaze settling on the garden where Thomas stood. That's where the prints had started.

Deborah watered the garden this morning before she left for work, and someone walked out of the garden, into the house, turned into a little girl as she made her way up the stairs. Then she smiled at me while she vanished.

He'd scribbled those words in his notebook. That little girl. Shit. Boyd hoped he'd just had some stress-induced hallucination. Anything, he thought, would be better than that girl being real.

"Whatever that was, your house is safe now," he said, the words sounding like a lie even to him. "We went through it good enough."

An hour more into the afternoon, Boyd drained his can and slammed it down onto his thigh. He didn't want his brother-in-law to see how much his hand still shook. He'd been through six beers and thought another might do him good.

"Got any more?" he asked. "It's been a hell of a day."

"Uh, sure," Kyle said, and went back into the house.

Tommy stood in the garden, looking back at Boyd, the boy's hair a mess. "Hey," Boyd called to him. "You okay, Tommy?"

The boy shook his head.

"Yeah," Boyd whispered. "Me neither."

[4]

His mom's Ford Escort rolled to a stop at the end of the long drive, gravel crunching beneath the tires. Thomas looked up. His dad didn't move from under the hood of the dirty feed truck, but the socket wrench went limp in his hand. Uncle Boyd had been gone an hour.

"What's wrong, Dad?" Thomas asked. He stood next to his father on the front bumper of the old truck. He knew he couldn't do much to help change the alternator except hold a light, or a bolt, or bring his dad beer, but he wanted to be close to him. They'd been through something today, and come out of it shaken but safe.

Besides, he was too damn scared to go back into the house.

His dad fit the socket on the last bolt that held the dirty gray engine part Thomas couldn't tell from the rest.

"She's late," his dad said. "That means she had to lock up late, and that means she'll be in a bad mood."

She'd been in a bad mood a lot lately.

Thomas's dad pushed the wrench (righty-tighty, lefty-loosey). The nut held fast, then popped, and he began to crank.

"Doesn't she like her job?" Thomas asked.

"She never wanted to go back to work," his dad explained, the wrench clicking in his hand. "She wanted to stay home and take care of you."

"So?" Thomas's eyes focused on his mother as she got out of the car and stormed up the porch steps to the house, the same porch steps that earlier today were dotted with muddy footprints.

His dad set the wrench on top of the radiator and looked at Thomas.

"So, farms aren't doing as well as they used to. We needed more money, and your mom wanted me to get a job."

"You have a job. You're a farmer."

His dad's shoulders slumped, and he looked toward the house; Thomas followed his gaze but couldn't see where he was looking.

"It doesn't pay the bills anymore. There was a teaching job open at the high school; that's what I went to college to do. Bet you didn't know that."

Thomas shook his head.

"Your mom really wanted me to get that job, but I didn't apply. If I started teaching, there'd go my days, some nights, some weekends." He grabbed his half-empty can of Miller Lite and drained it before setting it back on the engine. It fell through the empty spaces between all the engine parts and landed on the gravel with a hollow rattle. "Then I'd be a weekend farmer. We'd have to sell the hogs, the chickens, and Bessie and Doofus. I wouldn't be able to handle as many row crops, either. I'd be too busy."

"Then you wouldn't be a real farmer anymore?"

A grin played at his father's lips but didn't materialize. "Not like I want to be. She's mad that she's the one who got a job. She wants to paint and have another baby. It's my fault we don't have that right now."

His dad gently cupped Thomas's chin. When he moved his hand, the smear of grease he left felt heavy.

"Go get me a beer from the cooler, okay? I put a Dr Pepper in there for you."

Thomas smiled, although he didn't feel like smiling. He jumped down from the big truck's bumper and walked to the machine shed, its corrugated tin walls nailed to bare studs. Dust danced in the light that streamed through the dirty windows, a pane of glass missing here and there. Drill press, air compressor, band saw, and machines Thomas didn't know dotted the floor. The shed usually reeked of oil and dust, but today? Today it smelled like his mom's garden in the spring.

Thomas's steps slowed as he neared the cooler Dad had placed next to the engine from the old tractor. A plate holding a piece of cake sat on the lid, a sliver of chocolate curling from the top.

He froze, the machine shop air suddenly thick. Bare footprints from the girl-sized feet that walked up the stairs to his room were visible on the dirty concrete floor.

"Where are you?" Thomas whispered.

Each dusty corner, each cobweb that ran up the wall studs, each shadow cast by a stack of junk his dad would never work on held a secret. Something lurked in that darkness, something Thomas couldn't explain.

He cleared his throat. "I know you're here," he said, his voice shaky. "I know you were in my house today."

He stopped and listened for anything; his father grunted outside as he pulled the alternator from the old truck.

"I'm not eating your cake," he said flatly, picking up the plate and setting it on the concrete floor. Thomas opened the cooler and grabbed a beer and a soda. "I know what this is. It's—" He stopped and looked back at the truck. His father was still under the hood.

"—poop." His voice came out in a whisper. "You're trying to make me eat poop, and I'm not doing it."

A girl's giggle rang through the shed. Thomas turned and ran back into the sunlight.

[5]

"Are you sure you don't want any ice cream and cake?" his mom asked as he set his dinner dish in the sink.

Cake? No. No cake ever again.

"I don't, Mom," he said, his stomach a ball of nails. "I'm going to bed."

His mom set her fork on her plate—tines down, because that's what proper people do—and looked at Thomas.

"Do you feel okay, honey?"

Thomas nodded. "Yeah. Just tired, that's all." He paused, his attention at the window over the sink. His dad still leaned over the engine of the blue-and-red grain truck. "How come Dad didn't come in for supper?"

His mom's eyes dropped to her plate. "He really needs to get that truck running."

No, he doesn't. That truck was for the harvest, and the harvest was three months away. Dad just didn't want to come inside.

"Good night, Mom," Thomas said, and walked toward the stairs, wondering if it was time to start worrying about his parents getting a divorce.

[6]

Thomas didn't realize he'd fallen asleep until he woke in his bed, and night had fallen. His right hand instinctively swept across his mouth, wiping away drool. The house was dark and quiet. He slowly pushed himself up. The fresh, earthy scent of the garden filled the room, but it wasn't coming from outside. It couldn't. The air-conditioning was on, the windows shut.

Creeping vines of fear crawled over him, pinning him to the bed.

"Where are you?" he asked into the night, his heartbeat loud to him in the dead quiet. "I can smell you."

"What do I smell like?" came from the darkness as feet shuffled in the room, but Thomas couldn't tell from where; the sound came from all around.

"The garden," he said. "Show yourself."

"I'm here," a little voice said. A girl's voice. The voice from the answering machine. That voice was in his room. "Can't you see me?"

A soft glow grew in the window, and a small figure stepped into his bedroom. It was the fairy, but she was different. She had the same white dress and a round, smiling face framed with red hair. But the fairy was a tiny woman. This was a child.

"Hello," she said.

"Are you the fairy?" he asked.

The girl stood in front of the window where the fairy had stood four years before. It was the same person, wasn't it? But the fairy was small. This girl was eight, maybe nine years old, and close to the same height as Thomas.

"Yes, I am." She grabbed the hem of her skirt, stepped one foot behind the other and curtsied. "But I'm also me."

"That doesn't make any sense," Thomas said, his hands clenching fistfuls of bedsheets. "Why are you here?"

"I'm your friend, Thomas." The girl's voice, soft and sweet. She giggled again. "I'm here to warn you."

"About what?" Sweat beaded across Thomas's forehead.

She laughed, but there was no humor in it. It was the cackle of a movie villain.

"Dauðr is coming, Thomas. It's coming here, to your house, and you must be prepared because it's coming to eat you alive." The laugh disappeared from her voice. "Let me show you what it can do."

[7]

Suddenly Thomas was someplace else.

He stood waist-deep in prairie grass and flowers, the pink, yellow, and blue blooms so electric he was afraid to touch them. A sparkling red bird fluttered in a deep blue sky. In the distance, a calm sea stretched to the horizon; boats sailed on that sea, but were too far away for Thomas to see what they looked like. The gentle salt wind wafted a mingling of scents over him—lilac and cinnamon and rain on hot asphalt.

He opened his mouth to shout for someone, anyone, but words didn't come. The air tasted of Twizzlers, then of winter, then of smoke. The landscape melted.

This isn't real, he thought. It can't be real.

Suddenly, on the hill where Thomas stood gazing across the fields of flowers dotted with trees, the trees burst into flames. Snow began to fall in great clumps but melted before it touched the ground. In the distance, the sea boiled. Prairie flowers ignited and disappeared as the flames ate them alive. Snow changed to ash and buried the land in gray.

The world whizzed by in fast-forward. Smoke rose from craters of fire that burst through the ground, the once-green fields of flowers and trees now bald and ash covered, the few remaining trees bone-white and limbless. Charcoal clouds stretched over what had once been the calm sea but was now dry and littered with ancient boats and the skeletons of unfamiliar creatures. Thomas coughed. The air burned his lungs.

"Where am I?"

"My home," a voice said. A hand, smooth and comforting, laced its fingers in his. Thomas jumped and screamed. It was the girl from his room.

"Wha-what happened?" Thomas coughed again and spat onto the dusty ground. I'm dreaming. I have to be dreaming.

"You're not dreaming, Thomas," she said.

"This can't be your home. This can't be anybody's home. This place is—"

"Dead," she said. The grip on his hand tightened and he squeezed back. He needed this hand in his—this soft, solid hand—or Thomas knew his mind would unravel.

"My world was once green and blue—"

"—and tasted like Twizzlers," Thomas said. "What happened?"

She breathed deeply, then coughed from the smoke.

"Dauðr, the Death," she finally said. "It is always empty, always hungry. It feeds on worlds, leaving dust and smoke and sadness." The girl motioned forward. "Come."

A road, as gray as the landscape, ran under his feet and snaked down the hill, sometimes buried in dunes of slate-colored dust. Something moved in the distance, but he couldn't tell what.

Smoke sent him into a fit of coughing. The girl pulled Thomas's pajama shirt to his mouth to try and filter out the polluted air, and they started down the road. A fire sprang from a fissure next to the road, igniting a smooth, barkless tree; Thomas jumped, his sweat-matted hair heavy on his head.

"Dauðr is power," she said. "All-consuming power. It eats whatever is growing. It sucks energy, leaving death."

They continued in silence. With the distant sea gone, the plains seemed endless. They passed through a field of boulders. Then Thomas saw them—filthy, ragged people bound to those boulders with rusted chains. They moaned, swaying as if caught in a breeze, but no breeze graced this awful place.

"Who are they?" Compassion pulled from deep inside. Save them. Set them free.

A man, his teeth long gone, stood and leaned toward him, arms spread like a zombie's. Thomas jumped back, but the man had pulled the short chains tight, and he dropped into the dust. The gust of air from the chained man's fall struck Thomas with the stink of rot and death.

"Help. Help me," came through the man's crusty beard, the stench of blood reaching Thomas's nose. He gagged. "Please. Please kill me," the man said.

"No," Thomas said. His head started to swim. "I can't."

"Kill me," another voice said.

"No. Kill me."

"Me."

"Me. Kill me," the rough voices called down the road.

"No," Thomas moaned. "I can't kill anyone. I'm lost. I don't even know where I am."

The girl held fast to Thomas's hand to keep him from running.

The crusty man rose to his knees before Thomas; fresh blood dripped from his wrists where the manacles bound him to the stone.

"Land of da fairies," the man said, a cough splattering blood near Thomas's feet. He pointed at the girl who held Thomas's hand. "Her land. Ain't this a fuckin' paradise."

"Why are you here?" Thomas asked.

The man cackled, more blood spraying the dry ground. "Ate fairy food. Next thing I know, I'm here. The fairy played with me for a while, then this—" He coughed. "Then the thing with the teeth came and turned this place into hell."

The girl's grip relaxed, and Thomas's hand fell to his side. He looked at her. Why are you smiling?

He turned back to the bloody man. "What's the thing with teeth?" he asked.

The bloody man's eyes grew large, terror gripping his face. "It's behind you."

Thomas swung around. The girl had vanished; in her place a black wave of smoke curled on top of itself, rolling toward Thomas. He fell to his knees and screamed. A slit opened in the wave, and row after row of dripping needle teeth gleamed through the black- ness. The thing's hot, fetid breath crashed into him with the stench of a sun-swollen carcass.

Thomas woke, covered in vomit.

[8]

When Thomas's eyes opened again, his mom was sitting next to his bed, dabbing his forehead with a wet cloth. His dad sat on a chair in the corner of the room.

"Hey, you okay, champ?" his dad said, hopping to his feet to join his mom at the bedside.

Thomas tried to sit, but the room began to spin. He dropped back onto his pillow. His skin was hot, tight, as if he'd been in the sun too long.

"Mom?"

His mom held the cloth to Thomas's lips before moving it back to his forehead.

"Shhh. Don't talk, baby," she whispered. "You woke with a fever. It's gone down, but you're sick. Just lie there."

"I'm not sick," he mumbled.

"Kill me. Please, kill me," the bloody man had said.

No. No. Get me out of this place. Get me away from the bloody man. Get me away from the black. Get me away from the *teeth*.

"Hot," he said slowly, softly. "It's hot here, Mommy. It's hot. There's a monster, a monster with teeth. Help me. Get me home."

Thomas's mother kissed his forehead, then dabbed his face again.

"You're dreaming, honey. You're home in bed," she said. "And I know you're hot. I can get you some nice, cold Sprite, and a Tylenol. Would you like that?"

Thomas nodded slowly; his lids slid shut.

Home? I'm home?

"Have you seen the girl?" he mumbled before sleep grabbed him and dragged him under.

[9]

When Thomas woke again, sweat soaked his clothes. The girl, the dust, the bleeding man, the teeth. He sat bolt upright, eyes wide, heart pounding. He was still in bed. Thomas touched the sheets, then his pajama shirt. The cloth was real. He was really in his room. The nightmare was gone.

Thunder rumbled in the distance. A storm must be rolling through. The dark, which Thomas had always embraced, now frightened him; teeth lurked in the darkness. He slipped out of bed and stepped slowly toward his lamp. The lamp's shadow stood over him, and sometimes shadows lived. He reached to turn on the light, but a hand slapped his wrist.

"Don't," a voice said.

A scream leaped from his throat, but it died in the unnaturally thick air of his room. It was the girl from the dead world. The girl who was the fairy. Strength drained from Thomas's legs, and he began to fall backward. The girl's grip kept him on his feet.

"Shhh," she hissed. "You'll wake your parents."

She stepped from the shadows and took his hand, twisting her fingers in his. She wasn't the little girl anymore, and she wasn't the girl from the hell world. She was his age now and almost as tall.

"I want them awake," he mouthed, the words refusing to come out.

She shook her head. "They can't know what we're about to do."

Thomas pulled his hand from hers and sat on his bed. No. This isn't right. Always tell Mom and Dad. Always. "Why?" His fear was driven back by anger. "You sent me to that horrible burning place. That was awful. Why shouldn't I tell my parents everything?"

She stepped toward him, her eyes an ice-cold black in the dark room. Thomas didn't shrink away but was still. Despite the darkness that surrounded them, he could see her familiar face clearly, her red hair, her white dress.

She smelled like a garden.

"That burning place was my home," she said, her voice quiet but powerful. "The monster that destroyed it is coming. The burning will happen to your home tonight unless you come with me."

"The monster?" he whispered. "That thing with the teeth?"

The familiar knot formed in Thomas's stomach. Dauðr, the Death. The teeth. Row after row of needles, dripping with something vile. The gaping mouth, the rancid breath. She was right, it was Death.

She grasped his face, pulling it toward hers. "You saw it, didn't you? You saw the teeth?"

Thomas nodded. "What is it?"

She dropped his face and turned away. "It destroys everything it touches, and it's coming here, Thomas. It's coming here tonight. It's going to eat your world." She swung back to him. "You have to stop it," she said.

"How can I stop it? I'm ten years old."

A nervous giggle burst from her.

"I once told you you were special, Thomas. You are this thing's opposite, and opposites can't survive together. Your touch, your embrace, is poison to it." She gripped his shoulders. "Embrace it, stab it, combine your blood."

Blood? A hot flush swept over him, sweat rolled down his back. That mouth had filled the sky.

"I'm not getting close to that thing." His words sputtered out.

She cocked her head; her dark eyes burned into his. "But that is what you have to do. You have to share its space."

Thomas turned his head; he couldn't look into those eyes anymore. "Then what happens?"

"It goes away," she said. "Because if it doesn't, everyone you know dies. Your mother, your father, your friends. Everyone. Everyone dies, Thomas."

The darkness, the loneliness of night closed on him like a sack. Tremors shook his hands, but then the girl touched his arm, and the terror flitted away.

"Why is it coming to my house?" he finally asked.

The girl stared at Thomas through squinted eyes.

"The path to your world is easiest here because of you," she said. "You're a magnet drawing it toward you."

He shook his head. "How do you know this? Any of this?"

"I'm older than I look," she said. "And I've come here with what I know to stop this monster before it devours the universe." She raised her hand toward him. "Watch."

A lavender glow grew in her palm, then it flowed from her hand, caressing Thomas's forehead. A vision of the farm, gray and lifeless, flooded his mind.

The Guernseys, Bessie and Doofus, lay in the barnyard, nothing but dry, cracked hide pulled over bones. The fields were dust, and tortured souls knelt chained to the highway like the man with the bloody mouth.

His mom and dad, his uncle Boyd, neighbors, lay on the rural road in dirt-streaked rags, toothless, like the bleeding man. The monster Dauðr hung in the sky, licking its teeth with a forked black tongue.

"I don't want anyone to die," he said, or thought he did. Thomas didn't know. The tears on his cheeks fell onto the floor.

"Then," the girl said, slipping her warm, soft hand into his, "we have to go, now."

[10]

Sheriff Boyd Donally rolled over in the queen-sized bed he shared with his wife. His arm reached out but found only mattress. Maggie? Her name stirred somewhere in the meaningless tossing and turning he called sleep. He didn't sleep much, not really. A few hours of closed eyes separated by a few hours of dozing in front of the TV, or if the weather was right, maybe a while on the porch listening to those people who talk about ghosts and UFOs on AM radio.

"Maggie?" he said, the word, soft, muted.

He looked at the clock. 1:30 a.m. Maybe she'd gone downstairs for coffee. Come on, Boyd, you know her gout acts up sometimes and she can't sleep.

His eyes slid open, and reality pushed him fully awake. She wasn't in bed and wasn't downstairs. She was buried on a hilltop at Mt. Olive Cemetery and had been for a year. Boyd still woke most nights expecting to find her beside him.

"Goddammit."

His feet hit the carpet and Boyd pushed himself out of bed.

He settled onto the porch, the plastic cushion of his wicker chair wheezing beneath him. A slight breeze brought with it a nip of cool air. He placed a small radio on the table beside him, and cracked open a beer can, the sound loud in the darkness. It was too early for coffee, he supposed. Another beer wouldn't hurt.

He clicked on the radio, the volume just the way he liked it, the dial already on the right channel. Boyd found the show one night when driving back to the station from a two-car fatality on US 169. The host talked about the Bermuda Triangle, and Boyd was hooked.

He dropped his feet on the wicker footstool and took a drink, the cold liquid sending a chill through him.

"So, what you're telling me is the quantum physics people are right. Other dimensions exist parallel to ours." The host's voice was deep, the kind radio people called a "hired set of balls."

The guest on the other side of the call cleared his throat.

"Yes," he said. "There's a thin veil between our world and others. In some worlds, another Cap Freeman is right now interviewing another Gerald Anderson about *this* dimension. Other worlds look completely different."

A lighter clicked, an inhale from a fresh cigarette.

"How different?" Freeman asked, exhaling.

Boyd imagined the man in a dark studio, cigarette smoke swirling around his head.

"A world where Ronald Reagan is still president? A world where World War Three is raging?" Cap Freeman paused to laugh, a deep, rumbling chuckle. "Although those two might be the same world. What about a world where they've found a cure for cancer?"

"Yes," Anderson said. "All of the above and more."

"More?"

Boyd took a long drink of beer and stretched, sleep tapping his shoulder.

"Of course. A world where the Confederates won the Civil War. A world where the asteroid didn't kill the dinosaurs. A world where elves and fairies exist."

Freeman let go another long exhale of smoke. "Elves and fairies? Now we're getting into another topic altogether."

The cool breeze turned into a cold wind and the trees in Boyd's yard moaned in protest.

"Not really," Anderson said. "Cultures around the world, since the beginning of time, have passed on their stories of magic little people. European legends even have elves, diminutive malicious beings, able to grow in size to look indistinguishable from you or me. That's how they used their mischief to trick unsuspecting humans."

The half-empty can slid from Boyd's fingers and thunked on the old wooden porch, spilling the rest of his beer.

"These stories had to come from somewhere," Anderson continued. "Why not another dimension?"

"So, you're saying—" Freeman started, but Boyd's mind had gone somewhere else. Back to the Cavanaugh home, back to the unlikely muddy footprints that changed shape, shrinking from an adult to those of a child. A child with inhuman teeth.

Lightning flashed to the east, and Boyd looked up.

"There's a storm coming," he said mindlessly, picked up the radio, and walked back inside.

[11]

The floor groaned as Thomas stepped into the hallway, the open door to his mom and dad's room a black void. His mom kept the heavy shades drawn; like Thomas, she enjoyed the dark. At least he used to.

"Mom," he said, pausing at the door, waiting for a sound from the room—any sound to tell him his parents had heard the loose floorboard and were coming out to tell him everything was all right. Through his dad's light snoring, his mom's voice whispered, "Thomas?"

He opened his mouth to tell his mom a stranger was here, that a monster was coming, but the girl squeezed Thomas's hand and the words died. He turned toward the fairy girl.

"Shhh," she hissed, her eyes wide.

"Thomas, honey?" His mom's voice was heavy from sleep.

"Huh?" his dad grunted.

Get up, there's a stranger in the house, he tried to say, but the words didn't come. Purple light grew from the girl's hand and drifted into the bedroom; snoring followed.

His legs moved without his permission, and he had no choice but to walk down the hall on bare feet. They reached the end, and the girl hurried him down the stairs.

Outside, humidity turned the night to Jell-O, and a distant rumble announced a coming storm. One of the cows lowed; Thomas thought it was Doofus. The girl yanked Thomas's arm as he paused halfway through the barnyard.

"Come, Thomas," she said, her voice sharp. "We must hurry." She pulled at him, and they ran into the cornfield, Thomas's mind shrieking for her to stop, yet his body responding only to her commands.

Sharp, stiff leaves raked Thomas's skin. The corn. His dad always said never to go into the corn alone. It was easy to find your way out—you just had to follow the rows—but you never knew what hid there, waiting for a boy to get lost. A coyote yipped from somewhere inside the cornfield. This time his legs listened to him, and he stopped running. The girl pulled at him again, but he didn't move.

"No," he said, the word shaky but audible. A rumble in the sky was closer. "I'm going back to my house. I shouldn't be here."

A corn blade brushed his arm, the long, sharp leaf slicing a shallow furrow in his skin.

"It's coming," the girl said.

Thomas's feet moved backward; the dry, hard dirt clods jabbed his tender soles. The coyote yipped again, a few rows over now. The knot in his stomach grew into a boulder.

"Why?" he asked; panic fell from his voice by the fistful. "Why is this monster thing coming here?"

Her eyes pleaded with him to move. "Because it's weak, Thomas. It's so weak. It needs to feed."

"On what?"

The girl tugged at him, but he didn't move.

"Life," she said, leaning close and poking him in the chest. "It sucks out the thing that keeps your heart beating and eats it. People, plants, anything that breathes. Then its power grows so big it swallows your world."

He tried to yank his arm from her grip, but her fingers were too strong.

"No," he whispered.

She opened her mouth to speak, but a yip from the coyote silenced her. The dog-like beast was close, somewhere to Thomas's right. A sniff came from behind Thomas, the sound almost inaudible beneath the hammering of his heart.

"Go away," he said, the words a whisper. Something growled behind him, and he turned to face it. Hunched low between the rows of corn was the coyote; its ears laid back on its head, its teeth bared. Thomas's mind lurched. The coyote wore a piece of clothing; it looked like pajama pants.

"No." He jerked his body back toward the house to run, to get away from the monster, the coyote, whatever was coming in the night, but the girl rested a hand on his shoulder and the fear melted.

"It won't hurt you, Thomas," she said.

"Liar," he said, his voice small, flat.

A sound, a cork pop from a giant bottle of champagne, shook the night. A change in air pressure threw him to the ground. The coyote yelped and disappeared into the darkness.

The girl bent and whispered into his ear: "It's here."

She shoved something into his hand. He unfolded his fingers. The golden plastic snakehead from his Snake Mountain toy sat in his hand; it was what gave Snake Mountain its name.

"It's for luck," she said.

Lightning flashed in the distance.

"Come on," she urged. Thomas pushed himself off the clod-covered field onto weak, watery legs. Thunder growled in the distance. Was it one Mississippi, or two Mississippi? Either way, the storm grew closer.

The girl stood by him, looking into the clouds churning overhead, and the air smelled of rain, and something else—the sweet smell of rotting corn. Thunder clapped, and the ground shook; Thomas put out his arms to keep his balance. Something crashed in the corn, over, and over. Footsteps? Yes. Giant footsteps.

"Be brave, Thomas," the girl said. "It's coming this way." She walked beside him, her hand on his shoulder, but she sounded miles away.

"Don't make me do this," he whispered. "You can't make me do this."

"I'm not making you do anything," she whispered in his ear. "You want to do this. For your family. The monster has something I want, Thomas. You want to do it for *me*."

And in that moment he did want to do it for her.

Cornstalks parted in front of Thomas like waves before the bow of a great ship, the stalks withering as Dauðr pushed them aside. Then, two boot-clad feet stepped where the coyote had been, and Thomas almost fell to the dirt, his heart pounding. His dad stood in the parted corn about ten feet from them in the middle of a bed of wilted, blackened stalks at his feet.

"It's not real, Thomas," the girl said, her hand falling from his shoulder. "That's not your father."

His heart pounded hard. "Yeah, it is. It's my dad."

He stepped toward the man who stood before him. "Dad?"

The man nodded. Coyotes, six of them now, slunk out of the darkness and gathered by him, their eyes glowing green. The largest beast, ragged pajama pants hanging from it, brushed against the man's leg, its mouth open in a wicked grimace. Thomas stopped; his fingers tightened around the broken toy. Something was wrong with his dad. His arms were too long, his nose crooked. His—

Thomas's body shook; gooseflesh covered his arms.

"You're not my dad," Thomas said.

The farmer's grin grew, and his mouth—now too large for his face—opened slowly. Needle-like teeth, like the ones he'd seen in his dream, sprang from its gums. Row after row after row of them, like the corn they stood in. A deep laugh rolled from the mouth that was and was not his dad's.

Hands grabbed Thomas from behind and held him up.

"I'm here for you, Thomas." The girl's words fought their way into his mind. He reached back and grabbed her hand. "Don't worry about the animals. Focus on Dauðr." She squeezed his hand. "Embrace the monster. Embrace it and stab it with your snake. Draw blood."

Blood?

Thomas stepped forward with strength he didn't know he had, the girl following behind. The lesser coyotes, the ones that followed the alpha, cowered as the children approached. Thomas raised the arm with the snake, the other behind him, gripping the girl. The creature in the corn, the one that looked like his father, smiled, the demon teeth spread across its human face. The coyotes turned and bolted, all but the alpha. It cringed as Thomas stepped closer but bared its teeth.

"Just two more steps," the little girl said. "Just two more steps. Raise your talisman. Raise the snake."

Thomas's bare feet trod over rough clods, but he didn't feel the pain. He reached out to stab the monster with the snake, but the words "Kill the boy" came from it in a deep rumble, and the big coyote leaped.

The beast's canine teeth sank into Thomas's thigh and something warm and wet rushed down his leg—blood and urine. The coyote jerked backward, its teeth ripping at the meat of his thigh, and Thomas fell into the monster, screaming. The broken, jagged piece of Snake Mountain he'd imagined stabbing into the monster flew from his hand and disappeared into the darkness as he fell onto the creature that looked like his dad, grabbing its pants. He didn't draw blood; instead, he embraced the monster.

Then everything exploded.

Chapter Three  1990

[1]

BOBBY GARRETT SLEPT RESTLESSLY, the dream tossing him back and forth beneath his covers. The fourteen-year-old had never dreamed of corn, or farmers, or coyotes, at least not that he remembered later. His dream was loud and dark. Was it raining? Maybe? Then—

A scream ripped him from sleep, his plain white sheets soaked in sweat and his coal-black hair matted to his head. Bobby's eyes shot open, the dream still clear. The cornfield. The farmer. The monster. Bobby stood on four legs. The farmer, in dusty denim, towered over him.

"Kill the boy," the farmer said.

Death filled his thoughts, the chase, the leap, the taste of flesh rent by sharp yellow teeth, the warm gush of hot blood on his tongue, spurting from the sides of his snout.

The room swam into focus above him, his muscles frozen in taut bunches. Corn remained in his vision, only for a moment; stalks rose from the old, ratty shag carpeting in his room and through his television set. As his consciousness cleared, the cornstalks faded into the night, but the monster that looked like a ten-year-old boy stood over him holding a plastic snake, blood gushing from a ragged bite in his thigh.

The monster—a boy?

The leftover dream dissolved as footsteps hammered down the hall. Bobby's heavy bedroom door slammed against the wall and his mother ran into the room.

"Bobby," she called, running to his bedside.

He sat up, his heart hammering. She threw her arms around him.

"Bobby, baby." Her breath brushed his face; it stank of Pepsodent and Virginia Slims. "What happened?"

He ran a hand through his wet hair, his heart rate beginning to slow. "Just a bad dream, Mom. I'm okay, just sweaty."

She squeezed harder. "No, baby. No, you're not. Your pajamas are soaked through." She pulled back and dropped a hand to his sheets. "So's your bed. You need to change your clothes, honey." Her hand rose to his cheek. "You can change your sheets tomorrow. Why don't you come sleep with me tonight?"

His hand pushed hers away. "No, Mom, gross. I'm fourteen."

She backed away from her son, hands on her hips. "Don't talk to your mother like that." Her words were weak. "Who takes care of you?"

This again. "You do, Mom."

"And who stays home to teach you all your schoolwork, so you'll be a smart boy?" she asked, her hands on her hips.

His eyes dropped. "You do, Mom."

"And who keeps you home, safe from all those bad people in this world?"

Home, where he ate casseroles and learned all about math, and literature, and history—just the good history. No un-holy wars or riots for my baby, just the last six thousand years of humanity on this big, blue planet. He also watched *The 700 Club* with his mom while she smoked cigarettes and drank vodka tonics.

"Where's Dad?" he asked. He was never there when he needed him.

She straightened, arms crossing her chest. "He's at work, preparing for a conference."

"It's two o'clock in the morning."

"What are you trying to say, son?" Her voice shook, her eyes welled.

"Nothing, Mom, it's okay," he said. "I'll be there in a minute."

[2]

Fire and rain. Thomas lay in the dirt as fat, heavy drops pelted his battered body. A ringing deadened his ears; lightning flashed in the distance. The corn lay flat, the falling rain extinguishing the spots of yellow flame; the world around Thomas grew dark.

"Tommy," his dad yelled, but the dim noise ringing in his ears could be from anywhere. "Thomas."

The night grew deathly silent, the rain fell harder, leaving rows and rows of scorched, flattened stalks.

"Oh, dear God." It was another voice, a higher voice. His mom's. "Kyle, what happened?"

A thumb pulled Thomas's eye open. His mom's face swirled over him for a moment before the hazy world drifted into black.

"Call 9-1-1, Kyle," she ordered. "Call—"

[3]

The scent of sizzling bacon drifted up from downstairs. Bobby rolled over in his parents' bed. Pain throbbed in his right thigh as if he'd slammed it into a table. He pushed himself up, his aching arms and back evoking a moan, his body as sore as if he'd spent all day cleaning out the garage.

What happened? he wondered, until his dream wormed its way into his thoughts. A farmer, a monster, a cornfield, a coyote.

"I was a coyote?" he whispered as the dream began to drop from his memory piece by piece.

Bobby draped his legs over the side of the bed and sat still, taking in the morning. His mom was downstairs in the kitchen cooking breakfast. Where was his dad? Did his dad come home? Sometimes he didn't. More smells tickled his nose. Pancakes, and fried potatoes?

"Vera, honey," his dad said, his tone soft, as nonthreatening as a Smurf's. "Could I get some more coffee?"

Bobby zombie-walked to his own room to get dressed. His mom and dad always expected him to be dressed for breakfast.

When Bobby finally reached the kitchen, his mom was standing in front of the stove, tongs transferring slices of bacon from a cast-iron skillet to a plate layered with paper towels. His father sat at the kitchen table, napkin in his lap, suit jacket already on and ready for the day. "Always be on time and look like you belong there," was his dad's mantra, so when Bobby reached the faded linoleum of the kitchen he was already in a white shirt, black tie, black slacks, and polished black loafers. He was ready for another glorious day of homeschooling and probably wouldn't leave the house today, but his dad wouldn't be happy unless Bobby was dressed like he wanted to talk about Jesus.

His dad checked his watch.

"And three, two, one." He lowered his arm and smiled at his son. "You're right on time and lookin' sharp."

Lookin' sharp. Wow, Dad. Bobby pulled out his chair and sat at the kitchen table, a plate and silverware already in front of him, and an empty place setting next to him as usual. The Garrett family always left a spot at the table for Jesus.

His mom leaned over her husband's shoulder, a coffeepot in one hand. She kissed the back of his head and filled his cup.

"Got any plans today, son?" his dad asked.

Bobby's summer days were spent reading, listening to grunge low enough his folks wouldn't hear, and sneaking down to the creek to smoke cigarettes between homeschooling lessons that never, ever stopped, but his dad didn't need to know that.

"No, sir," he said. "No plans for today."

His dad spooned fried potatoes and onions onto his plate before moving on to a bowl of scrambled eggs. "Well, that's a good thing, Bobby boy," he said, tapping the slotted wooden spoon on his plate. "Because we're going on a trip."

Trip? The Garretts never went on trips. The Garretts never went on vacations. The Garretts never *went*. "What kind of trip?" he asked.

His mom leaned over Bobby, placed two pancakes on his plate, and upended the syrup bottle over the short stack. Lots of syrup, just the way he liked it. "Now come on, baby, Dad wants to take us someplace special," she said, her voice wavering. "We should let him. We love Daddy."

Bobby looked up at his mom's pinched face, then toward his dad, who was as calm as a fisherman. No, we don't love Daddy. "Sure," he said, not believing anything that came from his own mouth. "Sounds like fun."

His father grinned and held out his hands, palms up. Bobby reluctantly gripped one. His mother took his.

"Let us pray," his father said. "Lord Almighty, Maker of Heaven and Earth. Please bless this meal we are about to receive. We are all bad, we are all sinners, and do not deserve this bounty. Please remove the wickedness from our lives and lead us down the path of righteousness. There is always a place set at our table for our Lord. Amen."

"Amen," Bobby repeated, and cut into his pancakes.

[4]

A call woke Boyd after he'd finally gone back to sleep, Cap Freeman's guest talking fairies gave way to some yahoo going on about numerology. He didn't like being roused from sleep by the telephone, and he liked it even less now that he'd heard what Deputy Kirkhoff said.

Boyd pulled up to his sister and brother-in-law's farm for the second time in two days. What he saw was devastating. The cornfield—the whole damn cornfield, green and tall the last time he'd been there—lay pressed flat as if a hailstorm had beaten it to hell, except there had been no hailstorm. Just lightning and rain. The field lay black, scorched by fire. A few stalks remained upright but burned. Last night's rain took care of that. Pieces of a shredded anhydrous tank lay like eggshells across the destroyed field.

"Jesus."

He slipped the transmission into park and pushed himself out of the driver's seat. Deputy Glenn Kirkhoff jogged to the cruiser, notebook in hand.

An ambulance sat at the edge of the field, the blue lights on the roof still flashing. Two EMTs loaded a gurney into the back, then Debbie climbed in and an EMT followed her inside, shutting the door. The siren fired up, and the vehicle sped up the lane.

"It's bad, Sheriff," Kirkhoff said. "Anhydrous tank exploded, and what was left of the field caught fire, and the boy—"

"What about my nephew?" Boyd snapped.

Kirkhoff swallowed. "He's hurt. He was lying in the field right where the tank went off, but he didn't have a scratch on him. Except for the bite."

"Bite?"

"Yes, sir," Kirkhoff said. "Looked like a dog, or a coyote got to him. He's off to the hospital."

Boyd figured that. "I saw."

A car pulled onto the long gravel lane and sped toward them. He recognized the vehicle.

"Local press is here, Deputy. Keep them away from my brother-in-law."

Boyd quickened his pace toward Kyle, who stood teetering at the edge of the field, his white T-shirt and pale blue pajama pants streaked with blood.

"What the hell happened here, Kyle?" Boyd asked. The rain had stopped, but his black boots were thick with mud. "Looks like a war zone."

Kyle turned to face Boyd. Mud streaked his face except for a line beneath each eye washed clean by tears.

A handprint of blood sat in the center of his T-shirt.

"T-T-Tommy," he stuttered.

Boyd dropped his hands onto Kyle's shoulders. His brother-in-law wobbled on his feet; he might fall at any second.

"What happened to Tommy?" Boyd asked, his voice level and calm.

"He—" Kyle stopped, and looked at the sheriff, his eyes finally registering who he was talking to. "Boyd? Boyd. Thank God you're here."

"What happened?" he asked again. "What happened to my nephew?"

Kyle wobbled on unsteady legs and Boyd slipped an arm around his shoulders, walking him toward the cruiser as Deputy Kirkhoff corralled the local newspaper reporter. He dropped Kyle into the driver's seat and his brother-in-law's head fell into his hands.

"Kyle? Stay with me. What happened to Tommy?"

The eyes that rose to meet his were red and swollen, eyes that had seen things a parent should never see.

"Dead." His voice choked off. "He was dead."

Dead? Boyd's right arm shot forward to grab the car's roof and hold tight.

"What do you mean he was dead?"

"Dead, Boyd." Weakness saturated each word. "Debbie and me, we found him lying in the mud, the corn on fire all around him, but he wasn't touched. Not a burn mark on him."

Boyd had once arrested a guy hopped up on PCP who had pummeled him with fists that could no longer feel pain. That had hurt, but the punch in the gut Kyle hammered him with now was worse than that by a mile.

"Then why do you say he was dead?"

"He wasn't breathing." Kyle ran a forearm under his nose. "Then Debbie, she dropped down beside him and started mouth-to-mouth and pumping his chest and all that."

Kyle grabbed Boyd's free hand and squeezed. "She saved his life, Boyd. He woke up."

Pent-up anxiety whooshed out with an exhale. Debbie. Damn straight it was Debbie. She took a CPR class last summer. Hell, he'd taught it.

Over the roof of the Crown Vic, an argument between Kirkhoff and Jennifer Blair ended with the reporter storming around the deputy and stepping over the line of yellow police tape.

"The boy's going to be okay. He's alive and breathing, and he's in good hands," he told Kyle, pulling his brother-in-law back to his feet. "Now let's get to the house before that jackal corners us. I gotta put on my sheriff face and ask you some questions. It's best to do that at your own kitchen table with some coffee, because I haven't had mine yet."

Kyle nodded as Boyd tugged him forward.

"And some ham and eggs if you've got them." He draped an arm over Kyle's shoulders. "Don't worry, if you can't tell by my slim figure, I'm pretty good around a kitchen."

[5]

The four-person tent Bobby's dad had hammered into the hard, baked earth at the campground was going to be a hot, miserable mess to sleep in.

They were at Smithville Lake, Bobby knew from the signs, but they sure as heck couldn't see the lake from here. All he could see were trees and other tents.

"Ooooh. Yes, yes," a woman's voice moaned from one of them, an orange nylon tent two spots over. "Harder. Harder. Hit me. *HIT ME.*"

The sharp slap of skin-on-skin snapped in the air. The woman screamed in pain before moaning, "yes," again.

Bobby's legs kicked beneath him as he sat on the tailgate of the station wagon, sweat already beading on his upper lip. I know what you're doing in there, he thought.

Naughty, naughty.

Bobby's mom cleared her throat and glared at his dad, then nodded toward Bobby. His dad sat in a lawn chair drinking beer, his eyes on the orange tent.

"Ohhh, Gawwwwd," moaned the tent.

"Todd," his mom said, the word carrying. She cleared her throat again. "Todd?"

His dad turned toward her. "Yes?" Then shook his head like he'd only just noticed Bobby was there.

"Oh, shoot," his dad said. "Hey son." He pointed to the five-gallon water jug where Bobby rested his arm. "Why don't you go fill that up at the shower house? There should be a spigot marked 'Potable Water.' Make sure you fill it up from that one. Okay, pal?"

Bobby lifted the empty jug, his ears still on the orange tent. "What's *potable* mean?"

"It means—"

"Oh, oh, oh," the woman's shrill voice split the air.

"It means it's safe to drink." His dad downed the beer and tossed it into the firepit. "If it doesn't say *potable*, it could give us some kind of bacteria or parasite." He dropped his feet off the cooler and pulled out another beer. "We have enough parasites in this world, son. We don't need to personally feed them."

Maybe you could pay as much attention to your family as you are the orange tent, Bobby thought as he grabbed the jug and slid off the tailgate. The hammer his father used to drive in the tent stakes sat on the picnic table, a sixteen-ouncer, its handle smooth from little use. Bobby saw his fingers wrap around that handle and lift it. An electric cord hung from the hammer. No, no. This was wrong. Not a hammer. I'm not going to kill my parents with a hammer.

"Bobby?" his father said from outside his vision.

But you will kill them, a strange voice said in his head.

But I will kill them.

Wait. What?

Bobby had heard all sorts of voices when he knew nobody had spoken, mostly his own, and sometimes Scooby Doo said things to him when he wasn't even watching TV. But this voice was different. It seemed more real than the other voices but distant at the same time.

He concentrated on his father, but good ol' Dad's head was full of images of Tonja at work screaming at him to hit her while they did it on the conference table. And his mom? She was worried about missing her stories if they stayed through Monday. That Tad Martin was up to something.

Pathetic.

Who are you? Bobby asked inside his head.

Someone you need.

"Bobby?" his father snapped, and Bobby's vision faded, the hammer still on the table. He'd never touched it.

"What?"

"What the heck are you doing, son?" his father asked. "It was like you went someplace else. You're not playing with Ouija boards or listening to that Ozzy Osborne, are you?"

Bobby slowly shook his head. "No, sir." The words were soft and quiet.

His father took another drink of beer. "Good. That stuff's evil, son. That's what we're here to protect you from. Now," he said, "go get that water."

Hello? he pushed with his mind, but the voice never responded. It didn't need to. Oh, heck no. The voice had already told him what he was going to do: *Kill them.*

His folks were asking for it, really.

"Now remember where we are," his mom called after him as he started down the trail. "I don't want you getting lost."

I'm not a damn baby, Bobby thought. "Okay, Mom," he said. He hurried around a bend and disappeared from the view of the temporary Casa de Garrett. His mom was no more likeable than his dad.

He paused for a moment to hear one last scream from the orange tent before the show was over.

At least for now.

A few tents and RVs appeared around the bend, a shower house in the middle of them. Bobby didn't like the look of the shower house, which possibly contained strange, naked men. A sign fastened to the building read "Potable Water." His dad was right, of course. He always thought he was right.

He set the jug down beneath the spigot and turned it on; water shot out and into the jug. Bobby's stomach clenched when that something inside his brain that told him what people were thinking before they even said it tapped a little dance on the inside of his skull. Someone lurked nearby, he could sense it. Just like his mom and dad had told him, it was somebody bad.

A fist-sized chunk of concrete lay next to the building. He wrapped his fingers around it and picked it up.

"Whatcha going to do with that, kid?" a teenage boy said from behind him.

Bobby jumped slightly and turned to face the boy. A lanky kid about his age stood a few feet from him, his shorts too short, his stained Batman T-shirt faded. The boy leaned against the wall of the shower house and grinned at Bobby with a smile that cut a crooked line across his face.

Again, Bobby's stomach clenched. That boy was what his mom would call a "nogoodnik." Go away, he thought. Go away, go away, go away.

Hey, Bobby said to the voice, but it was gone, as if it were never there.

"I'm going to throw it into the lake to watch it splash," Bobby said. "And I'm not a kid."

The boy laughed. "Well, how old are you? I'm sixteen."

"Yeah, right," Bobby said. "I'm fourteen." He shook his head. "I gotta go. I have to take this water back to my camp."

Bobby leaned over the jug, staring at the water gurgling in the jug, hoping like heck it filled up fast.

It didn't.

"You wanna see a dead body?" the boy asked.

Bobby froze. "You do *not* have a dead body."

The boy laughed again, the sound like metal on metal. "Naw. It's not a dead body. It's just a snapping turtle."

"You're crazy," Bobby said. "Snapping turtles are dangerous."

Even before the frown grew on the boy, Bobby felt that was the wrong thing to say.

The boy glared at him, his eyes flat, angry. "I'm not crazy. I'm just having fun and danger's part of the fun. So, you wanna have fun?"

Fun?

"No fun," his mom would say. "Fun leads to bad things, Bobby. You don't want to be a bad boy when you grow up, do you?" If you knew I smoked, Mother, you'd know I already have fun.

He looked at this boy. He was exactly the kind of person his mom and dad kept him "safe" from. Ha.

Go with him.

Shit, Bobby screamed into his head. *Who are you?*

Only the thing you need.

"Sure," Bobby said, squeezing the chunk of concrete hard enough his knuckles grew white. Bobby turned off the water. "Let's go."

The stained-shirt boy led Bobby through a copse of trees and into a thick patch of undergrowth. Oh, that boy was a nogoodnik all right. It oozed off him with a scent Bobby couldn't really smell, not with his nose, but it was there nonetheless. The lake opened before them; blue-gray water lapped a rocky shore. The morning was quiet, save for the faint hum of a motorboat on another part of the water. The smell of dead fish drifted past. It seemed the real world was a hundred miles away.

"Where's the turtle?" Bobby asked, his already upset stomach crawling like it was alive.

"There's no turtle." The boy turned, his body inches away from Bobby's. Bobby could feel the boy's heartbeat, feel his heat as their chests pressed together. The boy's breath brushed Bobby's face with the sour reek of Funyuns.

No. No-no-no. This is bad. This is wrong. I have to go. I have to go. Tendrils of fear wormed through him, freezing his body. Bobby couldn't move.

"Wha-what are you doing?" Bobby stuttered, his mind, clear at the water faucet, now scrambled like a plate of eggs.

You know what to do.

A hand cupped Bobby's scrotum through his thin polyester shorts. The boy gently rolled Bobby's testicles in his hand. The sensation shot through him; his skin flushed, his penis grew at the touch. No. Bad-bad-bad, rushed through Bobby's head, but the touch, the caress.

He shivered.

Do it, Bobby.

"I told you I wanted to have fun. You want to have fun, right?" The boy moved his hand to the elastic waistband of Bobby's shorts and pushed it down into the underpants. His fingers grasped Bobby's penis.

Do it, Bobby.

Wrong. Wrong, wrong, wrong. Thoughts rushed to his mom, so close. What would his mom say?

Do it.

The boy looked Bobby hard in the eyes, his crooked grin with a dusting of mustache morphed into a smile, a wicked, wicked smile. Under the dark shade of the trees, the boy looked like Batman's Joker.

Do it.

"She'd say you're bad," Bobby said aloud. "She'd tell you what you are. A nogoodnik."

Do it now.

"No good, what?" the boy asked as Bobby pulled back his right hand, the fist-sized piece of concrete still wrapped in his fingers and smashed it into the boy's temple. The thud echoed across the waves. The boy staggered backward, his hand sliding from Bobby's shorts. Blood gushed from the boy's scalp, splattering Bobby's arm.

Bobby grabbed the boy's Batman T-shirt, holding him up.

"You're bad," Bobby said. He pulled the chunk of concrete back, poised behind him. "You're a bad boy."

Bobby struck him again, and again, and again. The boy's eyes crossed as Bobby brought the concrete down on his nose; the cartilage crunched under the mass of rock, splitting the boy's face. He collapsed backward, an eye fell free of its crushed socket as his body splashed into Smithville Lake. Bobby watched until the boy stopped making bubbles in the murky, red-stained water, then he dropped the bloody concrete in after him.

[6]

The reporter tapped on the door, but Boyd ignored her and whisked six eggs and a splash of milk, pouring them into a warm skillet. A few minutes later, Boyd stirred the eggs and scraped them onto a plate. He set it on the table in front of Kyle. Kyle didn't move, his eyes glazed over.

The reporter tapped on the door again and Boyd leveled a look through the window.

She didn't knock again.

"Where'd that anhydrous tank come from?" Boyd asked, filling his plate before sitting across from Kyle. "That yours?"

The plate of eggs sat untouched.

"Kyle?"

Kyle leaned back in his chair and took in Boyd, the glaze in his eyes still there.

"What?"

"The anhydrous tank. Did it come from your property?"

His head shook slowly. "No. No, it didn't. I think it came from Trent Lahone's place."

The black leather-bound notebook lay next to Boyd's plate. He scratched notes into it.

"Then how did it get into your field?"

Kyle pushed out an audible exhale. "I gotta go," he said, pushing his chair back, the wooden legs screeching across the tiles. "I gotta go see Tommy."

"No," Boyd snapped, and Kyle sat still. "You don't. He's got doctors and his mother. Not a damn thing you can do there. What you need to do is try and help me make some kind of sense out of this." Boyd jabbed a forkful of eggs. "I'll drive you to the hospital myself, just as soon as we're done. Lord knows you're in no shape to get there by yourself."

Kyle's shoulders slumped, the wind taken out of him. "Yeah, okay." He scratched the graying stubble on his chin. Boyd had never seen Kyle look like something out of a zombie movie before. "Where do you want to start?"

"I guess at the beginning," Boyd said through a mouthful of eggs. "What exactly happened here last night?"

Kyle leaned forward, his elbows resting on the table. "The explosion woke us up," he said. "There was the boom and a big flash of light. Stuff fell off the walls." He ran a hand through matted hair. "Debbie went to check on Tommy, and he wasn't in his room. We found him out in the field."

"How close to the explosion?" Boyd asked.

"I don't know. But if Tommy caused it—"

"If Tommy caused it, he'd be in more pieces than a box of Legos." Boyd paused and lifted a knife to start on the ham. "I don't believe for a second Tommy was involved in this. He's just too good a kid. He must have seen something or heard something and went outside to check."

"No." Kyle sat up straight. "He wouldn't do that. If that was the case, he'd have come and got me." His words dried as he spoke. "Or not."

"What do you mean?"

Kyle sipped his coffee. "He didn't come get me when he saw the footprints. He went into the house himself."

"So," Boyd said. "You're saying he might have gone off on his own?"

Kyle nodded and turned his face toward his plate.

Boyd chewed. Something was wrong here. Somebody would have had to steal a tank of anhydrous ammonia, move it to this property without anyone noticing, and explode it. Tommy was ten years old. He wouldn't have the reason; he wouldn't know how.

"You and Debbie cure this yourselves?" Boyd asked, holding up a piece of ham with his fork.

"No." Kyle stood, walked to the coffeepot, and refilled his cup. He held the pot out to Boyd, who nodded. "Picked it up at Nadler's. It good?"

Boyd stuffed the piece into his mouth. "Sure is." He chewed in silence as Kyle walked back to the table to refill his cup. "Everything going okay around here? The farm? Debbie?"

Kyle held his coffee cup in both hands.

"Farm's losing money. Most are. Then the ag job at the high school came up and I passed on it."

"That when Debbie started at the library?"

Kyle nodded.

"And she resents you for that?"

"Yeah."

Boyd's knife screeched on the plate as it passed through the ham. "This affect Tommy in any way? He act out? Sass mouth? Get in fights with his buddies? Anything strange?"

"No. Not that I can think of. Boyd, I really need to get to the hospital."

The sheriff lay his silverware on the now-empty plate and pushed himself to his feet.

"I know. Things are going to be all right. I'll find out what happened here, that's my job. And the ER doctor and nurses will take good care of my nephew, that's their job."

He stepped next to Kyle and slapped him on the arm.

"I'll clean this up," he said. "You go on upstairs to change your clothes and wash your face. You look terrible."

[7]

The campground was dead, as dead as the boy, everyone off fishing, or hiking, or napping. The shower house stood still, a concrete affront to nature. The men's entrance was open, revealing a black hole into the building. Bobby took a deep breath and stepped inside; dim light filtered in from vents under the eaves. He exhaled. The men's side was empty, but he already knew that.

The blood on his hands didn't want to come off. Bobby scrubbed his face hard because it was tough to make out details in such little light, and the mirror was only a polished sheet of metal screwed into the wall over the sink. The blood under his fingernails was the hardest to remove. He knew that was the part of today he'd remember. Not a bad boy touching his penis. Not bashing the boy's skull with a chunk of concrete. Not even the voice inside his head. But the blood under his nails that didn't want to come off.

A shout echoed from outside, hammering Bobby to the spot.

"Ronald," a woman's voice yelled. "Ronald Johnson. Honey, please come back to the tent. We're going to have hotdogs."

So, Ronald was lost. A relaxed smile crossed Bobby's face. Maybe that's your name, Mr. "You wanna see a dead body?" Is it, Ronald?

He shut off the water faucet and walked outside. The woman stood by the door, her eyes eager. When she saw Bobby, her face fell slack.

"Oh, sorry. I'm looking for my son, Ronald. He's about your age, wearing a Batman T-shirt. Have you seen him?"

Have I seen him? "Yes, ma'am," he said. "Just a few minutes ago. He said he was going to go play with a turtle down by the lake." He pointed toward the trees where the bad boy lay in the water.

Her face brightened. "Oh, thank you. Thank you. You're such a nice boy," she said, and hurried down the trail that led to the lake.

Bobby lifted the full water jug and went back to camp.

"Where have you been, boy?" his dad said when Bobby came into view, gripping the jug handle in both hands. His dad didn't get out of his chair to help. "Cheese and Rice, son, I give you one little job and it takes you a month of Sundays to get it done."

Kschlip, kschlip, kschlip came from the picnic table where his mom sliced onions for the hamburgers. "I was getting worried about you, honey," she said, not looking up from the table. "What took you so long?"

Wanna see a dead body?

He plucked a stray bit of onion off the cutting board and popped it into his mouth.

"Nothing really," he said. "I just made a friend."

[8]

Sirens cut through the late-afternoon air as Bobby's dad took the burgers off the grill.

Jason Offutt

"Something's happening," his mom said. "I'm glad we're here instead of out there. Out there's full of dangerous, nasty people. Don't you forget that, Bobby."

Bobby choked back a laugh and spooned cold potato salad onto his paper plate next to the baked beans. There were, he thought. But not anymore.

Right?

Right?

The voice was silent. Had I ever heard it?

Bobby's dad walked a plate of burgers to the table, the meat probably still pink on the inside because that's how Todd Garrett liked it, by God. Then he pulled another beer from the cooler, because that's what Todd Garrett liked too.

"Boy," his dad said. "Before you fix your plate you are to set out a plate for our Lord and Savior Jesus Christ."

"But Dad." Bobby held up a paper plate. "Would the Lord eat off this?"

"The Lord was humble son, He—"

"I wonder what all those sirens are about," his mom said, cutting off her husband before he got too angry. "Sounds like they're coming closer."

"Traffic accident out on the highway," Todd said. "Or degenerates. They're everywhere." He pointed at the orange tent. "Even places where a man takes his family."

Before eating, the three held hands. "Lord Almighty, Maker of Heaven and Earth," his dad said. "Please bless this beautiful food we are about to nourish our bodies with, bodies created by you, our most heavenly Father. Please forgive us our wicked ways and lead us down the path of righteousness, leading us from temptation. There is always a place set at our table for our Lord. Amen."

"Amen," Bobby said, pulling a bun from the package and building his hamburger.

"Maybe somebody got murdered," Bobby said, a giggle somewhere near the surface.

His mom dropped her fork.

"What on earth would make you say that, son?" his dad asked through a mouthful of potato salad.

Bobby shrugged. "I don't know. Anything can happen at a place like this."

"Well," his dad said. "There might be sexual degenerates here, but I certainly wouldn't take my family to a place where someone could get murdered. I mean, it's not like we went to Kansas City."

A laugh burst from Bobby. "Then I guess you should have left me at home."

"Robert Garret," his mother started, but two men in tan law-enforcement uniforms, one tall and thin, the other shorter and thick around the shoulders, appeared on the trail that led from the shower house and approached their table.

"Evening folks," the tall officer said, approaching the picnic table. "I'm Deputy Martens with the Clay County Sheriff's Department. This is Deputy Gonnor."

A jolt ran up Bobby, straight from his solar plexus to his brain leaving him with a wide, tight smile. A giggle bubbled out.

His dad glared at Bobby before turning toward the deputies.

"Evening, officers," he said. "What can we help you with?"

Deputy Martens approached the table and rested his right foot on the empty end of the bench. Deputy Gonnor stood back, thumbs in his belt.

"There's a dead boy," Martens said. "Ronald Johnson. Sixteen. His mother found him floating in the lake. Appears to have been attacked."

Bobby's mom inhaled sharply. Bobby's dad shook his head. "Here? Here? What kind of place is the parks department running here, officer?"

The deputy nodded to Bobby. "The mother said she was directed to the body by a boy about your age. About your size. About your hair color. Do you know anything about Ronald Johnson's death?"

"Now see here," Bobby's dad sputtered.

"Yes, sir," Bobby said.

The deputy dropped his boot to the dusty ground. "What can you tell me?" He pulled a notebook and pen from his shirt pocket. "What's your name, son?"

Giggles racked Bobby's thin frame; the smile never left. "Bobby," he said. "Robert Garrett. Ronald took me to the edge of the lake and played with my dick."

A stifled yelp came from his mom.

His dad's half-eaten burger dropped to his plate. "My God, what are you talking about, Bobby?" The beer, the shock, slurred his words.

Have another beer, Dad.

"And?" the deputy asked, his shoulders rigid.

Bobby bit into his hamburger and chewed slowly; a spot of ketchup oozed out the corner of his mouth. He didn't wipe it off.

"The boy was bad. He was real bad," Bobby said, his voice wavering with more giggles. He couldn't stop them now. They came out in jumpy waves. "So, I hit him in the head with a piece of concrete because a voice in my head told me to. His face cracked open like a Halloween pumpkin, and he fell in the lake."

A laugh burst from Bobby. Deputy Gonnor stepped closer.

"Then the water got all red." He laughed out loud again; he couldn't stop it and didn't want to. "I killed him. I killed him because he was bad." He turned his face to Deputy Martens, his expression blank. "You can never tell a person's motivations until they have a hand in your pants."

The air seemed to go from his mother, the wind sounding like a deflating balloon.

Bobby's dad tried to stand, but his legs wouldn't let him. "Bobby. Son. Please tell this man the truth. Please tell him you were joking. Please tell him that, Bobby."

"This is a serious thing to admit," the deputy said to Bobby. "Are you sure you're telling the truth?"

He lifted up his wrists. "The truth, the whole truth, and nothing but the truth."

"Bobby, no." His mother's words nearly inaudible.

Deputy Gonnor approached Bobby and grabbed his right wrist, turning him and grabbing his left wrist.

Bobby didn't struggle.

"I'm afraid we're going to have to take your son to the station to question him further," Deputy Martens said, facing Bobby's parents, the click of the cuffs around their son's slim wrists loud in the late afternoon.

"Are you arresting him?" Bobby's dad asked.

"No sir," Deputy Gonnor said. "Procedure. If we find your son's story corresponds with the evidence, it's likely we'll arrest him. You'll be allowed to come to the station as well, but I'd let your wife drive."

Tears streamed down his dad's flushed cheeks. "No, Bobby. You didn't do this. We didn't teach you to do this."

"Neither did Jesus," Bobby said. The smile never wavered. "But I did it anyway. Please take me away, Deputy. Ronald Johnson touched my dick. He was a bad boy, so I bashed in his head with a chunk of concrete. I killed Ronald Johnson. I'm ready to go."

Bobby's dad reached feebly for his son, but Bobby stepped closer to Deputy Martens.

The deputy pulled a business card from his chest pocket and set it on the picnic table.

"This is where your son will be held," he said, and walked away, Bobby escorted by Deputy Gonnor.

A scream tore from Bobby's mom as his dad tried to hold her when the deputy led Bobby down the trail and out of sight.

[9]

Thomas woke in a bright, white hospital room, his mom and dad sitting in cold metal chairs at the edge of his bed. An IV tube snaked from his right arm to a plastic bag of clear liquid, and wires sprang from beneath his hospital gown and attached to a machine beside the bed. Every few seconds the machine beeped.

"Where am I?" he asked, his voice dry and hoarse.

His mom nearly leaped from her chair. "Tommy," she gasped. "Tommy, baby." She took his hands in hers.

"Why are you so dirty?" Tommy asked.

His dad moved to the other side of the bed and took Thomas's other hand in his large, rough ones.

"Son."

His dad was crying. His dad didn't cry. What happened?

"I'm in the hospital," he said. "Why am I in the hospital?"

"You don't remember?" his mom asked.

Tommy shook his head. The movement made the room start to spin, and he pressed his head deeper into the pillow to make it stop.

"There was an explosion, honey," his mom said. "You were in the explosion, out in the cornfield. There's a bite on your leg. The

EMT said it looked like a dog bite, or a coyote's. Do you remember that?"

"No," he whispered.

His dad squeezed Thomas's hand. "That's okay, son. It'll come back. What's important is the doctor said you're going to be all right. You're one tough kid. Your mom—" His words shook.

"Did the right thing," a lady's voice finished for him.

A doctor walked in, so young her face was still without wrinkles.

"And you should thank your lucky stars she was loving enough to take a CPR class." She paused and laid a hand on Tommy's arm. "It's good to see you awake."

His dad smiled at his mom over Thomas's bed, and she smiled back. Thomas hadn't seen that in a while.

"You don't need to stay here long," the doctor said, addressing Thomas. "We're going to move you upstairs for today, maybe tomorrow too. Then you can go home, after the rabies shots. They're not fun, but necessary. Don't hate me for it. But because of your mother's fast action, you're going to be just fine."

Thomas closed his eyes and took a deep breath and thought, *She can't read the future.*

Chapter Four  1994

[1]

THE NURSES AT SISTERS OF Mercy Hospital were mean—whom Thomas's mom would call strict, but Thomas thought "royal bitches" fit better. He never said this aloud, oh no.

He knew what that would get him.

Nurse Carroll sat in a plastic chair in the fifth-floor common room, her legs crossed, a yellow legal pad on a wooden clipboard on her lap. Six patients sat less straight-backed, less confident, less like they cared one bit.

A familiar frown pulled the corners of Nurse Carroll's mouth, and she scribbled on her notepad.

"We have a new member in our little group," she said, looking at the collection of teenagers doing their best not to look back at her. "Robert Garrett. Mr. Garrett, do you know why you're here?"

"Bobby," the new kid said softly. "Call me Bobby."

"Okay, Bobby," Nurse Carroll said. "Do you know why you are here?"

Bobby shook his head, as if trying to dislodge a memory. He looked around the room. Everyone but Thomas looked away. "I hit a boy in the head with concrete until he fell in the water and drowned," he said flatly.

"And do you remember why you did that?" Nurse Carroll asked.

Bobby shrugged. "Because he was bad."

Nurse Carroll took a breath and let it out slowly. "How was he bad, Mr. Garrett?"

Thomas sat up straighter when Bobby laughed. Nobody, not even the violent stabby patients, gave attitude to Nurse Carroll.

"He took me into the trees and shoved his hand down my pants." Bobby stopped, his eyes dropping to his hands. "He touched my—my thing."

A boy named Mitchell snorted. Nurse Carroll glared at him like she wanted to cut someone, then turned back to Bobby and faked a slight smile.

"And how did that make you feel?"

"How did that make me feel?" burst from Bobby, his head turned up, staring into Nurse Carroll's eyes. "This kid I didn't know stuck his hand down my pants and fingered my dick. How do you think that made me feel?"

Thomas sucked in a breath and held it. Nobody yelled at Nurse Carroll. Nobody.

She never looked down as she wrote.

"There's no need to get excited, Mr. Garrett." Nurse Carroll folded the bottom right corner of Bobby's page before flipping to a fresh one. "You're safe here."

Bobby shrugged, the fire apparently gone. "He was just bad, so I made him not be bad anymore."

Her frown returned. "And how do you feel now?"

Thomas flinched as Mitchell started to rock in his chair next to him. Bekka moaned and slapped herself. Something about Bobby was terrifying.

"Sad, Nurse Carroll," he said. "I feel sad."

She made one final note, the scratch of her pen the only sound in the room.

"Thank you, Robert."

Nurse Carroll's eyes, like blue lasers, cut across the circle and settled on Thomas.

"How about you, Mr. Cavanaugh? Would you like to tell us why you're here," Nurse Carroll asked, but it wasn't a question.

He leaned back in his plastic chair, just like the others. The circle of patients all wore the same white polyester and cotton short-sleeved shirts, long pants, and slip-on shoes. No shoestrings here. No siree.

Thomas had been here three weeks, and every Tuesday and Thursday he'd participated in this circle, listening to people talk about what they had done to be sentenced to this stupid hospital. Johnny had found his mother dead in the bathtub from a heart attack and lived with her body in the house for three weeks. After Jillian's stepfather raped her one too many times—her mother too weak from chemotherapy to stop him—she shoved a screwdriver through the asshole's eye and scrambled his brain. Mitchell liked to cut people, and when he couldn't find people to cut, he cut himself; his arms were crisscrossed with thin white scars. Bekka just liked to set things on fire—like her grandma's house.

Thomas woke almost every night screaming because of something he couldn't remember. Unlike most of the other patients in this ward, his parents put him in here voluntarily. It had been four years since the incident and seeing a therapist twice a week hadn't helped. He could leave whenever he wanted, but what he wanted was to stop screaming at night because of the events in a cornfield. He didn't want to remember those events. Oh, no.

Whatever made him wake screaming, he didn't want to remember that at all.

"The reason I'm here today is the same as it was on Tuesday," Thomas said, his voice tired. Too tired for a fourteen-year-old.

"But Mr. Garrett wasn't here on Tuesday," Nurse Carroll said. "Please, Mr. Cavanaugh."

He exhaled. "I was in an explosion when I was ten." He closed his eyes and tried to concentrate, but he couldn't remember more than he'd already shared. "There was a coyote, and a smiling man, and somebody else. Somebody behind me."

"Have you remembered who that was?" Nurse Carroll asked, her legs crossed tightly. While playing cards, Johnny had told Thomas he'd like to get up under that skirt, but that was just gross. Totally.

Thomas shook his head. "No."

Nurse Carroll scrawled something on her notepad. "What do you remember next?"

Next? She asks that every time, and every time I don't know.

"I was dead," he said flatly. "There wasn't a white light. There wasn't a tunnel. I didn't see Jesus."

Jillian giggled at the mention of Jesus.

"It was just dark, and I woke up to my mother performing CPR."

He paused and looked around the group; everyone's eyes were looking down at their lap, as usual, except the new kid. Bobby Garrett's eyes smoldered as they reached into his. A stab, like a pinprick, poked behind Thomas's eyes, jabbing into his brain, growing, spreading outward like plant roots. He wanted to slam his eyes shut, but they wouldn't close. Memories, He-Man, Star Trek, helping his dad on the truck, the plate with the shit, the fairy.

A grin touched Bobby's lips when Nurse Carroll stood. "That's all for today," she said, blocking Bobby from Thomas's line of sight. The pain vanished and Thomas slumped in his chair, his breath coming hard. "We'll pick up here tomorrow." And she walked toward the nurse's station.

When Thomas looked up, Bobby had already gone.

[2]

Thomas's screams jerked him awake. He shot up and swung his feet to the floor. Sweat soaked his hair, his lungs strained to catch a breath. The memory of the dream—like the memory of the night he died—was empty.

The hall lights, dimmed for sleep, glowed steadily through the small window in the door. The widow was wire mesh, nothing glass in this ward. Nope, nope, nope. Nothing a patient could use to harm themselves or others.

Nurse Carroll gave him a notebook, not the spiral kind with a metal coil a creative person could use to inflict all sorts of damage but a black-and-white speckled composition notebook he couldn't hurt himself with. She also handed him a blue felt-tip pen. Everything at Sisters of Mercy was rounded, cushioned, and practically covered in bubble wrap. Safety first.

"This is for your dreams, Mr. Cavanaugh," she had said after his first Tuesday session. Tears invaded his story that day, and he stopped early. "I don't remember," he repeated, over and over. Nurse Carroll slipped the notebook from beneath her wooden clipboard and handed it to him. "We dream every night but forget most of them. Some we remember right when we wake, but they quickly dissolve." She placed the marker in his hand. "Keep these on the stand next to your bed, and as soon as you wake, record what you remember. This may help lead us to where we need to go."

He kept the notebook on the nightstand and every time he woke screaming, the horror of darkness still pressing against him, he put the pen to paper, and let his hand move. He drew circles. Always circles.

Circles with teeth.

[3]

Breakfast in the psych ward at Sisters of Mercy was usually some combination of oatmeal, powdered eggs, fried potatoes, sausages, and/or cereal with a cup of milk or juice. Orderlies served it in the rec room on cafeteria tables wheeled out from a large closet and unfolded by Ted the janitor. There was no coffee, there was no tea. Caffeine made people jumpy, and that's one of the many things the nurses at Sisters of Mercy did not want. Thomas accepted his tray of eggs, potatoes, and sausages and a plastic cup of milk. He sat at the farthest end of the farthest table from the nurses' station. They could watch him cry, they could watch him sleep, they could watch him poop, but for some reason Thomas didn't want the nurse on duty to watch him eat. Jillian slid her tray onto the table across from Thomas: oatmeal and raisins with a cup of apple juice for her.

She tried to smile, but her eyes twitched like a rabbit's.

"Hey," Thomas said. "I like your hair today."

It was usually flat and lay across her eyes like a sheepdog's, but something was different about it that day. Staring at her oatmeal, Jillian swiped a lock of red hair behind her ear. Her cheeks flared pink. Gingers could never hide their emotions.

"Thank you," she said, squeezing a small plastic packet of maple syrup onto her oatmeal. "The nurse. Uh, not Nurse Carroll, Madison, the young one, she, uh, cut my bangs," she said, stirring her breakfast with a plastic spoon.

Given another place, another situation, Thomas may have thought Jillian liked him, but he woke every night screaming, and from what he could hear down the hall from behind his locked door, so did she. Her bastard stepfather didn't just leave bruises—those were long gone; he'd left much deeper marks.

"Well, it looks nice."

"The easiest way to get a girl's attention is to say something nice about the way she looks," his mom had told Thomas before last semester's eighth-grade dance. That was before no one could take the screaming anymore and he wound up at Sisters of Mercy.

"Thank you," Jillian said, looking up from her breakfast, the spoon still stirring.

But his mom never told him what to do after he had their attention. He stabbed his reconstituted eggs and took a bite.

"What do you think of the new guy?"

"Oh, my gosh," shot from her mouth, her left hand stretched across the table to touch Thomas's arm. She realized what she'd done and pulled it back. Thomas didn't know what he'd expected, but he hadn't expected that. Her face grew pink again; so did his. "He's creepy."

Yeah, he is.

"He talks about 'bad people' a lot," she said, her voice low. There was something else there. Excitement? Maybe. "He thinks everyone's bad but him. You don't have problems. I don't have problems. That guy has problems."

Thomas hid his mouth in his wrist to mask his laughter, but Jillian saw it and smiled. The smile was gentle, beautiful. Damn that son of a bitch who put her in here.

Then the smile fell. "But I was talking with Bekka after showers, and, and—" Jillian stopped, her voice seemingly choked by a fist.

Thomas leaned closer. "What?" he whispered.

Jillian looked around the room before speaking. "She told me he asked her to play UNO, and he told her not to play a Draw Four."

"Yeah?" Thomas said. "Nobody wants to get hit with a Draw Four."

She stirred the spoon through her breakfast.

"No. She hadn't played the card. It was still in her hand. She was going to play the Draw Four, but Bobby looked at her with those scary eyes of his and said, 'Play the blue seven.'"

"So?"

"Don't you get it?" she said, shoving a spoon of oatmeal into her mouth. "She was going to play the Draw Four, and he knew she had a blue seven. He *knew* which cards she had. He knew."

Wow. That was loud. Thomas looked around. Nurse Madison, on duty at the nurses' station, looked up from her magazine and frowned. Thomas's attention dropped back to Jillian.

"What are you saying?" he whispered. "He's psychic? Mind reading isn't real."

Jillian fell quiet, stabbing her oatmeal. Thomas toyed with his eggs a few moments before changing the subject.

"I have my one-on-ones with Johnny," he said. "Afterward he talks about porking Nurse Carroll."

Jillian laughed out loud; a raisin flew from her mouth and landed on the table. She immediately hid her face in her hands. Thomas didn't turn from her because he knew what he'd see: the few people in the room looking at them. He didn't care.

The pink flush was slow to leave her face.

"I'm getting out of here soon," he said, pushing his fork through his food.

"But you're still screaming at night."

"It's been five months. If this place hasn't fixed me by now, it isn't going to." Thomas's attention dropped to his plate. He sawed at the over-microwaved sausage patty with his fork. Fixed? What is *fixed?* I feel fine, except at night when the . . . the what comes? What is it? Why can't I remember?

"I'm getting out of here in a month," Jillian said softly, staring at her food. "I'm going to live with my aunt."

Thomas hadn't told anyone he was here voluntarily. He didn't think anyone would accept him if he did.

"You think, maybe, we could do something?" Jillian continued. "You know, like when we get out. See a movie or something?"

Thomas froze. A date? Jillian was asking him to go out on a date?

"Yeah," he said. "Sure."

It wasn't until much later he realized the mental ward of a hospital probably wasn't the best place to meet girls.

[4]

The screaming from the kid who died dragged Bobby from sleep like it did every night, breaking the dream of his parents lying bloody and lifeless in the basement. In the dream, Bobby stood over them holding the heavy lamp that usually sat on his bedside table. He always woke with a smile.

The room was cold. It was at least ninety degrees outside in the Missouri summer, so why the hell did it have to be so cold in here? Bobby stood and walked to the wire window on the padded door.

"Hey, kid," he said into the dim light of the hall. It was never dark at Sisters of Mercy. "You. Kid who died in the cornfield."

Silence.

"I know you're awake."

"What do you want, Bobby?"

Bobby leaned into the door padding, trying to get as close to the dead kid as possible. He could feel him better that way; he knew the boy had sat up.

"Do you know why you scream at night?" Bobby asked.

The dead kid was processing the question, he knew. In his head he just knew. This was a mystery. A mystery for the boy, for his parents, for Dr. Tameron, Nurse Carroll, everyone. Everyone but—

But who? Bobby's mind felt someone else. Someone other than the people here at the hospital. The dead-alive boy had met a little girl who changed his life.

A little girl that wasn't a little girl.

"No," Thomas said. "I don't."

Bobby grinned. "I do."

The dead kid's face appeared in the mesh window of his own door. "What do you mean?"

"I know why you scream," Bobby said, his voice low.

A second went by, then two.

"No," the kid said. "You don't. Now leave me alone." His face disappeared from the window.

"It's the mouth," Bobby whispered in a snake-like hiss. He didn't know what the mouth was, but he knew the boy thought about it, and he knew it was good, wickedly good. Bobby wondered if that mouth was the one that spoke to him at the lake. "The mouth with all the teeth. It came that night. It killed you, Thomas Cavanaugh. It killed you dead."

Bobby hadn't known about the mouth with the teeth, it just came to him. Things always came to Bobby right when he needed them. Like that chunk of concrete when he'd met the bad boy.

"What are you talking about?" Thomas asked, his voice growing impatient.

"The girl led you to Dauðr, and that monster killed you in the cornfield," Bobby said. It was all coming to him from somewhere, a place he woke from one night in wet sheets, a place in the corn, a place where blood flooded his mouth. "But it's gone now, Thomas. You can sleep. Lie down and go to sleep. You won't scream anymore."

Bobby knew that wasn't true. Now that he had sensed this monster Dauðr through the dead-alive boy—something the dead-alive boy named Thomas couldn't even remember—Bobby felt almost happy. Dauðr was far, far away, but not too far away to speak to him. *You were there.* Bobby dropped onto his bed and pulled the white sheet up to his neck. He slept.

[5]

"I haven't screamed in a week," Thomas told his parents when they came to visit. They sat in the rec room; all the plastic chairs pushed under two-person tables, the cafeteria tables wiped down, folded, and wheeled back into their locked closet. Mitchell and Bobby played checkers in the corner.

"I want to come home."

"That's great, Tommy," his dad said, hands in his lap. His dad was always uncomfortable in this room. "If you're sure."

Thomas nodded. "I had private therapy, group therapy, they tried me on six different pills, and finally it's gone." He looked into his parents' faces. "I know this is costing you guys a lot, even with insurance. I—"

His mom reached across the table and gently took Thomas's hands in hers.

"We're doing okay," she said. "With the money your dad's going to make teaching, and with the farmland we sold—"

"You sold the farm?" Thomas shouted. Mitchell and Bobby turned to look at him. Nurse Carroll stirred at the nurses' station. Thomas pulled his hands out of his mother's grip.

"No touching," Thomas said, softer. "Rec room rules."

"We didn't sell the farm, son," his dad said. "But now that I'm going to teach, I won't have enough time for as many row crops, so I sold the acres down by the river."

That was Grandpa Cavanaugh's land.

"I thought you said that would mean you weren't a real farmer." Thomas knew the words were harsh, but he meant them.

His dad opened his mouth to speak, but his mom touched his arm, and he stopped.

"Did you sell it because I'm in here?" he asked. "I'm cured. I'm coming home. You can buy it back." Anger flushed Thomas's face. *It's my fault.*

His dad smiled and shook his head. "You had nothing to do with this, son, even though I'd sell the whole farm to take care of you and your mom. The farm isn't paying for itself, and the way things look it isn't going to. I knew I'd probably have to do this someday."

Thomas's sudden rage began to drain. His dad was right; now maybe the house would be happier. He smiled a lie at them.

"Take me home," he said.

[6]

Damn it. The dead-alive boy was going home. Bobby sat at the desk in his room drawing circles on a legal pad with a red crayon, the only writing instrument Nurse Carroll would allow him. Cavanaugh hadn't told him.

Hell, no.

They weren't friends, and something deep inside Bobby told him they never would be. The whispers had told him, coming from nowhere, from no one, like they always did. They had hit in a violent shove, a shove only high emotion could muster. Other thoughts drifted to Bobby in gentle waves.

From his parents? Were Mommy and Daddy Cavanaugh here to pick up their baby boy?

Mommy. No, that's not right. He called her Mom, and her name was a D-something. Denise? No, no. Deb? Debbie? Deborah? Yes, Deborah. And his dad? Kyle. That sucker's mind was as open as a twenty-four-hour grocery store.

Bobby rose from the desk, his feet moving on their own before stopping at the open doorway to his one-bed padded paradise. He sensed the dead-alive boy before he walked past Bobby's door.

"See you soon, Tommy boy," Bobby called after him, walking back to his desk before Thomas could react.

Bobby picked up his crayon and frowned. The circles he'd drawn had smiles, all filled with needle-sharp teeth Bobby couldn't remember drawing.

[7]

Thomas found Jillian in her room reading a dystopian YA novel. She sat up when he appeared at her open door. He couldn't walk in; it was against the rules.

"Hi," she said, trying to smooth her messy hair.

"Hey." Thomas didn't know what to say. Well, he knew *what* to say; he just didn't know *how* to say it. How do you tell a girl you're probably never going to see her again? "My parents came to get me."

Her face fell slack. "Today? You're going home today?"

He nodded. Thomas didn't know why, but at that moment he realized he liked her back. A lump formed in his throat. "Yeah," he said, then coughed into his fist. "They just told me. I'm going to— well, you know—miss you."

A tear rolled down Jillian's face. "Me too." She rustled through some papers, and handed Thomas a small notebook, and a blue felt-tip marker. "Give me your address so I can write to you."

Thomas smiled and wrote it down. "That'll be nice," he said.

[8]

Bobby sat on the edge of the thin mattress of the hospital bed, his cold, dark eyes staring blankly into the hallway. Something bounced around his head. A name. Dauðr? Bobby didn't know what Dauðr meant, not exactly, but the dead-alive boy was afraid of it. No, he was terrified of it. That only made the concept even more delicious. The image in Tommy boy's mind looked like a farmer standing in a cornfield, thunder crashing in the distance, lightning electrifying the night. That image. That dark, wet, terror-filled image was what latched on to Bobby. He knew that image.

I was there.

Thomas passed by Bobby's door on his way to his parents, who stood whispering in the common room, wondering if taking little Tommy was the right thing to do.

Ha, Bobby thought. I've seen inside his head. Your boy ain't right.

He closed his eyes and watched the Cavanaughs being escorted out of the mental ward of Sisters of Mercy and toward the elevator to sign all the discharge papers downstairs. The elevator door shut, and Bobby's eyes popped open.

"Jillian," he said and stood. He knew what Cavanaugh thought. He knew what Johnny thought (oh the things that boy wanted to do with Nurse Carroll). He could even read what Nurse Carroll thought, and Nurse Carroll was afraid of him. Scared. But Jillian? Bobby couldn't see inside her head. Not at all.

He stepped into the hall.

Bobby found the red-haired girl lying on her bed reading. He stopped outside her open door but didn't step in. Nope, nope, nope. Ward policy. Don't go into another patient's room.

"Hello, Jillian."

Her head snapped toward him, her eyes hard.

"Go away, Bobby," she said, and turned back to her book.

"Your boyfriend's gone, Jillian." He licked his upper lip. "Who are you going to share breakfast with now?"

She slid a piece of paper in as a bookmark and held the book in both hands. She sat up and glared at him.

"You don't have the right to use my name."

Oh, this is fun. So fun. So very, very fun. But why can't I read your stupid thoughts?

"I see things," he said, leaning against the door frame.

"So do I," Jillian said. "Like, right now, I see an asshole."

A rush of anger blew over him, but Bobby clenched his fists and choked it back.

"Your boyfriend has experienced things," he said, his teeth clenched. "A storm. A farmer, a bad, bad farmer. A coyote." Bobby stopped and inhaled, the vague memory of running on four legs, the endless energy, the strength, the sharp teeth, the taste of blood. "The bad farmer is called the Dauðr."

The book Jillian held slipped from her hands and slapped onto the floor.

Yes. Oh, yessy yes, yes. She knows something. She knows it, she knows it, she knows it.

He wrapped his arms across his chest and squeezed, trying to hold in the giggles. "You know that name, don't you? Dauðr. What does that mean?"

Jillian fished the book from the floor with shaking hands, never breaking eye contact. The stifled laughter in Bobby's chest was almost painful.

"You know," he said, trying to keep his voice down. The nurses couldn't come by now. Bobby was having too much fun. "Will you tell me? Please?"

"Shut up." Her words held no force.

"I can't quite figure you out, Jill-I-Anne," he said. "I have a way of knowing things. I know Bekka thinks you're a bitch. I know your little boyfriend is so in love with you he almost pisses himself whenever he talks to you. And I know I can't read you. Why?"

Jillian shot to her feet.

"Because I don't want you to, *Robert*." She stepped toward him, her hands in fists at her side. "You're a pestilence. A bug. An infestation. And I will—"

A flash of lavender fire burst from her hands.

Bobby stepped back. Did I see that?

"—not—"

The door to her room rattled.

"—be poisoned by you."

Jillian was in front of Bobby in a blur of motion and the door slammed in his face, the metal surface less than an inch from his nose. He stood outside the door until Nurse Madison came down the hall and shooed him to his own room, where he crawled beneath his covers.

He hadn't seen the door coming toward him. With Jillian, he couldn't see anything at all.

PART
3

Chapter Five  1999

[1]

THOMAS SAT ON A CRACKED plastic chair in Griffon Coin Laundry drinking rum and Coke through the straw of a forty-four-ounce convenience-store cup. Thomas's screams had stopped in 1994, but not the dreams. Nightmares of a black figure pulling him through the dark cornfield; coyotes yipping from the shadows. Did the coyotes chase them? No. Something else was out there. Something dark, looming, something that was all teeth.

Teeth like needles, like a lizard's or a dragon's.

He took a deep drink and set the cup on the concrete floor. The laundromat was quiet, save for the dryer with his clothes.

The cheap Bacardi knock-off flavored his drink, but barely; he had homework, so he poured it weak. Thomas leaned back, pawing through his psychology textbook, highlighted from past users. The door of the laundromat opened, and a family tumbled in, a mother with four children. He flipped to chapter 3: Erikson's Stages of Psychosocial Development. Professor Allison hadn't scheduled a quiz on the reading, but that didn't mean she wouldn't give one.

A hot wind brushed his arms, and Thomas looked up. The entry door, on a pneumatic hinge, automatically closed behind the family. There was no wind.

The oldest child, a boy, sat next to his mother on a bench, eyes pinned to his lime-green Game Boy Color. Two of the girls sat at a small table with a deck of UNO cards. The mother's fingers fidgeted, her face drawn and pale. Thomas's gaze darted around the laundry. There'd been another child, he was sure of it.

He flipped a page with his thumb and focused on his textbook.

The scent of a spring garden drifted past.

No.

A few lines down the page, his eyes passed over the words "Trust vs. Mistrust: Psychosocial Stage 1," and the skin of his neck crawled, bristling his hair; a push, almost like a physical intrusion into his thoughts, rushed into his head.

He knew that feeling.

His fists locked on the textbook, his gaze darting around the room. The machines agitated and spun, the older UNO girl played a red Draw Two, the boy jabbed buttons on his Game Boy, and the mother—oh, God, the mother. The skin drew back on her face, her mouth frozen in a clown grimace, her eyes bulged from their sockets.

When you leave a window open, you never know what may come through.

"Goddammit," he hissed. The boy looked up from his Game Boy, but only for a moment.

Hello, Thomas. The little girl's words forced their way inside his head.

He nearly shouted but instead turned to look behind him. The little girl from his room, the little girl from the cornfield, stood only a few feet from him. Her red hair hung in a loose ponytail, her white dress the same she'd worn the night he died. Thomas was twenty years old, but she was still a child. The textbook slid from his hand and slapped closed onto the floor.

The girl laughed; a scent drifted from her, the musty, claustrophobic smell of a cornfield. She giggled.

I want to say hello. She cocked her head and bit her bottom lip. *It's been so long, so very long, Thomas. I've missed you.*

The buzzer on Thomas's dryer sounded; a slight burst of urine soaked into his already dirty boxers. He jumped to his feet, but when he turned to face the girl again, she was gone.

Shaky hands grabbed the textbook and shoved it into his duffel bag; he stuffed his clothes in after it. Flinging the strap over his shoulder, he picked up his drink, threw open the door, and stepped into a world of silence.

No cars moved on the street, no pedestrians on the sidewalk. No horns, no yelling, no trill of pigeons. A sheet of paper caught by the wind hung unmoving in the air.

"What the hell?" It was a whisper.

Then a noise, the giggle of a child, came from behind him. The hair on his head bristled and he turned, stepping back inside the building. The dryers, the washers, the children playing UNO were frozen. The little girl stood in the center of the laundry and smiled at Thomas.

A shout burst from him as he fell backward out the door into the honking of a car horn, the laugh of two women emerging from a coffee shop, each with a to-go cup of something.

Thomas landed with an *oof* on top of his duffel, the drink in his hand still trapped in Styrofoam. A shadow loomed over him. The girl? The last time she was here, all hell had broken loose.

[2]

It took four beers for Boyd to ask Kyle about Thomas. His nephew had become a sensitive subject.

"He's okay, I guess," Kyle said, leaning back in one of the reclining deck chairs Deborah bought a few years back. "Still struggling in college. Still delivering sandwiches, far as I know."

The crack of a beer tab, loud in the early evening.

Boyd took a drink. "College isn't for everyone," he said. "The world needs mechanics, electricians, plumbers. We'd be in shit shape without plumbers."

Kyle cradled his own beer in both hands, his attention on the field. Soybeans this summer, the spot where the anhydrous tank blew still bare after so many years. "He's got so much potential." The aluminum can crinkled in Kyle's hands. "He just, he just—"

"He just needs to figure it out, that's all," Boyd said. "All you need is for him to be happy. You don't need him to save the world."

Kyle fished another beer from the twelve-pack between them, and rolled the sweating can between his palms before answering. "Maybe I do. I want him to do better than I did."

Boyd upended his can, draining it. "That's your problem, not his," he said. "I know what you're going to say. I don't have any kids of my own, so how do I know?" The can slipped and fell to the porch with a clank. "I had a dad too, you know. He worked as a police officer in St. Joseph thirty years before setting roots back down in the country. He didn't want me to do this. He wanted me to be a doctor."

Boyd grunted as he bent to grab his empty can.

"But that wasn't going to happen," he continued. "I just wished he'd lived long enough to see me become sheriff. That might have been okay with him."

Kyle moved to hand Boyd another can. "You think he'd have voted for you?"

"Not a chance," he said, waving off the beer. Boyd grunted as he pushed himself to his feet. The dinner of pork steak and fried potatoes had filled about as much room as he had to fill.

His brother-in-law held the beer can out again. This time Boyd took it.

"What's the hurry, anyway?" Kyle asked. "It's a nice night."

The sheriff slid his felt hat onto his head, the rim pushed up to his hairline.

"It is, but I need to head for home. KC's playing tonight. You know the Royals won't lose unless I watch."

"How many games you catch a year?"

A grin teased the corners of his mouth. "Every single one."

[3]

The day seemed normal. Traffic, pedestrians, someone shouting, "Hey, Kenny, wait up," somewhere down the street. A pigeon fluttered to rest on a streetlamp over his head. What the hell had happened in the laundromat?

The shadow above him loomed closer.

"Thomas?" A voice called from above. "Thomas Cavanaugh?"

He looked up. A woman stood over him, her features silhouetted by the sun.

"Uh, yeah."

She brushed a loose string of hair behind her ear.

"You don't remember me?" A hand moved to her face. "Oh, no. You don't, do you?"

Thomas pulled himself to sitting. Dear God. It was Jillian.

"Jillian," he whispered. "You're—you're grown up."

A laugh, the sound of a breeze through wind chimes, drifted from her and she held out a hand to him. He took it, and she pulled him to his feet.

"That happens. It's been five years." She cocked her head as she inspected his face. "But it doesn't seem like it. I always felt you were with me."

A nudge, like the one he'd felt in the laundromat pushed into his mind and the little girl's voice was there for only a moment. *Bye-bye*, she said, then was gone.

"Come on," Jillian said. "There's a coffee shop down the street." Before Thomas could say anything, she looped an arm through his. He bent and grabbed his duffel bag before she led him away.

Jillian ordered an Earl Grey tea; Thomas worked on his rum and Coke, hoping like hell he could hold his act together. They sat down at a little round table next to the front window.

"How come you stopped writing letters?" Thomas asked. His thumbnail, which needed trimming, made shallow cuts in the Styrofoam cup.

Jillian pulled her hair out of her face and tucked it behind her right ear, a motion he'd seen over and over at Sisters of Mercy. She forced a smile.

She'd never smiled much at the hospital, but of course there was never much reason to smile.

"My Aunt Jackie got me out of the hospital like she promised," Jillian said. "But I lost your letters in the move."

"You knew my last name," Thomas said. "You knew where I lived. You could have found my address." He took a long drink of rum and Coke. The rum was doing its trick; he could hardly taste it anymore.

Jillian looked down at her tea.

"I'm sorry. I'd been out of the hospital for more than a year. I moved to a new town, a new high school. I had a lot to get used to. Then I, I—" She stopped, raising and lowering the tea bag a few times. "After a few months I just got embarrassed that it had been so long since I'd contacted you. It was easier not to try." She looked up from her drink. "I've missed you, Thomas."

A shiver ran through him. Those were the exact words the little girl in Griffon Coin Laundry had said just minutes ago.

A couple holding hands walked by on the sidewalk. A bird lit on the back of a bench, then flew away. Thomas breathed deeply. The soft aroma of brewing coffee settled in the air; the tension began to bleed away. Everything's fine, dude. The world is a normal place. It's normal.

Thomas's gaze flitted nervously back and forth between Jillian and the window; he half expected the little girl to press her face to the glass and smile at him, her goblin mouth sending piss down his legs.

Jillian reached across the small table and grasped Thomas's hands. Her hands felt soft, warm. The darkness, the panic, slowly began to pass. He looked into her eyes. Was there concern? Yes, of course she's concerned. I'm sweating.

"Did you ever see that movie we'd talked about?" she asked. "*Ace Ventura*, right?"

Thomas took a deep breath and let it out slowly. "Not at the theater," he said as calmly as he could muster, "but yeah, I saw it." A frown washed over his face. "You?"

Jillian shook her head. "No. I never did." She bit her bottom lip.

Thomas tried to control his breathing. In and out. Just in and out. "I have it, you know. *Ace Ventura* on VHS. It's back at my apartment."

<hr />

As the opening credits rolled, she climbed on top of him and peeled off his clothes; Thomas wasn't going to say no.

She was eager, almost hungry. Thomas had not expected that from a girl who'd been through what she had. That was years ago, but still, it left a mark.

Jillian moved in a week later. They never watched the movie.

[4]

The Ford Taurus, a 'ninety-five, Boyd figured, weaved across Route N, the driver either lost, stupid, half-asleep, or drunk off his ass. Maybe all the above. Except, as his headlights hit the rear of the car, Boyd thought he knew who it belonged to. Light evergreen metallic, "Clinton/Gore '96" sticker faded and peeling on the left rear bumper. It swerved into the left lane, its tires grinding gravel on the thin shoulder before the driver over-corrected and jerked it hard to the right. The passenger tires hit the right shoulder, gravel dust misting into the early-evening air.

No. Can't be.

He grabbed the mic and clicked the push-to-talk bar. "Dispatch, this is Boyd."

"Yes, Sheriff," the voice crackled from the other end. Aaron worked the board tonight.

"Run me a plate." He pressed the accelerator, hard enough to read the plate but not too close. "Missouri—five, five, five—Bravo, Romeo, India."

Slight static ran across the speaker before the dispatcher said, "yes."

"Missouri—five, five, five—Bravo, Romeo, India belongs to an El-vin R. Miller, sixty-seven, Easton, Missouri."

Holy cow. Boyd eased up on the accelerator, letting the Taurus move a safer distance ahead. No way.

"Sir?" Aaron asked. "Everything okay?"

Boyd hesitated before he clicked into the mic. "Everything's fine. Thanks, dispatch. Over."

But nothing was fine. Elvin Miller drifting all over the highway like he was drunk?

Boyd flipped on the flashing lights and hit the siren. The Taurus's brake lights lit red, and the vehicle slowed, finally coming to a rest half on the shoulder, half in the ditch.

The snap of the safety strap on Boyd's holster clicked as he stepped from his car onto the graying asphalt of the rural highway. Elvin, or whoever it was, had the car in park, he hoped. At least it wasn't moving anymore. Boyd hated stops like this. Sure, when he was a deputy, guns-blazing, Dirty Harry stuff was fun, but now he just wanted to get home and watch the baseball game. Boyd grabbed his Maglite.

He moved closer; the driver's-side window was down.

"Elvin?" Boyd said, his voice even. "Is that you?"

"Boyd?" the driver barked back.

Goddammit, Elvin. What have you gotten yourself into? "Yeah, it's Boyd, Elvin. You got anyone else in that car?"

"Naw, Booooyd," Elvin slurred. "Got nobody. Just me and my buddy, Jim."

Boyd stepped closer to the car, quiet for such a large man.

"Who's Jim, Elvin?" Boyd called out, gripping the handle of his service revolver. Academy stuff.

"Jim Beam, baby," Elvin slurred. His right hand slapped the dash.

Is that crazy bastard laughing? No, Boyd realized, Elvin Miller was crying.

"I'm coming up to your door, Elvin," Boyd said. "Gotta tell ya, you're making me a little nervous out here, buddy. Everything okay?"

Elvin's shoulders slumped, and a hand started toward the open window. Boyd began to pull his weapon from the holster, hoping like hell he didn't have to shoot Elvin Miller.

Elvin's hand pushed through the window in slow motion as if it went through something solid. His hand held a half-empty fifth of bourbon.

Fucking Jim Beam.

The bottle dropped to the pavement onto its side, the copper liquid spilling out onto the highway.

Boyd released the grip on his revolver and clicked on his flashlight, stepping even with the window. The back seat was empty. Elvin was alone.

Thank you, Christ.

"What's going on, Elvin?" he asked, slipping the pistol back into the holster. "You've, uh, you've been drinking tonight."

The man's eyes looked up to meet Boyd's. Streaked with red in Boyd's flashlight, his cheeks wet from tears.

"When's the last time you tied one on?" Boyd asked, resting his left elbow casually on the Taurus's roof, his right hand holding the flashlight. "Fifteen years? Twenty?"

Elvin raised his thin arm above his face and waved. "Twenty, twenty-two. Twenty-two years." His head slumped forward onto the steering wheel. "I've been sober twenty-two years." His body shook with sobs. The next words came out in a whisper: "Twenty-two years."

Boyd shook his head. Jesus Christ. "What happened?" He reached into the car and rested a hand on the drunken man's shoulder. "Why tonight, Elvin?"

A drunken sigh seeped from Elvin; his head lolled back toward the headrest. "Goddammit," he slurred. "My boy's dead. She told me. She told me my boy is dead."

"Tanner? Tanner's been gone since 1992."

"I know," Elvin's eyes latched onto Boyd's. "He died in Iraq because of that goddamned Saddam Hussein and that friggin' George Bush. Blown up by a roadside bomb for no reason, Boyd. No reason. She came tonight. She came by the house and told me, she showed me Tanner. He was in the back of a Humvee. A woman walked out on the dirt road and the soldier driving it stopped. Then that woman blew up. You ever see an Iraqi with red hair? That red-haired woman blew up, Boyd. Tanner's face was gone, and—"

Boyd's hat tipped back against the door frame as he leaned in closer. The bourbon was sour on the man's breath.

"*She* told you? Who is *she?*"

Elvin exhaled and dropped deeper into the driver's seat. "Wha-what?"

"Who is *she? Who* told you?"

"The little girl," Elvin said.

Little girl? Boyd leaned hard onto the window frame of the Taurus. "What little girl?"

Tears welled again, Elvin's face pulled tight. "The little girl with red hair. She wore a white dress streaked with, with blood. It was covered in blood," he whispered. "The girl with the smile. The smile of needles. I think she's the devil, Boyd."

[5]

Boyd drove the patrol cruiser in silence with Elvin drifting in and out of sleep in the passenger seat. The drunken man should be in the back of the squad car in cuffs on his way to lockup, but Boyd was headed for Elvin's house. He'd call dispatch later and have the morning shift pick up the Taurus and take it to Elvin's place. Elvin wasn't at fault tonight. Not really. Boyd thought he knew who was.

The sheriff's grip tightened on the wheel as he counted the dash lines in the center of the highway. Fourteen, fifteen, sixteen. Anything to keep his mind off what Elvin, drunken Elvin, had told him. Boyd knew his hands would shake like Elvin's if he took them off the steering wheel.

Elvin had threatened to kill his wife twenty-two years ago and woke the next morning with the worst curse of a drunk—he remembered everything. That night he attended the local AA meeting and never drank again.

Until today.

The girl.

The little girl with the smile of needles.

The little girl had stood in his nephew's bedroom, her white dress streaked with dirt and sweat and blood, her mop of red hair pulled back in a ponytail. That day. Today. Needles. Her teeth were sharp needles.

A light appeared through a stand of elms: Elvin's house, where Loraine waited for her husband. A tug, somewhere in the back of Boyd's head, shook off the beer he'd had at Kyle and Debbie's. It was the same tug that told him to check the trunk when he pulled over anyone who didn't look local. The tug that led him to that girl's body in the well on the Sanderson property.

Damn it.

He turned into the gravel lane leading to Elvin's house and parked next to an old Chevy pickup; the house was lit like the Millers expected company.

"Gomma, gomma," Elvin mumbled, his face pressed against the window; a line of drool leaked down the glass.

"Elvin." Boyd laid a heavy hand on the man's shoulder and shook. "Elvin. Wake up. You're home."

His passenger shifted, then sat up straight. "Loraine," Elvin mumbled, his eyes wild, the scent of bourbon heavy in the cab. He scratched at the handle and threw the door open.

"Shit," Boyd hissed, and burst after Elvin, who stumbled up the porch steps and into the house; the screen door slammed behind him. Boyd followed and stepped into a nightmare.

Blood pooled on the floor; a spray pattern splattered the floral-print couch and the ceiling. The stench of copper was heavy. Elvin fell to his knees on the hardwood, dropping to his elbows in front of Loraine, an ax next to her in a red, murky puddle, her face split.

"Loraine," Elvin wailed, reaching out to hold a hand that couldn't hold back. "Lorrraaaainnne."

"Jesus." That was all Boyd could muster.

He reached for his shoulder mic but stopped as his hand neared it. On the wall, past the body of Loraine, past a pile of what he assumed were Elvin's gore-soaked clothes, was a picture painted in blood.

Boyd moved forward, only a step, keeping Elvin in front of him. The drawing, painted by a small hand, was childish: a circle and two lines for lips curved into a smile.

It wasn't a friendly smile. It was a smile of thin, pointed needles.

Chapter Six  1999

[1]

JILLIAN'S FEET, WARM FROM A night under a thick comforter, slipped under Thomas's T-shirt and slid up his back. She pushed and nearly shoved him out of bed.

"Get up," she half moaned, half whined, still half asleep.

The words floated somewhere outside Thomas's closed eyelids, their attachment to reality tenuous. A hand grabbed his shoulder and shook.

Oh, God, don't do that. Pain lanced through his head; his stomach lurched. The alarm clock beeped in the background, barely audible. Shut that thing off, please.

"Thomas," Jillian said, her voice impatient. "Get up. You've got work."

"Just five more minutes," he whispered. Even that hurt his head. Thursday Dollar Shot Night at the Inn-B-Tween was never a good idea.

"You're going to be late."

Thomas slid across sheets that probably should be washed and stopped at the edge of the mattress. He opened his eyes. His dirty underwear and socks were half under the bed next to his rarely opened anthropology textbook and an old Domino's pizza box. She pushed harder.

"Okay, okay. I'm going." His stomach sped things up. "I gotta throw up first."

Every crack, every pothole, every uneven surface sent sharp stabs through his brain and churned his stomach as Thomas drove his old, rusty silver Toyota Camry toward Murph's American Sammiches.

He barely made it into a parking lot three blocks away from work before he threw open the door and the scrambled eggs and coffee Jillian had talked him into splattered on the old, faded asphalt, the seat belt holding him steady, bile and tequila coating his mouth, his teeth fuzzy. He stopped at a gas station and bought aspirin and something to drink then made his way back onto Belt Highway at 9:47 a.m. He pulled into Murph's American Sammiches thirteen minutes later, the sight of the black-and-white building painful in the mid-morning sunlight.

"You gotta have a job, son," his dad had told him when he left for college in nearby St. Joseph a year ago. "Mom and I are helping you with tuition, and we'll send you home with food whenever you come visit, but we're not paying for beer and rubbers."

Thomas's first college job was sweeping up popcorn at the movie theater, hoping one day he'd run into Jillian. Back when he was fourteen, she'd closed a letter with "And maybe we can go to the movies!" She never sent her address, and never sent another letter.

Murph's American Sammiches came next. Thomas liked that gig better; he didn't really have to talk to people.

His cell phone alarm started to beep. He popped open a container of peppermint Tic Tacs and threw four or five into his mouth to drown out the smell of tequila and vomit. It was time to go to work.

[2]

Bobby stood looking out his second-floor bedroom window at the enormous oak tree that brushed his window in a wind. When he was younger, he'd lie in bed during storms, clutching his pillow as the tips of those limbs scraped across the glass like the clawed fingers of some demon. His parents eventually stopped coming to his room when he called, his dad telling him to quit being such a baby.

He was home. No more juvie, no more mental hospitals, no more loonies waking him screaming every night. Home. Home with his mom and dad, who jumped if he surprised them and could never look him in the eyes. His dad stuttered; he'd never stuttered before, and his mom dropped things whenever Bobby stepped into a room with her. She hadn't done that before either, or had she? All those pills and treatments, and the occasional ass reaming by those naughty boys in prison scrambled the last of Bobby's circuits his parents hadn't already scrambled. He knew growing up under his mom and dad's "protection" from all the bad people, their world of six thousand years, their leave-a-plate-for-Jesus didn't do him any favors. That's why the hospital finally let him go. Bobby knew he was messed up, but he'd learned how to hide it. Smile, nod, keep your voice low, tell them what you did was bad, tell them you're sorry, don't make any sudden movements, and read the Bible. Nurse Carroll loved him for it. She wrote a recommendation Circuit Court Judge Kerry Bingham thought was good enough to let Bobby out of the court system.

"Bobby, honey," his mom called up the stairs. "Lunch will be ready in an hour."

He pulled the heavy old curtains closed, throwing the room into darkness, save for the lamp next to his bed.

Bobby didn't have to smell what his mom cooked. He read it in her mind. Casserole again. Noodles and goop, or rice and goop, or maybe potatoes and goop. Goopy, goopy goop. That's all she ever cooked anymore.

"What are we having, Ma?" he yelled back from his bedroom at the top of the stairs, even though he knew she'd say, "tuna noodle casserole."

Nothing. Not a sound. His mom stood at the bottom of the dark brown wooden staircase biting her lower lip, wondering if Bobby was going to kill her tonight. She wondered that a lot, Bobby knew. Just like he knew his dad was banging the office manager at work, Tonja, who had two kids and whose husband traveled. Bobby sometimes wished he knew how he knew these things. They just popped into his head uninvited, but he worried that if he thought about it too much, the power might turn itself off.

He didn't want that.

"Tuna noodle casserole," his mom said, finally.

Bobby stared at the Green Day poster behind his lamp. Yeah, he'd thought Dookie was cool once, but he was all grown up now. He thought he should take the poster down.

"With crumbled potato chips on top?" he called.

More silence. Damn you woman, speak up. "Yes," she finally said.

Bobby ripped Billie Joe Armstrong's snarling, mascara-wearing face off the wall. Put on a decent shirt, Billie.

"Original Lay's, right? Not Ruffles. I freakin' hate Ruffles."

"No, Bobby, honey. No Ruffles. Lay's, just like you like them." Her voice sounded thin, farther away. She had moved from the staircase and stood cowering at the entrance to the dining room, an unlit Virginia Slims pinched between her fingers.

He stretched his shoulders and picked up the heavy lamp on the nightstand, his dark eyes glaring at himself in the mirror. The light shone upward, casting Norman Bates shadows across his grim face.

"Just like you like them, Bobby, honey," he mocked and jerked the lamp chord from the outlet, throwing his face into darkness.

"Good," he said. "I'll be right down."

<hr />

Bobby pranced down the stairs, gripping the lamp like a club. He ripped off the lampshade and tossed it onto the dining-room table. His mom had moved again, into the kitchen. He walked in and found her standing by the sink, pouring herself a vodka tonic. A big one.

"Hello, *Mother.*"

She froze; the stirring spoon tinked against the glass. She turned toward her son's voice slowly. Bobby stood just feet from her, his smile a cut across her face. The cigarette dropped to the kitchen floor.

"Wha-what are you doing, B-B-Bobby?"

He slung the lamp over his shoulder. "Trying to lighten your mood, Mom."

"Bobby, honey. You're, you're—"

"I'm what, Mommy? Frightening you?" He slapped the lamp into the palm of his hand. She jumped at the sound. "Everything frightens you. You're weak, Mo-ther. Pathetic."

Tears dripped down her cheeks. "Bobby, honey. Why are you saying these awful things? I, I lu-lu-love y—"

"I lu-lu-lu." Bobby took another step forward, his eyes bulging from excitement. "That was from a song, wasn't it? The Day My Momma Died?"

Bobby's mother screamed as he pulled his arm back and swung the metal lamp in a tall ark toward her skull. It connected with a dull thump, like he had dropped a melon, and she crumbled to the linoleum. She never moved again.

Damn it.

Where was the fight? Where was the begging? He'd wanted to say, "Thanks for letting me go to jail. I thank you, and the convicts that raped my ass thank you," but she fell instead, so he swung the lamp, smashing it into her skull again, and again, and again. The side of her head finally caved in, the blood and brains that flew from her shattered skull stuck to the microwave and Mr. Coffee like cake batter stirred by an electric mixer. Her body lay on the floor, blood seeping through her graying hair.

"Well, darn," he spat through heaving breaths. "You spilled your drink, Ma. Who's going to clean up that mess?"

A laugh burst from him. This time the laugh was real, loud, and it came from deep inside. The lamp slid from his hand and landed on the floor with a thunk. Bobby dropped to one knee and steadied himself against the kitchen counter, giggles gripping his chest. It was hard to breathe. "Holy cow," he said between heaves. All the home-schooling, all the proper dress, all the babying, all the Jay-sus. All the goddamned casseroles, the whining, and her putting up with his dad's bullshit. It was gone. "That was awesome. Why the hell didn't I do that before?"

Tears ran down his face, but not from sorrow. This was too funny to be sad, to miss his Mo-ther. His eyes shot to the clock on the stove. It was 10:00 a.m. His dad came home for lunch at 11:00 on the dot. Daddy couldn't resist his tuna and goop. Supper was different. His dad was always late; he had to have enough time to play hide the salami with Tonja in the break room on the table where his employees ate lunch.

Bobby stood and picked up the lamp, the base dripping with blood. He pulled a chair behind the kitchen door, sat, and waited. His dad always came in through the kitchen door. The first thing Daddy would see coming home would be his faithful bride's brains splattered across the floor. Then what would he do? Bobby wondered. Scream probably. He always was a little bitch.

Bobby's stomach rumbled. But he didn't want tuna casserole. He wanted a sandwich. He needed his strength before killing his dad.

[3]

"You're late, Cavanaugh," Barry barked as Thomas walked through the back door, the screen banging shut behind him.

He looked at his cell phone; it read 10:01:45 a.m.

"By less than two minutes. Nobody's going to die if they don't get their Fat Elvis hoagie before 10:05," Thomas said. Barry was cool, but as Thomas struggled to see him without the world wavering, he wondered just how cool.

Barry pointed a hairy arm at him. "Don't get smart."

Don't get up in my ass, Thomas thought but didn't say. "You don't have to respect your boss," Kyle had told him. "He or she might be an asshole. He or she might be an idiot. But you *have* to do what they say."

"Sorry, Barry," Thomas said. "I'll be on time tomorrow."

Barry nodded. "Fine. Whatever. Just get going. You've got an order up, on the South Side."

The South Side of St. Joseph was dodgy. Hookers, gangs, meth. Good God. He grabbed a black and white sandwich bag, insulated to keep the food warm, and looked at the ticket. A Bierock and onion rings? A human body shouldn't be able to tolerate that much grease this early in the day. The address was Carlyle Street, down by the stockyards.

Just great.

[4]

Where is that little putz whacker? Bobby Garrett paced the foyer of his boyhood home, his dad's fuzzy old-man slippers silent on the immaculate wooden floors.

"Hey, Mom. How's that casserole coming?" he shouted toward the kitchen, a laugh quickly followed. Bobby stomped through the lower floor of the house, pounding the heels of his hands onto his temples.

No attention. You can't draw attention to this house. That's the worst.

The yard looked awful. That was okay.

In this neighborhood a mowed lawn was a suspicious lawn. Mr. Harrington down the street kept his yard cut to three and a half inches. Yep, suspicious as hell. Bobby thought he should break in and have a look around one night when the old fart was at his prayer meeting, or at the VFW hall. Probably had a pot grow or something in there.

Bobby shuffled back to the front door, his hands deep his pants pockets. It was 10:20 a.m. He called right when that goddamned sandwich shop opened and ordered one of those closed ground-beef-and-cheese sandwiches he couldn't get in the hospital or in prison. His mom's cooking was good enough, he guessed, but she was gone now, and sandwiches weren't her specialty; good ol' Mom was a casserole woman, born and bred. Murph's American Sammiches would have to be his friend until he found someone to cook casseroles for him.

Bobby giggled again.

He looked back out the window, his eye invisible through the curtain slit, and waited for the sandwich guy. At 10:25, he still wasn't there.

Five more minutes and I get the sandwich for free, Bobby thought, although he didn't care about that. His mom and dad had plenty of money around the house, and they sure as heck weren't going to use it. A small 1980s car rolled by slowly, rust getting the better of its once red paint. The driver, a gray-haired old woman dangling a cigarette out the window, wasn't the delivery guy. But he was getting close—Bobby felt it.

Yeah, he felt it. A gnawing began somewhere in the back of Bobby's head like a mouse had invaded his skull and started nibbling at his brain. The gnawing grew stronger and stronger. It was the delivery guy. He'd just driven by the tattoo parlor. He'd be at the Garrett house in five minutes. Something else tickled Bobby's brain, he just didn't know what it was.

[5]

Carlyle Street could be the location of a zombie movie. The few cars parked on the street were older models, some on flats, one on blocks. Behind rusty gates, four great greystone houses with wide lawns that had long ago gone to seed sat at the head of the street, a street that apparently had been affluent about a hundred years ago. Today, the fine citizens of St. Joseph had largely abandoned Carlyle, and Thomas almost expected at least one or two vampires to lurk there. Smaller Victorians, still two-story and Scooby Doo haunted, formed a small cluster, their lawns no better cared for. The occasional mowed lawn looked like the part on an ugly head of hair. No human walked the crumbling sidewalks, raised in places from tree roots planted too close too long ago. Two men in baggy shorts and with unkempt gray beards, the only people out today, sat on a flower-print couch on a front porch drinking Natural Light beer from cans.

White paint peeled from the wooden porch of 4244 Carlyle Street like bark off a birch tree. Thomas checked the address on the receipt again. Yep, 4244 Carlyle.

I need a new job.

[6]

A Toyota Camry pulled slowly in front of the house at 10:28 a.m. and parked, a magnetic Murph's American Sammiches sticker on the door.

It's about damn time.

The delivery driver, a guy about Bobby's height but thicker around the shoulders, stepped from the car and pulled a black-and-white bag after him.

"Clock's a tickin'," Bobby said, not realizing his tongue involuntarily licked his bottom lip.

The deliveryman rushed around the car and up the driveway that was more gravel than concrete now. His black shirt and cap read "Murph's." The man took the porch steps two at a time and knocked on the screen door, not knowing Bobby stood less than two feet away. The man—he seemed familiar—reached out his right fist and knocked again.

I know this person, Bobby thought. He pushed his face into the musty curtain, his left eye inches from the window, the reek of burning tuna noodle casserole heavy in the air. He hoped it covered the smell of blood from the kitchen. Bobby thought he really should clean up his mom before his dad got home.

The deliveryman raised his fist to knock again. Bobby slid open the deadbolt lock and pulled the door open enough to take his food.

"Is that my sandwich?" he asked, his eyes dancing around the man's face. Oh, yes. I know him.

"Bierock and, and onion rings," the delivery guy said. He unzipped the bag and held up a paper sack with Bobby's lunch. "Eight ninety-five," he said, the words coming out slowly.

He recognizes me, but he doesn't know why. Bobby reached into the right pocket of his slacks and pulled out a bill he'd taken from the Ziploc bag of pin money that lay hidden beneath the granny panties in Mother's top dresser drawer. There was more than just pin money in there, he knew, but whatever problem Mother was hoarding for—she probably knew about Tonja, dumbass—it was over now.

"Keep it," Bobby said.

The delivery guy took the bill, and Bobby snatched the bag, slamming the door and locking the deadbolt, his eye fixed in the seam of the curtain. The deliveryman all but ran off the porch and back to his car before Bobby's hand grew limp and the sandwich bag dropped to the floor.

It was the dead-alive boy.

[7]

Thomas's legs wobbled as he lurched into the driveway, his energy gone, drained. He knew that man, and Thomas knew the creepy bastard recognized him too.

Eyes burned into the back of Thomas's neck as he crossed the drive and stepped onto the street. Is he watching me from behind the curtain? Had he memorized my license plate?

Stop it. It's all in your head.

Thomas fumbled with his key ring before he found the right one, a fat key with a black rubber bow. The key scratched the paint above the keyhole as Thomas tried to fit it into the lock. When the key finally found home and Thomas unlocked the door, he fell into the driver's seat, the taste of vomit rising in his throat.

"No," he whispered. But yes. He knew that face. He knew that voice. He knew those eyes. "That was Bobby, from the Sisters of Mercy."

Corn. The cornfield, with its razor leaves and coyotes, rumbled through his memory. The little girl. Dauðr. The teeth. The monster. It all rushed back. A coyote at the feet of a farmer surrounded by corn, its eyes blazing green. And it wore . . . pajama pants? For a moment, just a moment, the coyote looked like Bobby.

Chapter Seven 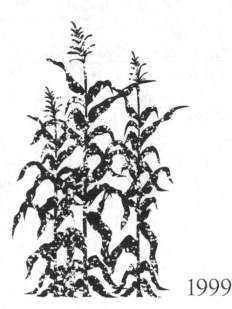 1999

[1]

THE BIEROCK WAS DELICIOUS. Bobby stood at the front door, safely behind the thick curtain that hung over the long pane of glass that wasn't a safety feature in this neighborhood. He took another bite. The roll, still soft and warm, yielded easily to his teeth. The aroma, the flavor of melted Swiss and ground beef, drowned out the smell of blood coagulating in the kitchen, although it couldn't do anything to erase the reek of burned tuna noodle casserole.

Greasy lips broke into a grin. The dead-alive boy was afraid be-cause Bobby knew something about him. Dauðr. Tom, Tommy. No, Thomas. The boy went by Thomas. Bobby felt Dauðr before, back when he shared a floor at Sisters of Mercy with Thomas. What was it? Four years ago, or five?

No, wait a minute. I felt something before that. The voice that talked to me when that bad Johnson boy grabbed my Johnson. Was that Dauðr? Was Dauðr my friendly little voice?

Bobby's eyes slid shut and crawled deep inside his head, the sandwich momentarily forgotten. A vast plane of black opened before him as it sometimes did when he let his mind go. He swayed as he stood before the door; he didn't know exactly where he went when his thoughts left his body, but it looked like the universe, so that's what he called it.

Stars appeared in the distance, growing sharper as he flew. The dust, maybe clouds of hydrogen, drifted in and out of his view as he traveled. Planets approached and zipped past, some blue and green and full of life, others giants made of gas, great rings of rock and ice-circled some; most were barren balls of rock, wastes of mass. Bobby's consciousness followed a path once made by the dead-alive boy. Dauðr, the Beast, the Monster of the Night, was still out there, alone, hungry. It stirred again somewhere far away, somewhere Bobby thought he could find.

The planet Bobby found spun alone, brown, dusty, its atmosphere thin but still thick enough for life to breathe. The star it circled was close enough to warm its oceans, if it had any. This land was dead, and its killer remained, waiting to be set free, waiting to feed again, to be strong again. But waiting for whom?

"Me," Bobby whispered.

But he sensed it also waited for someone else. It was the boy. It waited for Thomas.

Whatever. He took another bite of the sandwich. Oh, yes. That tasted good.

Thomas stopped his car in the parking lot of an old brick warehouse on Carter Street. His head dropped forward, the Murph's American Sammiches cap tipped back by the steering wheel. The air-conditioning on high did nothing to slow the sweat that ran in rivulets down his skin.

Of all the people sentenced to Sisters of Mercy, Bobby was the only one who scared him.

The cell phone buzzed in his pocket, sending him sitting up straight. Thomas grabbed the phone with a shaking hand; the caller ID read, "Murph's." Thomas clicked "accept" and put the phone to his ear.

"Where the hell are you, Tom?" Barry sounded more worried than angry. "Everything okay?"

No, dude. No, it's not.

"Uh, yeah, fine. Everything's fine." He took a deep breath and exhaled slowly, something his mom taught him to do when he was a kid, when he couldn't stop being angry. The smell of manure from the nearby stockyards was so much like the smell of home.

"The address was just hard to find. No numbers on most of the houses on that street." It was a lie, but Barry would never know. He couldn't imagine his boss driving his new BMW to shitsville. "The sandwich wasn't late. I got the money."

Barry was silent for a moment. "Well, good. I got orders backing up, and all the other drivers just went out. Get your ass back here."

All the other drivers meant Donna and Terry, but Thomas knew what it was like in the shop when one of the drivers dicked off. Everyone got behind, and Barry had to let sandwiches go for free. Then Barry wasn't happy, and when Barry wasn't happy, he didn't take deep breaths; he made sure no one else was happy.

"I'll be back ASAP," Thomas said, then paused. "Just don't send me back to that address, Barry. Please, please Barry, promise me."

"Tom, you know I can't—" Barry started, but Thomas cut him off.

"Fucking promise me, Barry."

"Okay, okay," Barry said. "Jesus, Cavanaugh, I'll send you to Beirut or some hellhole next time if it'll make you more comfortable. Now get back here. We got a big order for Golden Oaks Retirement Villa. I hope you can handle that one."

[3]

The day disappeared. Thomas made his sandwich runs to places like US Bank with a ten-foot-long muffuletta for the whole office, and a dorm room with a single-serving meatball sub and a bag of salt-and-vinegar chips. Each run through a dreamlike fog, Bobby Garrett riding shotgun on every trip, his one googly eye through the crack in the door undressing Thomas's soul. He managed a thank-you when the branch manager at US Bank gave him a $30 tip. He thought about taking Jillian out to dinner, but he didn't know if he'd have a job tomorrow. Barry hadn't talked to him since the phone call.

"You okay?" Donna asked as Thomas slid his punch card into the time clock.

The card hit home with a heavy click, and he slipped it back into its slot.

Donna leaned against the wall, her long brown hair sticking out from under her black Murph's cap. Thomas had nearly asked her out one day. She'd wanted him to, rumor had it, and restaurant rumors are always true, right? But he'd run into Jillian as he rushed out of Griffon Coin Laundry later that day, and romantic thoughts of Donna went poof.

He nodded. "Yeah, I'm okay."

She plucked her card from the rack and punched out. "Barry said you freaked out this morning. What happened?"

"I delivered a sandwich to a guy I used to know."

"So?"

Thomas opened the back door to the shop and let Donna out first, the mid-September day sweltering. The employee section of the parking lot was behind the restaurant.

"He killed a guy once." Thomas stopped, the Toyota still about twenty feet away. He looked at Donna, her dark brown eyes soft, caring. "I guess I just didn't feel comfortable, that's all."

She touched his forearm. "It's okay to be scared," she said. "Everybody gets scared."

A tingle ran through Thomas; his heartbeat quickened. A wave of guilt ran through him immediately. Jillian was at home, waiting for him.

"Yeah, I was a little scared." He held up an index finger. "Just don't tell anybody. I'll lose points on my Guy Card."

Donna smiled. "I didn't know those things were real."

Thomas started walking toward his Toyota. "Oh, yes they are," he said over his shoulder, not looking back. "And mine registers somewhere between John Rambo and James Bond. Don't blow it for me."

[4]

"Jillian," he called down the long hall that led into his apartment over Finnegan's Antiques and Fineries. "Jillian," he said again. "I'm home."

Nothing. Her last class was over at 4:00 p.m. It was 5:30. She should be here. He rounded the corner that led into the living room, where she stood in his Ramones T-shirt and apparently nothing else.

Her smile fell when Thomas stepped into the room. "What happened?" she asked.

"I need a beer," he said, walking past her into the kitchen area only separated from the living room by stained linoleum. He pulled a can from the gold refrigerator, a relic from the early 1970s. "Want one?"

"No." She sat on the couch, her legs beneath her. "What happened?"

The crisp pop of a beer tab sent foam across his knuckles. Thomas kicked the refrigerator door closed and sat on the couch, apart from Jillian, the can of Milwaukee's Best in his hand.

"I saw somebody today," he said flatly. "Somebody I never wanted to see again."

She turned sideways; the bottom of the shirt pulled high up her thighs. "Anybody I'd know?"

Thomas took a drink. The beer was cheap, but at least it was cold. "Bobby. I saw Bobby."

If Jillian felt anything, anything at all, her face didn't betray it. "Bobby Garrett? From Sisters of Mercy?"

Thomas nodded. That's not the reaction he'd expected. Hell, he didn't know what he'd expected, but nothing sure wasn't it.

"What was he doing?"

"He didn't do anything," Thomas said. "He ordered a sandwich and I delivered it."

"What's so bad about that? That's your job, you know." She tried to smile but failed miserably. Then Thomas saw it; her hands shook.

"He recognized me."

"It's been five years, Tom," she said. The shake had reached her voice. "I'm sure he didn't know who you were."

"He recognized me. And why wouldn't he? I mean, I recognized him too."

She pulled Thomas's beer from his hand and took a drink. "So?"

"He's insane, Jilly. He scares me. He scares the life out of me. And from the looks of things, he scares the life out of you too."

Jillian handed Thomas back his beer and walked to the bedroom. "I'm going out for Chinese," she said. "You want egg rolls or crab Rangoon?"

Thomas shot up and followed her.

"Wait. You're not just going to shut this down. Your hands are shaking, for Christ's sake." He set the beer can on his night table and wrapped his arms around her. She struggled against him as she pulled on her jeans. When they were up, she melted into his arms. Thomas held her tight. "Talk to me."

She looked up, and Thomas could see tears in her eyes, although she'd wiped most of them onto his shirt.

"Bobby talked to me the day you left Sisters of Mercy," she said.

He tried to read her face. It was blank.

"About what?"

Jillian ran a sleeve across her nose and sniffled. "He knew things, Thomas. About you."

"Me?" A cold shiver ran across Thomas's back. "What things?"

Jillian pulled back to button her blue jeans.

"He knew about that night in the corn. He knew about the rain, the monster that looked like a farmer, the coyote." The sobs started again, harder. She fell into his chest. "He talked like he was there, like he saw it, like he experienced it himself." When she looked up again, the tears were gone. "I think he did."

This time Thomas stepped away, his hands still on her shoulders.

"That's crazy talk. He couldn't have been there," Thomas said. Surprise suddenly grasped his face. "But, I never told you about that night, Jilly."

Jillian's hands moved behind her head, tying her long hair into a ponytail with a hair tie.

"First off, never, ever tell someone who's been in a mental hospital that what they say is 'crazy talk.' You should know that. Second, of course you told me. How would I know if you hadn't told me? Third, you didn't see him. You didn't hear him. I think, I think . . ." Her voice trailed off.

Thomas bent to look into her eyes. "What do you think?"

"I think he really was there. I don't know how, I don't know why, but I think he was the coyote that bit you."

The coyote with pajama pants.

Jillian pulled a twenty-dollar bill from her top dresser drawer and slipped it into her back pocket. "That should be enough," she said. "And since you didn't say, I'm getting you crab Rangoon."

And she left.

Thomas woke that night screaming for the first time in five years. His right thigh throbbed although it hadn't throbbed since the coyote bite had healed, leaving a jagged scar. He sat up in bed; sweat soaked the sheets.

"Jilly." He reached next to him, expecting to find Jillian's left shoulder. She always slept on her side, facing him. Her face was the first thing he saw every morning, but not today. Her side of the bed was empty. Thomas fingered the switch on the bedside lamp. He was alone in the bedroom. His eyes froze on the dresser; the top two drawers, her drawers, were open.

He slid out of bed and slowly approached the dresser; the draw-ers were empty.

"Jillian," he called, stepping into the living room/kitchen. He flipped on the light. The apartment was empty.

Jillian was gone.

Chapter Eight  2005

[1]

THE HOOD OF THE BLUE 2004 Cadillac CTS clicked shut. The
owner, a crabby old biddy named Natalia Swanson, would bite his
head off if there was so much as a smudge on the paint, so Thomas
was careful; he even wiped off smudges he didn't make.

The clock on the shop wall in the back building of Smithmeyer
Luxury Auto Center read 5:17 p.m. Thomas rubbed his hands on a
blue shop towel. He could have been out of there seventeen minutes
ago and down at Tennyson's Bar and Grill around the corner from
his apartment building (Carrington Arms, if you can believe that),
draining a few pints, but he wanted the Caddy back in the hands of

Mrs. Natalia "I Don't Poop" Swanson, and the hell out of Smithmeyer's shop.

"You done with the Caddy, Tom?" the shop supervisor asked when Thomas stepped up to his station.

Thomas nodded. Done, and done.

"Get this thing outta here, Mike. That old woman's going to kill me."

He handed Mike the keys and checked out. He'd never wanted his out-of-college job to revolve around a time clock, and except for his short stint on the farm, helping out while his dad recovered from a heart attack, that's all he'd ever had. His goal in college had been to teach high-school English. Hell, he figured one or two of the kids might even give a damn about Hemingway, or Lewis, or Morrison. He scrubbed at the grease on his hands, arms, and face, the gritty pumice in the industrial Orange Goop shredding the grime and some of his skin, but it was thorough—except for the grease under his fingernails. Thomas always had a problem there.

He threw on his jacket and zipped it, covering the navy Smithmeyer Luxury Auto Center work shirt with TOM stitched on the left breast in red thread. He'd never wanted a job where his name was stitched on his shirt either.

Once he'd wanted a job that would change the world. He was pretty sure fixing cars he couldn't afford for people he didn't like wasn't it.

The old Camry squeaked to a stop next to a gas pump in front of Speedy's Quick Mart. Thomas's credit card slid with a beep through the card reader on the front of the pump, the words "Remove quickly" replaced by "Do you want a receipt?" in green digital letters. The nozzle clinked into the filler neck, pumping gas.

A clerk and a teenage kid in a stocking cap were the only people inside the store. The kid paid for a soda, pushed open the glass door, and dropped his skateboard on the pavement. Something made Thomas edgy. The boy, probably fourteen and harmless as a puppy, pushed off and glided on the longboard down the sidewalk, disappearing around a corner. A breath snuck out. Relax, Tommy Boy. Relax. Ever since he discovered Bobby was still alive and kicking, the day Jillian left, Thomas had tried to stay low, out of sight. Thomas didn't want to attract attention. He never wanted to see that mad bastard again.

Gallons clicked off as Thomas leaned on the driver's-side door, his hands in his jacket pockets, the late fall evening chill but not cold. After-work traffic began to grow on the street behind him. People would soon stop here for gas, booze, lottery tickets, and smokes. When the handle clicked, the receipt didn't come. He reached out to punch the call button, when the words, "Pick up receipt inside" scrolled across the screen.

"Inside?" he said toward the shop. "Pretty inconvenient for a convenience store."

A guy in a stained Kansas City Chiefs jacket stepped into the store in front of Thomas; the smell of cigarettes rolled off him. The clerk sat behind the counter reading a Stephen King book.

Smoke Man stepped up to the rack of gum and breath mints at the counter and the clerk set down the book, the one with the claw on the cover. Smoke Man laid four loaves of bread, six cans of soup, a tub of butter, and two gallons of milk on the counter.

A movement, just a flicker, caught Thomas's eye. The clerk's book lay next to the "Take a Penny" bowl. The cover of the paperback jumped—a blister bulged from the center, and the scene swam into life. Rain swept a newspaper boat along a cracked gray curb, green claws reached through a sewer grate.

What the hell is happening?

The claw pushed through the bulge on the book cover, the blister squeaking like stretched latex. It flexed in its freedom; rainwater ran from the cover and cascaded onto the convenience-store floor.

"That all, Abe?" the clerk asked like his book hadn't just come to life.

Jesus Christ. Don't you see that?

The claw turned upward and gave Thomas the finger.

"Yep. That's it," Smoke Man said, his words slurred.

The clerk ran a bar code reader over each item, then held out his right hand. "Card, please," he said.

The man held out a food-stamp card, and the clerk took it and rang up. The scaly green claw pulled farther from the paperback cover with a screech. Thomas winced as it reached and plucked the food-stamp card from the clerk's hand and returned it to Smoke Man.

"Oh," the man said stiffly, like he'd rehearsed it and delivered that line more than once. "I just realized. I don't need any of that. Can I return it, and get four Powerballs, a pint of Everclear, two packs of Pall Malls, and the change?"

The clerk handled the transaction like it was routine because it was. His eyes glanced at Thomas. For a moment, they glowed red.

A shake rattled through Thomas.

A frown crossed the clerk's face. "You okay, buddy?"

Smoke Man nodded as he filled out his lottery tickets. "You bet I am, baby."

Thomas nodded as the claw spider-crawled across the counter and back onto the cover of the novel.

The book slammed shut with a slap. He swallowed a scream.

He's going to win, said a voice that slid easily into Thomas's head.

That voice. The little girl. He'd dreaded hearing that voice again since the day he'd seen Bobby six years ago. Abe and his stinky clothes, his lottery tickets, his smokes, and his grain alcohol coughed a laugh and shuffled away from the counter.

He's going to win more than $42 million tonight.

Thomas turned slowly as the clerk pushed the packaged food off to the side. The store was empty except for the clerk and Thomas. No little girl. No fairy. No monsters crawling from the cover of a paperback. The clerk looked at Thomas, his face blank, beaten down. Thomas understood that feeling.

"May I help you?" the clerk asked.

*Then—*the little girl started.

Thomas's eyes snapped shut. *Go away.*

The voice was directly behind him. Or was it? That little girl could be anywhere, or nowhere. *None of this is real,* Thomas realized. *What if I've just had a tumor all these years?*

A giggle. *Don't you want to know what happens to Abe?* she asked.

No, I don't. Just buzz off.

Another giggle. *You don't have a tumor, you know.*

The clerk's expression changed. A hand slid under the counter, where he either had an alarm buzzer or a piece.

"May I help you?" he asked again.

You'd better answer him, Thomas. You've been acting strange, and he has a .38-caliber pistol under the counter. His body temperature has risen, so he thinks you're a threat. He doesn't know you very well, does he?

I said buzz off, kid. You don't scare me anymore.

"I need my receipt. I'm on—" Thomas turned and looked back at the pumping station, "—pump two."

The clerk relaxed, punched a button on the cash register, and ripped off Thomas's receipt.

"Thanks," Thomas said. He took the strip of thermal paper and walked out the door.

[2]

Ten minutes later, at Tennyson's, Jim the bartender started pouring a pint of Boulevard Single-Wide IPA the moment Thomas sat at the bar. Being a regular had its benefits.

"Need a menu, Tom?" Jim asked, setting the glass of cloudy amber beer on a drink napkin. Thomas waved him off and downed the beer, signaling for a second.

"Whoa," Jim said. "Rough day?"

Thomas ran a hand through his hair. It stuck up at odd angles. What the hell happened? The cover of the Stephen King novel came to life and no one else noticed.

Jim sat another beer in front of him. Thomas grabbed it, the cold glass comforting in his hand.

"Would you like the usual?" Jim asked.

Thomas nodded. A Philly burger and house fries sounded good, or did it? Shit. What had happened? A shiver shook him. The book cover poured rainwater onto the floor of a convenience store, then the little girl spoke to him. He took a long drink from the second beer. The girl was back. Jesus Christ, she was back. What does she want?

Jim punched the food order into his computer; a waitress would deliver his sandwich to the bar in fifteen to twenty minutes with a smile, and a "Good to see you tonight, Tommy." More benefits.

Thomas peeled off his jacket and draped it over the back of the barstool, his work shirt traded in for a clean green polo. A movement to his right caught his eye as more people filed into the bar. The barstool next to him squeaked; someone pulled it out and sat.

The person next to Thomas picked up the drink menu.

She wants to tell you something. Thomas froze; the din of the bar was still there, but to Thomas it had mostly disappeared. The conversation, laughs, knives and forks scraping across plates, the football game on TV. It was all gone. The voice was back, here in the bar, but it wasn't *the* voice. The words had been spoken by a grown woman—a grown woman who sounded familiar.

I've missed you, Thomas, the new voice piped into his head.

Go away. I don't want you here.

I think you do, she said.

Where are you?

The tap on his shoulder almost sent him out of his seat. His hand shot forward and grabbed the bar, stopping him from crashing backward into a waitress. The once familiar nervous knot he hadn't felt since childhood gripped his stomach and didn't let up. He swung toward the person who sat beside him. It was a woman wearing blue jeans and a Ramones T-shirt. It was Jillian.

"It's me," she said. "It's always been me."

[3]

Jillian walked beside Thomas, his jacket big on her. He held his dinner, untouched, in a white to-go bag that swung between them.

"What happened to you?" he asked, a chill in his voice matching the one in the fall night. "You just disappeared."

Thomas took two more steps before he realized she was no longer beside him. Jillian stood, looking at the pavement, her hands stuffed in his jacket pockets.

"I went home," she said.

"I didn't think you had a home." The words were jagged, harsh, but she didn't seem to notice.

"It's far away." She took a step toward him. When he didn't move back toward her, she took another, until she could reach out and touch him but didn't. "It was Bobby. Bobby is evil. There's no other way to describe him. The fact that he's out there, in this town, frightened me. So, I just ran. I had to go home."

A pot of screw-you began to boil inside Thomas. "Who are you?" he asked. "Or should I say *what* are you?"

Her eyes shot toward the street. Thomas wanted to reach out and shake her, but he held his arms close to him, his hands in fists. "Answer me, Jillian, or whatever your name is. What are you?" *Are you the fairy I saw in my mother's garden?*

Her gaze slowly turned back to Thomas. *Yes,* her voice said in his mind.

The little girl who led me into the cornfield?

She nodded.

The little girl in the laundry?

Yes.

"Are you," he said aloud, his voice growing heavy, "are you even Jillian? Are you the girl I met at Sisters of Mercy?"

She nodded again, then pushed her hair behind her ear. Yeah, she was the same Jillian. "I went to Sisters of Mercy to be with you, Thomas. I don't have a stepfather. I was never raped. I never killed anyone with a screwdriver. I made up those stories to be there—with you." She stared into Thomas's face with soft, kind eyes. "I needed you. I am Jillian, but I am also all those other things."

Thomas took a step back. "That's not possible. What are you?"

"I am fae," she said, her voice soft.

"Fae? Does that mean fairy, because that's what I saw in the garden."

"Yes. You were right all along."

"Fairies don't exist," he said. "Don't you go to church?"

She laughed. "No."

"Me neither," he said. "What does *fae* mean?"

She shuffled closer to him. "I'm like you, but not like you. I can do . . . things. Things you would call magic, but it's not. There's no such thing as magic. Some people can do things, others can't. You never could hit a curveball, others can. We're all different. People have called those like me elementals, fairies, devils, but we are what we are."

The knot wrenched his guts.

"Are you human at all?" he hissed. "Even a little?"

She smiled. Her teeth nearly glowing in the lamp-lit city night. "Yes. I can be. I am, for you."

"I don't understand."

Jillian shook her head. "You don't have to. Not really. Just love me. I know you do. I can feel it. It radiates off you like a fever." She gently wrapped her arms around Thomas's neck and pulled his face to hers. She kissed him. He didn't resist.

[4]

The first thing Thomas saw when his eyes opened was the clock: it was 3:48 a.m. The second thing was the dinner on his dresser, uneaten, still in its to-go bag from Tennyson's. Jillian lay next to him, her leg wrapped over his. Was it Jillian? Yes. It was Jillian. But, he wondered, who was Jillian? The girl in the mental hospital? The woman who disappeared from his life? The child who held his hand as they walked into the cornfield to face some kind of monster that still haunted him?

The streetlamps glowed through his open window. He could feel her, see her body as she lay under the comforter, smell her scent. She was real. She was not this fae thing she'd claimed on the street. She couldn't be. Thomas turned toward her. Jillian moaned softly in her sleep and rolled away from him, her long red hair like slate in the moonlight.

He slowly pulled himself out of bed. Jillian groaned but didn't wake. Thomas grabbed his supper, walked into the kitchen, and dropped it into the garbage.

⸺⸻⸻

At 4:00 a.m. the world below Thomas's fifth-floor apartment ticked slowly by. A pickup cruised down Taylor Street—a responsible grownup going to work or a college student going home. Then the sound of bare feet on linoleum padded its way into the kitchen.

"Come back to bed," Jillian said as she stepped behind Thomas and wrapped her arms around his waist.

Who are you?

"You've known me since you were young," she said, gliding around to face him, her arm never leaving his body. "I'm Jillian."

"Is that your real name?"

She shook her head. "No."

"Then what is it?"

Jillian looked away, the streetlight through the window casting harsh shadows over her face. "You shouldn't know it."

He leaned his shoulder into the wall as he glared at her. "Why?"

Jillian's soft, warm hands released him, and she stepped back.

"You just shouldn't." She shook her head. "It doesn't really matter."

He moved closer. "After what you've put me through, don't tell me I shouldn't know your real name. Are you a celebrity? A criminal? A Disney princess? What?"

She turned to avoid his gaze. "It's nothing like that."

Fingers strong from twisting wrenches gently tipped her chin to face him; Thomas studied her face. It was the same face he'd known from his apartment above the antique shop years ago. The exact same face. Tiny creases had grown at the corners of Thomas's mouth and eyes over the past six years, along with a few strands of gray that appeared on his temples. She hadn't changed. She hadn't changed at all.

"Would laugh lines make you more comfortable?"

She knows what I'm thinking. Of course, she knows.

"Can you do that?"

Jillian nodded, and suddenly they were there, lines at the corners of her eyes and her lips. Thomas thought she looked even more beautiful. She smiled, and the lines became more pronounced.

"Thank you," she said.

"Then you *are* one of them," he said, his voice soft.

"I was your fairy in the garden," she said. "I asked you to be quiet so your mother wouldn't know. She would have ruined everything. Do you remember?"

Thomas nodded. "But how? The fairy was so—"

"Small?" Jillian reached toward Thomas's face and brought her hand down over his eyes. "Don't peek. Please don't peek until I say. I don't want you to scream at what you see."

"I'm a grown man," he said, although his eyes remained closed. "I won't scream."

He felt a change in air pressure against his ears.

"Okay," a voice said. It was Jillian's, or like Jillian's, but smaller. He could hear it, it was audible—barely, but it was also inside his head.

Thomas opened his eyes. The little woman who stepped from behind a stalk of corn in his mother's garden stood on the kitchen windowsill next to a dead potted plant he never remembered to water. It was the little woman in the white dress, with hair as red as a crayon.

"Do you believe me now?" she asked.

He grabbed the back of a chair to steady himself.

"Thomas?" the fairy said.

The air pressure changed again.

Hands, small and strong, grabbed his shoulders; strength flowed into him. Thomas pushed himself back to full height and looked at the thing that held on to him. She was now the little girl from his room, the little girl from the cornfield, the little girl from Griffon Coin Laundry. The girl stood before him wearing the same knee-length white dress and the same haircut.

"Recognize me?" the girl asked.

Thomas nodded. "Jillian?" he asked. "How old are you?"

The little girl's smile was Jillian's. "As old as I want to be," she said.

This was wrong. Everything to do with Jillian was wrong. He'd known that when he saw her face at Tennyson's. Now, as he stood in his dark kitchen with the little girl who convinced him as a child to fight the devil or something damn near like it, he knew it was worse than wrong.

"Why'd you come back?" he whispered.

A pop filled the room and she'd become Jillian again. "I missed you. I told you that."

Thomas steeled himself and breathed deeply.

"No. There's another reason. There has to be another reason." He grasped her shoulders with both hands. "Back in the cornfield . . . the night I died . . ."

He stopped. Her expression never changed.

"You told me that thing had destroyed your world and was coming to mine. You took me somewhere. Where was it?"

She melted into him, her head burrowing into his shoulder. "My world. As it was before Dauðr destroyed it, and after. It was once fresh, green, and glorious. It was the wellspring of life in the universe, and now it is a dusty husk. That's what will happen to your world unless we act."

"Wellspring of life in the universe? That sounds like Garden of Eden gibberish."

Jillian smiled up at him. "If that's what you want to call it. It's where all life began, and now it is a dead place, murdered, and the murderer is hungry again. It's here. It entered your world. It's weak now but getting stronger. Everyone is going to die."

"Well, if everyone's going to die, I guess it doesn't matter if I know your name."

Her mouth frowned, but her eyes didn't. "Alfhild. It's Alfhild."

"Alfhild?" he said. "What does that mean?

"It means 'Battle of Elves.'"

Chapter Nine  2005

BOBBY SAT IN HIS FATHER'S overstuffed recliner reading the newspaper he stole off Mr. Harrington's walkway while the old man was out for his morning coffee at Denny's, or Dunkin' Donuts, or wherever the hell old men go for coffee on a Wednesday. The chair wasn't comfortable.

The front page was garbage. City council this, public library that. Not like the front page when Mom and Dad Garrett went to the Great Beyond. WELL-RESPECTED COUPLE BUTCHERED IN THEIR OWN HOME BY UNGRATEFUL SON. No. That headline didn't happen at all. The Garretts' "circle of friends" included a woman from work his dad was sleeping with and a woman with dementia his mom played bridge with occasionally. Work called asking for his dad once and Bobby told the unconcerned secretary Todd Garrett had suddenly retired and decided to travel the country in an RV with his wife, so please mail his last check to the house, thank you very much. Neither parent had siblings, and both sets of grandparents were dead. Bobby wasn't just an only child, he was an only Garrett.

"Boring," Bobby said into the big, empty house as he flipped to page A2. A headline at the bottom of the page, in 28-point type, read, POPE BENEDICT XVI SAYS DEVIL IS ALIVE AND WELL AND LIVING IN HOLLYWOOD.

"Well, hello there," Bobby said.

The page crinkled as he folded it.

VATICAN CITY–Movies like "The Exorcist," "The Amityville Horror" and the recently released "Cursed," have one major thing in common, according to Pope Benedict XVI–they're all designed to intentionally bring Satan into the lives of everyday people.

"These movies glorify evil," Pope Benedict said, addressing the Church at Easter Mass. "When people rejoice in this celebration of Satan, it opens a window, and once that window is open, they cannot imagine what may come through it."

The paper fell to Bobby's lap as the quote rambled through his head. The image of an open window, something dark and wicked sending tendrils of black mist inside, touching, testing, before they coalesced into fingers and arms that drag a beast into the room.

I've heard that before, Bobby thought, then said aloud, "Where?"

He stood, the paper dropping to a floor cluttered with Murph's bags and dirty clothes.

"Where did the window come from?" Bobby shouted, his voice echoing in the empty space. No answer returned, not that he thought it would. His mom and dad talked to him sometimes, but that was usually when he tried to sleep. They stood by his bed, whispering to him. Bobby never knew what they said.

"Bueller?" he said into the empty house. "Bueller?"

Nothing.

"How can being dead make you even more boring?"

Window. Window, window, window. Where'd I get the image of a window?

He wandered through the ground floor of the house; his dad's study with its dark wood and a layer of dirt on a neatly organized desk, the dining room with the walnut table they used only once a year for Christmas, his mom's sunroom in the back of the house, all the blinds up, the view of the small waterway blocked by a row of trees. On to his backyard, with its three-feet-high grass probably home to snakes, or maybe velociraptors. He had visions of this house exploding and setting fire to the lawn he was never going to cut. He hoped that just like his visions of cracking his mom and dad's skulls open came true, one day this one would come true too.

Bobby's scattered random thoughts fell into the right slots.

"When you leave a window open, you never know what may come in," he whispered.

He knew where he'd heard those words—from the boy. The dead-alive boy. The boy who delivered a sandwich to this house. He didn't just scream at Sisters of Mercy, sometimes the dead-alive boy spat words into his hazy gray padded cell. The boy named Thomas.

A laugh, from somewhere deep down, bubbled to the surface. Bobby ran into the kitchen and threw open the refrigerator. He kept two things in there: beer and mustard. He opened a beer bottle with a twist and walked upstairs to open all the windows in his room. He had an invitation to send.

[2]

Bobby was lying in bed with the covers up to his neck when his dad visited in the night, the crescent-shaped dent the lamp left in the man's forehead stained dark with dried blood. In the mornings, Bobby never remembered if these visits were real or dreams, but by then it didn't matter. His dad rarely came alone; his mom was usually with him, sometimes looking away from Bobby with empty eye sockets, other times carrying a casserole dish of writhing maggots. Often his dad said, "We miss you, son. Come join us." Not this time. This time he stood next to Bobby's bed wearing a plastic St. Patrick's Day derby, his face expressionless. Flies buzzed around the dried wound. Bobby pulled his covers tighter; his father wanted something, but Bobby didn't know what.

He never found out. The memory of his father's visit was gone when he woke in the morning.

[3]

A tiny knock struck Bobby's front door, the hollow rap strange in the old house. He lay on the couch—shoes on—and listened. The fat guy from *Home Improvement* who hosted *Family Feud* made it hard to hear the knock, thank you very much.

Knock, knock, knock.

Was this the answer to his invitation?

"Hello," a high, thin voice called.

Knock, knock, knock.

He sat up, the *Home Improvement* guy said something that may have been a joke, but Bobby never found him funny.

"Who is it?" Bobby asked the door, his voice little more than a whisper.

A breeze, cold and sharp, flicked Bobby's cheek, then was gone. *Go to her,* whispered past his ear. His breathing froze for one moment, then two. He knew that voice; it spoke to him when he was fourteen, the day he hit the Johnson boy with a chunk of concrete.

He jumped to his feet.

"Hello?"

Hurry.

This time the voice in his head was louder. His legs moved on their own, pushing him toward the front door. His left hand reached out and unlocked the deadbolt, his right jerked the door handle. The door swung open. A small girl stood there. She wore a green beret, a green skirt and white shirt, and a green sash covered in patches draped over her right shoulder. She stood at the top of the steps leading down to the walk. She smiled; a black gap showed a missing tooth.

"Hi." She coughed into her hand and straightened her shoulders, the script ready in her head. "Hello. My name is Millie Novák and I am a Girl Scout in Troop Number two seventy-one." She paused and glanced back at her mother who sat on the street in a new Hyundai, then again at Bobby. "Would you like to buy some Girl Scout cookies? They cost three dollars a package. I—"

Take her, Bobby, the voice said, the words nearly shoving him forward.

He wasn't alone in the house anymore; something else was here, something he'd felt long ago. Dauðr. The voice was called Dauðr. He was sure.

"Yes. Yes, I will take her," he mumbled.

"Sir?" the Scout asked, trying to look past Bobby, but couldn't see into the house. He'd blocked the crack in the door with his body. She bit her lower lip. A little nervous, are you, honey? No need. This won't take long. He smiled, an easy, lying smile. The kind of smile people trusted, especially if they didn't look at his eyes. Bobby's cold, dark eyes made people uncomfortable.

We need her, the voice said.

"Sure, I'd like some cookies." Bobby squatted down to her eye level. "I like Tagalongs, but I think your mommy needs to come up here too. You can never be too safe in a strange neighborhood." A car engine down the street revved. It was the Madsen kid working on his Camaro. Bobby grew a smile.

The Scout nodded and smiled back; her pearly little teeth shone bright, except the missing incisor right on top. She turned and waved at her mother, who stepped out of the car and walked toward the house, clutching her cell phone like a lifeline.

Millie's mommy, a pretty thing, probably thirty-one or thirty-two, jogged up the steps to Bobby's porch, and he turned to face her, half his body still hidden by the door. The heavy lamp that had tap-danced on his mom and dad's heads sat on a small table against the wall, a lamp just like the one Miss Scarlet used to kill Mr. Boddy in the conservatory. Or was that a candlestick? Whatever. Bobby always won at Clue.

A wave of absolute chaos smashed into Bobby's mind: Mommy's thoughts were a jumble. Sell cookies, meet Chris and Amy for lunch, Millie's dance practice today at five, stop by the store to pick up pasta for supper, Gabe's out of town tomorrow, take his truck in for an oil change—

Bobby shook his head harder than he'd intended and looked up at the Scout's mother.

"Sorry, ma'am," he said. "But with so many bad people in this world today, I don't feel comfortable talking with a child without a parent around. I hope that's okay."

She blushed slightly and seemed to relax. "No," she said. "That's fine. I should have come to the door with her, but she wanted to do it herself."

His trustworthy, lying smile never wavered. "Of course."

"Mommy," the girl said softly, tugging at the leg of her khaki capris. Mommy bent toward her. "This house smells funny," the girl whispered, but Bobby heard it.

Why are you waiting? the voice asked.

The woman's cell phone played the *Golden Girls* "Thank you for being a friend . . ." across the porch. Jesus Christ, Bobby thought. Bashing in your brain is much too good for you.

"Oh, excuse me," she said, pulling her mobile phone to her ear and backing to the porch railing.

Take them now, the voice howled.

Bobby's smile vanished.

"No," he hissed under his breath. His face grew hot; blood pounded in his temples.

Take them now, take them now, take–them–now.

He sucked in a cleansing breath that didn't do a damn bit of good and looked back at the Girl Scout, her eyes now filled with fear. "I need to see the order sheet," he said, keeping his voice level.

"No, no, Chris. We're not quite to Carter. That's next. We'll—" She stopped and looked up and down the street. "No. There's not much here. Okay, okay. We'll meet you at Hyde Park and go from there."

Bobby plucked the brightly colored brochure from the girl's hands and waited for her mommy to get off the phone.

"Like I said, I really like Tagalongs," he told the Girl Scout again, pointing at the peanut-butter cookie covered in chocolate. "But those Samoas look pretty good, too. Which do you like best?"

She shrugged. "I dunno."

Her mother slid the phone into her purse and walked toward her daughter and Bobby.

"The Double Dutch are pretty new," the girl said. "They look good. Lots of chocolate."

The smile returned as Bobby nodded.

"Yes, they sure do, Millie." He rose and held his hand out to the mother. "Ma'am, do you have a pen? I'm going to order some cookies from young Millie here."

Now, the voice screamed.

He winced at the pain.

The mother didn't notice as she rustled in her purse. "I've got one in here somewhere."

"Oh, that's all right," Bobby said, his smile so tight it hurt. "I've got one in the house. Let's go get it?"

The woman looked up from her purse as Bobby's fist flew at the side of her head. It landed with a crunch and she staggered, moaning.

The little girl's scream came out as a squeak, buried under the rumble of the Madsen boy's Camaro down the street. Bobby grabbed her mommy's hair in one hand, the girl's in the other, and yanked them inside the house. His leg shot out and slammed the door shut, the sound of the Madsen boy's car suddenly deadened by the thick, wood paneled walls of the old house.

He bashed her mommy's head into the wooden door frame, and she crumpled. He tossed the Scout on top of her.

"Wha—" Millie's mother mumbled, her eyes glassy.

"Shut up," Bobby snapped, lifting the lamp from the round table. Oh, the lamp. The solid antique lamp. Good for bashin' in brains.

The Scout's arms hugged the woman's waist; her body shook with sobs.

"Don't hurt my little girl," the woman said. "Please, oh, God, don't hurt my little girl."

The lamp popped when he slapped it into the palm of his left hand.

"Oh, I'm not going to hurt anybody." He paused. "What's your name?"

"Kar—Karen," she stuttered.

He nodded.

"Karen. Okay, Karen."

He stepped toward her, and she scooted through the litter of garbage toward the living room, her ass leaving a trail on the dusty floor.

"You know, Karen," he said, "I must apologize."

Millie the Girl Scout's sobs became a siren of a wail as she crawled next to her mother. Bobby swung his left hand in a circle.

"For what?" he said. "You're supposed to ask for what?"

"F-f-for what?" she managed. Tears dragged mascara down her cheeks.

"Well, there we go," he said. "For a number of things, actually. One, this place is a mess. If you can imagine, I don't entertain often. I kind of let this place get away from me."

He lifted the metal lamp and rested it on his shoulder.

"Two, I've changed my mind about the cookies. And—"

Kill them.

Bobby stopped, looming over his mommy and her Scout. He slapped himself on the side of the head.

"I'm doing it," he barked. "What else do you want from me?"

"I didn't say anything." The woman was shaking now. Oh, how she shook.

Bobby waved a hand at her. "Thank you. That's the last thing I need to apologize for. I wasn't talking to you. I was talking to the voice in my head that told me to kill you."

The woman screamed as Bobby brought the base of the lamp down on top of her head. She screamed again when he brought it down a second time, but the sound died with her. The little girl wailed.

He lowered the lamp and looked down at the Girl Scout, who would never deliver cookies again.

"You know," he said, as casually as if he'd asked how school was today, "they sure knew how to make lamps back in the day."

The girl screamed again when Bobby slung the old lamp over his head, the cord dangling behind him, and brought it down on her.

Early the next morning, he drove Karen's Hyundai to a nearby nature park, barren of people at that time of day, set it on fire, and walked home. When he got there, police were waiting.

[4]

A blue-and-white St. Joseph Police Department SUV sat on the street across from Bobby's house. The passenger door opened, and a uniformed officer stepped out, followed by a second from the driver's side. Bobby froze, the instinct to flee pulled at him hard. The officer looked at a photo, then back up at Bobby. He threw a brusque wave and Bobby nearly shat.

Don't run, jumped into his head. It was the voice again. The voice of the dark creature he'd invited into his home. The voice that told him "*You know what to do*" the day the Johnson boy tried to molest him. A warmth washed over him, and the fear, the panic, dissolved. The voice was his friend.

What did you do? Bobby thought to the darkness.

Helped you. Now, approach these men.

An unwanted smile formed on Bobby's face, and he walked toward the officers, hands loose at his sides.

"Mr. Garrett?" the first officer asked.

Bobby smiled as he walked up to the man and stopped, his shoulders relaxed. *They do not see you as a threat. Greet them.*

"Yes. Hello, officers," Bobby said, his voice smooth, even. "What can I help you with?"

The first police officer pulled a photograph from beneath the one on top, which Bobby saw was of him.

"We're looking for a missing mother and daughter," he said. The other officer walked around the vehicle and stood opposite his partner, giving Bobby no room to run if he chose to. He showed the photo to Bobby. Karen and Millie Novák looked a lot better in that picture than they did in his basement lying in sticky pools of their own blood. "Have you seen them?"

Don't lie to these men.

Bobby's mouth moved, although he didn't feel in complete control of it.

"Yes, sir. They stopped at my house yesterday selling Girl Scout cookies. I hope there's nothing wrong."

The second officer produced a notepad and scratched down some words.

"At what time?" the first police officer asked.

Bobby shrugged. "I don't know. Sometime right before lunch. Sorry, but I can't give you the exact time."

"That's fine. Did they say anything to you, apart from selling cookies?"

He shook his head. "No, sir."

Yes, she did.

"Oh, wait. The mother answered her telephone while I was looking at the sales sheet."

"Do you remember what she said?" he asked.

Bobby did. Bobby remembered everything. "She was talking about meeting another Girl Scout mom at a park somewhere in town, but she wanted to stop at another house or two first."

Officer Number Two wrote this down. "Any idea which way they were going?" he asked.

"No, but this is a dead-end street," Bobby said, pointing toward the south. "There's only one occupied house that way."

"We'll stop there," Officer One said. "Is there anything else you can remember from yesterday? Any strange vehicles on the street? Anyone in the neighborhood you didn't know?"

They're going to leave.

Officer One stopped moving.

Bobby glanced at Officer Two; both police officers stood, motionless, their eyes glazed over for a strangely long time. They didn't seem to breathe.

Then both men started moving as suddenly as they'd stopped.

"Anyone in the neighborhood you didn't know?" Officer One repeated.

What did you do? Bobby thought.

Bobby shook his head. "No. I'm afraid I've told you all I know except I didn't buy any cookies. I hope that's not illegal."

The monster said in his head, *I told them they were finished here.*

The first officer smiled and handed Bobby a card.

"No, Mr. Garrett. If you think of anything, anything at all that relates to Karen and Millie Novák, please give us a call."

Bobby waved as the police officers climbed back into their SUV and continued down Carlyle Street. He thought his new friend may come in handy.

[5]

When Bobby went back inside, he realized the Girl Scout was right—the place smelled funny. Apparently, the stench of decaying bodies is difficult to remove from a house.

Squirts of Febreze went with him as he walked through the living room, occasionally stopping and sniffing. The floral scent dominated the air, but the underlying odor of rotting flesh wouldn't go away. He'd tried Natural, Clean, Fruity, and Exotic, and they all masked the stench enough to make it bearable to sit downstairs to watch *Everybody Loves Raymond* on Monday nights, but the sweet taint of death remained.

He hoped the police didn't come back.

Bobby sniffed the sleeve of his shirt but couldn't tell if the rot had permeated his clothes. It couldn't be his mom and dad. They'd been dead for five or six years by now. They were just dried, leathery skin stretched over old bones, propped up against the basement wall. His father wore a green plastic derby with a sticker on the front that read, "Kiss Me, I'm Irish." His mom wore Groucho glasses to cover her empty sockets.

Bobby laughed every time he went down there.

No, the smell was from the Girl Scout who knocked on his door to—spy on me, he thought. He took a second to clear his mind. I mean, "to sell cookies." It was probably her mom too. Mommy looked like the kind of person who asked to see the manager. It would make sense that she would stink up his house.

He waved the Febreze bottle around the foyer again, squirting the odor-masking liquid heavily around the door. It was nearly 8 p.m.; the driver from Murph's American Sammiches would be here soon, and he didn't want them to catch a whiff of anything.

[6]

Bobby wasn't sure what woke him, the jab in the side or the barking from Mrs. Bethany's little ankle-biting Taco Bell dog down the street. Something pointy poked him in the ribs again. It felt like a finger, but it couldn't be a finger. He was alone.

He belched; the half Guido Frito he'd eaten had given him a stomachache.

"Get up," said a tiny high-pitched voice. *A voice that wanted to sell you cookies before you hit me in the face with a lamp.*

Bobby scrambled up and away from the probing finger, bedsheets tangled around his legs. The Girl Scout stood inches from him, the green beret sideways on her head. He remembered her hat had twisted that way when the lamp slammed against her face. Bobby stumbled as he swung and connected with only her jaw. He'd had to choke her to death, for God's sake. Bobby hated choking, that was for hired goons and lunatics, not for him.

"Millie? You—you're dead," Bobby sputtered.

The Girl Scout grinned, her shiny, straight teeth now a mess of jagged, bloody stumps—except the missing incisor, which would never come in.

She reached out to poke him again, and Bobby scooted away, the side of the bed ending beneath him. He crashed to the floor, tangled in sheets. The hardwood floor of the old house connected with the back of Bobby's head when he struck; his vision swam.

"Millie is dead, Robert," the tiny voice said. "But I'm not Millie. I'm the reason you left the window open. I'm the one you invited into your house."

Small feet in patent leather shoes moved from the opposite side of the bed, visible to Bobby through the dust bunnies. The little shoes slowly shuffled toward him as he yanked at the sheets that bound his legs. The Girl Scout walked around the corner and stood over Bobby's prone form, her green sash dotted with patches and spots of her blood. The shoes clomped to a stop at his face; Bobby quit struggling.

"Are you—" He swallowed and started again. "Are you Dauðr?"

She smiled down at him with that mouth of shattered teeth.

Cold rained over him like sleet and Bobby shivered, gooseflesh rising on his skin.

"Do you hear the beast?" the dead Scout asked.

Beast?

"The dog?" Bobby asked.

"Yes." It came out *yeth* through her shattered teeth. "Do you know why it's barking?"

"Because it's a d-d-dog," he stuttered.

The Girl Scout's right foot stomped inches from Bobby's nose. He recoiled.

"No. Because it smells the woman in the basement. It smells what's left of my mommy, and it wants some. It's scratching at the window. Hard."

"What do you want?" Bobby's words came out in a whimper.

The Girl Scout bent toward him, and Bobby kicked at the sheets wrapped around his legs, only twisting them tighter.

"I want you to kill it." The girl's voice sounded—what? Excited? "Kill it before it brings its master (math-ter), and you are taken away. I can't have that, not yet. I need you, Robert Garrett."

"I-I-I—" Bobby whined.

The Girl Scout smiled, her broken mouth caked with crusted blood.

"Go," the dead girl said. "Go before I crush your useless testicles beneath my feet."

A scream ripped from his lungs as the little monster stomped those hard leather shoes on the wood floor.

Clomp, clomp, clomp.

He stood but fell into the hallway, his legs still tied in the sheets. He tore himself free and tumbled down the stairs.

———❦———

Bobby snuck quietly out the kitchen door, the same door he'd waited behind six years ago for dear old Dad to come home to a beating. The dog, a Chihuahua or some other kind of bug-eyed rat that made too much goddamned noise, sniffed around the basement window scratching and yipping.

No one could see into the basement—after he dragged his mom and dad down there, he'd duct taped garbage bags to the window— but that shitty little dog sure could smell, and now there was something new down there. Fresh meat.

"Hey," Bobby hissed at the dog. "Hey, dummy."

The dog sniffed the window and barked again. Bobby closed the distance between them but stumbled over his own feet and slammed against the house. The rat dog bared its teeth.

"Hey," he said louder. "I have food."

He held what was left of his foot-long Guido Frito, an Italian sausage hoagie stuffed with Fritos corn chips, and broke off a small piece of sausage.

"Take it. It won't give you a stomachache like it did me, you little monster. You won't be alive that long."

A piece of sausage landed a few feet away from the dog, who ignored it.

"God, you're stupid," Bobby whispered, and broke off another piece, tossing it right at the dog. It landed about a foot from the little bastard and rolled closer. The dog stopped scratching the window and looked around. It smelled the sausage and sniffed its way toward the meat, gulping it down in two bites. The dog sniffed again, walked to the first piece, and ate it too. Then it looked at Bobby and wagged its tail.

"Good boy."

Mrs. Bethany's dog followed Bobby to the garage. Bobby fumbled with the key to the side door, and when it finally creaked open, he stepped inside.

The little dog followed him.

It yelped when he snatched it off the floor and yelped again when he held it like a little fat baseball bat and swung it toward the garage wall. The second yelp was quieter than the first. Bobby swung it again, this time against a support beam. The dog's neck snapped, and the little yapping beast went limp.

"That's what you get for snooping, Taco Bell dog," Bobby said, his breathing heavy from . . . exertion? Nerves? He didn't know.

A smile dragged across his face. Mrs. Bethany had threatened to call the police when she caught Bobby peeing in her bushes when he was fourteen. That wasn't nice. Not nice at all. He grabbed the dead, bleeding dog by its collar, the neck lolling like a broken doll's, and stepped from the garage, shutting the side door behind him, the rest of the sandwich under his arm.

After Bobby shoved the dead crap factory into Mrs. Bethany's mailbox, the lights of the nearly deserted street dim in front of her house, he put a hand over his mouth to keep from laughing out loud and ran home to serve his new master.

Chapter Ten  2005

THE MORNING LIGHT SHONE THROUGH the half-open curtain, flooding Thomas's bedroom in a warm glow. Jillian lay next to him, her red hair cascading across the white pillowcase, her body beneath the covers moving gently with each breath.

At least she has to breathe, Thomas thought.

Jillian didn't stir when he slipped from under the covers and went into the kitchen. It was Friday morning, and he was up in time for work. Thomas had never missed a day during his more than three years at Smithmeyer Luxury Auto Center. Not for illness, not for a hangover, not for his dad's heart attack. "It was a mild one, thank

God," his mom had told him over the phone the afternoon his dad dropped to one knee in the yard, then collapsed. "They're already moving him out of the ER. He's going to be fine." So, Thomas stayed at work and went back into the shop the next day, visiting his dad at St. Joseph Regional Hospital on the west side of town after work.

But today, he wasn't going in.

"Yeah, Mike," he said into the telephone receiver, his voice soft. "I'm sorry, but I'm going to have to stay home today." Thomas audibly sucked in breath, then let it out slowly. "Migraine. Yeah, yeah, I get them every few years. I was due."

He paused; Mike's wife suffered from migraines, and Thomas had heard all about it.

"Listen, I gotta go take my meds and lie down, Mike. Yeah, thanks. A wet, warm towel over my forehead sounds good. I'll do that now. Thanks again. See you Monday."

Thomas slipped the phone back on the wall hook and started a pot of coffee.

He sat in a chair in the corner of the bedroom watching Jillian sleep, a coffee mug in his hands. She finally woke at 8:47 a.m., rolled over, grunted, and farted once, just like a real woman. Is she a real woman? She sat up and stretched, her smile white and clean.

"How long have you been watching me?" she asked.

Thomas took a sip of coffee. "Two hours," he said.

"Weirdo." Jillian pulled back her unkempt hair—like a real woman—and crawled out of bed wearing his Ramones shirt. That shirt bothered him. It was his shirt. She took it when she left, but it looked brand new; she'd had it for six years.

Jillian took Thomas's hand and gently pulled him from the chair. "I'm hungry," she said. "Got any bacon?"

Thomas had bacon and eggs and the ingredients for pancakes. No box mixes in his place. His mom taught him to cook from scratch and, unintentionally, how to hide a bottle of vodka. When his dad couldn't slow down his drinking, his mother inadvertently tried to keep up, she just didn't want anyone to know.

Thomas cracked an egg into a bowl and tossed the shell into the sink. He'd added vanilla, baking powder, and a few shakes of salt when Jillian slid next to him and wrapped an arm around his waist.

"You need any help?"

"A cup of milk," he said, nodding his head toward the refrigerator as he measured the ingredients and poured them into the bowl. He gave her a whisk and put a skillet on the stove.

The bacon went into another skillet, and soon the little apartment smelled like home. Ten minutes later, they sat at the small table in his kitchen and stared at each other.

"What are we doing, Jillian?" Thomas asked, the food forgotten on his plate. This woman, this person, this thing, had been part of his life since he was six years old. She was a part of him. But was she a good part?

A grin broke above her forkful of pancake. "Having breakfast," she said, then stuck the fork into her mouth, pulling it out clean. "Having a yummy breakfast."

He shook his head. "Not breakfast. You dropped an anvil on my head last night." He paused and looked at her with a piercing squint. "You understand metaphors, don't you?"

She sat her fork on her plate and dabbed syrup from the corners of her mouth with a paper napkin. "I can't tell if you're kidding or not," she said. "Don't tease me like that."

That was normal, wasn't it? Something was different about Jillian this morning, though. Something subtle.

"Sorry," he said. "I'm just having a hard time wrapping my head around everything."

Jillian smiled and reached across the small table, grasping his rough hands in her soft, warm ones. "I'm not going to disappear again. I'm sorry I did that to you. I was just, just—"

"Just what?"

She frowned. "Terrified. It was Bobby. Bobby's not just bad, he's wrong. He's—" she paused and looked at her empty plate. "He's a door. An entrance, a path. Everyone, everything that comes here from the elsewhere needs a door like Bobby. Bobby's a beacon, and something wicked has seen that beacon and latched on to it. It has come here."

"Dauðr?" Thomas asked, a tremor in his voice. "You said last night it was here. It got through."

"Yes." Tears grew in her eyes. She wiped the back of her hand across her face to take them away. "It's here. It smelled Bobby, and Bobby smelled it back. He let it in."

Thomas pulled his hands away and went over to the coffeemaker holding a cup that read "Beer Mug in Training." Mike had given him that coffee cup last Christmas.

"And what about you? Do you need one of these beacons to visit here?" Memories of his dream flooded his mind. Smoky plains and gray dust, the stunted, burnt trees, and the bloody man, begging. The teeth.

"Yes," she said.

He filled the mug, then waved the pot in her direction. She nodded, and he poured the last of the coffee into the cup on the table in front of her.

"What is it *you* need to come here?" he asked.

Her smile returned as she stood and took the coffeepot out of Thomas's hand, setting it on the Formica tabletop. She laced her fingers behind his neck. "You, Thomas Cavanaugh. I need you. I've always needed you."

"So, the first time you came here was—"

"In your mother's garden while she sang a Leesa Loman song."

"That part I remember," he said. A shiver ran through him. "What else don't I know?"

"We all know very little outside our own senses, Thomas. That includes me." Jillian buried her face in his shoulder. "The entity that's here now, with Bobby, that wants—no, *needs* to eat your world. That's what I know." She pulled her head from his chest, her eyes red. She released Thomas and wiped her eyes across the sleeve of her shirt. "And I also know that you're mine, and I'm yours. I couldn't be here if that wasn't so."

Thomas wanted to sit, to simply drop onto the chair where he ate breakfast every morning and rest his head on the table, but Jillian grasped his hand. Her touch kept him on his feet, her strength pouring into his limbs.

"Are we going to do something about this Dauðr monster?" he asked. "Like last time?"

"Yes," she said. "But we have to find it first."

[2]

Bobby sat on the front porch in the rocking chair his mother liked to sit in and read, before Bobby crushed her skull with a lamp.

A corn chip fell from the last bite of his Murph's Guido Frito. Bobby picked it off his lap and popped it into his mouth. His stomach didn't hurt this morning. Hell, why would it? His world was finally starting to make sense. Bobby leaned full into the chair and started to rock.

Mrs. Bethany tapped her walker along her cracked sidewalk to the mailbox; she pinched an envelope next to the walker handle in her claw-like hand. He didn't want to miss this. Mrs. Bethany reached the silver mailbox and leaned on the walker to lift the red flag.

The old woman's hand reached the lid and pulled it open; the dog's head lolled outward on its snapped neck. Her screams reached all the way down the street.

"Woof," Bobby said, his face pulled into a grimace. That stupid dog would have spoiled Bobby's fun by barking at what was in his basement. That wasn't going to happen. No dog, nobody and nothing, were going to spoil Bobby's fun. Now that Bobby had a new friend, the fun was just getting started.

Friend. He didn't know if the little girl in the white shirt and green sash was his friend. She scared him. Dead people that walked and talked would do that, he supposed. The Girl Scout had given him something to do today, something he didn't want to do. She'd walked up behind Bobby as he stood at the foyer door, peering into the morning, waiting for Mrs. Bethany to make her daily walk to the mailbox, and she'd touched him. Her cold, dead little fingers brushed his bare arm like little shriveled sausages. Bobby had jumped and stifled a shriek, turning to see the Girl Scout, her face flecked with dried, crusted blood. That's a hell of a thing see at six o'clock in the morning.

Then she told him to get a job. The little monster—what else could it be? It's a monster—said through its broken mouth, "Find a place (it came out *plathe*) with many people. Become one of them.

Blend with the surroundings." Blend with the surroundings? If he was going to work somewhere, he wanted to know why. He almost asked the Girl Scout; the words were on his lips when the little bitch did something to him. He didn't know what, but the thing's eyes rolled back into its head for only a second, and damn if pain didn't lance through Bobby's skull. His temples throbbed like he'd drank too much beer last night instead of what he did do, which was kill that little dog.

So, he'd said, "sure," and walked onto the porch, the pain slowly dissipating the farther he walked. He shut the door.

[3]

"I know where Bobby lives," Thomas said, staring at the ceiling. He and Jillian lay in his bed, her naked body pressed against his. "If he's this beacon, won't Dauðr be there with him?"

"Maybe," she said, twisting her finger in his scant patch of chest hair. "Probably. If we can find it. You went to his house once, years ago. How do you know he still lives there?"

"I don't, but it's a place to start," Thomas said, rolling onto his left side and looking into her face, her delicate, freckled face. "How long did it take you to find me?"

"Months," she said. "I lived in an apartment, going out to look for you when I felt you nearby. That may be what Dauðr's doing too. It may not have found Bobby yet."

"Or it may have."

She nodded; a frown creased her face. "Yes, but I don't think so. I can feel the monster, but it's not strong enough for me to find it. If it had found Bobby, I think it would be stronger."

Dear God. What did I get into?

"What kind of danger will we be in if we wait until you can pinpoint this thing?"

Her face showed no emotion. "I'd be too late to stop it from destroying your Earth."

[4]

Bobby shaved in the shower. That little girl followed him into the bathroom; her stained Girl Scout uniform stunk, or maybe it was just her. The thing's flesh had started to rot. Yes, he knew this walking, talking monster was dead, and whatever inhabited her now was not the little girl who just wanted to sell him cookies—Double Dutch or some other flavor. Something was inside her, something he was now sure wasn't really a friend, and he didn't know what it wanted.

Hot water cascaded over Bobby's black hair. The steam cleared his head, at least enough to try and think. Oh, yeah, it felt good to think. He'd spent years under the influence of so much psychiatric medication he couldn't think, not really. Everything had been all fuzzy. He felt free now, but he had a feeling the little monster didn't like that.

A small shadow fell across the mildewed shower curtain; Bobby turned his eyes. That was it. He was thinking in the shower, and she didn't like it, so she came to watch him, to babysit him. Bobby stuck out his tongue from behind the curtain. He wasn't going to give the Girl Scout the satisfaction of knowing she bothered him. But whatever that thing was standing outside the shower, it looked like an eight-year-old girl, and Bobby wasn't the kind of guy to let an eight-year-old girl watch him take a shower. That was creepy.

"Go away," he said, staring at the ceiling, the popcorn plaster starting to flake. "I need some privacy in here."

He turned toward the shadow; it was gone. Bobby hadn't thought that would work.

Black mildew lined the tiles and the curtain. Nice housekeeping, Mom, he thought, then laughed. He lathered himself as best he could with what he had, but the soap was useless, a ball of chips from used bars that stretched back to the years when Bobby's parents were still alive. A job? That thing wanted him to get a job in a high-traffic place. Why not? Dressing his mother and father in funny hats and glasses had gotten boring after so many years. He placed one of his mother's last pink plastic disposable razors in the shower caddy and turned off the water. The money he'd found in the house and drained from his parents' bank accounts had grown thin. The cookie girl was right, he needed a job. But something quiet and whiny that sounded like his mom told Bobby to run.

[5]

While she'd hunted for Thomas, Jillian had lived in the Starlight Motel, near a dilapidated airport. The airport had been a transportation hub sometime around the Korean War, but now it was only a hub for the homeless, drug addicts, and other people society had abandoned. But the motel was cared for, or at least remembered; the marquee beneath the dark Starlight Motel sign read "Vacancy." A wooded creek that cut through the nearby neighborhood on Carlyle Street ran behind the motel. Thomas figured as a kid he might have played in a creek like that, but in this shitty section of town, now he wouldn't go near it. Probably filled with needles and used rubbers.

Thomas pulled his Toyota into a lot and parked in front of the office. In this part of town, he'd expected graffiti and scattered trash. Three cars sat in the Starlight lot with Thomas's Toyota—a Hyundai, a Scion, and a Ford. All clean, all parked in marked spots, and not one of them on blocks.

"This is an abandoned motel," Thomas said, turning off the engine. "You live in an abandoned motel."

Jillian pulled the handle and swung open the door. "Not abandoned—repurposed," she said and got out of the car. She swayed for a moment, grabbing the door for support.

"Hey, you okay?" Thomas asked, shutting his door and rounding the car.

Jillian smiled at him. "Yes, I just got a little light-headed, that's all."

"Are you sure?" Thomas asked.

Jillian grabbed his hand and pulled him across the parking lot.

"Yes," she said. "And this isn't a motel, it's an apartment building that rents by the month."

"Why not something better?" he asked. "At least something cheap in a better neighborhood."

Jillian shook her head; her long hair tied in a tight ponytail swung in a slight arc.

"I don't have money to pay rent," she said. "However, I can pay rent in paper I make to look like money. The drug users who run this place won't notice; the type of people who operate places like your apartment building would."

She led him past a swimming pool, the paint new, the water clean. A "No lifeguard on duty, Swim safely!" sign hung on the gate of a chain-link fence closing off the pool from the lot. Deck chairs dotted the concrete.

"Nice," Thomas said. "No bodies floating in the pool."

Jillian ignored him and walked faster.

"Hey," he said. "That was funny. What—"

She stopped walking and swung around. "Something's wrong. I can feel it. We have to hurry."

She pulled a key from her pocket; a diamond-shaped green plastic fob with gold lettering dangled from the ring. Thomas slowed his pace as Jillian jogged up the steps to the second floor. A police siren fired up close by. She unlocked the door to 201 and stepped in.

After glancing around for people lurking outside in the darkness, Thomas followed her, shut the door, and threw the bolt.

The soft yellow glow of a desk lamp that still sported a tungsten bulb highlighted the deep forest green of the bed comforter. Maroon wallpaper that started halfway up the wall seemed to grow out of the dark brown paneling. Pastel portraits of sailing ships hung over the bed. It was a motel room from 1974. The place was a dump, but at least there weren't bullet holes in the walls.

"Decorate it yourself?"

Jillian ignored him and rushed into the bathroom. Thomas followed. She knelt next to the toilet, a wall tile in her hand.

"What are you doing?" he asked.

She reached into the hole in the wall and pulled out a bundle wrapped in brown paper held fast with a rubber band.

"It's important," she said, tucking the package under her arm and setting the tile back into place. "I took it from your house."

She stood and brushed her hands off on her clothes. "It meant something to you once. This gave you strength when we battled Dauðr." Jillian paused and looked into Thomas's eyes. Her breathing came hard. She was frightened.

"What is it?" Thomas asked, his voice soft, unsure.

Jillian shoved the small package into his hand and leaned forward on her tiptoes; her lips grazed his stubbly cheek.

"I feel it now," she whispered. "Dauðr is near. We have to leave."

"Oh, shit," Thomas said, and he followed her into the outer room.

[6]

The kitchen door's old hinges creaked, the sound raking through the still morning. Bobby winced as the door opened to reveal an empty kitchen. Images of the dead Girl Scout crawled through his brain like cockroaches scattering when the lights turn on. It was here. Bobby knew the thing was here somewhere, lurking, waiting for him. He'd expected it to be in the kitchen, but it wasn't. Where was it? A floorboard beneath the linoleum whined when he stepped into the kitchen and swung the door shut, the old stiff hinges screaming again. It was behind the door.

"You wanted to run."

Bobby jerked at the sudden sound, dropping the neighbor's newspaper to the floor. The stench from the Girl Scout's rotting body was thick in the air, thick enough to push him backward.

"No," he stammered. "No, no. I didn't. I just—"

"You lie, Robert. You were going to leave uth," it said through the Scout's broken mouth. The monster's lower lip dangled from its face, a graying worm that hung over the slack skin of its sagging chin. The lip jiggled as it spoke. "That will not happen."

Bobby wanted to beg this monster to let him go, but his mouth, dry as a drunk's, wouldn't work.

"You are bound to me, Robert."

Bobby's eyes focused on the dead creature's face. A fly landed on its cheek and rubbed its forelegs. "You can never leave us."

The fly moved, crawling over the rotting skin, pausing to probe an oozing, festering sore. It moved slowly into a nostril and disappeared; the Girl Scout didn't flinch. "You will not disappoint me again."

[7]

A white wave washed over Jillian's face before her knees buckled and she dropped to the dirty carpet.

"Hey," Thomas said, kneeling next to her; he wrapped an arm around her shoulders. Jillian leaned into him. His rough hand slid gently beneath her chin, tilting her face to his. "Jillian?"

Her eyelids opened, but her eyes rolled before they stopped and focused on him. "Dauðr. It's so close." Her hands latched on to Thomas's biceps, her grip tight. "It's found Bobby. Oh, Thomas. It's so much stronger than I thought."

Jillian was light in his arms as he lifted her and set her on her feet. They hurried from 201 and into the night, Thomas's arm around Jillian's slim waist.

"Where are they?" he asked, half-carrying her across the parking lot. The police siren had been joined by another. His Toyota seemed miles away.

"Close," she said. "It's not safe here."

A man, his eyes wild, naked except for filthy shorts despite the fall temperatures, shot around the corner of the old motel office. His wide, bloodshot eyes locked on Thomas and Jillian. He shouted something Thomas couldn't make out.

Thomas unlocked the Toyota's passenger-side door and lowered Jillian in, slamming the door behind her.

The man shouted again.

When Thomas looked up, the man ran toward him. The worn shocks groaned when Thomas launched himself over the hood to get away from the wild man, who was now chasing him with a knife he'd pulled from somewhere.

"Habba slab," the sprinting man jabbered.

The key hit the lock at an angle and twisted from Thomas's hand; the key ring landed on the concrete.

"Shit."

Thomas's stomach lurched as he dropped to the ground and reached for the key ring, which had landed next to a piece of rusty rebar. The slapping of the wild man's feet closed in, and Thomas grabbed the bar, jumping to his feet. He swung the rod across his body. It connected with the man's arm, and the knife flew into the night.

The man yelled, his body spinning away from Thomas. He tripped over his own feet and pitched onto the pavement, his stick-like legs still running.

The bar clanged on the concrete and Thomas unlocked and opened the driver's door. He dropped inside and started the car.

"You lived here?" he said. "For months?"

Jillian nodded. Thomas threw the car into gear and shot onto Bentley Boulevard, past the jabbering man and away from the Starlight Motel.

A police car shot past him in the opposite direction. A few seconds later, so did a second. He eased his foot off the accelerator, adrenalin eased off his heart.

"How close is Dauðr?" he asked, his words strained as he fought for air.

"Down the stream," she said. "The stream behind the motel."

The stream? Thomas couldn't tell what that meant.

"If you can feel these things, why didn't you feel it earlier?"

"I don't know, Thomas," she said, now sitting up straight. Jillian leaned against the dusty dash. "But we have to go. Go, go, go."

He lifted the brown paper package Jillian held. "What is this?" he asked.

"Open it later."

He ignored her. The old rubber band snapped under the fingers of his right hand while he steered with his left. He shook open the long thin paper bag, which had once held whiskey or a forty-ounce bottle of beer, and a curved piece of plastic fell into the empty drink holder.

"Oh, my God," he whispered.

Inside the bag that'd been tucked into a hole in the wall of the shitty motel bathroom was the golden plastic snakehead from Skeletor's Snake Mountain play set.

He hadn't seen that since, since—

"Dauðr," he whispered.

"This is your talisman," Jillian said, pressing the hard plastic into his hand like she had so many years before when he battled something evil, something that looked like his father. "This will give you strength."

Thomas started to speak, but Jillian shook her head. "Keep it safe," she said. "Keep it with you always." She squeezed his hand tight. "Promise me."

He started to pull away, but the strength in her hands was solid. "Promise me, Thomas Cavanaugh."

"Okay," he said. "I promise."

"Always. Promise me always."

"Yes, always. I'll keep it with me always."

She released him. "Good, now let's go home. This place is dangerous. We need a plan."

Home, he thought.

She called my apartment home.

[8]

Thomas stared at Jillian over his small kitchen table, his hands bunched into one big fist to keep them from shaking.

"Why didn't we go tonight?" he asked, trying to make eye contact with Jillian, who avoided it. "We were close."

She shook her head and picked at the tuna sandwich on the plate in front of her.

"We couldn't." She looked up at Thomas. "It's not strong yet, but it's stronger than I anticipated. Bobby must have killed for it. The monster gets more powerful when it feeds. I told you that."

"No, you didn't," he said.

She waved him off. "You were young. A lot went on. You died." She paused to take a bite and a chunk of tuna dressed with mayonnaise dropped onto the plate. "I wasn't ready."

Not ready? "Seriously? If we're doing this, whatever it is we're doing, you have to be ready."

She dropped the sandwich onto her plate. "Don't you think I know that, *Thomas?*" she said, her words hard. "We need a plan. Yes, a plan. Dauðr was looking for you tonight. It would have found us. We need to surprise it."

Thomas stood and went to the refrigerator, leaning against it before opening the door and grabbing a beer. "And how do we do that?" he asked.

"By not thinking about it." She stood and walked to him, running her hand down his arm. "Can you do that? Can you not think about it?"

He cracked open the tab. "I don't think so." Thomas took a long gulp before speaking again. "How do you suggest I stop thinking about the monster that killed me?"

She pulled the can from his hand and sat it on the table. "I can help," she said, wrapping her arms around him and pulling him tightly to her. "Let's go to bed. Everything will become clearer in the morning. By then, I'll have a plan."

A slight purple glow grew in Thomas's periphery but faded quickly. A warmth spread through his body, and a yawn overtook him.

"Yeah," he said. "I think you're right. Let's go to bed."

Jillian pulled his arm over her shoulders and helped him to the bedroom.

Chapter Eleven  2005

BOYD SWALLOWED THE LAST BIT of his cold coffee, the old mug stained from too much use, not enough washing. The file open on his desk was curious. No, not curious. Frustrating. Carrie Mc-Masters, a twenty-seven-year-old woman from Rushville, a 303-population pimple on the ass cheek of Missouri, came home early from her job as a dental hygienist in St. Joe, fixed a pot-roast dinner for her husband—John, twenty-six, a pharmacist in Atchison, Kansas—and when he arrived home and sat down for dinner, she slashed his throat with a carving knife. After, she ate the pot roast and completed a five-hundred-piece jigsaw puzzle on the bloody dining-room table before calling 9-1-1. No record of domestic dispute, no fights overheard by the neighbors, and both sides of the family claim Carrie and John were as happy as the day they met. The couple still held hands as they shopped at Walmart.

There wasn't enough coffee in the station for this.

A tap on the door frame to Boyd's office announced Kirkhoff. "Boss?"

"Morning, Glenn."

The sergeant lifted the pot in his hand. Boyd thought the promotion looked good on him. "More coffee?"

"I might hold out for something stronger," Boyd said, flipping a page to the crime-scene photographs. Blood. Jesus H. Christ, so much blood.

"Kind of early for that," Kirkhoff said, filling the sheriff's cup.

Boyd studied the first photo; the knife went right through John McMasters's neck. No sawing, no hacking. If Carrie had sharpened that knife, she made it a razor. "Early? What are you, my mother?" He looked at Kirkhoff. "Was there any infidelity?"

The sergeant shook his head. "Not that anyone can tell, and we've asked around, looked at phone records, searched for a burner phone, email, all that sort of thing. If either one was cheating, they were good at it."

"Hmm," Boyd grunted.

"And boss?"

His eyes met Glenn's.

"She says she doesn't remember it. Nothing after showing up for work that morning. She says she sure as hell doesn't remember killing her husband."

The next photo, a wide shot, was of the McMasters' dining room. Carrie finished the puzzle, no doubt about that. Grant Wood's *Fall*

Plowing, Boyd was pretty sure. Wood had been a favorite of Boyd's for a long time. Nice Midwestern boy. John's body was leaned back in his chair, his neck opened like a smile. The butcher knife lay in front of him, next to the plate with his fork as if Carrie had set his place with it.

The platter with the remaining roast, potatoes, carrots, and onion sat beside it, covered in John's blood.

And she ate her fill. Dear God.

Boyd pushed his thumb between the wide shot and the next photo, but his thumb wouldn't flip the picture over. A red mark, nothing more than a smudge on the wall in the photo, stopped him.

"What's this?" he asked.

Kirkhoff set the coffeepot on the sheriff's desk and came around to Boyd's side. "That's blood," he said.

Boyd lowered the photo. "Of course, it's blood. Did Aaron get any photos of whatever this blood looks like?"

"Sorry, boss," Kirkhoff said, sliding the stack of photos into his hands. "No, no, no, no. Yes." He held up an eight-by-ten picture of the bloody wall.

"Goddammit." Boyd's hand moved slowly. He didn't want to see this picture. He didn't want to touch it. He didn't want this photograph in his office. He didn't want this photograph to exist. A drawing in blood, centered on a white wall, the focus crisp as the snap of a potato chip. Kirkhoff was right, blood. A painting in blood. It was childish: a circle and two lines for lips curved into a smile.

It wasn't a friendly smile. It was a smile of thin, pointed needles.

"You okay, Sheriff?" Kirkhoff asked.

He'd seen this painting. The night he saw Loraine Miller's skull split like a log. Damn right he'd seen this painting.

"Sheriff?" Kirkhoff's hand shook Boyd's shoulder. "Boyd? Are you all right?"

Get a grip, Boyd. Get a grip. There hadn't been a photo of this in the press and, as far as he knew, no one outside his department knew the painting on Elvin Miller's living-room wall—or this one, a painting exactly like it—existed.

Boyd pointed at his office door. "Get Crossroads Correctional Center on the phone."

Kirkhoff backed away, picking up the coffeepot. "Sure. Why, boss?"

"I gotta drive to Cameron and interview a prisoner there," he said, pushing himself to his feet, the old wooden chair rollers squealing. "Tell them I'll be there in about thirty-five, forty minutes."

"Okay," Kirkhoff said. "Which prisoner?"

Boyd crammed his hat on his head before grabbing his coffee. "Elvin Miller."

[2]

Boyd exited Interstate 29 for US 36 East on his way to Cameron, Missouri, a city of barely nine thousand people, to the Crossroads Correctional Center, a maximum-security prison Elvin had called home for the past five years. Boyd testified at the trial; Elvin claimed he didn't remember killing his spouse, just like Carrie, but Elvin had split open his wife and bled her dry. Just like Carrie. But there was something neither Boyd nor Elvin mentioned in the trial. The little girl with the teeth. By that time, Elvin claimed he didn't remember the girl or killing Loraine.

"There's a connection here," Boyd said into the cab of the Crown Vic.

He pulled into a Phillips 66 station on the east side of the Platte River and parked out front. He didn't need gas, he didn't want anything to eat, but he sure as hell could use another cup of coffee.

Twenty minutes later, he pulled into the prison parking lot.

Boyd hated prisons. No matter how new or how well kept, they always stank. Sweat, piss, blood, desperation, depression, and sometimes hope. He couldn't handle that last one. Walking to Crossroads Correctional Center's big beige administration building, its green metal roof hard and unyielding under the glaring sun and the three stories of tinted glass staring down at him, he didn't want to smell hope.

Hope was for people who had a chance; of all the degenerates he'd sent here, only one deserved hope. And that was the one he was there to see.

Boyd didn't know why, but he never believed Elvin Miller deserved to be in jail. He'd been a drunk who'd turned his life around for twenty-two years to become a good citizen, a good man. Then, out of the blue, the man butchered his wife with an ax. He even admitted to the killing, although he couldn't remember doing it.

Something about the case never sat well with Boyd. It was the bloody hand painting of the girl with the smile of needles. He'd seen that girl, and in his kin's own home. He'd never told anyone, but he was going to today.

Boyd hit the buzzer next to the door with his thumb.

"Yes?" a tinny voice asked over the speaker.

"Sheriff Boyd Donally, Buchanan County," he said. He pissed a half hour ago at Phillips 66, and damn if he didn't have to go again. Getting old is a bitch. "I'm here to interview an inmate. My deputy should have called."

The mic clicked off for a moment, then two, then three.

Boyd pictured the jailer shuffling around a desk for a note someone else wrote and failed to tell anyone about.

The speaker clicked. "Yes, Sheriff," the voice said from the other side. The door's locking mechanism opened with a clunk. "Please report to the front desk."

He pulled open the tinted reinforced-glass door and went inside.

A few minutes later, Boyd stood outside the interrogation room where Elvin Miller sat in a metal chair, his wrists secured by metal cuffs latched to a metal table. A plastic cup of water sat between his hands.

"Those cuffs really aren't necessary," Boyd said to the guard who had escorted him. A Corporal Besser, by his name tag and rank insignia. "He's no danger to me."

Besser nodded. "No, probably not, Sheriff. Procedure. You know how that goes."

Elvin didn't seem to know Boyd was watching him through the dark glass. The man looked older than he remembered, grayer, more tired. Elvin stared at his cup.

"How's he been, Corporal?" Boyd asked.

"His health, sir?"

No, dummy. Why the heck should I ask about that? "His behavior during incarceration. Is he a troublemaker? A loner? A degenerate?"

"No, not any of those," Besser said. "He's friendly enough, works in the library. Taught a couple of guys to read. He holds AA and NA meetings twice a week. He doesn't really seem like the kind of guy who'd chop up his wife."

Those words hit Boyd harder than he'd expected.

"No," he said. "Don't suppose he does." Boyd nodded toward the keypad on the door, ten buttons and one red Cylon eye of a light on its face. "Would you mind?"

Corporal Besser smiled at Boyd and punched in a code. The pad beeped, and the red light turned green.

"Just hit the buzzer on the inner keypad and I'll come get you when you're ready."

Boyd thanked him and stepped into the interview room. Elvin glanced up, greeting Boyd with a smile.

"Boyd. Boyd Donally." Elvin moved to stand and shake Boyd's hand, but the chains caught. The smile never faded. He shook his head and sat back down. "I've been in here five years, and I still haven't gotten used to chains and cuffs and these things around my ankles." He looked up at Boyd, who'd never seen a more honest sadness on another human face. "Walked into my cell door the other day. Walked right into it, expecting it to be open. What a silly goose."

Silly goose. Boyd was certain that kind of talk would get somebody eaten alive in prison, but for some reason, he thought Elvin was just fine.

He motioned to the chair across from the man who split Loraine's head like he was slicing an orange. A blood orange.

"May I?" he asked.

Elvin pulled back a laugh. "A person kind of loses all manners in a place like this," he said. "I'm sorry. Of course, please, sit down."

The chair legs covered in rubber boots moved soundlessly across the concrete floor, and Boyd lowered himself onto the metal seat.

"Now, Boyd," Elvin said, rolling the plastic cup in his palms. "I know you're not here for a social call."

Boyd took his felt hat off and placed it on the table. He laid his leather-bound notebook and pen from his breast pocket next to it. Even though he'd ruminated over how to approach this meeting every inch of the drive from St. Joseph, he never figured out what he was going to say.

"No, Elvin. This isn't a social call." He clicked the pen, and opened the notebook, flipping past his last traffic stop to a blank page. "This is about the night I pulled you over."

The cup dropped to the table and overturned; water ran onto Elvin's lap. He didn't flinch, his eyes straight ahead, unblinking.

"The night I murdered Loraine."

Boyd's stomach rolled, a gurgle loud enough he could hear it.

"Yes. That night."

Boyd dropped the pen and opened the notebook to the back page and pulled out the photograph he'd tucked there and unfolded it.

"Take a look at this," Boyd said, louder than he'd intended. The photo was of the crime scene where Carrie McMasters slit her loving husband John's throat, of the wall with the drawing in blood. The drawing so like the one that loomed over Elvin's living room six years ago.

"Nooo," Elvin moaned, his arms tossing the handcuffs back and forth, the table jerking them. He shoved his slippered feet against the table, pulling to break free. "Nooooooo."

The door beeped, and Corporal Besser pushed in, hand on his weapon. Boyd held up his palm, and Besser stopped.

"Elvin," Boyd said, his voice as calm as if he were a six-pack in. "This is not your house."

Elvin propped his foot against the heavy table for leverage and threw his weight back. The chains caught, and he fell to the floor, hanging from his arms.

"Jesus, Elvin." Boyd rose and rounded the table to pull him up, Elvin's fight suddenly out of him. "The corporal about shot your sorry ass. Calm yourself."

Boyd straightened Elvin's chair with his foot and dropped the limp man into it.

"What is this drawing?" Boyd asked, his face pressed close to Elvin's. "Our photographer took that photo at a murder last night over in Rushville. The drawing's the same as the one in your house six years ago. What the hell happened then, Elvin? Who's the little girl? Who's the girl with the teeth?"

Tears racked the man, the sobs hard. He crumbled into Boyd's arms.

"We're done here, Sheriff," Besser said, laying a hand on Boyd's shoulder.

Boyd ignored him.

"What really happened, Elvin?" he said, hands clutching the man's arms.

Elvin's face was slack, white as milk. "The girl," he whispered.

A drop of drool grew in the corner of Elvin's mouth.

"You never mentioned her in the trial. Did you see her?" Boyd shook him. "What did she look like? Who was she? What did she want?"

Tears streaked Elvin's face. His mouth moved, but nothing came out.

"Elvin," Boyd barked into his face. "You can tell me, because I saw her too. I saw her just as clear as I'm seeing you now."

"She. She—" Elvin moaned. Besser dropped a heavy hand onto Boyd's shoulder.

He shook the man off.

"She crawled from out . . . from the split in Loraine's head." He grabbed Boyd's cheeks; his fingernails dug into the sheriff's skin. "She'd told me, in my head, she'd told me to get the ax. She did. She told me. I heard her. Then she told me Loraine was doing it with Donnie Glasgow the next farm over. And I, I had to stop it. I had to stop it, Boyd."

Snot ran down the man's face, running in streaks over his prison clothing. It dripped onto Boyd's hands. "She told me. Oh, God, Boyd, she told me it would all be better if I taught Loraine a lesson. A serious lesson, and she whispered. Oh—" Then he looked up, his forehead red. "I did. I did, Boyd. I taught her a lesson. Then—" He swallowed, the tears flowing again. "Then the girl came out of Loraine's head, and she drew the face on the wall with my wife's blood, and she smiled at me. Her smile was full of needles."

Corporal Besser pulled Boyd away from Elvin. Their eyes met. Boyd's flared, but he shook out the anger. He was finished.

"Sorry," Boyd said. "But I had to know that."

Besser keyed open the door. "I'll have to write a report about this."

Boyd slid his notebook and pen back into his pocket and retrieved his hat, which had fallen to the floor.

"Yes, you do. You need to," he said, and left the interview room. Elvin Miller's wails followed him down the hall.

[3]

Hills appeared on US 36 around Stewartsville; the Buchanan County Sheriff's Crown Victoria rolled over them past the town of 733 at 65 mph, sliding to the left of a Peterbilt truck hauling frozen chicken, slowing as it climbed a slope.

The conversation at the prison had left Boyd with more questions than he had before the visit. The girl had crawled from the split in Loraine's face?

Jesus Christ, Elvin. The girl, the little girl, innocent in her white dress and red ponytail, stood in the center of Thomas's room before dropping Boyd's life into unknown horror, but Elvin's? Elvin's girl crawled from the ruined face of his wife, blood streaking her hair, her face, soaking into her dress before revealing her secret, that she's no normal girl at all. Her smile was full of needles.

A shudder ran through Boyd. His car slowed until the truck pulled into his peripheral vision. He felt the driver's gaze on him. He glanced at the trucker, who glared into his car.

"Damn it," Boyd hissed. While thinking about Elvin, he'd lost track of the rig beside him. Sloppy driving. He punched the accelerator, pushing the cruiser ahead of the tractor trailer. A pickup with stock racks hauling pigs pulled in behind Boyd as he passed the semi, a short line of vehicles following it, a garbage truck among them.

He reached for the coffee he'd bought at the Phillips 66 an hour and a half ago as he neared the top of the rise and signaled to turn into the driving lane. Then he crested the hill. His heart jumped and the coffee cup fell to the floor.

Oh, hell.

A girl stood on the center line.

"Shit." Boyd's voice was less than a whisper when he slung the wheel back to the left. The cruiser sliced across the highway, missing the girl by inches, her eyes boring into his as the car's tires screeched black marks across the highway, her red hair whipped in the wind. The girl's hand, white as a china doll's, rose as the Crown Vic slogged by in slow motion. She waved, her lips parting. Row after row of needles sparkled in the yellow midday sun.

Boyd's screams drowned out the scanner that suddenly sparked to life; the cruiser hit the wide, green median, tires gouging the still damp grass.

Fields on either side of the four-lane highway blurred into a Claude Monet painting. The big rig jackknifed and for a second, only a second, the words "Glorioso's Pollo Congelado" and the logo of a smiling rooster stood still in midair before the trailer flipped. The back gate burst open, and boxes of rock-hard pollo parts smashed into car windshields. The trailer slammed the garbage truck into the pickup hauling pigs, the screech of metal-on-metal piercing even through the closed squad-car windows.

"No," Boyd grunted through clenched teeth, his fists tight on the wheel.

The pickup flipped over the hood of the patrol vehicle, the four hogs bouncing over the grass.

"Shhiiiiiiiitttt." The patrol car slammed into the pickup and sat still; cold, stale coffee splattered across the sheriff's legs. Another car hit the median; the driver slammed on her brakes and came to a stop in the grass.

The radio spat static before Kirkhoff's voice came over. "Dispatch, send somebody down to Faucett. Looks like a neighbor cut down a guy's tree and he's mad as hell. Just a—"

The sheriff leaned forward and grabbed the mic. Pain lanced his left shoulder.

"Ow, goddammit," he groaned.

"This is dispatch," the deputy at the other end came over. "That you, Sheriff?"

He squeezed the mic. "Yeah. We need boots out on US 36, just west of Stewartsville."

Don't say little girl. Don't ever mention the little girl.

He leaned back; pain stabbed his shoulder again. Someone outside the car screamed.

A mic clicked. "What the hell's going on, Boyd?" It was Kirkhoff.

"Jesus," he wheezed. "Collision. A big one. A semi hauling frozen food, a garbage truck, a couple of cars and a pickup carrying pigs—"

A Yorkshire barrow, about three hundred pounds by the look of it, appeared in his window. It rubbed its soft, flat nose across the glass, leaving a trail, like a giant, snotty slug.

"—and me. I got a strain, or a sprain, or I might have broken my damn collarbone, but I'll live. Some of these people might not. Get deputies, highway patrol, emergency personnel out here immediately."

His hand with the mic dropped into his lap, then the radio broke into dispatch barking orders. Boyd's head hit the rest behind it, the pig snorted outside the window. Two more pink-white hogs sniffed around the garbage truck, lying on its side.

I gotta get out there. Pain made Boyd wince as he unlatched his seat belt.

"Get out of here, porky," Boyd grunted at the pig, lifting his bulk from the car with his right arm, his left shoulder screaming. The pig didn't move. Boyd walked around it.

Smoke billowed from a fire blocked by the tractor trailer, four pigs ran loose on the median, trucks lay on their side.

But no sign of the little girl. He'd seen her. She'd been there, he was sure of it.

"I'm going to get your ass, you demon," he said.

No one was close enough to hear him.

[4]

Sirens became the soundtrack of the morning by the time Boyd made his way to the semi. He was sure the farmer in the pig truck had a concussion but would be okay. His pigs had already forgotten they'd gone airborne; they were feasting on rancid garbage the trash truck had spilled across the median. A man in a business suit cried

Jason Offutt

from behind the wheel of a BMW, smoke rolling from under the hood. Blood ran into the man's eye from a scalp wound.

"Help me," the man yelled. "Officer. Officer, help me. I'm bleeding."

Boyd turned toward him. "Ambulances are on the way, buddy," he said. "Suck it up."

A spate of curse words followed by "lawyer" came from the BMW, but Boyd kept walking.

The Peterbilt lay on its side; the big red truck leaking more fluids than a dying patient. Boyd stepped through the red and green and black streams gushing onto the highway. He remembered that when he'd jerked the wheel of the cruiser away from the Glorioso's Pollo Congelado, the trucker swerved too. He'd swerved to avoid hitting something, and there'd been only one thing in the road.

The trucker was young, maybe twenty-five by the looks of him. He was just a kid. He lay on the pavement, half out of the cab, a pool of blood beneath his fractured head.

The sheriff knelt and reached toward the man's arm. Touch his wrist. Look for a pulse.

He pulled back his hand and slid the hat from his head. There was no use. The driver was dead.

"Why did you swerve? What did you see?" Boyd asked the dead man. "Did you see—"

The words caught in Boyd's throat. Beyond the driver's head, beyond the sticky, crimson puddle, a child's drawing decorated the graying asphalt.

—the girl? his mind finished.

A breeze, unnatural and hot, cradled Boyd. The hair on his neck prickled, the skin of his testicles drew tight.

A finger painting in blood.

It was childish: a circle, two lines for lips curved into a smile.

Of course, it wasn't a friendly smile. It was a smile of thin, pointed needles.

Boyd raked a heavy black boot through the red pool seeping from the driver's head, dragging it over the finger painting, turning the death grin into a smear.

Sirens reached the bloody mess on the highway, deputies and the highway patrol there to put the world in order again. EMTs cared for the injured. The farmer still shouted at his pigs. Boyd leaned against the roof of the truck's cab, the poor driver's blood on his shoes, the girl with the smile nowhere to be seen.

"Come at me again," he said into the chaos. "Next time I'll run you down."

Chapter Twelve  2005

[1]

THE NEWSPAPER BOBBY STOLE FROM his neighbor's lawn
was sprawled across his kitchen table, the classifieds spread wide.
Bobby ran his pen hand across the pages, smudging his heel black
with ink, and looked for any job he was qualified for. Most jobs required at least a high-school diploma, which Bobby didn't have, or it
required a skill he didn't have.

Spending his teen years drugged in prisons and mental institu-
tions didn't aid in resumé building. His hand traveled down a newspaper column and stopped. The mall advertised for new security
guards. He circled the ad in red.

WANTED: Rolling Meadows Shopping Mall is staffing for Part-
and Full-Time Security Guards. Successful candidates will be
responsible for ensuring the security of businesses and the safety
of employees and customers. This is a great opportunity to gain
experience in a security environment. No experience necessary.
Security license, criminal background check, and drug test required.
An equal opportunity employer.

Criminal background check? Equal opportunity employer my
ass. Fourteen. He was fourteen when he'd hit that bad Johnson boy
in the head with a fist-sized ball of concrete. But would anybody
know that? Can they even look at my juvenile record? He didn't
want to take the chance, and scratched out the ad. That would have
been perfect, he thought. Big place, lots of people, a position no
one notices. He could have walked around the mall all day, scoping
out the bitchy teenage girls and their prick-faced little boyfriends,
grinning at which one he'd kill first. That crazy Girl Scout would be
happy about that. Bobby almost laughed. Crazy? Who am I calling
crazy? Dauðr may come from hell, but it didn't spend five years in a
loony bin.

What bothered him most about Dauðr wasn't the rotting shell it
inhabited but its blankness. He knew it was a monster; a monster that
now lived—lived? Ha—in his house, but Bobby didn't know anything
about Dauðr. Its past, its present, its hopes, its fears—it was blank.
Just like he didn't know anything about that skinny red-haired girl
from the hospital. Jillian. She woke up screaming just like Thomas,
the dead-alive boy, but she was different. She was blank, too.

The smell of decay slowly wafted through the air. He swallowed
an urge to gag. Dauðr's shoes had fallen off months ago and its steps
were soundless; the little girl monster had terrified him more than

once when it appeared silently next to his bed or behind him while he watched the annoying mother from *Everybody Loves Raymond.* But now Bobby always knew when it was coming because of its stench.

"Would you stand in the other room?" Bobby said aloud, never looking up from the newspaper. "You smell bad."

"Then get me someone else," the thing said, the sound that pushed through the rotted vocal cords no more than a wheeze.

Another body?

"Yes."

It's too risky.

"Then don't complain about the way I smell," it said. Bobby could see it from the corner of his eye, standing between the table and the back door, like it expected him to run away. That thought wasn't wrong. "Have those papers told you anything?"

Bobby shook his head. "There's not much here for me."

Dauðr cackled. "There's not much you're good at, Robert. You never tried to get better at anything, except killing. Go get me another body, another female body. One that's alive this time."

Fuck you.

"That's why I was drawn to you," it said, stepping closer; the stench of death hugged Bobby's face, prodding, probing for every pinpoint to enter, to stick with him always. A wave of dizziness swept over him. "You're a killer, Robert. You hate this race of weak puppets as much as I do. You want them dead, Robert, all of them. We're alike, you and me. We're part of one another. We always have been. Do you remember the corn?"

Bobby's face dropped into his hands. *Shut up. Shut up. Shut up.*

"We're meant to be together, Robert," it hissed through its ruined mouth as it moved closer, its fetid breath caressing the side of Bobby's face.

Tears welled. "No. I don't want you here anymore. Please go away."

"You know I can't do that, Robert. We've been together since the beginning. It was I who brought you to the cornfield into the body of the dog-beast. I felt you through the ether, Robert. We're bonded. Together forever."

Small, stick-like fingers slid across his cheek; the bone that broke through the decaying flesh raked thin scratches in his skin. His muscles froze. A deep cold spread slowly, the hair rose on the skin of his arms.

"Forever," Dauðr whispered.

A scream burst from deep down inside Bobby and didn't stop for a long time.

[2]

The light of the Saturday-morning sun filtered through the bedroom curtains. Thomas's arm reached toward Jillian's side. The comforter and sheets were twisted, the pillow dented, but Jillian was gone.

He sat up, his body sluggish. Gone? The scent of coffee dragged him from bed and into the living room, where Jillian stood.

She's still here.

Thomas stepped behind her and wrapped his arms around her waist; she leaned in to him.

"Good morning," he said.

She took a long, slow sip of coffee, black, like she liked it, and tried to snuggle more deeply into him.

"Good morning," she said at last.

The smell of her hair, lavender and lemon, drifted up to him. He'd always felt at home in that smell, it was like sunshine.

"You're up early." That was a stupid thing to say, he thought. Like saying "You got a haircut" to someone who obviously just got a haircut. "Everything okay?"

She set her coffee mug on the windowsill and turned to face Thomas, crushing herself into him with strength someone her size shouldn't possess.

"I'm scared," she said into his chest, then looked into his face, her eyes red and puffy from tears.

"Why? Scared of what?"

She looked up at him; the hint of a grin played at the corners of her mouth for only a moment. "You don't remember last night?"

Last night? He tried to bring the night into focus and it flooded his mind at once: the crappy motel, the broken toy—his broken toy—Bobby.

Oh God, Bobby.

"We're going after this Dauðr thing, aren't we?" he said, the words flat. "We were close yesterday, weren't we?"

Once the memories began, they didn't stop. What had happened to him as a child left some kind of evil on the Cavanaugh farm. The cornfield—where his mom and dad found his dead body amid the leveled, scorched corn—still wouldn't grow crops. It wouldn't grow anything, the black dirt burned out, bereft even of weeds. Something evil had come and stained the earth.

"The motel's not that far from Carlyle Street. That's where this Dauðr is, isn't it? It's at Bobby's house?" he spat. "Jillian, we should have gone yesterday."

"I—"

He grabbed her arms. "Why didn't we do this *yesterday?*"

Jillian jerked out of his grasp. "I said I didn't feel like it," she snapped.

Thomas's jaw clenched and he turned from her, staring out the window; a few white cumulus clouds dotted the blue morning sky. A woman in a red coat stepped from the doughnut shop down the street, across from Tennyson's, and disappeared around the corner.

"You're right, we should go," she whispered. "Are you ready?" She reached around him and patted the legs of his boxer shorts. "Your talisman. Where's your talisman?"

Thomas tried to nudge her away.

"I don't have pockets in my underwear," he said. "It's in my jeans back in the bedroom. They're on the chair next to the bed."

"No," Jillian hissed, shaking her hands loose from his grip. "I said, 'Keep it with you always.' You promised me."

Thomas turned. "I'll get it, okay? I'll get it." He walked into the bedroom and pulled on his jeans, patting a lump in his front pocket. "Here it is. The head from Snake Mountain, in my pocket. Happy?"

She pulled on her own clothes and used a hair tie to gather her hair into a ponytail. "No. I'm not. You're questioning me. Stop it."

He turned on her. "This is bullshit. You pulled something with me last night to get me to go to sleep instead of tracking down this—" he put his fingers in air quotes "—dark monster of time and space, when we could have done it then. What gives?"

She stomped to the coffeemaker and filled two travel mugs, walking back to Thomas and slapping one into his hands.

"I have my reasons," she said. "We kill it today."

[3]

The job Bobby found turned out to be at the mall anyway.

WANTED: Rolling Meadows Shopping Mall is staffing for two Full-Time custodial engineers . . .

Custodial engineers. Whatever. *Custodial engineer* was just a fancy name for janitor. They were the people who mopped around him as he sat doped up in juvenile jail before his parents transferred him to Sisters of Mercy. He could push a mop and a broom, and he could clean toilets, at least for a while. Janitors were like security guards and busboys and photographers. People like that were just part of the scenery; they did their jobs, and nobody noticed. None of the hundreds of people that came to the mall every day would even really see him.

Nope, not one.

He pulled his father's Cadillac into the parking lot at Rolling Meadows Shopping Mall. Few cars dotted the mall lot this early in the morning. Cars in the back were probably employee vehicles; the few at the front belonged to mall walkers. Teenagers were in school at this hour, and the delinquents who shopped at Hot Topic were still sleeping one off. Everybody else had jobs. Except Bobby, and he was going to fix that *toot sweet.*

Electronic doors slid open, and he walked in dressed in black slacks, white Oxford shirt, and black tie. When he'd adjusted the clip-on under his collar back at home, the decaying beast in the mirror behind him, Bobby thought he looked like one of those Mormon missionary kids sent to bicycle around the cities of the world to spread the word of Jesus Christ. He wanted to laugh at the image but couldn't. A flap of cheek had fallen off the thing in the Girl Scout clothes and landed on Bobby's floor. That took any humor out of his day. He sprayed Febreze over his clothes to hide the scent of death and went out the kitchen door.

The mall directory stood at the entrance near a chain restaurant, the back-lit pane of plastic with a pastel orange, green, blue, and pink map directing shoppers to a department store, a bath store, and Mr. Wok. Bobby traced a finger along the main level and found a hallway to the "Mall Offices" that started between Chickin Lickin and Missouri Wireless and emptied out between Hava Java and a vitamin joint.

"That's it," Bobby said, too low for the mind-numbed zombies walking past him to hear. He pulled his hand into the shape of a gun and shot at a pair of seventy-year-old women who marched past him wearing lavender and pink jogging clothes and new tennis shoes. You'll be the first to go, ladies, Bobby thought, then quickly stuffed his hands in his pockets. A security guard he didn't qualify to become might have seen that, and Crazy Shooting Guy isn't fit for a job at this mall, mister. His eyes scanned the walls and ceiling. Cameras were everywhere.

Eyes in the sky. Dumb, Bobby. Dumb, dumb, dumb, he told himself.

He buried his chin in his shirt and made his way toward the mall offices. Along the way, wide-open mouths of shops sold thousand-dollar flat-screen televisions, chocolate-covered coffee beans, kitchen appliances, and lacy underwear that didn't cover the parts underwear was supposed to cover. It hurt Bobby's stomach. Nobody needed this. Nobody. Especially not these people.

A couple in their late thirties dressed like they wanted to be twenty again caught Bobby's attention. He didn't know why, but something froze his feet to the tiles he hoped to someday wax, and he watched the couple stand at the Chickin Lickin counter and argue with the clerk about the amount of mayonnaise on the man's Grilled Chickin Deluxe breakfast sandwich.

"What is this?" the man asked the clerk, holding open a biscuit that held a grilled chicken breast, slice of American cheese, scrambled eggs, and mayonnaise, just like it said on the glowing sign behind the seventeen-year-old clerk's head. "Do you see all this mayonnaise?" the man said, his voice rising.

The young clerk pointed behind him, to the menu over his head. "The sign says what the sandwich comes with, sir," he said slowly, and clearly, "and the Chickin Lickin Grilled Chickin' Deluxe breakfast sandwich comes with mayonnaise."

The man leaned hard on the counter, his wife standing behind him with her arms folded under her breasts. "I'd like to see the manager, now," he said.

The clerk smiled. "I *am* the manager. If you have any more complaints, please contact our corporate office." He pointed behind him again. "The website URL is on the sign."

Mr. and Mrs. Jerkface took their breakfast sandwiches and walked far down the food court before they sat at a bench and ate the food, mayonnaise and all.

Bobby changed his mind. The old ladies trying to keep their waddle off by walking around the mall weren't the first he'd kill for Dauðr. It was people like this. He'd kill the old ladies second.

The mall office manager, Terri Gerki, led Bobby through a room of monitors. A semi-buff security guard sat in front of them watching a couple walk into a Dillard's changing room, a young mother push an infant in a stroller, and Mr. and Mrs. Jerkface finish breakfast, leaving their wrappers on the food court table instead of throwing them in the trash bin a few feet away.

The security guy is getting off on this, Bobby realized. He's going to masturbate on break. Bobby paused and closed his eyes. Not to the pretty brunette stealing underwear in the changing room, but the young mom. He's got a thing for mothers.

"And this is Dale, our chief of security," Terri said, motioning to the man with an erection hidden under his desk.

Dale didn't stand as he held out his hand to Bobby. Bobby took it.

"Nice to meet you," Dale said, then pulled back his hand.

Won't shake your hand ever again, Dale, boy-o, Bobby thought. Nope. Not without gloves.

"Same," Bobby said. "Thanks."

Terri took Bobby through a hallway only employees and wannabe employees ever saw and seated him at a line of chairs already occupied by four other people. She held out an application.

"Do you have a pen?" she asked.

What kind of idiot doesn't have a pen? He reached into his front pants pocket and pulled out a blue Bic biro.

"Right here," he said, holding it up like he'd just found a sucker. She nodded and sat behind a desk, doing her best to ignore everyone in the room.

The application took Bobby a little too long to complete. He knew that, but he'd never filled out a job application before. He almost laughed out loud at, "Are you currently employed?" but he checked, "yes." It was easy to check "yes" or "no" to questions like "Do you have any custodial experience?" (yes) and "Have you ever been convicted of a misdemeanor/felony?" (no). But the Employment Background was hard to forge. Place of Employment? Address? Start/End Date? Supervisor? As Bobby sat in a room with four other applicants, he closed his eyes, and just let himself know things.

The rest came easy. Two Mexican men in polos and Dockers, the overweight white twentysomething in overalls, and the jittery white woman who kept scratching the tattoo on her arm gave him all the information he needed. Bobby smiled and filled out his application.

Terri liked it.

"Your application looks good," she said from across her desk. "I see you've worked at Walmart, and Missouri Western State Community College. So, you're used to heavy traffic."

Heavy traffic? Bobby smiled. "Yes, ma'am," he said.

Terri slid the application into the stacked storage trays on her desk.

"When can you start?"

⸻

Bobby drove toward Carlyle Street, knowing that right at that moment security-dude Dale stood in the employee restroom with the door locked, sliding his hand up and down his engorged penis, leaning on his left arm over the toilet while the young mom in a University of Missouri sweatshirt danced in his head.

Dale, you're a pervert, Bobby thought. I hope you're at work when the fun starts.

A job in a busy, crowded place. That's what the monster wanted. Then maybe it'll leave me alone. But Bobby knew it wouldn't. That dead Girl Scout would never leave him alone. Not until it was finished with him.

Two blocks from home, the Caddy sputtered, and the engine died. It coasted for half a block before it stopped on the side of the street near the bridge. Bobby pounded on the steering wheel. The needle on the gas gauge sat at E.

But, he thought, I filled it up just the other day.

"Fuck."

[4]

The crumbling asphalt parking lot near Carlyle Street where Thomas had sat panicking in this same car six years ago was now choked with even more weeds, yellowed and brittle as the season drifted through fall. Thomas could smell the slight hint of manure from the stockyards even with the windows up. The Toyota idled at the stop sign. Just one little left turn and they'd be on Bobby's street. The four greystone houses at the park-like entrance to Carlyle Street looked like artifacts from some earlier age. A time of peace, prosperity, and gluttony. That was a long, long time ago, though. There was nothing peaceful about Carlyle Street.

Not today, not ever again.

Thomas jumped slightly when Jillian touched his arm. "You okay?" she asked, her face tight with worry.

No, he thought. Not at all.

"Yeah," he lied. "Just nervous, that's all."

The six-inch piece of plastic snake felt like it didn't belong in his front pocket; it poked his thigh uncomfortably. He pulled it out and held it in front of him.

"And just how is this broken toy going to protect me?" he asked. "It's a piece of garbage."

Jillian leaned over and kissed his cheek. A warm flush grew over him.

"It's not just a broken piece of plastic," she said. "It's a symbol. A symbol of strength. A symbol of victory."

"But this is Skeletor's. Skeletor was the bad guy. He never won."

A slight smile broke through. "Your He-Man never destroyed Skeletor," she said. "Good never vanquished evil in your cartoon's world. Skeletor always defeated himself."

That sounds like bullshit.

"It's not bullshit." Her hand reached out and grabbed the hand that held the toy; the snake began to glow. "It is the kind of magic that protects children from being hurt in a fall, the magic that protects them from the monster under the bed."

His hand grew warm. Thomas didn't want to be there, in that car with Jillian, seeking death. He wanted to be home in bed.

"I thought you said there was no such thing as magic," Thomas said. Jillian didn't respond. "If this monster is capable of destroying all life on a planet, why doesn't it just do it? Why aren't we dead already?"

Her hand tightened over his. "Devouring my world satiated the monster and it slept, rested, until it hungered again. It woke weak, too weak to move without help. It found help and came through to your cornfield."

"Bobby," Thomas whispered.

"Yes, but you sent it away weak and it slept more. Now it's rested, and everything you know will die if we don't stop it from feeding again." The words hung heavy in the car. "I don't know how many deaths Bobby fed it, but it will want more and more. Slowly at first, then as its power grows, Dauðr will demand to feed off more deaths until nothing remains."

Silence permeated the cab of the car. Then Jillian suddenly laughed. "Well, let's go, hero," she said. "I'm hungry too."

Like on his first visit to Bobby's street, abandoned cars sat on blocks where horses and buggies once carried men in suits and women in fancy dresses to cotillions, or whatever the hell rich people did back in 1900. Were these the same cars as six years ago? As Thomas's Toyota moved slowly past them, one car looked out of place. An older model pale yellow Cadillac Eldorado was parked near the curb at an odd angle, but unlike the other cars on this street, this big, luxury box on wheels appeared well cared for. No rust. No dents. All four tires still inflated.

"Someone's walking," Jillian said, pointing out the window.

A man, tall and thin, strode awkwardly off to the side of the road, hands in the pockets of his black slacks, eyes at his feet. Mormon missionary? crossed Thomas's mind. Bits of gravel and broken asphalt cracked and popped under the Toyota's tires, and Thomas slowed to roll over a small bridge that spanned a thin creek shaded by thick trees.

The same creek that probably ran behind the Starlight Motel, Thomas thought.

The man stepped farther over to let the car pass.

"It's Bobby," she said.

"How do you know?" Thomas asked.

"I made him run out of gas."

Thomas cast her a sideways glance. "You what?"

The Toyota crept slower, and the man loomed larger in the window as they approached. The walk, the slumped shoulders, the black hair, the face. He knew that face.

"Bobby," he whispered, and shoved his foot onto the brake. The car squealed and came to a sudden stop. Bobby the Killer. Bobby the Beacon.

The man turned his head, his bangs almost in his eyes, and looked squarely at Thomas. His mouth dropped open, and he ran.

"Go," Jillian hissed, but Thomas had already thrown the car into park and jumped out the door.

[5]

Worthless goddamned car ran out of goddamned gas.

A vehicle slowly pulled behind Bobby, bits of gravel and broken asphalt cracking and popping under its tires, loud in the dead morning. Keep moving, assholes. What did Dauðr plan? Machine guns? A bazooka?

No, Bobby realized. Too flashy. Too expensive.

Too much room for error. If this monster wanted him to kill people, lots of people in a place like the mall, it had to be subtle. He just didn't know how.

The car appeared in his peripheral vision as it pulled beside him, matching his gait. Keep moving, folks. Nothing to see here. The nose of the car moved slightly ahead of Bobby, then the car, a Toyota, squealed as the driver applied the brakes. Bobby's head instinctually snapped toward that sound, and his world changed.

The dead-alive boy and that blank girl Jillian stared at him from the car wearing pathetic, weak faces.

The girl screamed his name. The dead-alive boy threw open his door and dashed around the car toward him.

A yelp escaped Bobby's lips.

A rush of thought poured into his head. No. Oh, no, no, no. The dead-alive boy is here to kill Dauðr. He grabbed the sides of his head. Not now. Not *now*. The people at the mall. They're bad. They're all bad. But the Girl Scout. No. It's, it's—it's a nightmare. The image of the small skeletal monster loomed large in his head, and a jolt of pain caused him to stumble, just for a step.

It knows.

Bobby took a deep breath before shooting across the road and heading down toward the creek.

[6]

Bobby simply disappeared. Dust rose as Thomas slid to a stop at the end of the bridge.

"He was here." Thomas looked back at Jillian. "He was just here."

She jogged by Thomas, grabbing his hand.

"Come on," she said, pulling him along. "He went down here."

A vague path led between two bushes and toward the creek. Thomas followed Jillian between the bushes and into a dark world populated with the tinkling of running water and the earthy scent of dead leaves.

His eyes shot to his right, under the bridge, expecting Bobby to be lurking in the darkness, but no one was there. He paused and listened. A twig snapped around a bend in the creek. Jillian dropped his hand and darted toward the sound, jumping over stones that made a dry path over the water and then running along the far shore.

"Shit," Thomas hissed and ran after her. He missed the first stone and splashed into the slowly moving water, soaking his shoe and pants leg to mid-shin.

A canopy of trees kept the creek bed hidden during the summer, but in late fall, the leafless branches let the sun stream in. Bobby was down here, somewhere.

"Jillian, wait," Thomas said, splashing through the stream.

She paused long enough for Thomas to catch up, and they rounded a thicket-clogged bend. A rock the size of a skull whistled past Thomas's head.

Bobby stood on a wide, flat stone, eyes wide.

Goddammit. Thomas shoved his hand in his pocket and gripped the relic from Snake Mountain. No strength, no power, no confidence. He didn't feel anything.

Bobby ran away.

Jillian took off again, and Thomas followed, the plastic snake bouncing in his pocket as they ran.

"Bobby, stop," Thomas yelled. "You don't want this." Although deep down, Thomas knew Bobby wanted whatever Dauðr had planned. He wanted it bad.

Bobby disappeared around another bend, dashing through familiar territory where Thomas and Jillian had to watch their step. They reached the bend and stopped. An invisible weight almost crushed Thomas to the ground, but he stayed on his feet. Jillian stopped next to him; a wall of stench sucked at their wind. The day grayed, but through the bare branches the sky stretched wide and blue over the dark world of the creek bed. Bobby clambered up the bank and into the backyard of a house, a three-story Victorian that loomed like a barren mountain peak.

A small figure stood at the top of the trail Bobby scaled. He reached the top and sprinted past it.

"Dear God," Thomas wheezed.

What had once been a girl of about eight or nine stood at the edge of the lawn, her green pleated skirt filthy, a once-white shirt stained with dried blood. A green sash dotted with patches and pins hung limply across her chest. The girl tried to smile, but her face had been crushed by something heavy long ago, her teeth jagged tombstones poking through a ruined, fleshless mouth.

Thomas screamed.

"Thomas," Jillian yelled, but her voice fell silently on his ears. She pulled at him. "Thomas."

Kill it. Kill it, his mind begged. Thomas pushed a shaking hand back into his pocket and pulled out the plastic snake. It felt small and useless in his hand.

Its bones shook, only for a second, then darkness spread over the little monster, a shadow, black as a back alley. It seemed to burst from the creature, engulfing it in an inky void, pouring over itself, growing, an incoming tidal wave of night. Fiery wind tore from the sky.

"No, Thomas," Jillian pleaded, pulling his arm. "Not now. It was ready for us. Run, Thomas, run."

A smile ripped through the thing of nightmares as it leaned forward. Rows and rows of needle teeth as long as swords opened over Thomas and Jillian, ichor dripping from them in a poisonous rain.

"Welcome," it said, the voice deep and soulless. The monster laughed as Jillian pulled Thomas toward her and they ran back down the creek bed.

[7]

Bobby leaned on the kitchen table, the taste of vomit splashing the back of his throat, when Dauðr shuffled through the kitchen doorway on decaying legs, dragging the scent of death with it.

I threw a rock at him, right at his head. How did it miss? He should be dead.

He should be dead.

Dauðr ignored his thoughts.

"You did what you said you'd do." The monster's voice, grating like two rocks rubbed together, turned Bobby's legs into weak pegs. He held onto the table to keep from falling to the floor.

Dauðr paused and cocked its head. A nudge, like a finger trying to find a soft spot in the rind of an orange, dug at Bobby's brain.

"You will now be at this place, this mall quite often, wearing a uniform, yes?"

Bobby nodded. Nausea gripped him. The finger dug deeper, teasing Bobby's olfactory nerve. Goosing it, stroking it. Suddenly, he smelled everything. Gases gurgling and sighing inside the sieve of a body. The built-up shit in the Girl Scout's colon, and the stain that leaked out when he bashed her face with the lamp. Stale blood. And—oh shit. No. No, no, no—the insect larvae feasting inside the ruined corpse.

The worms crawl in, the worms crawl out—

A belch worked its way up Bobby's throat followed by a stream of vomit that burst from his lips, spewing across the dusty table and splashing onto the floor. He looked over the mess, some of his breakfast still recognizable.

Dauðr paid him no heed.

"Hundreds of people will be there each day?" it said. "Not enough, but enough to start with." It stepped closer to the table, its drying ligaments creaking under the strain.

"Wha-what do you want me to do?" Bobby asked, his breath heavy and thick with bile; his stomach threatened to come up again.

"Kill them," it said. "Kill them all. I will feast off their energy and become stronger. Then, Robert. I can reward you."

The little monster walked around the table, its index finger making swirls in Bobby's vomit.

"And your new friends. They want to stop us, Robert. We can't have that." It stopped opposite Bobby, its eyes nothing more than prunes. "Do you know who your new friends are, Robert?"

"No," he said, panting. "No, I—"

The finger dug into his gut; more vomit spilled onto the table.

"That's a lie, Robert," it said. "You know who they are."

He slid into a chair, vomit dripping from his chin. Dauðr's shrunken, puckered eyes glared at him.

"I know them from the mental hospital," he said. "We were all kids, but I know the boy died. He died trying to kill you."

The beast's mouth opened wide; Bobby's sphincter threatened to let go. "If he died, why is he still alive? He's only a human." It picked at a piece of jerkied arm flesh and peeled it away from the bone. "And you humans are so fragile."

Bobby wiped the sleeve of his white shirt across the wet mess on his chin. "I don't know," he said. "But I know he wants to try to kill you again."

The ceramic/glass top of the stove suddenly exploded, shards of glass scattering across the kitchen. Bobby fell backward and lay splayed across the floor, no energy left to stand. Dauðr raised its arms, and the microwave flew from its shelf, straining momentarily on the plug still firmly fixed in the wall socket before it flew across the room, smashing into the wall. The flimsy plastic door popped from its hinges.

"You brought them here, Robert," it shouted as loudly as the rotting lungs would allow, its anger beating a pulse through the kitchen. "You brought them to me."

The refrigerator teetered back and forth, Bobby in its path. He howled and scooted across the floor, his heels skidding in the pool of vomit. His back finally hit the basement door. He reached up, turned the handle, and opened it, spilling down the stairs to the dirty concrete floor.

The refrigerator crashed hard above him, raining ancient dust from the cobweb-filled basement ceiling. The door he fell through slammed shut.

Help me. Oh, God, help me.

Tears streaked the dirt on Bobby's face. He rolled to his belly and crawled through the dust to the far corner of the room, to the spot under the window where Mrs. Bethany's tiny bug-eyed yip-yip dog had scratched. He crawled to his mother.

"Mom," he whimpered. "Mommy." Bobby dropped to the floor before the dried, mummified corpse of Vera Garrett. He laid his head in her bony lap and fell into blackness.

[8]

The Toyota idled in the parking lot behind the Carrington Arms until it ran out of gas and sputtered to silence. Thomas sat in the driver's seat, his face wet with tears, aching fingers gripping the steering wheel. Jillian's hand was cold on his.

"Thomas," she said, her voice soft but with strength behind it. Deep, ancient strength. "Let's go inside. I'll fix you something to eat."

His eyes stared straight ahead at the brick wall of the apartment building; a sign bleeding rust from bolts that held it to the wall read, "Private Lot. Violators Will Be Toed." He'd always laughed at the misspelling and had once inserted a W with a black marker that nature had since erased. Today he didn't see the misspelling, the sign, or even the wall. Thomas saw only death dressed in rotting flesh and the sash of a Girl Scout.

Jillian shook his arm. "Come on."

He turned toward her, his face pale, his eyes swollen and red. She wrapped both hands around his and gently pried them from the wheel.

"You need to lie down. And try to sleep."

"Screw you," he whispered.

"Excuse me?"

His face grew red with anger. "We needed to kill that thing. Why did you run?"

"It was too powerful," she said.

"No, *Jillian*," Thomas snapped. "It wasn't too powerful, it was a Girl Scout. We had it. We could have finished it, but you ran. Why?"

"Bobby—"

Thomas cut off her words. "Bobby was pissing himself. He couldn't wait to get away from us. He was no threat. Neither was that dead kid. We could have finished it. We could have *finished* it."

"Shut up, Thomas," she said, through clenched teeth.

"No. No. I've accepted a lot of the BS that's come out of your mouth. I've followed you around like a goddamned puppy, doing what you want to do, but now—"

The rest of the words froze in his mouth. Jillian smiled at him. She smiled; that weird red rash she'd get glowed on her skin. The smile grew, and the sound of a balloon stretched too far squealed in the car; the corners of her mouth reached her ears and her long, thin, misshapen lips parted. Her mouth was full of needles, Jillian's eyes solid black.

"I said shut up," she said, her voice too deep to be Jillian's.

Thomas screamed and slapped at the door handle, his fingers unable to find purchase. When he looked back, Jillian was Jillian again. She reached toward Thomas, and he pressed himself against the car door.

"Oh, baby," she said, her voice soft, caring, normal. "Baby, I'm sorry. I'm so sorry."

"What the—who . . . what are you?"

His hand landed on the handle and the door swung open. He fell onto the pavement. She leaned out the driver's-side door, and a lavender glow engulfed Thomas.

The panic, the terror, melted.

"You're not afraid," she said.

Afraid? As he lay on the cold asphalt, his fear of that monster, of Jillian, faded.

"This did not happen," Jillian continued.

This did not happen.

"You're asleep, my love. This was a bad dream, that's all."

Thomas woke screaming. His eyes shot open, and he sat up; the room was dark, although the light from the setting sun shone through the open doorway. He was in bed—his bed.

How did I get here?

He remembered teeth. A girl with teeth.

Jillian appeared in the doorway wearing an apron.

"Honey, what's wrong?" she asked.

Shit. He threw himself out of bed opposite of Jillian, his hands defensively in front of him.

"Whoa." She raised her own hands, palms up. "You must have had a dream. A bad one." Jillian approached slowly. Thomas's heart was hammering.

She reached up and cupped his cheek; his face was hot. Thomas relaxed at her touch. "I have something for that," she said. "You hungry?"

The smell of fried chicken wafted through his apartment. He didn't struggle as Jillian led him into the kitchen, his brain still fuzzy with sleep, Bobby and the horror in the Girl Scout uniform momentarily forgotten. The girl with the teeth still lurked near the surface.

"You were tired," she said, her arm around him, supporting his body more than he realized. "Let's get you some food. You'll feel better."

He nodded and let Jillian walk him to the kitchen table. He fell into a seat. A golden-brown thigh, mashed potatoes, and a steaming pile of lima beans sat on a plate in front of him.

"Fried chicken?" he said, the image and smells finally combining in his brain. Why do I feel like this?

"You bet it is, honey," she said, and put a fork into his hand.

"This looks great, Ji-Jil-Jillian," he said, his tongue thick in his mouth. "This is my favorite meal, you know?"

She grinned, the new lines around her lips more pronounced than Thomas remembered. "I would say it was an old family recipe, but that wouldn't be true. We ate what the trees and grasses would give us," she said. "It was all good, but not fried chicken and mashed potatoes good. Now, eat."

He slid his fork into the potatoes, making sure to scoop some beans like he'd done when his mom made this meal every couple of weeks growing up.

"Oh," he said through a mouthful of food. "This tastes just like—"

"Mom's?" Jillian finished for him. "You sure know how to compliment a girl."

He took another forkful of potatoes and lima beans before turning his attention to the chicken.

"My favorite piece. How did you know?"

Jillian shook her head. "If you don't know by now, you're pretty dense."

The table fell silent as Jillian focused on her beans, a few flecks of roasted red bell pepper beating Deborah Cavanaugh on presentation.

"You've never cooked for me before," Thomas said.

Jillian laid her fork on the plate, tines down, and dabbed her mouth with a paper towel, her gaze cold.

"I mean, I like cooking. I like cooking for you," he said. "I'm not some 'woman cook for me' Neanderthal. I, you know—"

Her hand reached across the table and held his, the warmth from it unnatural. "I've never cooked for you because I can't." Her voice faint, distant. "Never accept food from fae folk, Thomas, or you'll drift off to their fairy land, and you may never see your own world again."

"Ha." He coughed, a fleck of crust from his mouth hitting the table. "That's—"

His words froze in his mouth as Jillian's body began to dissolve like static on an old TV.

"Wha—"

Bobby, the snake head, the dead Girl Scout, Dauðr suddenly sprang to the front of his thoughts.

"I—" he started, but something was wrong here, dead wrong. His kitchen swayed, as if trying to keep its balance. The walls leaned inward toward each other. Jillian wasn't there anymore, not really; fuzz shaped like a woman sat in a chair that was no longer a chair.

The next thing he knew, he was in hell.

Chapter Thirteen  Ālfheimr

GRAY DUST FILLED THE AIR. Thomas lay on ground that had been baked into an unforgiving brick by relentless heat. A rock stabbed his ribs, but he hardly registered it. He tried to push himself to his knees, but his arms wouldn't move. Thomas dropped back to the hard ground, and a cough sent a black spat into the dust. Grit stung his eyes.

Dear God, where am I? The world hung heavily over him in a gray sheet. What the hell happened?

Jillian. Jillian had brought him home, and he was sleepy. So sleepy. Jillian.

A hand, gray with a layer of dust, appeared in front of him and grasped his own.

"Are you all right?"

Jillian?

His eyes scanned the land around him.

Craters pocked the earth, some spewed smoke. They didn't look like impact craters; these craters came from below, from the earth sinking into itself, and something burned there, crackling. That crackling, like frozen food dropped into hot grease, sounded familiar, a favorite memory from childhood, of his mother standing in a kitchen, the heat from the stove beading sweat on her upper lip. She'd pick up the crackling bits with metal tongs and lay them on a plate covered in paper towels.

The sound was of frying chicken.

Chicken.

Jillian had prepared chicken for him, and then he'd found himself here.

Holy Jesus.

Thomas rolled to his side, the feeling coming back into his arms. They were on a hill. A road, buried in places by piles of windblown gray dirt, stretched down to plains dotted with boulders. The memory of a face flashed in his head—a toothless face flecked with blood. The panic grew stronger, and Thomas pushed again, trying to stand.

I've been here before. The night I died.

Filthy people, beaten, bloody, had been chained to the boulders lining the road that night, waiting for the evil, the monster called Dauðr, Death, to devour them. "Ate *fairy food*," the bloody man had told Thomas. "Next thing I know, I'm here. The fairy played with me for a while, then this. Then the thing with the teeth came and turned this place into hell."

Jillian cooked chicken, and he ate it, then the world went fuzzy. Damn it.

"Next thing I know, I'm here," the bloody man had said. "Then the thing with the teeth came and turned this place into hell."

The hand holding his squeezed. "Thomas. Are you all right?"

His head moved toward the voice in slow motion. Jillian lay next to him, her hair stained gray with dust, the lines around her eyes crusted in it. He was back in the dream, but this time Thomas knew it wasn't a dream.

"What did you do?" he wheezed. "What the hell did you do to me?"

A cough shot from her mouth, blowing dirt from the ground in front of her face. Through that, she managed to smile.

"So, you're okay?"

Jillian rolled toward him, her face close to his. Sweat streaks stained the dirt on her cheeks black. *Why are we here?* Pain sliced through his ribs. Jesus Christ, the ground was hard.

"Why?" he asked. "Why did you bring me to this hellhole?"

Her hand pushed hair from his forehead. Dust rained down.

"I had to." She coughed again, like a heavy smoker. "I misjudged Bobby. I misjudged Dauðr. They knew we were there. They were waiting for us." She coughed again, her lungs rattling. "They're stronger than I imagined. We had to flee."

"Get me out of here," he hissed. "Get me out of here now."

Jillian pushed herself to her hands and knees, her limbs shaking with the effort. She paused, pulling her shirt over her nose. Another spasm of coughs racked her. "I can't, Thomas. Not yet," she wheezed, shaking her head. "We have to wait, but not here. We go lower, out of the wind, to the city."

Thomas forced himself to his knees, glaring at her. "No. You get me out of here. Pronto. I didn't give you permission to do whatever witchy voodoo you did to me. I've followed you. I've followed you my whole life and it's gotten me killed, stuck in a mental hospital, and had me dragging myself from shit job to shit job. Following you has ruined my life, *Jillian*." He paused, his next words came out hard. "Damn you. Damn your Dauðr monster. And damn this place. Send me home."

She raised a hand, and the fight went out of Thomas. Jillian stood slowly, tottering on her feet. When she steadied herself, she held a hand out to him.

"Come on, honey," she said. "Or we'll die here."

———※—————

Each step on the heat-baked road brought his memory closer. He'd walked this ground when he was ten, but it hadn't been this desolate, had it? Leafless trees in what may have once been a forest loomed beside the road, the road plunging into that dead world. The wind and the dust lessened at the bottom of the hill, but the heat of this desert did not. The trees, some blackened by a long-ago fire, thinned as they approached the boulder field where the bleeding man had squatted, bound in place. Great chunks of granite sat on each side of the road, and chains hung off them limply, like dead snakes. Humans once screamed at him from these chains, begging Thomas to kill them. Tears welled in his eyes. Thomas closed them and swallowed hard. He had to stop the tears; he knew he couldn't lose any moisture in this heat.

When he opened his eyes, he had stopped next to the first boulder, his hand in Jillian's. A lump distorted the windblown symmetry of a small dune at his feet. The chains from the rock disappeared into the sand; something was buried there. He knelt and brushed some of the dust away. Gray, dirt-filled sockets of a toothless human skull stared back at him. "Please," the bloody man had begged. "Kill me. Please, please kill me." The skullcap was missing; it appeared to have been bitten off by enormous, pointed teeth. The man got his wish. He was dead.

Jillian pulled on his arm. "Come on. We have a long way to go."

Thomas looked up at her. "I met that man," he said, his voice shaky. He took Jillian's hand again. "He begged me to kill him."

She started walking, Thomas in tow. "Did you?" she asked.

Thomas shook his head. "No, of course not."

She stared at him with cold eyes. "Just remember, Dauðr might look like a person, but it's not. It's not human at all. Not anymore. You can kill *that*; I know you can."

Of course it's not human. It's a dead Girl Scout, he thought.

They continued through the line of boulders and chains, an occasional skeletal arm or leg jutting from the dirt. Thomas remembered what else the bleeding man had said, "Land of da fairies. Ain't this a fuckin' paradise."

Mid-Buchannan High School—2006

The hallway smelled of popcorn; Bobby figured the concession stand must be getting ready for halftime. He pulled a stainless-steel cable tie tight around the handles of the south gymnasium doors, the north doors and the exterior locker room doors already snug as a bug in a deathtrap.

The grin on Bobby's face was almost painful.

A buzzer sounded and the crowd exploded in cheers. He chanced a look through the long, thin windows in the doors; Central-Buchanan just went up by three on court-warming night. Halftime was thirty-five seconds away.

"Man," Bobby whispered. "Somebody's getting laid tonight." A laugh took him. "Or not."

He tipped over an old, dented five-gallon can and gasoline rushed beneath the door, the pungent fumes overpowering the popcorn.

"Hey, mister. Whatcha doin'?"

A kid. Damn. Bobby swung his head in the direction of the voice. A boy of about eight stood just outside the door to the concession stand, a bottle of Coke in one hand, a paper sack of popcorn in the other.

Bobby's grin grew tighter as he backed away from the gasoline spill, lifting a road flare from his back pocket. He held the red stick beneath the black line, just like the YouTube video had told him to do—safety first—pulled off the cap and struck the cap's scratch surface over the igniter; a stumpy jet of white-and-yellow flame shot out.

The kid's eyes grew wide as Bobby tossed the flare onto the spreading pool of gasoline, a fire bursting to life and crawling beneath the door and into the gymnasium. The boy screamed and ran; popcorn flew everywhere.

"I hope you've got asbestos underwear," Bobby yelled after him, laughing as muffled screams began to flood the gym.

He secured the front door to the high school with another cable tie and walked to the edge of the parking lot, where he'd left his dad's Caddy next to a pole with a burned-out light. A siren wailed in the distance.

Shit. Somebody inside the gym must have called 9-1-1. Bunch of pussies. He scurried the final ten yards to the car and slid in.

"You did it," a scratchy voice said from the back seat.

Bobby cringed. "Yes."

"They're bunched at the doors, screaming," Dauðr said through the crushed mouth of the Girl Scout. Bobby looked at the little monster in the rearview mirror. It swayed, humming softly. "The first death. Oh, Robert, the power it brings me, and fear. Oh, the fear. Fear tastes good."

The big engine of the Cadillac came to life, and Bobby put it into reverse.

It didn't move.

"What? Stop doing that," he snapped at the creature in the back seat. "We have to go. The cops are coming."

Orange flames flickered in the windows of the school; smoke began to billow into the sky.

"Ooooh," the little monster said, gripping the back rest of Bobby's seat to keep itself steady. "They're falling now. Many. Sweet, sweet essence. Stay, Robert. I must drink it all. Death tastes better if I'm close."

No. No, no. He swung around in his seat.

"We can't be here when the cops come," he said.

The skeletal Girl Scout cocked her head like a puppy, a puppy from the third circle of hell.

"They'll know it was me. They'll turn, they'll follow me, and they'll catch me. Hell, I *smell* like gasoline. Then you—"

Dauðr patted Bobby's shoulder and a scream ripped from its throat. When the terror subsided, Dauðr removed the hand.

"Your authorities will not know you were here," the Girl Scout said. "And you must get me a living body sometime. A living female. My desires have changed."

"What do you need a living woman for?" he nearly asked, but the monster cut him short.

He looked in horror when the Girl Scout leaned back in the seat, and a swirling cloud engulfed his car. Faces grew and shrank in the mass, churning in a shadowy spin of death.

"These are the spirits of those killed in the fire, Robert," Dauðr moaned. "You brought them to me; you brought me strength."

Shadowy bodies of the dead flowed into the car, and soaked into the ancient monster. Dauðr began to glow.

As sheriff's cars, fire trucks, and ambulances came to rescue the people Bobby knew could no longer be rescued, he put the Caddy in gear and simply drove away.

Álfheimr

The road emerged from the field of dry dead trees and into a land that sloped downward toward an ancient seabed. The wind had dwindled, but dust remained, a haze in the air. The boulders peeled away, and the land flattened.

"I was here," Jillian said beside him. His body kept trying to stumble, but her hand helped him stay on his feet. "Before Dauðr turned my world into a desert, I was here. Salt spray in the air, birds running on the sand, children playing. You saw that world when you came before. It was beautiful."

"It was." Thomas's voice was choppy, rough, his anger buried but not gone. Jillian had hidden it from him. Why did you do that, Jillian? Why are we really here? He coughed to clear his throat. "Why did Dauðr come here?"

"My world was the cradle of all life," she said, her voice soft. "The earliest, the strongest of all living things were born here. Life spread throughout the void, but we were the first." Jillian stopped, tears turning her cheeks to mud. "Then Dauðr came and it fed. It swallowed what you call our souls."

Thomas swallowed; the grit-filled saliva scratched his throat. "And this thing chose my world next?"

Jillian nodded.

He waved an arm toward the horizon. "What happened to everyone who lived here?"

"Most died, but the ones who escaped are in hiding, mostly where you call home," she said, never looking at Thomas.

"Home? My home?" The words came out loud. "There are more of you? And they're in *my* world? What? Do you guys have a colony or something?"

She laughed slightly. "Nothing like that," she said. "We are integrated into your society. We are bank tellers and waiters, movie stars and newspaper delivery drivers."

"But not cooks?"

She waved her hand. "No. Never." Jillian pulled at his arm. "Everybody knows someone like me. Now, come on. We need to keep moving."

They marched for miles. As darkness morphed the slate gray sky into charcoal, Jillian led Thomas off the road and into a grove of dead, white trees. Thomas started to speak, but she lifted a finger to her lips and shook her head, just as she'd done in the garden when Thomas was a boy. He fell quiet and followed her. Dust drifted around them like fine snow.

A vibration rumbled through the ground, then stopped and started again.

"What's that?" Thomas asked. "It felt like a giant taking a walk."

Jillian increased her speed. "That's because it is."

She stopped, eventually. They could have walked off the road twenty feet or twenty miles. Thomas didn't know; everything here looked the same. He slumped against a tree after she released his hand. The rumble vibrated beneath his feet, through the tree; it seemed to move the air.

"It's closer," Thomas said, his throat raw and dry.

Jillian bent beside a mound and gently brushed the dirt away. Thomas tried to walk over to help her, but he couldn't move his legs. Jillian found a curved pink shell and began pushing against it. It rolled to its side, dust billowing into the air. A shallow bunker lay beneath.

"Come on," she said, and held out a hand. Thomas took it and she pulled him into the pit. The enormous shell fit easily back over the excavation, and Thomas lay on its floor.

"Sleep," Jillian said, brushing a glowing hand over his eyes.

He woke to a light shining above him, faint and white. Jillian sat next to him eating chili straight from a can with a white plastic spoon. She smiled and took another bite. They were in a hole in the ground, not a hobbit hole but homey enough. The walls, stacked with cans and bottles, were carved from the earth, a layer of dirt and rock formed the floor.

Something soft lay beneath him. As he gripped it, he realized it was a nylon sleeping bag.

"Drink up, handsome," Jillian said, motioning to a plastic bottle of water, an Ozarka Natural Spring Water label on the side. "You'll feel better."

"Is it safe to drink?" he asked. "Or will it spirit me away somewhere?"

She frowned. "No. I never touched it."

The water. Dear God, the water. It tasted better than anything he'd ever put in his mouth. After drinking, his muscles, though sore, moved easier. His head felt clear. Thomas lay back down.

Veins coursed through the hard ceiling above him, and they glowed. The shell wasn't just their shelter from the heat, and dust—it was the source of light.

She held a can of chili out to him, a spoon also in her hand. The appearance of this mass-produced product with its corporate logo designed by someone who would never visit here somehow seemed almost normal under the alien phosphorescent dome.

"How about this? Safe? You touched it," he said.

"I'd have to open the can, honey, and I didn't do that." She scraped the last spoonful of chili from her can. "I'm getting the impression you don't trust me anymore."

Thomas sat up, his head a foot below the shell, and took the can; the pull tab cracked in the small room. "No, Jillian. I don't," he said. "Not anymore. You've done too many things that don't make any sense. Then you drag me to this place." The toothless man's words echoed in his head. "You also got me killed when I was ten. I'm still trying to figure that one out."

She opened her mouth to answer, but he raised a hand to stop her. "Don't bother. I won't believe you anyway."

A huff blew from her, and she dropped her empty can and plastic spoon into a plastic grocery-store bag and stuffed it into a backpack.

"When Dauðr began to murder Álfheimr, we started making these shelters, stocking them. We needed places to hide."

Thomas shoveled in another spoonful of stew. "Okay, I'll bite. What's Álfheimr?"

A frown moved across her face. "This place has a name," she said. "Your world has a name, and I don't find the name Earth very exciting. It means 'dirt,' you know."

Jillian grunted before she continued. "Álfheimr means 'Land of the Elves,'" she said. "The word is Norse. My people and the ancients of your home interacted often. Trading, celebrating, marrying. The Norse accepted us more readily than others. We became—close."

"How close?" he asked between bites.

"Close," she said again, then cleared her throat. "Sjá Álfr dróttning. / Hefi hana marglóð kloth. / Hon gera minn brjóst með vilja, / Bera mik staðr ek eigi til munu vitumk."

Thomas slid his can between his legs and clapped, slow and steady. "Nice. Very nice. Kinda pretty. What did you say?"

"Are all human men so ignorant of their past?" she grouched. "This is a poem, an ancient poem, *Álfr Dróttning*."

When Thomas didn't answer, she huffed. "It means The Elf Queen. Behold the elf queen, / Clad in her golden gown. / She fills my breast with longing, / Carry me places I won't be found." She folded her arms and breathed heavily. "It's the plea of a Viking warrior for the queen of elves to take him here, to Álfheimr, where they can always be in love, without aging, without death."

They grew silent, the vibrations beneath them growing stronger.

"Then Dauðr came," Thomas said. "How'd that work out for them?"

She slammed fists into her thighs. "Please stop being like this, Thomas. Stop treating me like, like—"

"—the villain?" he finished for her.

Her eyes blazed lavender.

The ground shook, cans and water bottles fell.

"Shhh," she hissed, and rubbed her hands across the pink shell above them. The veins faded to black, the outside light casting a dull gray over the hole.

The vibrations—*thud, thud, thud*—sent dust into the air. Thomas opened his mouth to speak, but Jillian put a hand over it.

The thuds grew louder, and Thomas's body shook with each pounding.

A shriek, the wail of a thousand cats, split the air outside their shelter, and darkness grew over them.

"Be quiet," Jillian mouthed.

A long spindly shadow drifted over the translucent shell that protected them. It crashed to the ground, and the tremor threw Thomas onto his back. Another shadow moved above them.

"What is that?" The question tight, heavy.

"I beg you," she pleaded. "Shut up."

The next shadow slammed into the earth and the shell shifted above them.

Thomas grabbed Jillian's shoulders; her face stretched, her eye wide and panicked. "Those are—legs?" he whispered.

She nodded slowly, as if the muscles in her neck might make enough noise to give them away. Jillian's hand, slight and gentle, rose in front of Thomas's face, emitting a pale purple glow. His next words died inside; he no longer wanted to use them.

Another appendage passed overhead, dragging a thick, shadowy body behind it. The crash of the third leg beyond their shelter scattered bottles of water across the floor; an edge of the shell dropped behind Jillian, and the section above Thomas lifted, exposing them to the night.

The giant hovered directly above, its insectoid body the size of a city bus, its legs hoary, like a yeti crab. It raised its head, mandibles snapping open and shut; its shriek pushed Thomas to the floor of the shelter. Jillian grabbed his arm, pulling at him to get under the shell. He yanked back and she flew forward. They were both exposed, but he had to see this, he had to see everything.

Another leg swung overhead, the end—with pointed, serrated blades—slammed into the hard earth next to Thomas; the shockwave dropped him back into the pit.

"If it finds us, we're dead," Jillian hissed into his ear. "Dead, Thomas."

Another leg dropped, and the beast came fully into view. Its segmented tail wavered as it curved, arching over its back, a stinger as long as a backhoe arm glistened in the dying light.

What is it? Thomas thought he said but didn't.

A drop of liquid shook from the tip of the stinger, the bubble growing as it fell.

"Get in here," Jillian hissed, grabbing Thomas's shoulders and pulling. He didn't resist, the fight in him gone.

The monster smashed the shell, ragged shards scattering. Jillian screamed. The blades on the beast's legs shredded the shelter, piercing the sleeping bag Thomas had lain on. The liquid from its stinger hit the ground and splattered; a drop struck Thomas's arm.

Heat. Fire. Pain.

"Jesus Christ," he mouthed, because the words wouldn't come. The spot on his skin boiled.

Jillian grabbed Thomas by the shoulders. "Run," was all she said before she bolted from the shelter and disappeared into the falling dust.

Thomas rolled from the pit and into the night; talcum-like powder stuck to his skin. The monster wobbled above him, the walking-stick body on stories-tall legs an affront to physics. The white fur seemed alien on an insect, but its tail, the horrid tail of a scorpion, loomed over the trees, poison bubbling from the tip.

It stopped.

The monster's bulbous head twisted unnaturally to the right, then left. Thomas lay unmoving as the beast's antennae swung from side to side. The creature was searching for—him? Of all the things that pulled at his mind, the one that came with the richest clarity was his mother. His mom singing while weeding the garden. His mom humming, a thin paintbrush in her hand. His mom laughing at dinner over a silly story Thomas told her about school, and his dad laughing right along with her.

"Everyone you know dies." The words flowed into his head on a memory, a memory of long ago. The little girl, Jillian, when he first knew her. "Your mother, your father, your friends. Everyone. Everyone dies, Thomas."

No.

The creature leaned to its left, a leg crushing the remains of the shelter. Its head, as big as his dad's pickup, dropped toward him, its antennae sniffing, touching, probing, searching.

Thomas's eyes slammed shut as the antennae passed over him, his body covered by the steadily falling snow of fine, gray dust.

A snort, then the creature shifted, and a massive leg dropped to the ground, farther away this time. Then another, and another. Until the tremors became only noise in the background.

Atchison, Kansas—2009

A shiver went through Bobby, although he didn't know if it was due to the cold temperature of the Missouri River bridge between Winthrop, Missouri, and Atchison, Kansas, or because of what he was about to do. He knelt on a concrete pylon that held up the west end of the bridge with great steel legs. Bobby got atop the pylon by an aluminum extension ladder, its tips resting against the concrete base, and they'd better stay there, or he couldn't get back down. Below on one side was a current he knew he couldn't swim against and below on the other side were boulders and concrete. Neither side presented an option he wanted to explore.

And Bobby desperately wanted to get back down.

He opened the flap of his backpack and pulled out a ceramic jar, setting it gently onto the concrete before slipping welding goggles onto his forehead, and donning heatproof gloves. Lifting the lid off the pot, he poured the three-to-one mixture of aluminum powder and iron oxide around the plate that bolted the metal leg to the concrete.

Another shiver hit him.

Dauðr waited above, in the car. It couldn't feed, it told him, if it wasn't close enough. He wanted to hit someplace closer, like the mall, but the Girl Scout said no. It wasn't strong enough yet. It needed more of the energy it sucked from the dying before Bobby could try something closer to home. Damn thing.

Bobby scooted to the second enormous metal leg, dotted with rivets, and brought out a second ceramic jar, pouring it as he did the first.

A great breath escaped him, white fog dissipating into the night. Holy shit, Bobby. This is it. Are you ready? Are you *ready*? He chanted like an athlete getting pumped up for a game. Gonna get hot in here.

A big truck rumbled across the deck above him raining dust and flakes of rust; a car honked from somewhere.

Shit yes, I'm ready.

He scooted to the ladder, his foot finding tentative stability on a rung before he lowered his other foot and stood solidly, descending until his chest was level with the top of the concrete pylon. He wanted to be ready when he lit the thermite. Oh, yeah, baby. Gonna get *hot* in here.

More vehicles moved by above him. He didn't know how many lives he'd end for the monster, but it would be interesting to watch. The magnesium strips were the cherry on top of the thermite sundae he'd whipped up with a little help from his friend the internet. When ignited by magnesium, aluminum powder and iron oxide burns at more than 4,000 degrees Fahrenheit, hot enough to melt steel and send the decking, and any vehicles on top of it, into the frigid river.

It was December, after all. Merry Christmas.

The two grabber tools in his belt came up next, and he affixed a strip of magnesium in each claw before extending the tools to their full length. His hands shook. Jesus Christ, they should. Bobby's grip on the grabber tools was as tight as a banker's wallet as he moved the magnesium closer to the circle of thermite. He nudged the welding goggles over his eyes with his shoulder and touched the first strip.

The flame ignited. A searing, crackling yellow light burst from the base of the steel support. Bobby almost tumbled backward; the fall would have been deadly.

Would Dauðr feed on me? he wondered, although he knew that monster would.

"Cheese and Rice," he whined, his voice nearly soundless against the roar of the river, the hum of vehicles above, and the sizzle of the thermite eating into steel.

He steadied himself and lowered the second magnesium strip. The fire was instantaneous.

"I love science," he shouted into the night, dropping the grabbers, shimmying down the shaking ladder, and tossing it into the fast-moving river the moment he touched bottom.

The Girl Scout waited for him in the car, parked nearby at a Shell gas station on Utah Street. They watched together as vehicles coming home from work from the Missouri side, and ones going home from Kansas, leaned awkwardly when a third of the bridge collapsed.

The Scout laughed this time as it sucked the souls of the dead into the car. Tears filled Bobby's eyes. He didn't know how much more of this he could take.

Ālfheimr

A hand shook Thomas's shoulder. "Hey."

His eyes opened and were stung by a sprinkling of fine dust, the yeti-crab scorpion monster gone. Jillian knelt above him, her hair gray. He nodded, spilling more dust into his eyes. He sat and spat, rubbing his eyes on the inside of his shirt.

Jillian's fist struck his arm.

"Ow."

"You deserved that," Jillian said. She stood and reached toward him with a dusty hand.

Thomas didn't take it. "I want to go home."

She shook her head slowly. "There's something worse there."

"How? How could it be worse?" He put his face in his hands.

She tapped his shoulder, and he looked up, tears hot on his cheeks. A sudden cross breeze swept powder into a dust devil, the snowy figure of a ghost in the twilight.

The ground shook again, the monster's steps a light thunder in the distance.

"We have to leave. The city is too far to reach tonight, but there's another shelter close enough," she said. "Come on."

They walked back to the road, their old footprints wiped clean by the wind. Jillian wore a backpack with two cans of chili, a bag of beef jerky, and two bottles of water salvaged from the ruined shelter. Thomas carried a sleeping bag in the crook of one arm. Jillian's world was different at night; a world of shadows and lurking monsters. Thomas stood in the road, his hands in his pockets to hide their shaking; the dead, dusty world stretched in a painted canvas around him.

"That thing. That scorpion. Do you have other monsters like it?" he asked.

She turned to face him, her right cheek a shade of pink. "That's not our monster. It's Dauðr's pet. It's here to find anything it missed. It's like salting the ground." She continued walking.

Thomas followed. "I still don't understand why Dauðr is still alive."

She managed a weak smile. "We failed. We needed to merge your blood with Dauðr's, but the coyote bit you and you didn't get the chance to do that. You fell and your talisman dropped to the dirt."

"Blood?" he shouted. "You never told me that."

Jillian slowly nodded. "I did, when you were young."

"That part of my childhood's still kind of fuzzy," he said. "I don't want to remember that night very well."

She took his hand in hers. "You must, eventually. You have no choice."

The world of shadows closed in as they trudged through what must have once been a lush forest, the trees now mostly stripped of bark by the never-ending wind, the exposed wood bleached white as bone.

"What was this place?" Thomas asked, his voice loud in the dead, silent forest.

"The realm of Woodsdeep." Jillian stopped and patted the trunk of an ancient tree. The sound was deep, and hollow. "The home of the Ealbhar."

They stood for a few moments in silence.

"I don't know what that is," Thomas said.

"I think you'd call them cousins. They preferred the trees to the ocean. They rarely left them." She rapped the trunk with her knuckles. "They inhabited places like this."

Thomas touched the long-dead tree, the wood smooth as glass. "This tree?"

"Could it be?" she whispered, tapping more gently. The tone altered, became sharper, and she smiled. "Yes."

Her hand slipped inside the wood and an opening grew, as if it had always been visible.

"Now come." She disappeared inside, and the opening vanished behind her, the smooth tree whole again.

"What the hell?"

A few seconds later, her hand appeared as if it grew from the tree. It grabbed his arm and pulled him inside.

Thomas stood in darkness. A flashlight in Jillian's hand cast a beam down steps that spiraled through the roots of the tree. They walked until they reached a circle of a room, its ceiling the intricate, twisting roots of the tree, giving way to a smooth stone wall and a floor of polished crystal. The stale smell of dry rot and disuse filled the room.

"Whoa," he managed.

Jillian lifted a stool and sat, dropping the backpack to the ground. She removed the two bottles of water.

"An Álfrheima," she said, holding out a bottle to Thomas. "An elf home. A family of Ealbhar once lived here."

No paintings, no carvings, no art at all marked the smooth wall. A table and two stools were all that remained of whoever once called this place home. As he pulled up a stool and sat next to Jillian, he saw the table was carved with intricate writing that seemed familiar, but—

"Are those Norse runes?" he asked.

"Maybe." Jillian lowered her water bottle and offered a curious smile. "Or are they Álfr runes?"

He uncapped his bottle. "They really were that close?"

"Yes."

"Is that where this family went?" he asked. "Did the, the Eel-ba-har go to Norway?"

"Ealbhar, but you're getting better." Jillian offered Thomas some jerky from the pack, but he waved her off. "Some, but some went to your country, your state even. The people in Norway, Sweden, Finland, they have mostly forgotten us. All but the older ones. Some of them still remember, even those in your country."

Half the bottle of spring water disappeared before Thomas lowered it to the table and replaced the plastic cap.

"Why did you come to Missouri?"

She untied The North Face sleeping bag.

"Some areas between worlds are thin, some are thick." The bag unrolled onto the crystal floor, disturbing a thin layer of dust. "I came to Missouri, to your farm, because the area there is thin. It is a window, Thomas. And you know what happens when a window is open."

"You never know what may come in." The words were nearly inaudible.

"I came because you were there." She knelt on the shiny crystal floor and smoothed out the sleeping bag, the zipper loud in the underground room. "And so did Dauðr. It came because of you, and Bobby."

A tightness squeezed his chest. "None of this is *my* fault."

She gripped his hand hard enough that he winced. "No, it's not," she snapped. "Never think that. Dauðr would have come no matter who it smelled, or who was on the other side to help it through. If anyone is to blame, it's Bobby Garrett."

The light from the flashlight danced around the room like Jillian was playing with a cat. "I need to turn this off before the batteries die."

Die. That word was popular.

"Did Bobby help it through when it came in the corn? He was, what? Fourteen, or something?"

Jillian nodded. "Yes. He was with us that night, remember?"

The coyote.

"Yes. The coyote," Jillian said. "Now, please go to sleep."

St. Joseph—2012

The Cadillac sputtered as Bobby pulled it into the Rolling Meadow Shopping Mall parking lot and brought it to a stop in the employee section. The security cameras didn't monitor all the way out here. He was certain of it.

In his years working at the mall, he'd seen Mr. Head of Security Dale's screens enough to know what they saw and what they didn't. The one in the JCPenney changing rooms would probably get old Dale-o in trouble, but Bobby never snitched. He'd hate for Terri to hire someone competent.

A brown duffel bag he'd bought at JCPenney two months earlier sat in the seat beside him, stuffed with things old James Cash Penney never sold. He found the gas mask at the army surplus store, the hazmat suit at Walmart, and he whipped up the Ziploc bags of white powder in his own kitchen. Making the poison had been easy.

He just typed "how to make ricin" into Ask.com at the public library under the login name Jack Torrance, and a list of recipes popped up. Bobby even ordered the supplies online: Ricinus communis, seeds of the castor oil plant, which were supposed to keep moles out of people's lawns or something. Bobby didn't care; he just wanted the poison. He boiled the beans in two of his mom's big black pots, filtered out the oil, followed the directions he'd printed at the library on crisp, white paper he paid for in cash, and boom. He had a powder capable of killing everyone at Rolling Meadows Shopping Mall.

The zip of the duffel was loud, his nerves pulled as tight as fence wire. Getting the bag inside would be easy because he'd worked at the mall for years, sweeping dust and picking up other people's garbage. Scooting around the concourses, even with the squeaky mop bucket, he was invisible. A ghost—and that was perfect.

He circled the car to the passenger side, awkwardly hefting the bag from the seat.

The long stretch of pavement ended at the employee entrance, a ramp that took workers down into the bowels of the building instead of allowing them to mingle with the regular people upstairs. Bobby wore his blue janitor's uniform and a smile, the duffel hanging innocently off his shoulder. If anyone asked about the bag, he planned to tell them he had a date after work and didn't have time to go home to change.

Would anybody believe that?

He shook his head.

Was that Dauðr's voice reaching him out here? Or had he finally blown a gasket? The monster had grown stronger, sure, now holding the Girl Scout's skeleton together with the black shadow that freaked him right the hell out. The black shadow with the teeth. But all the way out here?

The keypad beeped as he typed in the passcode, and the door clicked, swinging open to the mall's underbelly. Terri stood near the loading dock talking with Thad, the dock manager.

Oh, shit. Oh, shit. Oh, shit. This was it. The plan. This was the plan Dauðr helped him construct. But Dauðr wasn't here.

I'm alone.

The blood rushed from his face; he could feel his skin bleach white in an instant. His knees wobbled when he passed Terri and Thad, who were too embroiled in an argument over what "that jackass assistant manager at Sears ordered this time" to pay him any attention. Invisible. A ghost.

The steel door to Climate Control, in the rear of Janitorial, was closed, as he expected. Bobby ducked behind a row of lockers, his breath coming fast. The door loomed over him. He was alone. He was still invisible. A specter.

His bladder grew heavy, although he knew he didn't have to pee.

"Did you go potty, honey?" His mom's voice, hollow, echoed in his head. Not his mother alive and making casseroles, but his mother dead, a mummy sitting on the basement floor wearing novelty glasses.

"Yes, I went potty, Mother."

His hand shook as it rose toward the handle, which turned easily in his hand. He opened the door and ducked inside, shutting and locking it behind him.

The hazmat suit from his duffel went on easily—he'd practiced with it in the mirror enough. It was the mask he worried about. Even sucking in a little of the grayish-white power would give him about two days to worry about his lungs filling with water before he shat himself to death. The mask sealed around his face, Bobby flicked the master switch that killed the fan to the air-conditioning.

All planned out, Bobby. Everything's going smoothly.

The panel accessing the main vent carrying cold air throughout the building came off easily, and Bobby dumped the Ziploc bags of death into the cold metal tube. Twenty of them. He hoped it would be enough.

Then he replaced the panel.

Death was ready to sweep through the mall, but his hand froze over the red master switch.

"Do I really want to do this?" His voice came out in a whimper. "Do I want to kill all these people for that stupid little monster?"

The parking lot had been relatively full. It was the Saturday before Mother's Day. These people were here to be sheep, and sheep were bad. Sheep didn't think, they followed the lead sheep, who didn't know where the hell it was going anyway. That's all these mall goers were: sheep.

Worse than sheep, Dauðr whispered in his head. *All these people are bad, Robert. Selfish. Pathetic. Perverts, like that Johnson boy, and Dale the security chief, who masturbates to young moms changing their clothes in a room that's supposed to be safe. Yes, they are bad. And yes, you want to do this. It was your idea after all.*

"Yes," Bobby said. "It was my idea."

As he threw the switch to kick on the fan that blew death throughout the mall, Bobby's penis grew hard.

Oh, yeah.

"Good-bye, mall walkers," he said, trying to push his dick into a comfortable position through the hazmat suit. "Good-bye, Dale."

And he left, winding his way up a utility staircase into the back of Party City and into the parking lot through a service door. No one saw him inside the mall. But outside, he walked from the building in full view of the surveillance cameras, a man of indeterminate size in a bulky white hazmat suit, his face obscured by a safety mask. There were no shouts, no alarms, no sirens. If the plan worked, and Bobby thought it would, no one would put two-and-two together for days, and by then there would be no evidence.

Nope. No evidence at all.

A pretty woman in her twenties, wearing a red dress, got out of her car, which was parked next to the Cadillac. Waiting for someone, Bobby figured, or going to the TGI Fridays in the next lot over. Sure. That lot was crowded; it was almost lunchtime. A few people looked over at the strange man in the hazmat suit, some pointed, but they lost interest quickly enough and went inside the restaurant.

A thought tickled the back of his brain. "Go get me another body," Dauðr had said when he left for the mall today—again. That little monster. "Remember, a female. One that's alive. We have things to do, me and you."

Dear God, what?

Bobby walked up behind the young woman, butterflies in his stomach. Butterflies? Who the hell came up with that? The gurgling in his stomach felt more like a belly full of Diet Coke and Mentos.

The woman took out an iPhone to do something. Check texts, the weather, to see how much the Warm Pretzels with Craft Beer Cheese Dipping Sauce cost at TGI Fridays. Bobby didn't care. She stood alone, her attention on the restaurant parking lot; whoever she waited for hadn't arrived. Here was that other body the walking skeleton had demanded for years.

Reward me, Bobby thought.

The tread of his shoes was silent as a spider as he approached the woman. The cameras of the mall and the shitty chain restaurant didn't point out this far. He slapped the mobile phone from her slim hand. The screen cracked against the pavement.

"Hey," she said, whipping around. Her eyes bulged at this monster in white, its eyes and proboscis those of an enormous insect. "What?"

A black-gloved fist slammed into the woman's face, destroying whatever scream had started to form. She dropped to the gray asphalt, landing on her buttocks.

"Why—" started to escape her bleeding lips, but Bobby put an index finger in front of the mask.

"Shhh," he hissed, the sound muffled. Her mouth opened to scream, but Bobby smashed a fist into it again. He pulled his hand back for another strike and she stopped. He slipped the Cadillac's key in the trunk lock and it popped open.

"Get in," he said, "and I won't kill you."

"But—" she started, trying to crawl away from him.

"Talk, and I will."

She shook her head and Bobby unzipped the duffel, sliding his hand inside. "My hand is on a shotgun. If you don't get in, I'll shoot you and be out of this stupid town before the echoes die."

Tears flowed down the woman's red, swelling face. She climbed into the trunk of the car and lay down on a bag of dry-cleaned garments that would never be opened. Bobby shut the trunk and slipped behind the wheel.

"Hey," someone called from the TGI Fridays parking lot, but Bobby pulled away and headed toward the interstate. He wouldn't stay on the interstate long, just enough so that anyone who saw him take the woman would point the police in exactly the wrong direction.

The old two-car garage door moaned as it crawled shut, its electric motor complaining like it wanted a raise and better working conditions. Bobby emerged from the Cadillac and stripped off his hazmat suit, the mask already in the dumpster of a Chinese restaurant, buried beneath bags of drippy kung pao chicken. He'd have to destroy the suit soon, hopefully today, since it wasn't a priority. Not anymore.

Bam, bam, bam; a palm slapped the interior of the trunk lid.

She was.

An unnatural chill ran through Bobby, a cold that burrowed deep inside him. The monster—his monster—was nearby. The image of the living skeleton lingered in the corners of his mind, lurking, watching.

"Hey," the woman in the trunk growled, her word muffled by the layer of Michigan steel.

I can still let her go, flitted around his head, a moth in an attic filled with cobwebs. Then this—a jab of pain shot through his skull, causing him to collapse onto the trunk.

"Hey, hey, hey," came louder, the slaps more urgent.

The pain evaporated, and Bobby stood. He couldn't release her. Dauðr wouldn't let him. The key slid into the lock, and it clicked. The trunk flew open, and the woman attempted to jump out, but her tight, stiff muscles made her stumble. She brandished an unwound metal hanger from Tonja's dry cleaning, the jagged end pointing at Bobby.

"I'm sorry," he said.

Confusion washed over her face. "For which part, dickhole?"

I deserve that. "For hitting you. Mom didn't raise me like that." She raised me to beat people to death with lamps.

The woman's hand holding the hanger shook, but not from fear. She was pissed.

"Who are you?"

He shook his head, a thatch of greasy black hair dropping over one eye. "I don't want you to know my name."

"I'm—" she started.

"I don't want to know your name either," he said.

"It's Marguerite Jenkins. Deal with it, bitch."

Bobby hit Marguerite again because she didn't want to go into his house.

"You're a terrible person," Marguerite spat at Bobby, as he pulled her across the short concrete sidewalk between the garage and the kitchen door. He yanked her up the steps toward the kitchen when her hand struck his temple, and he stumbled inside, pulling her in with him.

They tumbled onto the stained floor, Marguerite on top, her elbow in his gut. She shoved herself to her knees, her right hand balled into a fist.

"Shitty," she snapped. "Shitty, shitty, shitty."

Defeat her. The words cracked in his head like melting ice.

Marguerite's first punch struck his shoulder. The second his cheek.

"Goddammit," wheezed out as he pulled his arms from beneath her to cover his face. "Stop it."

A fist made it through and popped Bobby's nose. A scream burst from his blood-splattered his face.

"Ha." Marguerite hit him again. "Serves you right."

Then the bludgeoning stopped, but the woman sat still on his chest.

Bobby's arms spread enough to see; her eyes were huge, her face, pretty beneath the growing bruises, stretched into a soundless scream.

The Girl Scout stood in the periphery of his vision.

"You did well, Robert," it said, its voice nothing more than a frigid breeze.

The skeletal dwarf stepped closer, its body bones and ligaments. The woman didn't move, didn't flinch as Dauðr reached a skeletal hand to stroke her hair. The Girl Scout's mandible fell open, and the woman finally screamed, a high, horror-movie scream. Smoke, black and oily, rolled from Dauðr's gaping hole, caressing the woman's face, poking, probing, stroking, crawling into her mouth and up her nostrils until it was all inside. Inky blackness soaked into her eyes for only a moment before bleeding away, and thick, oily tears ran down her cheeks.

Bobby flinched when the Scout's bones clattered to the floor; the blood-stained sash tangled among them.

"Yes, Robert." The woman on his chest pinned his arms to the floor and grinned down on him. "You did well."

Ālfheimr

They left the elf home at some time in the morning. It was impossible to tell when. The perpetually gray sky and dusty air rendered the world timeless. And why not? Time is a human construction, and as Thomas kept discovering, humans don't know anything.

They ate canned food as they walked along the long, smooth ribbon of road. It dipped and drifted lower through the remains of a seaside village and into an ancient shore, the seabed dotted with the skeletons of enormous ocean beings and longships, their prows decorated with dragons and snakes.

A high cliff dotted with holes like a giant hive rose to the left, stone steps led to them. An amphitheater surrounded by black stone monoliths sat at the base of the cliff.

"We're here," Jillian said, taking his hand. An electric jolt shot up Thomas's arm. "Come."

They weren't alone. Thomas pulled back on Jillian's hand when they reached the bottom of the hill. People were there, moving around the stones, some chanting, others crying.

They're not people, Thomas kept telling himself, but it was difficult to believe. Pale, sad faces stared at the monoliths. The small flock of maybe twenty stood, dwarfed in the lee of the tall, smooth, black Stonehenge. Brown hair and blond, short and tall, all dressed in ill-fitting, worn clothing. Blue jeans and khakis, tennis shoes and loafers, T-shirts and button-downs. All could have been from thrift stores or stolen off clotheslines. They could have been beggars in downtown St. Joseph.

Maybe they were.

"Is this what elves normally look like?" Thomas asked.

"You mean like people?"

"Yes."

"Why not?" Jillian said. "Aren't we?"

A woman in a plaid jacket, despite the heat, turned her head toward Jillian as they walked past. The woman's eyes grew wide with—what? Fear? She scurried away as they approached.

"I want to go," Thomas whispered.

"No," was all Jillian said.

The people began to notice Jillian and Thomas and scattered, darting away from the monoliths. His eyes followed them; some disappeared into the hives, others popped from existence into thin air.

He started to speak, but Jillian raised a hand and the word died.

She stopped in front of a monument; veins in the rock glowed slightly in the gray day. The surface of the smooth, black stone began to swirl, and a picture emerged. A woman with red hair in a long, flowing, white dress sat on a rock, staring out across a mirrored sea, a breeze tugging at her hair.

A gull, or something like it, flew in the distance. Thomas stood still, his gaze affixed to the picture. A spot in the ocean swelled, green foam floating outward in concentric circles from the—what? The water continued to swell, like Godzilla ready to surface. The woman in the picture screamed; a thin wail reached Thomas's ears. An enormous crab, beige with orange-stained edges and black-tipped claws the size of cars, broke the water.

But the woman—Jillian.

Dear God, it's Jillian—wasn't screaming because of the crab, she screamed at something behind it. The scene changed from sunshine to darkness as a black cloud loomed over the beach, its center filled with teeth. The crab reached the sand and turned to face the darkness, but tendrils of black nothingness grew around the clicking beast. The darkness constricted, and the crab dropped to the sand, unmoving.

"Thomas." Jillian dropped a hand on his arm, and he jumped, his heart drumming. "You stopped breathing."

"What are these stones?" he wheezed, hands shaking.

She curled an arm around his waist.

"This is our history," she said, and guided him to another monument. They were alone now; the elf-people had fled. "It shows us the scenes we want to see. I brought you to these monuments to show you what you can't remember; the night in the corn."

A picture grew on the black stone, fuzzy at first, sharpening at the edges and growing inward. A field at night, the long rows of corn ending at a farmhouse. Two cows stood next to a barn eating hay from a large round bale turned on its side.

"That's my house," Thomas whispered.

Two figures ran from the house; a girl with red hair in a white dress held the hand of a brown-haired boy in pajamas. They dashed across a garden and into the cornfield.

"No," came from Thomas's lips.

Dogs—no, not dogs, coyotes—ran through the cornrows beside the children but out of sight, their yips now small and far away, but Thomas heard them. Another boy, taller than the young Thomas and with black hair, appeared in the corn dressed in blue pajamas. The boy's form shifted—the pajama shirt peeling off, the pants remaining—and became that of a coyote.

"That's Bobby," he whispered. "Bobby was in the cornfield. He—he became a coyote?"

"Just breathe, honey," Jillian said beside him. "Bobby's spirit was there. He's always been with you, Thomas. Always. His spirit merged with the coyote who bit you; he tasted your blood."

"How—" he wheezed. "Why?"

She held him tight. "All opposites are connected. Good/bad, yin/yang, pleasure/pain. You are special, my love, but so is Bobby. Bobby is connected to you as your shadow is to your feet."

The moving picture on the monolith swirled and grew clear again. They returned to the first stone.

The darkness that killed the giant crab flowed over the field, pulled itself into a tight ball and became a solid form: a white capsule, like a giant Tylenol, rolling on wheels. Thomas recognized this, an anhydrous ammonia tank. It moved by itself through the corn, toward a man, toward a figure that looked like his dad.

Jillian held him tight. "Remember, that never was your father," she said, but Thomas's mind was far away.

The moments reliving themselves on the surface of that stone, the long-stifled memories, all came back. The man who wasn't a man; the smile, the teeth; the terror of a ten-year-old; the teeth of the coyote that wasn't a coyote; and Snake Mountain. Little Thomas fell, blood soaking his pajama leg. He collided with the man-thing and the tank exploded.

The man-thing screamed and threw up its hands when Thomas attacked it, a black hand grew from the monster and wrapped in a fist around the anhydrous ammonia tank, and then fire filled the night.

"I remember," he told Jillian, the salt from his tears reaching his tongue. He licked his dusty lips clean. Oh, God, I remember it all.

"Thomas," came from somewhere. A hand grabbed his shoulders and shook. "Thomas."

He looked at Jillian standing over him, her hand still on his shoulder. "Why am I on the ground?"

St. Joseph—2014

Boyd sat in the creaky wooden office chair, the same chair under the same wide, oaken desk every Buchanan County sheriff since the 1930s had plopped their fat butts into. He flicked the raisins in his salad to the corner of the too-small piece of Tupperware Emily packed his lunch in.

He hated raisins.

Raisins were only good for children who didn't know any better and long-term convicts who had to make toilet wine out of something.

Emily.

She'd surprised the hell out of him.

Emily Kristiansen moved to town from Bemidji, Minnesota, and soon joined Debbie's Thursday night book club at the library because she didn't have anything better to do on a Thursday night. Two weeks later, Debbie set up a blind date. A month after that, Emily came over every night for dinner. Boyd cooked, until he didn't. Steak and potatoes turned into whitefish and shredded cabbage before he could say no.

Boyd lost twenty pounds, but as he poked at his lunch, all he wanted to do was go fishing, alone on his boat with a cooler of beer and roast beef sandwiches and a bag of Cool Ranch Doritos, and he didn't want to catch one damn fish.

Sergeant Kirkhoff knocked on the door, and Boyd popped a lid on the Tupperware before he did anything crazy, like finish that salad.

"Come on in, Glenn."

Kirkhoff hesitated. "I wouldn't interrupt lunch unless it was important."

A feeling of satisfaction grew over Boyd, the kind of satisfaction a person gets after finishing a good meal, which he had not. It was Kirkhoff. He'd made a good deputy, he made a good second-in-command, and someday he'd make a good sheriff.

"This lunch deserves interrupting," he said. "Come in and sit down."

Kirkhoff's Opie Taylor face beamed.

"Emily's been good for you, Boyd," Kirkhoff said. "You're lookin' like you could stick with this job for thirty years or more."

"Shit." Boyd dropped a paper napkin over the Tupperware, hiding it. "I've been in this job thirty years already." The chair groaned as he leaned back. "It's almost quittin' time, Glenn. You'd look good in this chair."

Kirkhoff leaned forward, laying a fax sheet on Boyd's desk.

"Election's coming up," Kirkhoff said. "Why don't you give it four more years, then I'll run if you got my back."

Boyd's laugh barked through the office. Deputy Aaron Shank shot a glance toward the office before grabbing his hat and heading out the door.

"Guaranteed, son," he said, taking a look at the fax. It was a missing person report from St. Joe. The face of a beautiful girl, college-aged maybe, smiled back at him. "What's going on?"

Before answering, Kirkhoff scratched at his beard.

"This is Marguerite Jenkins, twenty-two, of Savannah. Well, now twenty-four. She was supposed to meet a date." Kirkhoff pointed to a spot halfway down the report. "A Mitchell Tremblay, now twenty-six, of St. Joe. Never showed up. That was two years ago."

Boyd looked up. "Yeah. I remember this. Possibly connected to the Rolling Meadows Mall disaster. Never found her. You got a new lead?"

He shook his head. "Not really, but—"

The sheriff motioned him to hurry. "But?"

"Her mom called me. I know Margie. She's the baby sister of my best buddy from high school. Marguerite was a solid, likable kid. Responsible. She wouldn't disappear voluntarily. She'd have called her mom. And this Tremblay guy claims she never showed up for their date at TGI Fridays. He checked out, never been in trouble. Margie's mom went to a psychic down in Kansas City. He told her Margie's still alive."

"A psychic?" Boyd asked. "Well, what's she want us to do? She disappeared two years ago. And besides, it's not our jurisdiction."

Kirkhoff shrugged. "I guess—" His finger drifted closer to the bottom of the page. "It's because of me. She wants me to try and find her."

Boyd sat back down.

"All right. Fill me in."

"The St. Joe cops found her car in the back of Rolling Meadows Shopping Mall lot, purse still in it, her cell phone on the pavement, screen cracked to hell."

"What about—"

"Surveillance cameras?" Kirkhoff said. "No. They didn't hit that spot. Either Tremblay's lying, Margie decided to not be Margie, or somebody abducted her. Maybe the guy who did the mall."

Boyd pushed the fax sheet over the napkin. Those raisins couldn't get far enough away.

"Employees park back there?" he asked.

"Yeah, boss," Kirkhoff said, pushing himself to his feet. "I've already asked the mall manager to provide a list of everyone working within a twenty-four-hour period of Margie's disappearance."

The chair creaked as Boyd leaned forward. "You sure you don't want this job now?"

"No, Boyd," Kirkhoff said. "You gotta be ready first. Four more years, remember?"

As Kirkhoff took the fax sheet from the desk and walked into the squad room, Boyd thought he might be ready now.

Ālfheimr

Thomas scrunched his nose. The smell came from nowhere, but everywhere, and not from this dusty land—from somewhere else; it wasn't natural. Industrial cleaner, maybe.

The kind janitors use in factories. Sitting on the steps of a simple, elegant stone amphitheater, the crowd of—fairies? Elves? Hobgoblins?—long gone, he sniffed but still couldn't find the source.

Jillian sat next to him and pulled a bag of Twinkies from her backpack.

"Twinkies?" he asked.

She frowned. "Don't you like Twinkies?"

"Everyone likes Twinkies. But why do you have a bag of Twinkies?"

She ripped open the cellophane sack. The scent of sugar hung heavily in the air but couldn't drown out the stench of cleaning supplies.

"Why don't you take a bite and find out?"

Thomas hesitated. "The food looked good," the bleeding man had told him, "so why not?" Jillian had offered him food many times. He didn't eat the cake with the curl of chocolate on top that became a turd in the morning. He left the second piece of cake on his dad's beer cooler in the shop. It was the fried chicken and mashed potatoes he finally ate.

Then he woke in Fairyland.

"Are you taking me home?"

Jillian nodded. "Yes. That's why the Twinkies, they hold a magic all their own."

"Do they?"

She shook her head. "No."

"You once tried to feed me shit."

She held the Twinkie in front of his face. "It wouldn't have turned into shit if you'd just eaten it. Fairy food is special. It doesn't last long. I gave you chocolate cake, your stubbornness turned it to shit."

"Wait, this isn't shit, is it?"

"No, it's just a Twinkie." He opened his mouth slightly, and she pushed the pastry in. "It'll turn into shit the usual way."

Then the smell of industrial cleaner, or maybe hospital disinfectant, grew stronger. The Twinkie tasted like a Twinkie, moist, and spongy, but when Thomas swallowed the second bite, the world began to spin.

Jillian wrapped her arms around him as the hot, dusty, gray world of Ālfheimr disappeared into blackness, and he melted into a place filled with the chemical smell. The ground beneath him gave way, like sand sifting through a child's beach toy, and they fell.

PART
5

Chapter Fourteen  2016

[1]

THOMAS WAS DIMLY AWARE OF passing through a swirling void when suddenly he dropped through the ceiling of a shitty room in a shitty apartment. He landed on what was left of a table coming at him too fast. The shoddy pressed wood cracked when he struck it, shards flew across the room, pain jabbed his side, and he hit the floor.

Jillian landed beside him, groaning.

"Is traveling with you always like this?" Thomas moaned.

A feeble streetlight fought against the dirt that smeared the windows in the room. Jillian spat on the floor, her spit dark, bloody.

At least she bleeds.

"No," she wheezed. "Sometimes it's worse."

He pushed himself to sit, then froze.

A movement, the shake of a little nervous dog, started in a dark corner, then shimmied closer, the reek of hazardous chemicals growing with it.

"Da fug?" asked a shaky voice masked in darkness. The shaking wasn't fear. That dude was high. "Da fug are you? What the hell you come out the ceilin' for?"

Thomas grabbed Jillian's arm, his back pressing into the filthy, scarred wall, the hair of his scalp on end.

The voice paused, and the figure moved; what was left of a man stumbled into the dim yellow light. Tall and thin, his ribs stuck out from his hollow chest as if giant fingers gripped him from behind. This scarecrow man, a bushy hay pile of hair billowing over his head, leaned forward, his teeth rotted black stumps.

"Wha' you doin'?" he barked, his breath like a hamper. "Why you in mah house?"

This place was no house. A blanket lay on what was left of a moldy mattress. Fist-sized holes decorated walls that were half dark paneling, half dark red wallpaper scattered with bullet holes.

"Why you in mah house?" he repeated. Then, under his feet, Thomas saw it: a picture of a sailing ship.

Jillian's apartment?

"Hey, man," Thomas started, his voice as weak as bad coffee. We're going to die, Thomas was sure of it. "I'm sorry. This is all a mistake. We're not supposed to be here."

The man reached into the front pocket of his filthy, baggy jeans and pulled out a small-caliber pistol, the barrel gray in the scant light. He stepped closer, his skin pockmarked with acne, the industrial smell stronger.

"Assa damn straight you ain't supposed to be here. Be here in mah house."

"You can't rationalize with a person on meth," Uncle Boyd once said at dinner, the day after a meth cook attacked him during a raid. "Don't shout at them, don't cuss at them, and don't make any sudden movements. Those idiots are as unhinged as a human can be."

Thomas's skin crawled.

"Sir," Thomas said, but the man shook the pistol at him.

"Shu-up," Meth Man mumbled, then swung the gun at Jillian, his eyes locked on her like he'd never seen a woman before. "Why you, why you in mah house? You a demon. You a demon in mah house."

A leg of the table Thomas crashed through lay near his fingertips. He curled his fingers around the narrow end, the wood solid in his hand.

"You here to git me, devil woman?" The man's body jerked from involuntary muscle movements; a hand wiped snot across his upper lip. "But you woan. You woan. I git you firse."

He pulled back the gun's hammer, and Thomas moved. He brought the table leg down hard; Meth Man's stick-like forearm snapped, but he didn't scream. He didn't react. The impact dropped the pistol to the floor. Meth Man stood over it, his arm hanging like it had an extra joint.

Thomas pulled Jillian to her feet.

"You didn't have to do that," she said. "I could have handled Rodney."

"How did you know his name was Rodney?"

Jillian rolled her eyes.

"He was going to shoot you," Thomas said.

"Ya, I was," Meth Man said, seemingly impervious to the pain of his shattered forearm. "I was gon shoot that demon dead."

Thomas put the base of the table leg in the center of Meth Man's chest and shoved. The man, emaciated by cheap crank, dropped to the floor. Thomas bent and grabbed the pistol, the warm handle greasy in his hand.

"Come on," he said to Jillian and led her out the door, the cheap metal numbers 201 screwed into the wooden surface. She followed him into the parking lot, which was bathed in a single yellow light. He glanced at her: a strawberry mark was again on her face. It came and went when she used magic, he realized.

[2]

The YouTube video was glorious. Bobby sat in the dark; the light from his laptop flickered across his face as he watched a seven-year-old news report from St. Joseph's ABC station. The missing girl, Marguerite L. Jenkins, twenty-two, of Savannah, Missouri, just a blip on the talking-head radar. One missing pizza waitress lost among headlines blatantly profiting off the hundreds of binge-shopping sheep who went home from the mall with their Mother's Day purchases and died vomiting blood two days later. Marguerite was a forgotten casualty in a city of casualties, and Bobby couldn't be happier.

"Local hospitals report hundreds of deaths and hundreds more sickened from what's been identified as a terrorist attack," said the just-out-of-college reporter on KQ2. "Someone released the deadly poison ricin into the ventilation system at Rolling Meadows Shopping Mall the day before Mother's Day. So far, no suspects have been identified. Reporter Stephanie Giatti is live with mall office manager Terri Gerki. Stephanie?"

The floor moaned behind Bobby, and he lost track of the news report streaming on his laptop, the glow from the screen the only light in the master bedroom. It had become his office, where he slept, and where he hid from the world. All pictures, doilies, and scraps of his parents were long gone, burned in the firepit in the backyard.

Seven years. The monster in the woman's body wanted a death here and there, just enough to keep it satiated as it waited for something big, appetizers before the main course. The new body that fed on the mall deaths somehow grew into something less frightening. But the new plan, the plan made a line of drool escape Marguerite's mouth.

It was something special.

"Bobby, honey," Marguerite said, her voice light, sweet. He knew the monster was inside that body, that soft, supple body. He'd watched it take her, but damn. Warm, wet lips touched his ear; he didn't cringe. "When are you coming to bed?"

He turned, the laptop glow shining on Marguerite, standing behind him in one of his blue work shirts, her hair pulled back in a ponytail. Bobby knew what she was, he knew the unholy creature that dwelled within, but the beast had changed since it went inside her. Maybe because she was living when it did, but it acted like a girl. It *was* a girl. He grabbed her hand and gently squeezed.

"In a minute. I'm just reading more on attaching the detonators to the C-4. I don't want to blow us up."

"Oh, reading, reading, reading. That's all you ever do," she said, her lips in a pout. "You're ready, Bobby, honey. You're more than ready. You can do this, and you can do this soon. How about tomorrow? You know I believe in you."

Warmth grew over him. Dauðr still needed him to carry out the actual work, and as long as it needed him, he had Marguerite. But how long was that? The high school, the bridge, the mall all took planning, effort, and the demon fed off all those deaths. But it wanted something else before he took that next step, when he made St. Joseph, Missouri, explode in a great ball of fire. What was it? What did it want? Why did it need a living body?

Bobby didn't know.

But he knew that once Dauðr got what it really wanted, it wouldn't need him anymore, and Marguerite would be gone.

He closed the lid to his HP notebook, the room suddenly dim except for moonlight radiating through the open windows.

"Okay," he said, then stopped and watched this beautiful, beautiful monster unbutton his work shirt and let it drop to the floor.

"Hey," he said, protesting weakly as she pushed him onto the bed. "You haven't gotten pregnant, or anything, so that's not possible, right?"

The Marguerite monster rested a finger on his lips, and he no longer wanted to talk. "Of course, it's not," she said. "I wouldn't worry about that a bit."

[3]

The swollen corpse of a dog lay in a pit of frozen slime at the bottom of the Starlight Motel swimming pool.

"Oh," burst from Jillian, and she dropped to one knee. Thomas stopped in front of a concrete barrier covered in gang graffiti and wrapped an arm around her. It was freezing here, so different from her furnace world.

Had it been spring when we left? No, fall. Definitely not winter.

A woman in a velvet dress and faux-fur coat stood at the street corner chewing gum. Her breath rose in a white cloud.

"You okay?" the hooker asked.

"What's wrong?" Thomas took Jillian's chin in his hand and turned her face toward his.

Her teeth chattered. "We have to leave. That man was going to shoot us. *Shoot* us."

"Hey," the hooker said, her voice loud. "Is she comin' down from Rodney's stuff? Probably needs Tylenol and water. Lots of water."

The adrenaline pumping into Thomas's veins began to lose its magic. He started to shake like Meth Man. The cold didn't help.

Jillian pointed to a rusty 1970s Chevy Nova, the only car in the parking lot with tires.

"We have to leave now," Jillian said, her voice nearly too soft for him to hear. "Something big is going to happen, and it's going to happen soon. We have to stop it."

"Stop it?" Thomas said. "What? When?"

He hefted Jillian to her feet and walked her to the car, his legs threatening to collapse onto the crumbled, trash-covered pavement. He swerved around a patch of ice and tried the Nova's passenger-side door. It was unlocked.

"I don't know when to stop it," she said, dropping into the seat. "All I know is, it's going to happen, it's going to happen here in St. Joseph, and we can't stop it if we don't leave right now."

"Hey," the hooker yelled at him. "You better take care o' her."

Thomas waved at the woman and slid into the driver's seat, the pistol still in his hand.

"We don't have a key," he said.

Before he could bend down to try and hotwire the car, Jillian touched the dash and a burst of violet shot from her hand. Suddenly the old car sputtered to life.

"That was magic."

"No," Jillian said, her door clicking shut. "I told you, there's no such thing as magic. It's just something I can do. Now get us out of here."

The strawberry on her face nearly glowed.

"That thing on your face," Thomas said. "It's getting bigger."

Her hand slid over it. "A rash," she said. "It's just a rash."

"I've only seen it when you use your little magic thing. Is—"

She swung on him. "Mind your own damn business," she snapped. "Just drive."

The hooker at the corner barely moved when Thomas pulled the Nova onto Bentley Boulevard and drove away, the car puffing oil-filled smoke from the exhaust. The woman unwrapped another stick of gum and slid it into her mouth.

[4]

Emily's car, a sensible Ford Fusion hybrid, sat beneath the old elm tree in Boyd's yard, snow covering the hood. She'd been here a while. Her slim figure moved around his kitchen, visible through the open curtains when he pulled the cruiser up next to the Ford. Getting out of the car, he had to admit, was a bit easier without the extra pounds. If he kept losing weight, well, hell, he didn't like to think that far ahead.

"You're early," Emily said, as Boyd opened the front door. The kitchen of the small house was wide open to the rest of the floor. She walked to him in more of a glide than a walk, two Miller Lites in her hands. Her upper Minnesota accent was sexy as hell. Or at least Boyd thought so.

He nodded, sliding off his sheriff's hat and dropping it onto a wall peg, followed by his heavy winter coat.

"Stressful day," he said, taking a beer from Emily, the crack sprayed a thin splatter of foam over his hand. "It was weird."

Emily cracked open her beer. "Weird?"

The cold, crisp beer rolled over his tongue. He let it roll until half the can had disappeared.

"Yeah," he said, walking over to his recliner and dropping into it. "The whole day was like walking into a barroom before a fight breaks out. You know? Full of tension."

"Well, Mr. Sheriff Man, I don't know what it feels like to walk into a barroom before a fight breaks out, but you just described our family dinners back home." She took a drink of her beer before setting it on a coaster she'd already put on the coffee table. "Got a surprise for you."

Boyd wanted to tell her that law enforcement officers didn't like surprises. They usually ended with somebody's brains splattered on a wall, but he kept quiet.

She went into the kitchen and came back with a twelve-pack-sized cooler. He reached for it; she shooed his hand back. "Oh, don't you get all excited," she said. "It's not a prime rib, buster. But it's as close to one as you're going to get from me."

He grinned as he rolled the can in his hands. "Well, don't keep me guessing."

Emily sat on the couch and put the cooler on the coffee table. "I thought I'd spoil you tonight." She reached into the cooler and pulled out a gallon Ziploc bag. "Roast beef and horseradish on marbled rye. I also bought a bag of barbecue chips, but don't get too excited—they're baked."

She smiled; her teeth were white, but they weren't all straight. It gave her character. A fluttering danced in his chest. Not the heart-attack kind of fluttering he'd been pushing himself toward before

Debbie set up his date with Emily. An awkward date, sure, but it must have worked. Boyd looked at Emily; she was a pretty one. He wondered what she saw in a pig's ass like him.

"You sure know your way into a guy's heart."

Her laugh brought a smile to him. "Oh, holy buckets, Boyd. You eat too many of these—the way to your heart is a doctor sawing right through your chest. Now eat up."

She handed him a sandwich. It took a moment for him to take it.

"What's the matter, hon?" she asked.

He shrugged. "Nothing really. I just have a bad feeling the hard part of my day's not over yet."

[5]

"What did you do?" Thomas screamed at the windshield, years of dirt and cigarette smoke clouding the glass. He gripped the wheel with bare hands, wishing like hell he had gloves; the streetlight above them glowed yellow in the night. The Nova sat at a stop sign Thomas had stopped at before. The building at the intersection was gone, the weeds growing in the cracks gone. It was now a parking lot, but not a fresh one; the asphalt had been bleached gray by more than one summer. But Thomas's eyes weren't on the parking lot, with its "Parking: $5 an hour, $15 a day" sign at the entrance. His eyes were on the convenience store across the street.

"Gas—" he paused, glaring at the glowing red numbers that read $3.78. "Three dollars and seventy-eight cents? Gas is two sixty-seven. It's two sixty-seven. I just filled up my tank Wednesday. And that gas station wasn't there before. It wasn't there."

Thomas turned toward Jillian, his face pinched in confusion. Steam streamed from his nostrils in the frigid cab of the Nova.

"And your room. Your room was trashed. That Rodney claimed it was his place. I ask again, what did you *do*?"

Jillian touched his arm. He could feel the grit from Ālfheimr on their skin.

"Don't panic, Thomas," she said, calm as the counselors had been at Sisters of Mercy. "We can't do this if you panic."

He shook her hand off his arm. "And what exactly is 'this'?" he shouted, the sound like a slap. "What happened?

She sat back in the split vinyl seat. "Time," she said flatly. "Time moves differently in different places."

"Time? How differently?" Thomas pounded the old, dusty dash, his thoughts trying to coalesce. "Yeah, yeah, okay. I learned about this in college. The Haf, Haf, Hafele. The Hafele-Keating experiment. They put a clock on an airplane, and it moved slower than one on the ground. It had something to do with speed causing time, dialing. Dianetics. No. Dial— Dilation. Time dilation."

Jillian's shook her head; her red hair flopped in a greasy, lifeless mess.

"And you dropped out of college?"

"Focus," he growled, anger bringing his strength back. "What did you mean time moves differently in different places?"

She sucked in the icy air of the car and released it, her breath a cloud of fog. "Time moves much faster here than it does in Ālfheimr."

"And?" Thomas asked.

"It's not 2005 anymore," she said. "And it sure isn't autumn."

He slumped into the driver's seat like an inflatable doll losing air. The knot. Jesus Christ, the knot. It clutched his stomach, churning it, flipping it, twisting like a Rubik's Cube.

"Then what year is it?" His words came out in a growl.

Jillian shrugged. "I don't know. I just know whenever I cross over and come back, years have gone where only hours or days have passed for me."

He turned his head toward her, his eyes wet. "Then, when you left me—"

A horn honk behind them shocked Thomas up straight. A car with its right blinker on revved its motor behind them at the stop sign. Thomas slowly pushed the accelerator with his foot, and the Nova crept through the intersection.

"Where are we going?" Jillian asked.

"Home," Thomas said, tears running down his dirty face. "If we're in the future, I have to make sure my parents are okay."

[6]

Soft snoring purred from the left side of Bobby's bed. It was his mother and father's bed, technically, although he'd washed the sheets plenty since he and the monster had decided it was time for him to kill them. It had been, what, eight or nine years? Ten? Twenty? A thousand? He figured anything left of his mom and dad was long gone. He used to wonder if his dad had ever boinked Tonja in this bed when his mom was out shopping or playing bridge, but it didn't matter anymore. Marguerite was here now, and it was their bed. Bobby tried not to think of the monster inside her, lurking, a black spot of cancer on her soul. He was living with the devil, having dinner with it, watching it sleep. These thoughts went away when Marguerite was naked, moving up and down, back and forth on top of him. Whatever had been Marguerite was still inside that body somewhere. It may not ever come out again, but her personality, her life, had changed the soulless creature that inhabited her, at least on the outside. It smiled, it asked about his day, it ate, it slept, and unlike the Girl Scout, it didn't rot.

Bobby pushed out of bed slowly, not waking the pretty sleeping girl beside him. She was, what? Twenty-five? Twenty-six? Thirty? Was she still a girl? She still acted like a girl, especially when she made him do things, horrible things. Begging in that childish voice, lips pouting. But it always worked. He wanted to do things for her, for it. Chain a stranger in the basement, slip Drano into the iced-tea dispenser at the convenience store. Death fed the beast inside her, he knew, and she got off on it—*it* got off on it. He would work on the monster's next project right now.

Bobby stole into the hall on socked feet.

Black garbage bags stacked at the back door were filled with hundreds of empty Silly Putty eggshells and Vaseline jars, although some still sat on the table. That big, old kitchen table, with all three leaves in place, held Bobby's work—it was covered with snowmen. Dozens of homemade C-4 bombs—each comprising three wax-covered balls made of Vaseline, Silly Putty, cooking oil, and cornstarch—lay on the table. In movies, this explosive came in bricks, but the internet told him the C-4 worked better as a three-balled cascading bomb, and that's what Bobby wanted: whatever worked best. If what worked best looked like Frosty the Fucking Snowman, all the better. If he had time, he thought he might even put little hats on them. It was nearly Christmas, after all.

At the other end of the table, the faces of battery-powered alarm clocks stared blankly at Bobby, most of them purchased at thrift stores. The internet, the wonderful, all-knowing internet, told him how easy it was to make detonators "on the cheap!" So, clock radios that had once woken people for work all across town now lay in his kitchen, ready to give a jolt to those snowmen.

He knew he repulsed the real Marguerite, and that she was scared. She just wanted to go home. Maybe if he failed, Dauðr would let her go. Maybe the monster inside her would look for another way to motivate him.

No. He doubted that. Dauðr would use Marguerite, use her all up, before it went on to something else.

The follow-up to the Rolling Meadows Shopping Mall Disaster would happen, and it would happen soon—a big party at St. Joseph Children's Hospital. Bobby wanted to be ready. He cracked open a package of nine-volt batteries from the Dollar Store and fitted one into a partially disassembled clock. The LED flashed 12:00. He grinned, then mouthed *boom*. He set the alarm for 3:15 a.m. and set it aside. Three fifteen a.m. That's when all the bad stuff happened in *The Amityville Horror*. Bobby picked up another clock, wires dangling, and fitted in a battery. He sat hunched over the kitchen table, his black greasy hair hanging into his face as he twisted copper wires from old clocks and inserted them into the snowmen. The wires cut into the pads of Bobby's fingers.

Marguerite's bare feet made no noise on the stairs. She came into the kitchen. "How close are the bombs to being ready?" she asked, sliding her soft hands onto Bobby's shoulders. She rubbed, the dark thing inside controlling her motions. He could feel her tummy press into his back; it had started to get big.

Bobby set the armed explosive he was working on gently on the table and picked up another.

"They'll be ready tonight," he said, not turning to look at her.

Tonight. Do it tonight, fluttered through his thoughts.

Bobby inserted a battery into the clock and set the time. The old clocks weren't exactly efficient, so the bombs wouldn't go off together, but they didn't need to.

A minute here or there wouldn't matter when the world started to burn.

"Tonight?" he asked.

Marguerite slipped her hands around his chest and leaned into his ear. "Tonight," she whispered and licked his ear. "You need to rain hell tonight. You do it for me, and I'll do it for you."

Bobby turned to face Marguerite, whose once deep-brown eyes were now saturated with black. He ran a finger along her jawline and smiled a humorless smile. "That thing I like?" he asked.

The dark thing inside Marguerite kept her expression steady. "Twice, if you can handle it."

He slipped an arm around her and squeezed her butt cheek. "Tonight."

[7]

The old Nova's one headlight cut through the darkness, rolling over the hilly highway east of St. Joseph, patches of dirty snow on the shoulder. Thomas's mind was locked, focused on the road—and his parents. How many years had been yanked from beneath him? How many did his parents have left?

The memory of his dad's heart attack in 2002 stomped on Thomas like the giant scorpion.

They approached the lane to the Cavanaugh farm, or what was once the Cavanaugh farm, and Thomas slowed the Nova to a crawl, stopping when the headlight beam hit the mailbox painted in John Deere green. Cavanaugh, Rural Route 2, Box 63.

"You okay?" Jillian asked.

"No," he said, taking his foot off the brake and driving toward his boyhood home. "Not even close."

Their field, once thick with tall, green cornstalks, lay dead at the end of the gravel roadway; a few stubborn piles of brown snow remained where the anhydrous tank had exploded.

Memories flooded him as they grew closer to the house and outbuildings. Helping his mom in the garden, playing catch with his dad, running along this lane after he came home from Sisters of Mercy hoping the postal carrier brought a letter from Jillian. The old grain truck still sat at the side of the shed. A Pontiac, a model he'd never seen before, was parked next to a Ford F-150. A strange F-150, the edges rounder than he knew they should be.

"I don't think you want to do this," Jillian said.

Thomas gritted his teeth. "Stop telling me what I do and do not want," he said. "My parents probably think I'm dead." As they cruised to a stop at the edge of the lawn, he reached to kill the engine, but there wasn't a key. Jillian touched the dash, and the car died a slow, sputtering death.

"It'd be a dick move to turn back now."

Thomas opened the old, rusty door and stepped out; a slight breeze of freezing air sliced into him.

A motion-sensor light that was new to Thomas popped on when he stepped into the yard from the driveway. His breath came fast, bursts of fog as if he were puffing a cigar.

"I saw them last week," he said. "My mom made pork chops for dinner."

A hand dropped onto his arm, and he stopped.

"To you it was last week," Jillian said. "To them, it was years ago."

At that moment, this person next to him seemed tired, weak, not like the one who caused all the trouble in his life. He looked at her, her face still covered in dirt. Goddammit. She was still Jillian.

He took her hand in his and continued to move toward the porch. "I have to get you inside. You're freezing."

The steps to the kitchen door, the same steps where he'd once found muddy footprints, needed work. The third one sagged in the middle; it would snap before too many years. Before he mounted the first step, the door flew open and the screen door cracked against the wooden outside wall.

"Thomas." It was his mom; she ran onto the porch. Gray streaked her hair. "My God, Thomas." She ran down the steps, and wrapped her arms around him, squeezing hard. "Where have you been? Where have you been?"

Thomas's dad stepped onto the porch, his weatherworn face chiseled in granite. His mom pulled back from Thomas, her hands on his shoulders.

"Are you all right, baby?" she asked, the energy gone from her voice.

Thomas nodded. "I'm okay."

She squeezed him hard again. He heard a cough and looking up, over his mother's shoulder, he saw his dad approaching.

His dad wrapped his big arms around Thomas. "It's good to see you, boy," he said.

"Dad—" Thomas started, but his father shut him down.

"It's freezing out here, and you two are filthy," he said, nodding toward Jillian. "Get inside and clean up. Then we talk."

They'd showered in separate bathrooms, Jillian in the hall, Thomas in his parents'. He stopped at his old room, the room the fairy's muddy footprints had led to, the room where she'd appeared and dragged him into the cornfield to his death. He looked inside. No posters tacked to the wall, no Star Wars sheets on the bed. It wasn't his room anymore. his mom had taken it over for an art studio; an easel and stool sat in the center of the room, landscapes of the farm hanging from the walls. Thomas had to admit they were pretty good.

His bed remained, but it was shoved into a corner. My room's a guest room, and I'm a guest in my own home, he thought. As he walked downstairs, his feet coaxing the familiar creaks from the steps, he realized it wasn't his home anymore either.

He stepped into the kitchen, the air dead, the energy flat and cold as a mortuary. The kitchen was the same—black and white tiles in a checkboard, the scarred oak dining table, even the refrigerator—but his parents weren't. He sat down opposite his father, Jillian and his mom already at the table, cups of coffee in front of them. His mom was bigger than Jillian (taller, wider) but her clothes fit Jillian like she owned them. Thomas wore a pair of his dad's blue jeans and a flannel shirt. Thomas was roughly the same size as his father, just a little slimmer at the waist. The extra bulk of the pants hid the plastic snake in his front pocket.

Silence hung over the room like a dense fog, everyone afraid if they broke it, they might become lost. Thomas opened his mouth but stopped when headlights cut through the window. A few seconds crawled by, and a car door shut, then another.

"Were you expecting someone?" he asked.

His dad cleared his throat. "We called your Uncle Boyd while you were in the shower," he said. "If you two are in some kind of trouble, we thought he'd better be here."

"So, I come home, and you call the law?"

Porch steps creaked as feet moved up them. There were two sets. Uncle Boyd wasn't alone.

"I called your *uncle*, son." His dad waved toward the door.

"Knock, knock," Boyd said loud enough to hear through the kitchen door. "Anyone home?"

"Come on in," his dad said, never moving his eyes from Thomas.

The sheriff opened the door and stepped in, wearing a heavy coat with a Buchanan County Sheriff's badge insignia on the chest. Uncle Boyd was older, too, grayer, with less of a paunch. A thin blonde woman walked in with him; she shed her winter coat and clicked the door shut behind her.

Uncle Boyd had a girlfriend?

"It's good to see you, boy," Uncle Boyd said to Thomas, dropping a heavy hand on his shoulder. "We were all scared to death for you."

"Sit down, Boyd, Emily." His mom stood. "Can I get you something?"

Uncle Boyd took off his brown felt sheriff's hat and rested it on the counter before pulling out a chair and sitting at the table. Emily leaned against the counter. "Yes, Debbie. If this goes like it might, I think I'm going to need a beer," said Boyd.

"I could use one now," Emily said in a heavy Northern accent.

Uncle Boyd looked at his dad. "You all talked yet?"

His dad motioned to his mom to make it three beers. "No," he said. "When they got here in what looked like a demolition-derby car, they were caked with dirt. They just got cleaned up."

Uncle Boyd pulled a black leather notebook from his shirt pocket and flipped through a few pages before looking at Thomas directly. A chill ran through Thomas, but not from the cold; Uncle Boyd didn't give him a family look, he gave him a cop look.

"I ran the VIN on that car, Tommy. Looks like it belongs to a Tim Binnall of Pinehurst, Massachusetts. Reported stolen about ten years ago. You two been gone for eleven. You want to tell me what it's doing here?"

Eleven? Eleven years?

Thomas's hands slapped the table; his mom jumped. "It's 2016?" he asked.

"Yes," his mom said, setting three cans of Miller Lite on the table. She tried to hold back tears and failed. "What happened to you, baby? Where have you been?"

"We—" Thomas started, but his throat was as dry as Jillian's desert home. He lifted one of the beers and chugged it. When he returned the empty can to the table, tears pooled in his eyes. "We left in 2005."

His uncle Boyd nodded. "That's right. You left in 2005. You got a point?"

"But we didn't take that car ten years ago. We couldn't have taken it. Ten years ago, it was 1995."

A frown grew on Boyd's face.

His dad leaned forward on his elbows. "You're not making any sense, son. You want to try that again?"

"We stole the car." Jillian's voice quiet in the big kitchen. "But not from this Binnall person in Massachusetts. We stole it from a meth cook named Rodney at the Starlight Motel in St. Joseph."

"The Starlight?" Boyd snapped, unbelief in his voice. "What the hell were you doing in that hole? You're lucky you didn't get killed."

The lines on his mom's face grew deeper. "Are you on drugs?"

Thomas held up his hands, palms first. "No, Mom. No, I am not. I'm just—"

"Suspicious," Uncle Boyd said. He stuck his hand into his pants pocket and pulled out the pistol Thomas had left on the front seat. "This your meth head's, too?"

"Yes," Jillian said frankly. "It is. You'll probably still find him there with a broken arm. He's in room 201."

Boyd set the pistol on the table, close enough to him that no one else could reach for it first. "I'm not going to dance with you two," he said. "You disappeared eleven years ago and showed up here tonight in a stolen car with an unregistered gun, and your dad said you looked like you'd spent the last week in the desert. Now, you're going to tell me what the hell is going on and you're going to tell me now."

Emily's hands gently rested on Boyd's shoulders.

Thomas pushed his chair back, the legs scraping the floor. He walked slowly to the refrigerator and took out another can. The crack of the tab split the air like a gunshot.

"Mom," he said. "Do you remember when I was a kid and told you about the fairy in the garden?" He glanced at Jillian; she nodded once. He turned back to his mom. "I think I was about six. Do you remember?"

She shook her head like she was trying to dislodge something. "Fairy?" His mom paused, her face grew white, and she looked Thomas in the eyes. "Yes. I remember you telling me about the fairy," she said, her voice soft, unsure. "Wasn't it in the corn?"

He took a drink, the beer cold, his shredded nerves calmed, just slightly. "Yes," he said, leaning back against the refrigerator. "She was in the corn."

"You were singing a Leesa Loman song." Everyone turned and looked at Jillian. "'Where Are You Baby?'"

His mom's face grew slack. "That was my favorite song when you were little, Tommy."

Thomas stepped back to the table. "Uncle Boyd, do you remember the muddy footprints in the house?"

Confusion drained from Boyd's face along with his color as he remembered that day. "Yes."

"Do you remember what happened to those footprints when we got to the steps?"

Uncle Boyd swallowed, sweat started to bead on his forehead. "Well, I don't know if anything 'happened' to them, Tommy. They—"

"Got smaller," Thomas said. "They shrank from a woman's size to a child's size. You remember that, right?"

The can slipped from Boyd's hand as he started to lift it; the half-full beer clacked onto the table. He fumbled to grab it before it tipped over. "Now, Tommy. I don't know about that. I remember there was something strange about them, but—"

Thomas grabbed Jillian's leg and lifted her foot to the table. "If we had measured them, the prints in the kitchen would be exactly this size, and the ones on the steps—" He stopped and looked around the table. Everyone was confused and angry.

"The ones on the steps?" his dad said. "I remember them. They got small, like a child's." He placed his hands on the table and sat back in his chair. "What exactly are you getting at, Tommy?"

"We need to show them, Jillian."

"Show us what?" His mom's eyes widened, the fear now bewilderment. "What's happening?"

Jillian took a deep breath. "Are you sure we should?" she asked Thomas.

[8]

The Peterson kid at the hospital made Bobby wonder if he was doing the right thing. He hadn't cared about poisoning those mindless zombies in the mall as they bought garbage from the Gap and frilly underpants from Victoria's Secret no self-respecting human being should wear. They needed to be put down, but Tucker Peterson was different. Tucker Peterson was a good kid; he wasn't bad like that Johnson boy. Oh, no. Tucker Peterson was a good kid who had cancer. Pancreatic cancer. He read that from Tucker the first day he came in to clean the boy's room. Buried beneath thoughts of not being able to see *Captain America: Civil War* when it came out in the theater in April was the fact he had pancreatic cancer and probably wouldn't live until April anyway.

Bobby hunkered down low after the Rolling Meadows Mall Disaster, as the press called it. Disaster? Ha. Cops had talked to him, questioning him on the front porch of his house on Carlyle Street drinking iced tea Marguerite had made. Bobby wasn't scheduled to work at the mall the day of the Disaster. Nope. He was at home watching a *Cops* marathon on TBS. The *TV Guide* Bobby still had confirmed that. For some reason—and he knew the monster inside Marguerite was that reason—that was good enough for the St. Joseph Police officers, and they thanked him for the tea and drove away. A month later, Bobby started pushing a broom at St. Joseph Children's Hospital, and for him the world grew quiet as he worked on something that would make everyone forget about the Rolling Meadows Mall Disaster. Oh, yes.

The day he was assigned to the fourth floor was the day he'd met Tucker.

"Hey," the way-too-skinny bald boy in Room 468 said as Bobby pulled a clear trash bag full of old flowers and get-well cards from the bin.

Bobby looked up. He never made eye contact with patients. They were like baby animals on a farm. Don't name them, you might get attached. They were all going to die, the piglets, the calves, the lambs, the little bald boy wired to so many machines he looked like a cyborg.

"What?" Bobby asked, his voice low, eyes avoiding the boy's Lex Luthor head, the ghost-white skin, the body of a concentration-camp prisoner.

"What's your name?" the boy asked simply. His voice was weak, but probably as normal as he could muster. "My name's Tucker."

Bobby couldn't tell the boy's age. He might be twelve or eighteen, lying in that hospital bed under painfully white sheets, his identity wiped away by whatever had stripped his color, his hair, his hope. Tucker? Sounded like a guy who punched bears for a living, not someone who was going to die from cancer.

How much time did he have? Bobby wondered, then realized he shouldn't care.

"Bobby," he said. No one at St. Joseph Children's Hospital had asked him his name. To patients, family, doctors, Bobby was part of the scenery, like the elevator; if you pushed the right buttons, everything worked. Nurses talked to him. Some even tried to joke with him, but no one else knew his name, only the custodians he worked with. "My name's Bobby."

"Nice to meet you, Bobby," Tucker Peterson said, that sad, blank face managing a smile. "Would you do me a favor?"

Favor? Me? "What do you want?"

He pulled a crisp, tight twenty-dollar bill from a "Get Well Soon" card with Garfield on the front. "I'd really like a Snickers bar."

[9]

There were no lights or bells. No wavering spots in the air like in the movies. A sudden change in air pressure was all; everyone grabbed their ears as they popped when Jillian disappeared. Uncle Boyd pushed back from the table.

"What the hell?"

His mom screamed, and his dad just sat there, his expression blank. Emily backed away, leaning against a kitchen cabinet, one hand in her jeans pocket, the other wrapped around a beer can. Jillian reappeared seconds later, stepping from behind the floral centerpiece in the middle of the table, still dressed in his mom's clothes, but she was six inches tall, and her clothes would fit a doll.

"This is what I saw in the garden, Mom," he said. "I saw a fairy, this fairy."

Jillian perched herself on the saltshaker and waved.

"What is this?" his dad asked, his face drained, ashen.

"It's Jillian, Dad. She's not from here."

"No kidding," whistled out of Boyd. Thomas's uncle's face had grown red. He looked like he might punch someone.

Jillian vanished from the table in another pop, and a little girl—*the* little girl—appeared beside Thomas, in his mother's jeans and pink blouse now fit for a ten-year-old. The change in air pressure hit Thomas again. He opened his mouth to pop his ears. His mom jumped, but she didn't scream.

"I'm sorry I took your son from you, but we only spent two days in my world, eleven years for you," Jillian said, her voice high and tiny. "We've been hiding from the monster."

"Monster?" Boyd said, standing, his hand on the butt of his service revolver. "I've never seen a fairy in my life, but I have seen you. I did see those muddy footprints change size, and when I went upstairs, I saw you in Tommy's room." His voice began to shake. "Back then, your face was full of needle teeth. If there's any monster, I'd say it's you."

Thomas stepped forward. "Uncle Boyd, no. She's not a—"

"Monster," Emily finished. "Yes, she is."

Jillian stepped back, hiding behind Thomas.

"And you are?" Thomas asked Emily.

"She's—" Boyd began, but Emily shushed him.

"Oh, I can speak for myself, Mr. John McClane," she said. "My name's Emily Kristiansen and I'm Sheriff Boyd Donally's girlfriend, if it's any damn business of yours. I've seen her likes before, and she's a dark elf, that one."

"What are you talking about?" Thomas shouted, his face flush with anger, panic. "She's *my* girlfriend, and you both need to back off."

Boyd's jaw muscles clenched. "Do you know what your *girlfriend* is, Tommy?" Thomas started to speak, but his uncle cut him off. "She's a monster, and she has lizard teeth."

"Stop it," Thomas said, the strength gone from his voice, his face now pale.

A thought tugged at the back of his head telling him he'd seen those teeth, but he couldn't remember where.

"Boyd's right." Emily's beer can clanked on the counter as she stepped next to her boyfriend. "You don't grow up in the North-woods of Minnesota with oldies not so far removed from back home, and not have seen and heard some things," she said. "You betcha she's oh fer cute, but she's got teeth, and lots of them."

Boyd leaned forward. "You seen her teeth, Tommy? No?" He stared at Jillian. "Go ahead and flash 'em, sweetheart."

The pressure changed again, this time with a pop, and Jillian disappeared again, the little girl reappearing next to Boyd. He yelped and stumbled backward into the cabinets. His hand dropped from the pistol grip.

"No, Sheriff Boyd," Jillian said, her tone deep, ancient. "I'm not the monster. The monster we seek destroyed my world. It has made its way into your world. We must stop it, or everyone will die."

"You," Boyd said, his arm outstretched, shaking as he pointed at Jillian, "the monster is you."

Her smile glared at him.

Thomas's dad rose from the table.

"Would you just be grown-up Jillian again?" he said to the little girl. "You've made your point."

Another pop and she was back, sitting at the table as if she'd never moved.

Emily slapped Boyd on the shoulder. "Shoot the damn thing before it does something," she said, attempting to push his flaccid hand onto the handle of his revolver. "Pump some lead into this monster, Sheriff. If you think this older is here to save anything, it's her own ass."

Boyd's muscles suddenly relaxed, and he leaned against the table.

"I appreciate your concern, Emily," he said, his words steady, calculated. "But I'm not shooting anyone—yet." His head tipped toward Jillian. "I did see you in Tommy's room. I woke up screaming at the image of your smile for years. Those teeth." He choked back his anger. "Those teeth. You killed Loraine Miller."

"I did not," she said. "Elvin did."

"You." The sheriff ground his teeth. "You killed John McMasters."

"No," she said, her voice calm. "Carrie did."

"You," he bellowed, his voice sending Thomas's dad and mom back in their seats. "You tried to kill me on US 36 outside Stewartsville."

"No, it was an accident."

"Was it, now. How come you know all that, having been gone and all?" His hand grasped the handle of his service pistol. "When I saw that smiling-teeth picture drawn on the highway in the blood of a goddamned innocent truck driver, I swore I was going to end you." Sheriff Boyd Donally pulled his revolver and leveled it at Jillian—the little girl with the teeth.

"No," Thomas said, moving toward Jillian.

Boyd pulled the trigger, and the pistol went *click*. He pulled it again. *Click, click, click.*

Jillian held her hands over her head, palms facing the sheriff.

"I love your nephew, Sheriff," she said. "Which means I love your family. I won't do anything to harm any of you. You can stop trying to shoot me now."

"Oh, Jesus, Mary, and Joseph," Emily barked, stomping to the refrigerator and grabbing another beer. "Since this is turning into a shit show, I'm going to get drunk and pass out. Somebody wake me after she kills us all."

Everyone stared at Jillian. Thomas's mom was the first to speak.

"You came to my house as my son's girlfriend. I need to know who . . . or what you are. You said, 'your world.' What world? Are you a space alien?"

Jillian shrugged. "Yes, no, maybe. I don't know," she said. "My world is similar to yours; it's connected to yours. It's close."

"Mars?" Thomas's dad asked, his tone flat.

"No. Not physically close. Dimensionally close." She stopped and looked at him. "It's hard to explain."

"It's like Doctor Who visiting the Garden of Eden, Dad," Thomas said. "Or the Star Trek mirror universe. I think her world is ours, it's just behind a curtain. I've been there."

He turned to Jillian, who nodded along with him.

Emily migrated to sitting on the butcher block, swinging her legs beneath her, playing on her mobile phone as the others sat around the table staring at each other.

"If you told us this with a straight face, your mother and I would have had you back in the mental ward before morning," his dad said. "But you showed us." He turned to Jillian. "Jillian showed us, and I still don't believe it."

"Jesus Christ, Kyle," shot from Emily.

"Jillian is not dangerous," Thomas said, slipping his hand into Jillian's. "But there's something in St. Joe that is."

"This monster?" His uncle Boyd pushed his half-empty beer can away from him.

"Yes, the monster," Thomas said, his voice on the verge of pleading. "As much as Jillian is the fairy, this thing is the monster. We both saw it. It's in the body of a Girl Scout."

"A Girl Scout?" his dad asked.

Jillian's voice was soft but commanding. "It's not a Girl Scout, it's *inside* the Girl Scout. Inside her corpse. When we saw it, it was in an advanced stage of decomposition."

Thomas's mom threw herself to her feet, walked to the sink, and turned on the water, squirting in too much liquid dishwashing soap; hot sudsy water began to fill the basin.

"I don't believe a damn word that comes out of your mouth," Boyd said to Jillian.

"How long ago was this?" Kyle asked.

"I don't know. It was in 2005, however long ago that was," Thomas said without hesitation. It was the last year he really remembered.

Boyd hissed a "damn," and drummed his fingers on the table.

Jillian turned toward him.

"First," the sheriff said to Jillian. "Don't say a damn word. I don't know what you did to me, but whenever your witchy little spell is over, I'm going to shoot you in the face." He inhaled deeply before continuing. "A Girl Scout, a Millie something. Millie . . . Millie Novák, and her mother, Carley? No, Karen. They disappeared in St. Joe around that time. If I remember correctly, the last time they were seen was in a neighborhood down by the stockyards," he said, reaching to the mic on his shoulder. "I could find out quick enough, but—"

Thomas motioned before speaking, but a force pulled back his hand. He turned to Jillian. "I'm trying to defend you here. Stop trying to control me. I'm not some goddammed doll."

The room fell silent, the ticking of his mom's bird clock the only sound for one, two, three—

Jillian rested a hand on his forearm. "Sorry."

"So," Emily said, her words beginning to slur. "What's this so-called monster of yours going to do?"

Jillian looked at her and cocked her head. "It's going to kill people. Suck their life out," she said simply. "It's going to do this to a lot of people, the ground, the water, and the sky." She paused, worry filling her eyes. "Oh, no. Has it started already? It has, hasn't it?"

"What?" Thomas asked.

"Dauðr and Bobby," she said, turning toward Boyd. "Have there been any more mass deaths in or around St. Joseph in the past eleven years, Sheriff?"

Boyd stuck his shaking hands in his pants pockets. "Mass? Well, yeah, there was the high school. Mid-Buchannan. A fire during a basketball game back in, oh, maybe 2005 or 2006."

Thomas's mom shook her head. "That was just awful."

"What happened?" Thomas asked.

Boyd took a deep breath and sighed. "Somebody set the place on fire, but not before blocking all the doors. Nobody made it out of there alive."

"Jesus," Thomas whispered, then turned and looked at his uncle. "Were there any others?"

"A bridge collapsed," Thomas's dad said. "Right before Christmas."

Boyd nodded. "Yeah. That one's unsolved too."

The stomach knot that plagued Thomas as a kid gripped his insides. "Did people . . ." His voice faded.

"Die?" Boyd asked. "Twenty-seven. It was an Atchison County case, so I don't know much more, other than they never found out who did it."

"Bobby could have done it," Jillian said, looking at Thomas for confirmation.

"Or you," Emily said, raising her hands in mock excitement. "Oh, there's a monster, and it's going to kill us." Her hands lowered to the cabinet. "How come you know so damn much about what this thing is going to do unless you're in on it?"

Jillian crossed her legs, her hands in her lap. "What do you want from me?" she asked. "I've shown you what I am. I've warned you of the monster. All I want is your help."

"All we've seen are parlor tricks," Emily said. "And a 'monster'? What if you're the monster? I think you are. Boyd knows it's true."

"Hey," Thomas snapped. "Calm down."

Emily's eyes narrowed. "I am calm. But what I want to know next is why aren't the rest of you freaking out at this? Deborah? Kyle? You saw what this lady did, and she kidnapped your son. Does he look eleven years older? I'm asking because I have no idea."

Thomas stood. "We're wasting time, and we've already wasted eleven years. This beast, this thing, I saw it. It was the thing that killed me in the cornfield. It's already killed me once; it's going to do it again. But it's not going to kill just me. From what Jillian's said, it's going to go all out and claim a lot of people. It's going to do something epic."

"The mall," Uncle Boyd whispered.

"The mall? What do you mean?"

"The ricin attack," his dad said. "Somebody dumped homemade ricin into the ventilation system. It poisoned everyone in the mall. It killed around a hundred and fifty people. They never caught whoever did that either."

"One forty-seven," the sheriff finished, his hard eyes still on Jillian. "It's not my jurisdiction, but I was there. It was big, so a lot of us were called in. Sheriff, highway patrol, FBI. Everybody. Two days after the attack no one realized happened, fifteen people were dead. Two days after that, it was a hundred and forty-seven."

He fumbled with his beer can. "And Kyle's right. We never caught the guy, but someone in a white hazmat suit and protective mask walked out the employee entrance that day and disappeared out of range of any security cameras. It was well planned out. We had no leads, no suspects, nothing." Boyd stopped, his jaw muscles clinched.

"And a girl disappeared that day. A Marguerite Jenkins, twenty-two, from Savannah. She was waiting on a lunch date to show up while she stood in that parking lot across from TGI Fridays. Her car and shattered cell phone were found in just the spot where the security cameras don't reach."

Thomas didn't like where this was going.

"You two know anything about this?" Boyd asked.

Jillian nodded. "Yes," she said. "We know who did it."

A deep exhale escaped Thomas as he sat back, and told them all he knew about Bobby Garrett.

The candy bar cost $1.50. Bobby bought it at the gift shop from an old lady volunteer who smiled too much, and he got back on the elevator. He didn't know what he was doing buying that candy bar. He didn't interact with anyone. That was the plan. Sweep, mop, dump trash, dust the administrator's office, and run the waxing machine over the floors. Easy. Invisible. Do your job and go home, Bobby. Go home and work on the C-4. That's your real job. He gripped the candy bar in his pocket as gently as if he were holding a baby rabbit.

The elevator door opened on four, and Bobby stepped out, his hand in the front right pocket of his uniform. Invisible Bobby. That would be his name if he were a Batman villain. Invisible Bobby. He walked past people crying, people oblivious to their upcoming reality, and nurses who had better things to do than notice him. He walked into Room 468. The little bald boy lay in his tube-crossed bed and grinned.

"You got it?"

Bobby nodded, and pulled the Snickers bar from his pocket, the twenty-dollar bill wrapped around it. Tucker started to protest, but Bobby waved him off.

"Why'd you want this so bad?" Bobby asked.

Tucker peeled off the wrapper, the chocolate black in the darkened room.

"I'm going to die," the boy said. "They know it, I know it, but they won't let me eat what I want. This is my favorite candy bar."

Bobby's eyes drifted to the Mylar balloons of soccer balls and Spider-Man that stretched toward the ceiling.

"How long you got?"

Tucker shook his head. "Nobody really knows. A month maybe."

Maybe, Bobby thought. But probably a lot less.

"You want another one tomorrow?"

The boy's eyes sprang to life. "Yeah, I would."

"Tomorrow then," Bobby said, and left the room. Out in the hall, he became Invisible Bobby again.

Chapter Fifteen

2016

[1]

BOBBY FISHED IN HIS PANTS to push his erection to the side, his boner uncomfortable in his tighty-whities. He'd also had an erection when he loaded the ricin into the mall ventilation system before he unleashed a slow death on 147 people. Maybe this is normal, he thought.

The side door to his garage screeched on little-used hinges, and Bobby stepped into the freezing-cold barn-like building, four home-made snowman bombs cradled in shaking arms. Calm down, Bobby boy. He felt for the light switch with his shoulder, rubbing up and down like a cat. Eventually he caught the switch and clicked it on.

The room stayed dark.

"Damn it." Bobby felt his way to the rear of the car with his knees, and gently laid the explosives on the trunk. His erection throbbed in his jeans.

Wait, he told it. Just wait.

It took him ten trips to move all the explosives from the kitchen to the car and lay them in the front seat, on the floorboard, and across the back seat. He slowly shut the back door of the Caddy, red LEDs on the homemade timers all reading 11:42 p.m. His erection had grown painful. He pulled his pants down over his slim hips and jerked once, twice, three times and came on the car's pale yellow door. Bobby leaned on his left elbow against the glass and exhaled, the air shooting from his lungs in short, foggy bursts.

His lust subsided—lust for what? Death, Bobby, death—and the image of the bald white boy swam into focus.

I can't kill him. But Bobby shook his head. No. Tucker was a good kid, but he was weak, and everything weak deserved death. Besides, Tucker was dying of cancer. Bobby was doing him a favor.

"Bobby," Marguerite called from the kitchen, the door pushed open, her stupid body bulging slightly at the midsection of her stupid six-year-old red dress. She looked toward the garage, her rounding stomach now more than a pooch, and Bobby looked back. His mind lurched when he realized she was probably pregnant. Bobby shook his head slightly as if to send the thought flying. It didn't work.

"You're letting all the heat out," his dad would have yelled.

Bobby could see her in the light, and he knew she could see him, staring over the top of the Caddy. She—no, it—could probably see his dick still in his hand.

"Bobby, honey. I want to come, too."

"The seats are filled with—" He almost yelled "explosives," but stopped himself. He didn't want to tell the whole neighborhood. Not that anyone lived close by anymore. The nearest neighbor, Mrs. Bethany, died of a heart attack not long after she found her dog stuffed into the mailbox, and the Madsen boy with the loud car was sitting pretty in the Crossroads Correctional Center in Cameron. "—snowmen. The seats are filled with snowmen. There's no room."

She folded her arms beneath her breasts and stuck out her bottom lip. "Poopy," she huffed. "You never let me do anything fun."

Fun. Yeah, this was going to be fun. But Bobby knew before Dauðr started playing house inside her, Marguerite Jenkins's idea of fun was probably getting drunk on Moscow Mules out of copper cups and dancing with girlfriends at a club. Watching explosives shred a city was not on her to-do list, he was sure. To hell with her. It. Whatever.

The plan. It had taken Bobby years to come up with it. Had he been the one who came up with it? As he stood there staring at the thing in the red dress, his spunk crawling down the Cadillac door, he saw himself sitting at the kitchen table poring over maps of St. Joseph and hand-drawn diagrams of the children's hospital, where he pushed a mop bucket. Marguerite always looking over his shoulder, pointing out problems, offering suggestions, her boobs mashed into his shoulders. He never questioned her suggestions, never said no. Was this plan really his? Or was it Dauðr's?

Marguerite stuck her tongue out and stomped into the house, slamming the door behind her. Bobby folded his now flaccid penis into his underwear that hadn't been white in a long time and fastened his pants. It stomped inside, probably upstairs to their bedroom, to sit in his mother's desk chair staring into the night. Bobby caught it doing that almost every night when he woke to piss. It just sat quietly, looking into the darkness. He never questioned what it looked at; he never questioned Dauðr at all.

A grin crept over his face, the kind of grin that caused people to look away from him and step to the other side of the street. The car's back door moaned as he opened it again. He gently pulled an empty McDonald's bag from under a pile of explosives, picked up one of the deadly snowmen, and gently placed it inside the sack. He stuck a roll of duct tape he'd bought for tonight under his armpit and began to hum the theme song to *Gilligan's Island* to drown out his thoughts. Dauðr could always tell what he was thinking, and he wanted nothing more than it to think about a three-hour tour.

[2]

Thomas hadn't liked how anything had gone since he arrived at the old farmhouse.

Not at all.

Emily made her way to the sink and began to wash the dishes his mom had run the water for and forgotten about.

"She didn't have to drug us," she slurred. "She's a darkling, darling."

Jillian sat silent for a moment before she spoke, ignoring Emily, her eyes fixed on Boyd.

"No, Sheriff. No drugs. I'm fae. At least that's what the new agers call people like me." She toyed with her coffee mug, her eyes never blinking. "People have called us fairies, elves, gods, trolls, elementals, demons, monsters, husband, wife, lover and, yes, darklings." Jillian's words rattled off like a cadence. "I'm just like you, Sheriff. I eat, I drink, I laugh, I watch *My Name is Earl*, I poop, and if I drink too much my head hurts the next morning. The only difference between us is that I can walk through walls. Can you walk through walls, Sheriff?"

Thomas's dad coughed. "You're telling us something unbelievable," he said, the words hard as steel.

His mom reached out and grabbed his dad's right hand. He never looked away from Thomas. "I thought you'd failed again, son," he said. "I thought you were dead, or worse."

His mom squeezed her husband's hand. "I think what we all want to know is, what do we do now?"

Emily turned from the sink. "Pray, would be my suggestion," she said. "Or better yet, shoot her."

Jillian's cup slammed onto the table; lukewarm coffee sloshed out. "Why do you hate me?" she asked. "Or are you just afraid?"

Emily slid an arm around Boyd's shoulders and leaned over the table. "Both. One of your kind came to my grandpa's cabin on Blackduck Lake one fine summer's evening, begging for food. My grandpa was a widower, and this fine-looking young thing tossed some kind of spell over him, and he invited her in for the night, sending my folks and me home while she stayed. The little bitch winked at me too, just as I walked out the door."

Thomas crushed his empty aluminum can and dropped it on the table. "Some strange woman flirting with your grandpa—"

Emily's hands slapped the table. "Not some strange woman. A fae. I was the last one out the door, and she transformed into a little fairy just like this monster did tonight. That's when she winked."

[3]

"Marguerite," Bobby called when he walked through the kitchen door. She wasn't waiting for him there or downstairs at all.

"Go to hell," her voice called from upstairs, soft but angry. She must have her face shoved into a pillow.

She sure got pissy when she— "Got pregnant?" he whispered.

Bobby forced the *Gilligan's Island* theme to meld into *The Facts of Life* as he went into the basement, pulling the door from the kitchen open so slowly it hardly made a sound. The stairs creaked slightly. Bobby walked on tiptoes at the outside of the steps to keep the groaning of the old wood from the beast upstairs, but he knew the monster heard things it shouldn't.

He stopped at the bottom of the steps and flipped on the light. He'd spent his childhood playing here away from his parents, away from people. Running his trucks across the concrete floor, which was always dusty, drawing pictures of spaceships on half-used yellow legal pads. The basement had been part of his life. Now it would be part of other people's death. Behind the enormous old furnace, the Girl Scout's mom leaned against the dryer. His parents glared at him through empty sockets inside skeletal faces, the flesh long gone, the gray skin peeling off. He walked over to them, took off the plastic hat and Groucho glasses, and sat the party favors quietly on the dryer. They'd been dead a long time, and he'd finally bury them. It was about time to show some respect.

Bobby hummed the *Beverly Hillbillies* theme now. Let that asshole read my mind while it worries about a man named Jed. He nodded at his parents' corpses and went to the middle of the house; a load-bearing beam ran beneath the first floor of the old home. He slowly took the homemade explosive from the McDonald's bag and checked the wiring. Everything was still in place. The duct tape ripped when he pulled it off the roll, the noise too loud in the silent basement. He stopped and listened, but nothing moved upstairs. No voice berating him came down the steps. Bobby pulled off a piece of tape with his teeth and secured the snowman to the beam. The clock wired to the bomb read 11:50 p.m.; the alarm was set to 3:15 a.m. Bobby changed his hum to a whistle, and started *The Andy Griffith Show* theme, not too loud, but not too soft. He pushed his left thumb onto the "alarm set" button, and his right index finger on the one marked "hour," then "minute." The red light ran from 4, 5, 6, until Bobby stopped at 12:30 a.m.

He patted the bomb like one would a child's head, then turned toward the stairs.

A shiver ran through his body as a warm whoosh of arid wind pushed past. What the hell?

A giggle, slight and distant. Another shiver ran through his shoulders as he turned. A spot, red and wet, grew on the concrete wall above his parents as if an invisible hand were covered in paint. The spot grew into a handprint. The handprint of a child.

A hot, copper odor touched his nostrils. That wasn't paint. The red was blood. Bobby ran up the stairs and out the door.

[4]

The Cavanaugh kitchen sat quiet.

"What happened?" his mom asked, her face slack.

"My daddy found him the next morning, dead. His body shriveled, drained of every drop of liquid a human body should have." Emily pulled a chair next to Boyd's and plopped into it. "The coroner said he'd never seen a damn thing like it."

Jillian sat for a moment, eyes glazed, until Thomas squeezed her arm.

"I'm sorry that happened," Jillian said, the coffee cup back in her hands. "But that wasn't me."

"I'm sorry that happened." Emily snorted.

Uncle Boyd laid a big hand on her small one and squeezed.

"You sure this Bobby fella is responsible for the ricin deaths?" he asked, his face flushed, but from beer or anger, Thomas couldn't tell. "That'd be something I'd have to follow up on."

"He did it, Uncle Boyd," Thomas said. Jillian set a hand on his shoulder, and a calming, cool sensation sank into him like he'd stepped into a walk-in cooler. He looked at her smiling face and turned back to Boyd, his anger suddenly gone. "Jillian and I met at Sisters of Mercy, but we also met Bobby there. I wasn't crazy, Jillian wasn't crazy, but Bobby, Bobby was. The kind of crazy that counseling and pills can't make go away."

"The kind of crazy who could poison a mall full of innocent people?" his dad asked. "To set fire to a full gymnasium?"

Jillian nodded. "And more," she said. "But he wasn't acting alone, I'm sure. Bobby is dangerous, but to kill on such a grand scale, he had to have help."

Boyd's right eyebrow shot up. "Help? Where does Bobby's help figure in all your bullshit?"

"It's not bullshit, Uncle Boyd," Thomas snapped. "When we saw Bobby, we saw the corpse of a Girl Scout and . . . and it talked to us. Jesus, it talked to us."

Boyd ignored Thomas, his eyes trained on Jillian.

"There's no evidence this Bobby person did anything. Just your word, and I don't trust that one bit," he said. "I can't go arrest a man on suspicion of being in cahoots with an evil spirit. Not that I don't believe in evil spirits. I've seen evil because I've seen Miss Jillian's handiwork. Promised myself I'd take her out the next time I saw her. Now, can anyone tell me why I shouldn't do that right now?"

The mic attached to the right shoulder of Uncle Boyd's uniform cracked to life. He leaned toward it and pushed the push-to-talk button. "Sheriff Donally here."

"Because if you kill me . . ." Jillian's voice came through the mic as Uncle Boyd stared at her, his mouth open. Hers didn't move. ". . . the monster will succeed and we're all going to die. Thomas knows how to kill this beast, but he can't do it without me."

The Sheriff's face, the pink drained from it, hung slack. Uncle Boyd took a handkerchief from his back pocket and mopped his sweaty forehead. "You've made your point," he said softly. "I need to think for a second."

Boyd looked at the clock over the sink, a bird clock, with each hour chiming a different bird whistle. He took a few deep breaths and looked back across the table, his gaze shifting from Jillian to Thomas.

"You say this Bobby—what's his last name?"

"Garrett," Thomas said. "Robert Garrett."

"So, this Garrett boy carried out, but didn't necessarily orchestrate, the ricin attack, and the fire at the basketball game, and the bridge, and he's planning something else soon, something big in St. Joe. All that correct?"

"Yes," Jillian said. "Dauðr's power has grown. Its hunger is intense. The killing will start soon." She stopped. "I can feel it. It tears at me. I think it starts tonight." She stood suddenly. "We must go."

Boyd frowned. "You know where this Bobby fella lives?" he asked Thomas.

Thomas told his uncle the street, but not the house number. He couldn't remember it.

"I have his name, and general location, if he still lives there," Uncle Boyd said. "Whoever's manning the station tonight will get me to that house. It won't do any harm to go ask him a few questions. I'm going to go look around, and if I find anything, I'll make a call," Boyd said. "You want to come with me?"

Thomas shook his head. "No, Uncle Boyd. Jillian and I are going to hunt for Dauðr our own way."

Boyd nodded and stood, looking directly at Jillian. "This is not over, missy. I don't know what you did to my weapon, but I had it aimed straight at your heart. If what you pulled tonight turns out to be a big scam to distract me from your involvement in all this, I swear I will end you. Understand?"

"Uncle Bo—" Thomas began, but the sheriff ignored him.

"Can I get some coffee for the road, sis?" Boyd asked. "I think I'm going to need it."

Emily lifted her head from Boyd's shoulder, a string of drool following her.

"Me too," she said. "I'm going too."

[5]

"So," Thomas's mom said after Uncle Boyd scooped his sheriff's hat off the counter and walked out the screen door, Emily behind him. Her index finger traced the design on her coffee cup as she spoke, like she didn't know where she should look. "I know I asked this before, but what do we do now?"

Thomas stood and walked to the sink, pouring out the rest of his beer, the words "In-Sink-Erator" set in the ring around the mouth of the garbage disposal suddenly looking odd to him.

Through the window over the sink, he could see Uncle Boyd standing by his patrol cruiser, pissing Miller Lite in the glow of the motion-sensor light.

Emily was already in the car.

Thomas's dad rose, but Thomas waved his hand.

"Nothing," Thomas said. "You and Dad do nothing. Just stay here. And don't watch the local news."

Kyle balled his hands into fists. "What are *you* going to do, son?" he asked. "Everything tonight has been, it's been—"

"Crazy?" Thomas finished.

His dad nodded.

Thomas grabbed Rodney's pistol from the table; he had a feeling his uncle had forgotten it on purpose. Outside, the cruiser roared to life and headlights flashed in the kitchen as it turned and headed down the gravel lane.

Jillian put her arm through his.

"Boyd is looking for Bobby," Jillian said, her eyes directly on Thomas's father. "The other monster, Dauðr, it's not with Bobby anymore. He's off creating the destruction, the monster is doing something else."

"And how can you know that?" Thomas's father asked, his voice tired.

Thomas tried to speak, but the thought died in his head.

"Because in some ways I'm like Dauðr, Mr. Cavanaugh, and Thomas is much like Bobby," she said. "The four of us are connected. I hope your brother-in-law finds Bobby and stops him. It will make our job with Dauðr much easier."

Kyle started to talk, but Thomas cut him off.

"Dad." His hand dropped to the talisman in his pocket, the pistol clanking against it. "Please just stay home. I faced this thing once before."

His dad snorted. "From what you told us, that's the night you died."

[6]

Bobby changed into his blue janitor's uniform in the car in the back parking lot of St. Joseph Children's Hospital, light snow beginning to fall. He slid off his black slacks and draped them over the C-4 in the front seat to keep them from prying eyes. He'd parked far away from the hospital because of the security cameras. He didn't know why he was worried about them; all the recordings would be gone at 3:15 a.m. when the little snowmen blew the heck out of the town. It was just caution, the same caution that had told him to park in the blind spot of the security cameras at the mall near TGI Fridays, and that had worked. When years ago, he first looked up the Rolling Meadows Shopping Mall murders case on the internet, using an anonymous computer station at the library, a picture of him in his mask and hazmat suit popped up labeled "Person of Interest." That was it. Person of Interest. His plan—was it his plan?—had worked flawlessly.

The Cadillac sat next to Randolph's silver Kia Optima. Bobby wasn't thrilled that his supervisor was on the premises. Randolph treated Bobby well, like he was a person and not just a guy who only existed to mop up blood and piss. But he couldn't wait for Randolph to leave. The Cadillac was armed to take out city blocks at 3:15 a.m. It was midnight, and Bobby had a deadline. Get it? DEAD line. He laughed. Screw Randolph. If he took a janitorial shift at this time of night, that's his fault. Bobby just hoped he didn't run into him. It might be awkward.

He got out of the car and walked to the trunk, his shoes leaving prints in the new snow. His duffel was there. He also grabbed a wrench, a big Craftsman, and let it drop into his back pocket. A tickle in the back of his head told him that wrench might come in handy, and he learned a long time ago at Smithville Lake to listen to those tickles.

He walked through the doors that led to hallways that ran underneath the hospital, the doors janitorial services employees and delivery drivers were doomed to use—behind, beneath, out of sight. The smell of hospital disinfectant struck him as he entered the basement. The odor permeated everything in the hospital: the corridors, his clothes, the overpriced flowers at the gift shop. Everything. Bobby wondered if the smell went with him when he went home, but he knew the answer. It did. Aromas like the hospital's stench soak into anything and anyone until it just becomes part of them.

The delivery doors opened to a wide hallway that ended in a T. To the left was the cafeteria, and that meant employees (whatever janitors were on duty—Randolph among them—the hospital lunch ladies, interns, nurses) and the few family members still trolling the hospital to grab a bite while waiting for their child to die from leukemia, or a brain tumor, or whatever it was kids were into these days. To the right was the true underbelly of the hospital. The furnaces, the generators, the morgue, and storage, with big steel and concrete pillars that held all ten floors of St. Joseph Children's Hospital off the ground. He couldn't get to the pillar in the cafeteria. This wasn't like a normal hospital where the cafeteria closed after supper, letting all the hungry folk feast on boxed dinners of cold sandwiches and apples. This thing catered to the families of sick children, and it was always open. But everything else open to Bobby and his ring of keys should be quiet for the night.

The knock on the door to the downstairs women's restroom rang hollow. He waited, but no one cried out a "busy," "I'm in here," or "occupado." The handle turned easily, and Bobby pushed the door open to the three stalls. He clicked the lock in the middle of the knob. No poopus inturruptus this morning. Can't have any of that. Another door sat at the back of the bathroom between the row of sinks and the last stall. Bobby walked swiftly to it and pulled out the key ring attached to his belt by a chain, picking the key he'd marked with a glob of his mother's old pink nail polish. Inserting it into the lock, he swung the door open to a closet—a half closet, really. Stacks of toilet paper and paper towel rolls rose from the floor, wedged against a steel and concrete pillar. Bobby smiled. This was it. One out of eleven.

Bobby unzipped the duffel with more noise than he would have liked, amplified in the small space. The C-4 snowmen all huddled together like kittens trying to nurse. He gently lifted the first explosive from the bag: 12:15 turning to 12:16. His hands shook with excitement. Come on, Bobby. Come on. He pressed the bomb onto the concrete as he wrapped duct tape around the pillar, ripped off the piece from the roll, and stood back. The bomb stuck with silver efficiency.

"Is there anything duct tape can't do?" he whispered, then checked the time on the bomb against his watch. Both read 12:16.

Fourteen more minutes. And then the house, Dauðr, Marguerite, his mom and dad . . . boom.

Bobby zipped the duffel closed and stifled a giggle. He draped the strap over his shoulder. The thought of all the children from across the Midwest that lay sleeping above his head suddenly struck him. Children with parents and grandparents and friends and—

You never had any of that, Bobby. It was Dauðr's voice. Or was it? *That bad Johnson boy wanted to screw you, Bobby. People like him are here. Right here.*

Bobby shook his head. *Stop it. Just stop it. I—*

The bathroom door rattled. Someone knocked.

Bobby silently shut the closet door and removed his key.

"Hold on," he called toward the door, then checked his face in the mirror. Black half-moons clung to the skin below his eyes like leaches. *Damn, I look tired.* He leaned forward; the whites of his eyes were lined with the jagged lightning bolts of veins. *No kidding. Look what I'm living with.* He knew what existed inside Marguerite. It was what Mother always warned him about. Old Scratch. He was screwing the beast inside Marguerite—the devil.

Bobby turned the knob to the bathroom door and pulled it open to see Randolph. He expected to feel something, anything, regret at Randolph being here the night he was going to blow up the hospital, but he was wrong.

Fancy that.

"Bobby?" Randolph stood just outside the door, his hand on a mop. "What are you doing here?"

Killing you. "Callie called. She's sick. Wanted to know if I could cover her shift." *Lies. Lies. Lies.* But Bobby felt comfortable with that. The truth always tasted bad in his mouth.

Randolph frowned; his hairy jowls drooped like a cartoon dog's. "Callie's not scheduled for tonight. Connie is."

Bobby opened his hand and comically slapped his forehead. "Connie." *Bobby, you're an idiot. But a lucky idiot.* "Don't know why I said Callie. Connie called. Bad sushi or something."

"She should have contacted me," Randolph said, leaning forward on his mop. "What are you doing in the women's restroom? You don't have any cleaning supplies."

Bobby smiled. "I just came in," he said, the words now flowing from his mouth like they were true. "Hershey squirts. Somebody left a dumper in the men's john. It smells like the stockyards in there. It's almost 12:30 in the morning. I didn't think it would be a problem if

I used the girl's bathroom." He paused and shrugged his shoulders. "I locked the door."

Randolph frowned, the expression under his beard quickly turned into a smile.

"It's okay. I'm just a little concerned over Connie. Protocol is she calls me, not someone to fill in for her. But that's fine. I'll talk with her when she's better."

Really? It was that easy?

"Well, then," Bobby said. "I'd better get to work. That nuke in the men's room ain't going to clean itself."

[7]

Boyd's bladder decided it'd had enough. He pulled off Carter Street and eased the car to a silent stop behind an abandoned car wash. A rusty sign above the black, gaping entrance to the auto wash read "Lickity Slick," an obvious attempt at something sexual, but it was lost on Boyd.

"What are you doing, hon?" Emily asked. Boyd had hoped she'd fall asleep before they arrived. Just not his day.

"Just shakin' the snake," he said, opening the car door. A couple argued somewhere nearby. He hefted himself from the low seat and quickly eased the door shut. Nothing as obvious as a dome light needed to draw attention to the illegal public indecency in the St. Joseph city limits. Too much beer at Debbie and Kyle's, too much messed-up talk.

That'd be a hell of an end to the night, he figured, a St. Joe cop pulling up and arresting him for being over the limit and waving his dick around. Boyd stepped into dead, knee-high weeds and let it fly, steam escaping into the night. He'd learned long ago as a county deputy that when you're out in BFE and have to piss on the road, it's best to do it in the weeds. Keeps splatter off your shoes.

What the hell are you doing, Boyd? he wondered, sneaking a look at the cruiser, Emily leaning back in the passenger seat. You got it good, man. This is a goddamned fool's errand, and you know it.

Fairies. Monsters. Bullshit. But the image of Loraine Miller's head smashed open rushed through his mind. The smiley face on the wall. The girl with the teeth in Tommy's room, on the highway on the way back from Cameron, in Carrie McMasters's house when she killed her husband and finished a jigsaw puzzle covered in his blood. And Jillian. Jillian turning into that little girl right before his eyes.

Fairies do exist, goddammit.

Boyd zipped his pants and got back in the driver's seat. He pulled out of the crumbling Lickity Slick parking lot back onto Carter Street, the distinct scent of the nearby stockyards faint in the cold night. Carlyle Street was nearby.

Emily slid an arm over the computer and between the seat and the shotgun mount, resting it on Boyd's leg.

"What are you going to do when you find this Garrett fellow?" she asked, the slur she'd had at his sister's house gone.

The man's name was Robert Joseph Garrett, Donny back at the station had told him. Forty years old. No record except for a little something called murder back when he was fourteen. Killed another boy named Ronald Day Johnson, sixteen, at a lake campground in 1990. Bashed the kid's head in with a chunk of concrete. Spent time in a juvenile facility before a transfer to Sisters of Mercy Hospital in St. Joseph, where he stayed in the psych ward for about a year. Released because the doctors said so. Could this guy be capable of pulling off the ricin attack? The fire at the school? The bridge?

Donny said records showed he was questioned in the Rolling Meadows Shopping Mall case. Worked at the mall as a janitor, so he had access to the area where the killer delivered the ricin. Bobby wasn't scheduled to work that day, but that didn't mean anything.

Could Bobby have orchestrated all those murders? Fucking-A right he could. Maybe Tommy's right.

"I hope to just have a little chat," he said. A green-and-white street sign leaning off a pole like a drunk read "Carlyle St" through flakes of snow beginning to thicken in the headlights. "Damn it."

Boyd drove by the street entrance, hit the signal arm, and made a U-turn. Nobody looked twice at a cop making a U-turn, and given the amount of traffic that wasn't on Carter Street, nobody cared. He passed a convenience store and turned onto Carlyle.

"Well, if you're going to have a little chat, you'd better hope he's awake," Emily said. "It's twelve twenty in the morning."

The street looked abandoned. He drove past the large houses, mansions compared to the house where Boyd lived. This area of St. Joe was wealthy once, a long, long time ago. As Boyd drove down Carlyle and across a bridge, the overhanging trees creating a tunnel, he figured he could pick out the meth houses just by the couches on the front porch.

The cruiser's headlights cut a sharp slice into this dark road, most of the streetlights dead—no reason for the city to replace them.

"Hey," Emily said, pointing out the window. "You see that? That woman, the woman in the red dress with no coat. I think she's pregnant. She shouldn't be walking in this neighborhood."

Shit. He did not.

"Honey. If she's walking in this neighborhood and didn't yell for us when she saw law enforcement cruise by, there's a good reason for it."

"But—"

"Emily." His voice louder than he'd intended. "Sorry, but we need to focus. That girl didn't need us, or she'd have let us know it. We're on our way to 4244 Carlyle—" Boyd leaned forward to get a good look at the mailboxes as the cruiser crawled past; the first one he could read was 4002 "—and we're close. We ought to be there by twelve thirty. Maybe a few minutes before."

Boyd scratched the long-overgrown five-o'clock shadow on his chin and wondered what were his chances of getting Emily to stay in the car.

Chapter Sixteen  2016

[1]

BOBBY RIPPED DUCT TAPE OFF the roll and wrapped a strip over a deadly snowman, securing it to a support pillar between the hospital's two enormous diesel generators. One generator to keep the hospital running during a power outage, the other a backup. He patted the main generator, his palm against the full tank a flat slap.

"There's going to be a power outage in a couple of hours, fellas," Bobby said. "You boys ready?" He laughed; his voice echoed in the long room. Quiet. Quiet. Must be quiet.

Bobby stood still, listening. Nothing. The room was as silent as a funeral parlor, but Randolph wandered around the hospital somewhere, and Bobby didn't need to draw attention to himself. There was no reason for Bobby to be in the generator room. No reason at all, except to blow up the hospital. Bobby had done everything right so far. He knew it, but arming the hospital had taken longer than he'd expected, and Randolph showing his goateed face now might be a problem, one he didn't want to deal with.

Twelve twenty-five. Five minutes, just five minutes until his house went up in flames, and that monster was gone from his life. No more fear, no more pain, and no more sex. He wanted to see his house explode in an orange rain of fire, taking Dauðr back to hell, or wherever it came from. Hefting the duffel strap over his shoulder, Bobby hurried to the beige metal door that led back to the hallway, the bag bumping the backs of his thighs. He froze, the duffel swaying back and forth like a wrecking ball. Most of the explosives were still in the Caddy, lying beneath bits of Bobby's clothing, but there were still two in this bag. He'd hoped to see his house explode from the parking lot, but there was no way he'd get outside the building before the show. He didn't even know if he'd see the blast at this distance.

Bad planning, man. Bad planning.

Bobby reached for the door handle, but before he opened it, he knew Randolph was on the other side, looking for him. He took a deep breath and pulled open the door. Randolph was there, keys in his hand.

"Been looking for you, Bobby," Randolph said, a frown beneath the black goatee flecked with gray. "What are you doing in the generator room?"

Think, Bobby. Think.

"Just filling in for Connie, you know," Bobby said, the words coming out as smoothly as the truth.

Randolph hooked a ring filled with brass keys and fobs onto his belt and folded his arms across his large chest.

"Really," he began. "Funny thing is, Connie is in ICU right now, mopping the floor, just like she was scheduled to do. She feels fine. Said she hadn't talked to you for a week." He stared at Bobby, narrowing his eyes behind his black horn-rimmed hipster glasses. "Now, what are you doing in the generator room?"

Bobby stood half in, half out of the room, the door resting on his left shoulder. He set the duffel on the concrete floor and stood up straight, his expression as "aw shucks" as a redneck caricature in a B-movie.

"Sorry, Randolph," he said, his right hand drifting behind his back. "It's just that . . . well, I need the money. I wanted a few extra hours."

"I don't want to hear it, Bobby," Randolph interrupted. "You lied to me."

In less than five minutes, a slight tremor from his house exploding might just run through the concrete under their feet. Bobby tensed. He had to do one more thing in the hospital, then get outside to watch the show, and Randolph was in the way.

"Gosh, Randolph. I sure am sorry," Bobby said, his fingers wrapped around the handle of the Craftsman wrench in the back pocket of his janitor uniform.

"I ought to fire you for that, Bobby. I ought to—"

Bobby didn't let him finish.

He slammed the box end of the wrench against Randolph's temple. Blood splattered the wall, and Randolph's body crumpled into an ungainly pile on the floor.

Bobby swung his arm a second time and brought the wrench down squarely on his boss's forehead.

"I'm late," Bobby hissed, his hand still on the wrench handle, Randolph's blood dripping from his face. "I gotta go watch my house blow up, Ran-douche." He slammed the heavy piece of Craftsman steel against Randolph's skull again. Blood ran over the floor.

"Damn it," he said. "Now who's going to clean that up?"

[2]

The Buchanan County Sheriff's Department cruiser slowed to a crawl in front of 4244 Carlyle Street. Boyd pulled the car to the side of the road and stopped, the well-kept brakes silent as a nod. A turn of the key, and the car died, the huge engine capable of hitting 150 mph going from a soft purr to silence in seconds. Procedure was to keep the car running in case he had to leave in an instant, but procedure went out the door tonight.

The lights inside the house showed from every window, although Boyd couldn't see movement. The house still listed Todd and Vera Garrett on the title, even though Donny at the station couldn't find one trace of them, except they paid their bills on time. Seventeen years ago, the Garretts stopped using their credit cards and stopped voting. Except for Social Security checks that kept getting cashed, and the paid bills, Mr. and Mrs. Garrett had disappeared.

"Stay here," Boyd said, opening his door, although he knew he'd probably wasted his breath.

"Not on your life, baby," Emily said. "You need backup."

"Goddammit," rushed out, and Boyd lifted himself from the driver's seat and pushed the door shut without a sound.

Snow pelted his face as they got from his car and onto the sidewalk. He paused and listened. The neighborhood was quiet. Too quiet. Maybe all the drug dealers had seen the car with the cherries, or maybe they were at a Sudafed convention. They walked along the short path to the Garrett house, the tall, dead grass on either side long gone to seed, the imposing Victorian structure a horror movie come to life. Boyd slowly went up the snow-covered steps. The ancient, heavy front door hung wide open.

"Watch out, honey," he said to Emily. "This is suspicious as hell." He knocked on the slight wooden frame of the screen door.

"Hello," he said through the rusty screen. "This is Sheriff Boyd Donally. I'm looking for Robert Garrett."

He leaned close to Emily. "What time you got?"

She kissed his ear. "Twelve twenty-five."

Boyd wiped his mouth with the back of his hand. Sweat had formed there despite the cold, and his hand shook as he raised it toward his face. Something was wrong. Something about Bobby and his missing parents. Boyd had been a cop since he graduated high school back in 1974. It's all he'd ever wanted to be. Police academy in St. Joe, city cop up in Maryville, deputy in Buchanan County, then sheriff. He'd been on high-speed chases, broken open doors with a battering ram, and tackled a murder suspect waving a kitchen knife like it was a Fourth of July sparkler, but he'd never felt like this. Boyd knew something, deep, deep down, and he hated it.

For the first time since he was a kid, Boyd Donally was terrified.

"Get in the car, Emily," he said, his voice shaky.

She slapped his butt. "Not on your life."

Boyd cleared his throat.

"This is Buchanan County Sheriff Boyd Donally," he yelled into the house. "I need to speak with Robert Garrett."

Snow began to accumulate on the door's mesh.

"If you don't respond, I will step inside the house and search for him. Please respond now."

Nothing. The air inside the house was dead. A smell drifted onto the porch as the furnace kicked on, something brief but heavy enough to reach his nose. He sniffed. Light, floral. Febreze. He had the same kind in the cruiser because he'd spilled a beer in there once and had to take the presiding commissioner—the man who signed his paycheck—on a ride-along the next day. The shit worked. It covered up any smell that needed covering. Boyd reached inside his coat to his right shoulder and clicked the engage button of his walkie-talkie.

"Donny."

Static, and finally a voice. "Yes, Sheriff."

Boyd stared through the screen door.

A lamp lit the foyer, the shade on crooked, the metal base dented and encrusted with something that looked a little like rust. Nothing moved inside that house.

He was sure no one was home.

"Donny, I'm about to enter the residence at 4244 Carlyle. The front door is unlocked and wide open. Contact St. Joe police. Have them send a car down here. I'm pretty sure no one is here, but something's off. This could be a crime scene. I'd feel better with some company."

Static. "Will do." Donny clicked off. More static ran through the speaker before he spoke again. "Boyd, you're not going in there by yourself, are you? That'd be dangerous."

He looked down at Emily, her eyes still slightly glazed but bright at the same time. Snow flecked her hair. She grinned.

"I kind of have backup, Donny. I don't have much choi—" A scream wailed from deep inside the house and his voice died in his throat. An unmistakably female voice had said, "Help me." He was sure of it.

"I gotta go in," Boyd barked into the mic. "Somebody's in trouble. Call St. Joe PD *now*." He opened the screen door and stepped inside.

———— ✳✳ ————

The house needed a good cleaning. Old food bags from Murph's American Sammiches and Taco John's littered the floor of the foyer, and as Boyd could see through the arches that led left and right, the mess wasn't confined to the front room.

"Bobby," he called, not expecting a response. Either Bobby was gone or waiting, and if he was waiting, neither of them was going to enjoy it. Boyd stepped toward the dented lamp and bent forward, pulling a cheap pen from his breast pocket. The rusty spots flaked off at the flick of the pen. Blood. Old, dried blood. He shot up, his hand on his service weapon, a revolver he'd strapped to his side every workday for thirty years. With a thumb, he unhooked the leather clasp that held it snugly in its holster and wrapped his hand around the grip. Yes, something was wrong here.

His boots thumped through the dining room. Dust covered the few parts of the table not stacked with garbage, but Bobby wasn't there. Boyd inched his way toward the kitchen, keeping close to the wall, the pistol in front of him like a shield. A microwave with the door broken off lay on the floor, the refrigerator pushed over onto its front. But the table pulled his eyes wide. Empty Silly Putty containers and Vaseline jars? Bottles of cooking oil? Boxes of corn starch?

"Oh damn," he whispered. Wire cutters and nubs of plastic wire covers stripped from the empty shells of clock radios sat on one end of the table.

Something bad happened here.

The digital display on the stove stacked with pizza boxes read 12:26.

Boyd stepped into the room. A smell, something Febreze couldn't cover, rose from the wide-open basement door. Garbage? Feces? Boyd stepped over the trash and toward the door.

A figure stepped into the kitchen from a hallway, and Boyd's weapon snapped to his eye.

"Jesus Christ, Emily," he panted, his heart slamming against his ribs as he lowered the pistol. "I almost shot you. What the hell are you doing?"

Her face, white with fear, glared at Boyd's. "I'm sorry, baby," she said, the words almost not there. "I thought we could cover more ground this way. I don't think there's anyone upstairs."

The stove clock moved to 12:27 and a woman's voice moaned from the basement: "Help me."

"Stay with me," he said and approached the basement door. "We have to get that woman and get the hell out of here before something bad happens."

Her eyes grew wide. "What?"

He ignored her.

"Hello," he yelled down the steps. "I need to talk with Robert Garrett. This is Sheriff Boyd Donally. You are not yet a suspect in a crime, but we need to clear a few things up so you won't be." Boyd moved down the creaky steps, stopping when he reached the concrete floor. The light at the bottom of the steps was bright enough to cut any suspicious shadows. He took one step, his weapon clasped tightly in his hands. Boyd was comfortable with guns. Boyd had pulled this weapon once already tonight and had thanked God he didn't kill anyone.

This situation smelled like he just might.

"Bobby," he said, although he knew he'd get no answer. "Bobby Garrett, my patience is running thin. If you are in this house, you will speak to me. This is Sheriff Boyd Donally and I'm finished playing around. If you don't come out now, I'm going to take you in when I find you. Obstruction of justice, Bobby. Make it easy for yourself and talk to me. Now."

"Help me," the woman cried again, closer this time. Her voice. Goddammit. Boyd knew her voice. "Please help me."

Then it came to him.

No. It can't be.

Boyd moved around the big, old furnace in the center of the room with Emily in tow. She screamed.

"Jesus H. Christ," shot from his mouth in a whisper. A woman in a light blue dress, a trail of blood from her nose, stood next to three bodies, dry as firewood, that sat propped against the wall opposite the stairs. "No. You are not."

"We gotta get her out of here," Emily whispered. She stepped forward, but Boyd stuck an arm out to stop her.

"No," he said, his eyes on the woman in the blue dress.

"Boyd," the woman said. "I've missed you."

Emily stopped still. "You know her? Then damn it, grab her."

"No, Emily," he said, his voice flat. "That's my wife. She's been dead for years."

Boyd stepped closer slowly, oh so slowly. These people on the floor had died of head trauma; the skull of each had been cracked open with something heavy.

Like a metal lamp.

But Maggie? Maggie shouldn't be here.

"I don't know what you are," he said to the woman in the blue dress. "But you're not my Maggie. Please. Please go away." Sweat soaked Boyd's undershirt. He moved his pistol to eye level, Emily silent beside him.

The thing that looked like Maggie cackled, then exploded. The red mist of what the thing had been quickly dissipated and Boyd froze at what it left on the wall, a mark that glistened in fresh blood. A red handprint the size of the girl's.

"It's gone now, Boyd, honey," Emily said. "Stay with me."

He fingered the walkie-talkie again. "Donny," he said. "Come in, you sonabitch."

Static. Then a voice. "Sheriff?"

"You better tell me St. Joe PD is on its way to 4244 Carlyle Street now. Right now. I got bodies in the basement, and the name of the suspect."

"Sheriff?"

"Do you read, Donny?"

Static.

"Goddammit," he grumbled. "I lost contact with the station."

Emily rested a hand on his arm. Boyd grabbed her hand and turned toward the steps.

[3]

The lights of St. Joseph hung on the horizon. The old Chevy Nova, stolen more than a decade ago from some guy Thomas would never meet, moved jerkily down the highway like it didn't want to, snow growing thicker under the bald tires. Thomas hoped the car got them to town; he'd figure out the rest later.

An enormous green-and-yellow fireworks warehouse, the kind that dotted interstates across Missouri, loomed to the right, the giant inflatable gorilla strapped on the roof moving slightly in the falling snow. Fireworks were legal here 365 days a year. Thomas wondered if they should stop and buy something explosive just in case they needed it, but Jillian rested a hand on his thigh, and the thought disappeared.

Hell, it was closed anyway.

He knew she was directing his thoughts; he just didn't care—the world was coming to an end.

"Do you feel anything?" Thomas asked, leaning forward in the seat, both hands grasping the wheel as if strangling it. He glanced at her, the traffic on the interstate light, the stretch of highway straight but growing white. "Do you?"

She turned toward him, her eyes wide and wet. "Yes," she said, her voice soft, distant. "It's begun."

"What? What's begun?"

Jillian reached forward and rested her hands on the dash next to the sun-bleached Happy Meal toys superglued to the vinyl. Her eyes glazed over.

"Jillian?"

She shook her head. "I don't know. We have to get closer."

Thomas leaned back in the seat and pushed the struggling old engine as hard as he could, hoping they didn't slide off the road.

[4]

"Damn it, Donny." Boyd fiddled with the controls on the walkie. Static hissed like a lizard as they moved up the steps and into the kitchen. "Come in, come in. Donny."

Nothing. Emily latched her arms around his waist, something she couldn't do when they began dating, and buried her face in his shoulder.

They reached the first level and Boyd twisted, shrugging Emily off, both hands back on the gun. The revolver hovered in front of him, his finger tight on the trigger, too tight.

"That wasn't there before," Emily said, her voice trembling. She pointed at the kitchen wall. "What is this?"

He lost his balance and fell against the basement door. A bloody picture smeared the wall. The drawing, painted with a hand, was childish: a circle with two lines for lips curved into a smile. A smile of thin, pointed needles.

"We gotta get out of here," he said, his voice low and hollow.

"Why?"

A grandfather clock chimed somewhere in the house. Once. To mark the half hour: 12:30.

It never chimed again.

[5]

The floor shook as Bobby stepped into the fourth-floor hallway. The clock over the nurse's station read 12:30.

Aw, man. I missed it.

Tucker lay in his bed in Room 468, the dull, shadowless glow from the hallway and the bright red LEDs of the monitors strapped to the boy the only lights in the room. The kid's raspy breathing cut through the night, the rhythmic beep of the heart monitor his only company. The boy was days away from death, hours now, Bobby thought coldly.

"Bobby?" he asked in a soft voice.

Bobby went to the bed and pushed the rolling table out of his way; an insulated hospital cup of ice water and a stack of get-well cards sat on top. "Yeah, I'm here. How do you feel today?"

A deep laugh rattled in the boy's skeletal chest, and he reached up to wipe something dark from the corner of his mouth. Blood.

"Ready for anything," he said. "Bring on the girls."

The boy knew he was going to die; he was taking it with humor. Bobby wondered how he'd take the knowledge of his own death. Probably not with a smile, that's for sure. His left hand slid inside his uniform pocket, pulled out a candy bar, and set it in Tucker's hand.

"Brought you something."

Tucker lifted the candy so he could see it without moving his head.

"Hey, Bobby. Thanks." He struggled against the IV drip as he stretched for the table Bobby had pushed out of his reach. "Let me get you some money."

Geez, kid. Bobby touched the boy's shoulder, and gently eased him back onto the pillow.

"That's okay, Tucker. It's on me."

"You sure?" the boy asked, his voice weaker than Bobby had ever heard it. Tucker winced. The boy was in pain too. Lots of pain. He felt the kid wanted to die, and his feelings were never wrong.

"Yeah, I'm sure. Let's call it a going-away present."

Tucker frowned. "A going-away present? You, or me?"

Both, kid. Both. "Me. I'm moving on. Just thought I'd come up and say good-bye."

"But—" Tucker started. Bobby cut him off.

"I'm late as it is," he said, and started toward the door, then stopped and turned toward Tucker. "I'd eat that right now if I were you. You know what'll happen if a nurse catches you with it."

Tucker held up the Snickers bar. "Thanks, Bobby."

Bobby nodded and walked out the door. You don't need to thank me, kid, but I am doing you a favor.

[6]

"Car's overheating," Thomas said to Jillian, who was perched at the edge of the passenger seat, hands flat on the cracked, dusty dash. "It needs water, and a quart of oil wouldn't hurt."

"We don't have time," Jillian said.

Thomas steered the vehicle onto the off ramp and into the lot of Jesse's Last Stop convenience store. The car chugged to a stop and he put it in park.

"We don't have a choice," he said as Jillian pulled his hand off the steering wheel and grasped it tightly. "If we don't get the engine cooled down, we walk. I need to open the hood. In this weather, it shouldn't take long."

Jillian hovered her right hand over the dash, her eyes closed. A spark closed the gap between her hand and the cracked vinyl, a violet light flashed in the night, then went dim. Frost crystals formed on the windows. A slight crackling popped and tinged through the cab as the ice grew, like it needed any help.

"The car is now cool," she said. "We have to go."

Thomas stared at her, his breath coming out in visible puffs. The heat gauge that had seconds before been in the red, sat buried on Cold.

"We have to hurry."

He was reaching toward the gearshift, when Jillian screamed. Her arms shot to her sides, fingers digging into the shredded vinyl seat. She gasped. Thomas grabbed her shoulders.

"Jillian," he yelled. "What's wrong? What—"

"Thomas," she said softly, and turned toward him. Tears glistened in her eyes. "Your uncle and his girlfriend are dead."

"What?"

"Boyd and Emily. I saw a flash of yellow and orange, then I couldn't feel them anymore." She wiped her eyes on the shoulder of Deborah Cavanaugh's coat. "But I could feel Dauðr. It's stronger."

Uncle Boyd. Gone? Memories overwhelmed him. Sitting in Uncle Boyd's boat with fishing lines in the water, a Pepsi between his knees, and Uncle Boyd and his dad drinking beer. Uncle Boyd taking him to the Dairy Freeze for chocolate malts after Little League games.

His shoulders slumped.

The rusty door of the Nova groaned as Thomas tried to get out, but Jillian grabbed his arm.

"Where are you going?"

He tried to pull his arm from her grip, but she was too strong. "Let me go, I gotta call my folks."

"There's no time. Bobby has done something, is still doing something. If we don't act now, many more people will die." She took his stubbly chin in her hand and turned his face toward hers. "He's the reason your uncle is dead. Please. We have to go."

He sank into the seat, put the stolen Nova in reverse, and backed out of the parking space.

[7]

Sirens cut the night when Bobby burst from the loading doors and ran into the parking lot, his slick shoes nearly face-planting him onto the snowy pavement. A fire truck roared by the hospital, south toward Bobby's neighborhood. He thought he could make out the soft glow of a large fire, but it was too far out to tell. He knew it. The house had exploded, the monster was gone.

"Gone," he yelled into the night. "I am free."

He jogged across the asphalt to the Cadillac, his legs not used to that much exercise. He scanned the lot for anything. People, cops, monsters. Nothing. Just the employees' cars that had been scattered around the lot when he pulled in. The Caddy's windshield was now covered in a growing layer of white.

"I did it." He slowed and looked behind him, but only saw the hospital lit by spotlights on the grounds. "I did it," he shouted into the snow, and unlocked the door to the car. He gently laid the duffel in the back seat and shut the door.

The dash clock read 12:35 a.m. Two hours. That gave him just two hours to place the rest of the pretty little snowmen and get back here to see the show. And Bobby wanted to see this show; it would be glorious. He pulled a piece of yellow legal pad paper from the duffel, notes scrawled over it in his jagged script, and checked off "St. Joseph Children's Hospital" with a blue pen. "Amoco on Felix is next." He started the car and drove toward the gas station.

The monster may be gone, but Bobby knew he was too far in to stop.

Chapter Seventeen  2016

[1]

THE DEFROSTER FINALLY HEATED enough to melt the frost on the windshield by the time Thomas saw the Felix Avenue sign on Interstate 229; the old Nova sputtered and coughed like a smoker.

"Pull off here," Jillian said.

"Why?"

"Just do it."

He pulled the car onto the off ramp, and into downtown St. Joe, leaving a greasy trail in the air behind it. The St. Joseph Civic Arena and a Holiday Inn among old brick storefronts dominated the view from the highway.

"Bobby's down here somewhere," she said. "I don't know where, but I can feel him. He's close by. He's done something in this area. Something awful. What's down here?"

The car coughed down the off ramp.

"The arena, a couple hotels, those big grain bins down by the river, the hospital—"

"The hospital," Jillian said, then turned toward Thomas, her face blank. "He's done something to the hospital."

"Oh, no. No, no, no. That's a children's hospital." Thomas woke up in that hospital after his first fight with Dauðr had left him dead. "What the hell did he do to it?"

The well-lit ten-story structure flashed between the tall downtown buildings as Thomas coasted the again-overheated Nova down a hill lined with bars and pawn shops.

Jillian shook her head. "I don't know."

Thomas wiped the tears running down his face and turned right, toward the hospital, the old Nova picking up speed.

"The car's not going to make it," he said. "Can you do that purple glow thing to keep it going?"

She looked away from him and out the side window. "No, Thomas. I can't. The car's too far gone. Not even I can make the dead come back to life."

My mom could, Thomas thought as he took his foot off the gas and let the momentum take them as far as it could. She brought me back to life.

[2]

Bobby sat across the street from the Phillips 66 C-Store, the lights of the hospital in the rearview mirror. He waited for a pickup full of rednecks to leave. They had to be rednecks, there was a Confederate flag in the back window, and a "No Fat Chicks" sticker barely visible through the snow on the bumper. And there was the cowboy hat. Two men, one in the hat, the other looking like Larry the Cable Guy in a flannel shirt with no sleeves—in *this* weather?—walked from the convenience store, the cowboy carrying a microwave burrito and a bag of pork rinds. Larry carried a bag of beef jerky. The cowboy set the food on the dash, opened a cooler in the bed of the truck, and handed four beers to his buddy through the back window. He laughed and slapped the side of the truck.

"Come on," Bobby hissed. He sat behind the wheel of the Cadillac pulled to the side of the street, headlights off, the falling snow swirling in the glow of streetlights. The truck was in his way, wasting his time, and time was something Bobby didn't have. Three of his little explosive snowmen wired with old alarm clocks lay in the front seat. Minutes clicked away as the rednecks dicked around in *his* spot.

The cowboy finally lifted himself into the front seat, the tight Wrangler jeans pulled up his ass crack. A minute later—a full minute—the cowboy started the truck, and it crawled away from the gas pumps and out of the convenience store lot. Bobby flicked on the headlights and pulled in behind the truck, which went over the curb on its way out. He stopped the Caddy next to the cast-iron lids that led to the three underground gasoline tanks, blocking the view of the caps from the shop. He'd mapped his route well, marking where all the targets were in relation to the gas station clerks and the view of any cop who might drive by.

This station was risky, there was nothing to shield Bobby's work from anyone on the street, but it was late at night on a weekday with shitty weather. Nobody but rednecks with a hankerin' for microwave burritos would drive by at this hour.

Despite the planning, his first target, the Amoco station on Felix, had taken too long. The heavy iron lid had been too much for Bobby to lift on his own. He'd opened the hood to the Cadillac, looked under it like he'd planned, walked to the passenger side, which faced a brick enclosure for a dumpster, and stuck his fingers into the groove of the lid. It moved but didn't come off its cradle. He finally removed it with the tire iron, placed his friendly little package, pumped five gallons of gas, went inside, and bought a lottery ticket. He won two bucks. "Tonight's my lucky night," he told the clerk.

He now had a system, and this convenience store a mile from the children's hospital was going to go down like a glass of milk. Bobby got out, walked around the front, raised the long yellow hood, and looked underneath, pretending he knew what he was doing. He was safe.

Human beings are lazy, Bobby knew. If he looked like he was in trouble, people would actively avoid him, turning their gaze like he was a leper.

The tire tool was next. Opening the passenger door, he took the L-shaped metal wrench used for loosening lug nuts, bent and wedged the flat end inside a notch on the metal gas tank lid buried in the asphalt. One shove, and it lifted off the top of a tank that held eight thousand to ten thousand gallons of gasoline. Just an explosion waiting to happen.

Easy peasy, lemon squeezy.

Reaching inside the open door, Bobby pulled out a plastic grocery bag; his homemade C-4 and a detonator set for 3:15 a.m. lay in the bottom.

The bag slid into the hole that Bobby covered with the lid, part of the plastic bag wedged under the lid and filler cap. The bomb would hang like mistletoe over enough unleaded gasoline to blow up a city block with just a kiss—and there were two more tanks buried on either side of it. Kablooey.

A loud car creaked and clunked down the hill. He turned, and an old rusty Nova was pointed toward the parking lot. Bobby froze and watched the car grow closer, snow catching in his hair. Something was wrong about that car with one burned-out headlight, he just didn't know what. Dauðr was gone, blown up—or was it? Is that the monster? Could it be her? Bobby stepped in front of the Caddy and buried his face in the shadow of the hood. The front left tire of the old Nova thunked as it hit the curb—just like the stupid truck with the stupid redneck cowboy—and squealed to a stop on ruined brakes in the far corner of the Phillips 66 parking lot.

Smoke rolled from under the Nova's hood; its doors flew open and a man and a woman spilled out.

He didn't believe it.

A smile split Bobby's face. Jillian, the pixie girl from Sisters of Mercy, stood on the passenger side of the Nova, looking across the hood, her face pensive. He never could read her, but the other, oh yes, the other. He could read him. The dead-alive boy stepped out of the driver's side, looked across at Jillian, and nodded. Jillian stared across the hood of the old, ruined car at Bobby standing under the open hood of the Cadillac.

She's looking at me, rushed through Bobby's head. Is she looking at me?

Jillian hurried around the smoking Nova and stopped next to Thomas.

"I can't fix it this time," Jillian said loud enough Bobby could hear. "We'll have to go by foot."

The dead-alive boy grabbed Jillian's hand, and they abandoned the old car, running toward the hospital. St. Joseph Children's Hospital.

"What just happened?" Bobby said, his voice low as he slammed the hood shut. There were still two snowmen in sacks on the front seat. He'd planned to place one at another gas station, the other at Burton Propane, but this was better. The dead-alive boy and the elf girl.

They were going to get the last two snowmen no matter what.

He slid into the driver's seat and put the car in gear, slowly following his new targets down the street.

Jillian looked at me, she looked right at me. "No. Couldn't be," he said to himself.

The dash clock read 2:45 a.m.

[3]

A stitch stabbed Thomas's side, a gremlin hanging onto his ribs with a knife, his wind gone. Thomas ran cross-country in high school, but high school was a long, long time ago. His feet flapped to a stop, and he bent, wheezing, next to one of the black-and-rust lampposts that lit the sidewalks with pools of yellow light, snowflakes drifting in and out on his breath. For the first time ever, he wondered if he might be having a heart attack.

"Wait a sec." His hands dropped to his knees as he sucked air; the streetlight above him flickered, and swarmed with insects. He struggled to focus. No, not insects. Snow. It's winter. "Let me catch my breath. I just need a minute."

Jillian stopped and ran back to him; she grabbed his arm and pulled. He didn't budge.

"Come on," she pleaded. "We must go. I will help you if you need me to, but we must continue."

He looked up into her pleading eyes.

"No," he said. "I'll be ready in a second. Just winded, that's all."

She frowned and bit her bottom lip. "I don't know what's happening, but I know it's happening at the hospital, and it's happening soon. We have to stop it, or something awful will happen. Not just to everyone in that building," she said, pointing toward the hospital that looked to Thomas still miles away. "But to everyone in this town. And not just your people."

Jillian reached out and turned his face to hers with a soft hand. "Mine. My people too. Remember, Thomas, fae fled Ālfheimr. You saw them. Some are here."

She pulled at his arm again, and Thomas stood straight, his breath returning.

"I love you, you know," Jillian said. Leaning forward, she softly kissed his cheek.

Thomas nodded, and started running again, but slower, his muscles screaming against the cold. The hospital was still a few blocks away.

[4]

"Clock's ticking, people," Bobby barked into the cab of the Caddy as it slid silently two blocks behind his new targets, the lights off. The dead-alive boy had collapsed by a lamppost like he was dying—again. Bobby pushed the brake pedal and slammed his palms on the steering wheel.

"Come on, come on," he spat. "What're you doing? Making snow angels? Time's a wastin'."

The elf girl grabbed the dead-alive boy and probably did some fae voodoo on him. That had to be it, because the man stood and started jogging with her toward the hospital, where Bobby had duct-taped eleven homemade bombs to the core of the building, ready to "make boom" at 3:15 a.m. What the hell were these two dumbwits doing here? How did they know what he had done? How *could* they know?

But, Bobby knew they couldn't stop the fun, even if they knew where the snowmen were.

"You're too late," he said, kneading the steering wheel with both hands, twisting the cheap grip pad his father had wrapped over the wheel forever ago.

The dead-alive boy and the elf girl made it another block, their footprints following them in the snow, something Norman Rockwell would have painted if he painted pictures of people who'd be dead in a few minutes. Bobby eased his foot off the brake pedal and onto the accelerator. The Caddy crawled forward in the still night. It was the only car on this street. Good. Bobby knew a cop could screw up his plans something fierce.

The dash clock read 2:55 a.m.

[5]

St. Joseph Children's Hospital rose from a great sea of parking lots, a giant thumbs-up in the night. The old brick buildings of downtown St. Joseph seemed to be from another world, or at least another time. Thomas and Jillian stumbled off the street and into a lot. Thomas stopped and bent forward, his hands on his knees, breath coming hard.

"We're here, Thomas. Hurry, hurry."

I can do this. He dropped to one knee. I have to. "I'm—" He paused, chest heaving. "Coming." Thomas stood, wiping the sweat from his face with a coat sleeve. Jesus Christ, I'm dying.

He took a step toward Jillian and a big yellow car, an old-model Cadillac, shot into view, coming to rest after a snowy skid about ten yards away. The car stopped between them and the hospital.

"What the—" Thomas started. The driver's side door flew open, and a man with dark hair and blue coveralls stepped out. Thomas squinted. The man looked familiar. He looked like—

"Bobby," Thomas whispered.

Jillian grabbed his arm. "It's Bobby."

"What have you done, Bobby?" Thomas called out, his voice shaky.

The man, his bulging eyes darting, looked from Thomas to Jillian and licked his lips like a drunk as he stepped away from the vehicle, a tire iron in his right hand.

"What have you done, Bobby?" Bobby mocked in a falsetto voice. "What are you, my mother?" He touched his chin with an index finger. "Oh, no. You can't be my mother because I beat her skull in with a table lamp."

Thomas threw a protective arm across Jillian.

"Dear old Dad's too." Bobby scratched the back of his head with the metal tool. "You know what it's like when you're a grown-up and still live with Mommy and Daddy? It's embarrassing, Tommy. So, you either have to pack up and leave, or they do." He brought the tire iron down with a slap into his left palm.

"What'd you do to my uncle, Bobby?" Thomas said, taking a step forward, the cold now forgotten. "Sheriff Boyd Donally. He came looking for you. Jill says he's dead."

"I don't know anything about your uncle, Tommy," Bobby said, then stopped. A grin grew on his face. "The sheriff? Looking for me? Was he at *my* house?" He laughed. "Well, then I'm afraid he went boom," Bobby said, flaring the fingers of his left hand. "My house went away rather suddenly."

"You blew up your own house?"

"Don't worry. He wasn't alone. Dauðr was in there with him. Kablooey. Sayonara to that creeper." Bobby looked inside the Cadillac, then back toward Thomas. "Time's running thin for our little conversation," he said, slapping the tire iron into his left palm again. "If the dead-alive boy and the elf girl would please come closer, I'll tell you what I did, and where I did it. I'll even give you my car so you can get there faster. Thomas, you don't look like you can run very far. You need to keep up on your cardio."

Thomas reached into his pocket and pulled out Rodney the Meth Head's .25-caliber pistol. He pointed it at Bobby and pulled the trigger; the muzzle blast sliced through the silent night. The bullet struck the car door next to that crazy bastard, shattering the window; glass flew, and Bobby shrieked like a little girl. The tire iron fell to the pavement, the metal ringing as it clattered to a stop.

"Don't kill him," Jillian begged, grabbing his arm where snow had begun to collect. "We need him to tell us what he's done to the hospital."

Thomas shook her off. "I grew up with guns," he said, his body tense. "If I wanted him dead, he'd be dead."

Thomas turned back to Bobby. "What did you do to the hospital?" he asked the greasy man, his teeth clenched. Thomas stalked closer, the pistol aimed at Bobby's chest.

Bobby tried to shrink into the Cadillac under Thomas's approach, fear wiping his face blank.

"What did you do?" Thomas aimed at Bobby's shoulder and pulled the trigger. The hammer fell with a click. He pulled the trigger again. Rodney's pistol was empty.

Fuck.

He dropped the gun and rushed at Bobby Garrett.

Bobby was almost in the driver's seat when Thomas reached the car and grabbed him by his loose-fitting work uniform. He yanked backward, hips set firm on the side of the car, and lifted, throwing Bobby onto the concrete. Bobby skidded hands first in the snow, the concrete beneath shredding his palms.

Thomas pounced on him in an instant. "What have you done?" he screamed, planting the toe of his dad's boot into Bobby's side. The dull snap of cracking ribs punctuated the night.

A scream shot from Bobby. He rolled onto his hands and knees, holding up the bloody palm of his left hand, more blood smearing the surface of the lot.

"Stop," he wheezed. "Stop, please stop."

Thomas slung back his leg to kick Bobby again, but suddenly Jillian was there, pulling Thomas away.

"He has to tell us what he's done, Thomas," she said, her voice high and fast. "He has to be *able* to tell us."

Using the car, Bobby pulled himself to his feet, a bloody hand gripping his left side.

"I'm not telling you anything," he hissed, blood glistening on his bottom lip. Then he smiled. "Or maybe I should. It's too late for you to do anything about it now."

"What?" Thomas shouted, then Bobby bent low, scooped up the fallen tire iron and swung it in a clumsy arc toward Jillian's head. Thomas pushed her to the side, and the iron struck his upper arm. The force of the swing knocked Bobby off balance, and Thomas leveled a fist into the madman's stomach. Wind shot out of Bobby, and he started to fall, but Thomas grabbed the overall collar, holding him like a schoolyard bully holds a kid too small for his own good.

"Thomas," Jillian said, but he couldn't hear. The blood rush was too great, adrenaline coursing through his body. He couldn't stop.

His right arm flew forward, striking Bobby's face, the crunch of his nose breaking drowned by Jillian's screams. Blood flowed down Bobby's ruined face, but Thomas hit him again and again. Bobby's eyes jiggled like a cheap doll's, and his head reeled. Thomas pulled back his arm to hit Bobby again, but Jillian grabbed it with both hands and hung on it, dragging the arm down.

"What are you doing?" Jillian shouted; the sound was more like a growl than words. She shook her head, and the rage slipped from Thomas if it were just a passing thought.

His left hand slowly opened, and Bobby dropped in a bloody mess onto the concrete.

Jillian dropped to her knees next to him. "Bobby," she said softly. "What did you do? What's going to happen?"

A gurgle escaped his lips. Air bubbled through the blood pooling around his mouth.

"We need to know, Bobby." Jillian touched his forehead, and the bruised knots that had grown from the pounding of Thomas's fist began to soften and fade. "Please tell us."

"Isss," spilled out. A bloody string of spit ran onto his coveralls.

She leaned closer. Thomas tried to pull her back, but she shooed him off. "Please, Bobby. You will tell us. You have to."

His left eye crawled open. The right couldn't, it was swollen tight as a losing boxer's.

"Iss too late." A dark, empty smile pulled his lips back; he'd lost at least two teeth.

"Too late for what?"

"Ever-thin'."

Jillian wiped a hand over his bad eye; the swelling slowly disappeared. He coughed and blood came out in spurts.

"What?" she asked.

Bobby motioned a hand, pointing behind him. "The hos-hos-hospital. It go boom."

"Shit," Thomas spat.

"When, Bobby?" Jillian was on her feet now. "When?"

He stared at her with both eyes and opened his mouth, gaping like an idiot. "Boom," he said, louder, then cackled. The laugh jerked him in spasms, and he broke into more coughs.

Thomas and Jillian watched as Bobby vomited blood onto the gathering snow.

"Come on," Thomas urged, grabbing Jillian's shoulder. He threw himself into the open driver's-side door of Bobby's Cadillac and turned the key. The enormous old Cadillac engine roared to life. Jillian opened the passenger door, grabbed the two plastic grocery bags on the seat, and dropped into the car, the bags on her lap.

"Boom?" Thomas said. "Explosives? Is he going to blow up the hospital?"

Jillian was silent. Thomas turned to her; the rash on her face was back, this time a deeper red, angrier. She held a cascade stack of C-4 in each hand; a roughly made digital timer attached to each by duct tape and wires read 3:13. One suddenly turned silently to 3:14, the next clock changed a few seconds later.

"What do we do?" Jillian asked, her voice thin, almost missing.

"Set them on the floor," Thomas said. "Gently. Very gently. And run. Don't look back."

[6]

Thomas and Jillian threw open the doors to Bobby's Cadillac and bolted across the parking lot. Thomas didn't know where Jillian was—hopefully running in the opposite direction. He leaped over

Bobby's beaten, bloody form, a wet, red smile still on Bobby's face and the snow around him stained pink. Thomas's side hurt, his lungs burned. Thomas wasn't a runner anymore. He was a mechanic.

Three fourteen. When's it going off, Bobby? When? Do we still have time?

Thomas's boot slipped on the snow, and he almost went down. Flailing his arms, he caught his balance and looked forward. A woman? A woman stood in the freezing night. What the hell? She walked toward him wearing a tight red dress nearly white with snow, her face hidden by a mass of hair frozen white. She was halfway across the street walking directly toward him. And she had a belly. Not fat, pregnant. What was a pregnant woman in a date dress doing in downtown St. Joseph in the middle of a snowstorm?

The thought stopped there because that's when the world around Thomas exploded.

Chapter Eighteen  2016

[1]

IN THE FLEETING MOMENT BETWEEN panic and curiosity, anger and fear, Thomas thought the explosion must have been from the cascading bombs in Bobby's Cadillac. A wave of heat and pressure lifted Thomas and threw him past the woman, who kept walking, seemingly immune to the shock of the blast. He struck the asphalt of the street with his left shoulder—the same spot where Bobby had cracked him with the tire iron—the layer of snow did little to cushion his fall. His body flopped three, four, five times before slamming into the jagged concrete curb, his right ankle bent beneath him. Thomas screamed in pain and looked up, the night alive with fire.

The bumper of the Cadillac lay in the street; scorched slices of pale-yellow metal from the hood, roof, and quarter panels spread across the parking lot. The spot where he'd been standing raged with fire. A body—Bobby's or Jillian's. My God—lay scorched to the bone. Another explosion hit, but Thomas couldn't hear it, not really; the shock waves hit his eardrums like he was underwater.

The ground shook. A burst of yellow-orange flame lit the sky just beyond a gaggle of old brick buildings around the gas station where Thomas and Jillian had abandoned the Nova. A moment of yellow flashed through his mind. An old Cadillac had been parked by a gas pump. Bobby.

Dear God. Did he rig the whole town?

Another explosion rocked the night, the ground uncertain beneath him. Then another spurt of flame shot into the sky maybe a mile away, rocketing far into the night, followed by another, and another, a great ring of destruction.

"Goddammit." Thomas's word was buried beneath the chaos.

Huge balls of fire lit up downtown St. Joseph. Thomas pushed himself to his knees, his right ankle throbbing. The pregnant woman continued to walk through the parking lot, past the burning wreckage of the car, past the flaming corpse, over a spot where snow could no longer survive.

"Jillian," Thomas yelled, or thought he yelled, the sound of his voice dull and too hollow to be real.

A flash flew through his vision; Jillian crossed half the parking lot in seconds, stopping by the wreckage of a Kia Optima before turning and seeing him and the pregnant woman. Jillian's mouth moved, but Thomas could only hear the ringing in his ears.

She ran toward him as the ground cracked and she pulled him from the chasm that burst open, flames erupting where he lay a moment before. Jillian rolled him onto the sidewalk, his ankle absurdly swollen.

"Thomas," she called, but he couldn't hear her. The explosions deafened him. She cupped her palms over his ears and closed her eyes. Purple currents like those that cooled the old, stolen Nova crackled from her fingers and melted into Thomas's scalp. He looked up at her, his eyes and ears suddenly clear.

"Jillian," he whispered.

"Thomas? Can you hear me?"

He nodded, and she let go of his head, wrapped her arms around him, and held him tight. "Are you all right?"

"Yes," he said, his one-syllable word cut short by another explosion in the distance. "Except my ankle. I think it might be broken."

"It's not." Jillian gently wrapped her fingers over his grossly swollen ankle, gripping it as if it was a cantaloupe. The swelling slowly disappeared, and she released his leg.

"You can walk now," she said. "But I don't know if you can run."

Thomas grabbed Jillian's shoulders. "Wait. You can heal people? I died in that damn cornfield, Jillian."

She shrugged off his hands. "We don't have time for this."

He grabbed a fistful of her coat. "I died that night and you didn't *help* me?"

"I told you I can't revive the dead," she said.

His hand dropped from her coat, the wind knocked out of him. She grabbed his arm and pulled. "Come on."

Blocks of downtown buildings raged in flames, three-story structures built at the turn of the twentieth century burned like tinder. But the hospital stood.

"Maybe he didn't target the hospital," she said. "All those children—"

A rumble sounded. Not like the others; something deeper, something more powerful. The pregnant woman cackled in the distance. They turned to see her standing over Bobby's seared corpse, her back arched, arms pointed toward a sky painted with fire.

[2]

More explosions, and the grain silos near the river collapsed; fire danced in their remains. Thomas grabbed Jillian's hands, and together they stood.

"There might still be time," he said, another explosion in the distance drowning out his words.

Jillian looked at Thomas with wet eyes and slowly shook her head.

A low rumble from somewhere underground, followed by a second, a third, and a fourth. The hospital building, its ten stories of steel and concrete leaned drunkenly. Thomas stood, his gaze nailed to the scene. Another explosion and the foundation of the building thundered, then the cracked, fiery ground shook. Jillian grabbed Thomas's arm tightly. The hospital swayed and the eastern corner of the first floor disappeared into the ground. Another explosion thundered from beneath the pavement, and the building tilted backward. Something inside gave way, and the hospital collapsed onto itself; floor after floor crushing the one beneath it. Concrete dust blew in a great burst over the surrounding parking lots.

Jillian brought her coat sleeve over her mouth, her face buried in Thomas's shoulder; Thomas wrapped her in his arms, back turned to the grisly scene. A rush of hot air filled with dust blew over them like they were back in Álfheimr. He steeled his legs against the wind, keeping them upright. The shock wave blasted past them, but as

Thomas released Jillian and looked into the blazing night through squinted eyes—the air clogged with dust mingling with heavier snowfall—the woman still stood, her arms raised over her head.

"Come on." Jillian pulled at Thomas, her face tense and saturated with fear, her cheek nearly covered with the strawberry rash. "We have to finish this. It's her. What's inside her. She's Dauðr."

"Her?"

Another blast sounded in the distance, but Thomas hardly noticed. Jillian's words crept through his thoughts, his attention glued on the woman. "*She's* Dauðr?"

[3]

The woman stood still as the explosions spat fiery death into the sky, her body like the statue of an ancient goddess. She spread her fingers and her body began to sink, to fold over onto itself, as it dropped to the pavement, shedding like a snake skin from the jet-black silhouette that remained, arms to the sky.

"What's happening, Jillian?" Thomas's voice shook.

She didn't answer. Jillian stood next to Thomas, chin drooping, a trail of drool ready to fall.

The sirens grew closer.

Wind, icy cold, shot by Thomas, sweat from the heat of the fire froze in his clothes, frost covered his skin. A cloud of debris from the destroyed hospital spun around them, a dust devil of human faces crawling over each other through the swirling death, biting, snapping, a Lovecraftian horror. Thoughts of running, throwing up arms, tackling Jillian to the pavement and covering her with his body fell from his mind in icy chunks. The frigid tornado of—what?— Souls. Dear God, are those souls?

The tornado threw Thomas and Jillian to the pavement, snow-flakes falling on them again. The swirl of screaming souls, the dead pulled by Dauðr from the rubble of the hospital, weaved toward the monster, striking it, unwinding as if from a spool. The voices of the dead shrieked louder than any siren, any explosion, as the point of the tornado struck the monster in the chest. The impact bent the black shadow creature, but it didn't fall. Its knees didn't buckle. The monster, this ancient monster, absorbed them.

Thomas leaned into Jillian, who lay next to him. "What is it doing?" he shouted, his voice nearly inaudible over the shrieking.

The vortex tail whipped over their heads, a bald child howled past, his eyes sunken hollow pits, followed by a girl—ten? Twelve? Fourteen?—her fingernails raking Thomas's cheeks. The tornado spun back toward the black stain on the night, the tumult of the souls wailing as they slammed into Dauðr, pushing Thomas's face to the pavement, the stench of asphalt, fire, and blood flooded his nostrils.

A hand shook him. He turned his bleeding face to Jillian.

"It's feeding," she said, her voice strangely calm. "Dauðr is feeding. It's strong. It's ready to take its true form."

He buried his face in his hands. What are we doing here? This is madness. Hot tears ran over his skin; only then did he realize how cold it was. The tears melted streaks through the snow that clung to his skin.

Jillian grabbed his arm and shook.

"Can't you see them?" Her eyes bulged from her face.

See?

"The people." Jillian's mouth moved like it was full of peanut butter. "Can't you see them?"

"Yes." Thomas touched his face where the tornado girl had scratched him. His hand came back bloody.

"They're the dead." Her voice was weak and hollow. "The dead are moving. All those doctors and nurses. All the children." She stopped and swallowed. "All of them. Dauðr. It's drawing all of them to it."

Thomas's gaze shifted to Dauðr. The demon had changed. It was now the monster he'd seen as a child in the cornfield.

The monster from his nightmares turned and smiled at him.

[4]

You, a voice in Thomas's head thundered. He grabbed his scalp in both hands, and squeezed, trying to drive it out. *Thomas Eugene Cavanaugh. I am going to eat you. I am going to eat you alive.* He looked up; Dauðr's eyes blazed red.

A hand touched his shoulder. Jillian. She was now on her feet.

She shoved a hand under his right armpit, and tried to drag Thomas up. He didn't move.

"We have to go," she said.

Dauðr raised its hands to the heavens again, not the soft hands of the human woman who lay on the pavement at the monster's feet, but dark, misshapen claws. The air changed, and Thomas's ears popped. A rip, like God had pulled open a bag of potato chips, split the night.

Above the black hulking figure, the sky swirled, splitting the snowstorm with churning lights. Deep colors—navy, violet, green, indigo—churned in a whirlpool over the remains of the hospital.

"What the hell is happening?"

Jillian shook her head slowly, but she did not speak.

A dark shape dropped from the electric vortex and struck the asphalt.

"Holy shit," Thomas whispered.

A giant, black-clawed leg covered in the white fur of a yeti crab, jointed in four, five, six places, gained purchase and straightened. A second leg plunged through the twisting colors and struck the ground, crushing a car beneath it. More legs pushed open the hole, the swirling mass stretching to allow the thing to force its way through.

Jillian stood, pulling Thomas up with her. He grabbed her shoulders and turned her toward him. "Jillian," he shouted into her face, his thoughts spinning.

Her green gaze slowly crept up to him and finally focused on his brown one. "It's the end of everything, you know," she whispered. "Death, destruction. The total annihilation of your world."

He shook her, hard this time. "No." He was close to panic. "We saw this thing, this thing coming out of the sky. What is it doing *here?*"

The enormous creature slammed all its legs on the pavement, and Thomas's world shook like the hospital had fallen again. That thud. He'd heard that thud before. "This is the thing we hid from in Ālf, Ālf, Ā-"

"Ālfheimr," she finished for him.

"Yes."

Jillian nodded. "It is."

"We hid from it then, Jillian," he said, the words running from his mouth, stumbling over each other, "in your safe house, the hole in the ground. We can hide from it now. We can—" His words died in his mouth.

Jillian's face drifted toward his in slow motion.

"Yes," she said. "But we can't stop it."

The entire body of the thing fell through the vortex as if the sky had given birth to a *kaiju* monster. Its human-like eyes gazed into the fire, and a long, sectioned tail ending in a poisonous barb slammed into the pavement. Thomas's hand flew to the spot where that thing's poison had burned his skin; it still stung. The creature raised its enormous head and shrieked with a vertical mouth, its beak an octopus's. Its scream threw Thomas back to the ground.

The vortex flashed, the clouds churning as if the gods were fighting. An indigo hurricane dropped onto St. Joseph, vortices flaring open across the sky, forming gateways over the city. Clawed, hairy legs fell through the swirling holes.

"An invasion," he whispered.

Jillian pressed herself into Thomas's chest.

"That's what it is," she said, regaining her feet. "We need to go. Now."

Thomas didn't move. Jillian touched his forehead; the area around her fingers glowed a soft violet, and he turned his face toward hers.

"Where?" he asked. "Where the hell can we go?"

Thomas looked back at the creature that stumbled forward on unsure legs, one slipping in the snow. The legs of other damned beasts dangled from endless spots throughout the sky—it was the birth of demons. Jillian turned to face the monsters and yanked at Thomas again.

"Now."

His face turned back to Jillian, his mind cleared by the magic of the fae's touch. He smiled. "Okay," he said, his voice calm in the chaos.

Jillian helped him to his feet, and they ran.

[5]

A silver Kia Optima sat in a gravel parking lot across the street. The body of a man, cold enough the snow clung to it, lay sprawled on the roadside. Thomas released Jillian's hand, his boots skidding as he grabbed the driver's-side door handle. It was unlocked. Jillian ran to the passenger side and stopped. Her hand hovered over the handle.

"Ohhhh," whooshed from her. "It was in this car. Dauðr was in this car. That man—" She sucked in a heavy breath. "That man gave her a ride, then she ate him."

Thomas leaned into the car; the key was still in the ignition. The car started easily. "We can't do anything about that. Let's go."

The ground shook. The monster that loomed over the parking lot hammered a giant leg onto the pavement, then another, as it started to lope toward them, Bambi on ice. The beast's shrieks pierced the night, metal grating on metal, as the other creatures forced their way through the churning storm.

"Get in," Thomas yelled, and dropped into the driver's seat. He hit the wiper switch and the plastic blades swiped back and forth across the windshield, pushing away the snow. "Get in, dammit."

The car shook as the monster charged across the parking lot toward them, its multi-jointed legs flying like a badly constructed toy. The enormous creature's tail, a cudgel tipped in poison, crashed into a line of cars and sent them flying.

"Now," Thomas ordered, and Jillian sank into the passenger seat. Thomas slammed the gearshift into drive and jammed the accelerator into the floor. The Kia bounced over the curb and shot into the street as the monster pounded toward them. The beast hit the street and slipped on the snowy surface.

The steering wheel lurched to the left, yanking itself out of Thomas's hands. The car punched over another curb and jumped into one of the lots that surrounded the hospital.

"What are you doing?" Thomas yelled at Jillian, his muscles bunching as he pulled at the wheel. "It won't budge."

"That's because you're going to drive straight at Dauðr," Jillian said, her voice serious, deep.

A memory slammed into Thomas, a lost recollection. No, not lost, hidden. Jillian in the car, him yelling at her. Her face, it, it— split, growing into a smile that covered it, a smile with rows and rows of needle-like lizard teeth. That smile—

Thomas slammed on the brakes and the car skidded as it hit the patch that used to be Bobby, skidding to a stop before Dauðr, its inky black body darker than the night. Above, a second monster was now almost entirely pulled through the whirlpool in the sky.

Thomas turned and saw Jillian's face covered in that red rash.

"You're a monster," Thomas whispered, his old friend the knot in his gut. "You've always been a monster. That's why you didn't heal me when I died. You thought you didn't need me anymore."

The doors flung themselves open. An invisible hand grasped Thomas and threw him across the pavement into the demon storm.

A snap cracked in the night and his ankle folded beneath him. His scream split his throat.

Jillian knelt over Thomas; ice and bits of concrete swirled, pelting them.

The ground shook. Another demon beast dropped from the swirling skies and lifted itself on impossible legs. Its shriek raked at the moaning storm. It stumbled away through the fires and deeper into the city.

Dauðr loomed over Thomas.

"Dad," Thomas whispered.

A man stood in place of the wicked black figure. It was his dad, but not the dad they'd left at home on the farm, with graying hair and a thick waist, but the man they'd faced in the cornfield, the man's mouth with an impossible number of teeth.

"Hello, Thomas," the dad-thing said. "Remember me?"

Thomas grimaced in pain. "You're not my father." The words came out stronger than he felt. "And I'm not a child."

A triangular wedge opened across the monster's face, growing too large for his dad's head, and it smiled—the face full of glistening spikes, just like the ones in the Jillian memory. Above, another horror burst through the churning air, screaming, the sound of its birth from the universe a wet release of suction. Claw-tipped legs slammed to the ground all around Thomas. Jillian shouted something, but Dauðr took no notice, its eyes blazing red at Thomas. A nearby windbreak of blue spruce trees between lots collapsed, the trunks snapping like gunshots, the blue of the nettles sucked to brown.

"You sent me away." The voice was still his dad's, but deeper, dripping with bile. "And I was hungry. Oh, so hungry." A grumble, too deep for a human throat, rolled from the dad-creature. "I still am."

Jillian reached for Thomas and hefted him to his good foot. He wrapped an arm around her shoulders to keep from falling. Fear, the fear that drenched every inch, every cell of his body, faded, pushed back by hate.

The swirling snow changed to ash, and weakness spread through Thomas's limbs as if his energy, his life, were being drained.

Dauðr laughed. "You are a fine representative of your people, Thomas. Weak, pathetic. You are food. Mindless food. Mmm. You taste delicious."

Thomas clenched his fists, ready to move toward the dark stain that mocked his father, but Dauðr sprang forward; it grabbed Thomas by the throat and easily lifted him from the pavement. A cardinal fell from the sky and hit the concrete; a blue jay fell after, then a rain of dead winter birds drawn from their roosts fell around him.

Wind whipped around them as the thing's iron fingers clutched him. Thomas pulled at those fingers, but they wouldn't move. Strength drained from him.

Sirens and gunfire sounded somewhere in the distance.

A pull, somewhere deep inside Thomas, dragged him closer to Dauðr—but his body didn't move. A glossy thread, drawn out by the palm of the monster's hand, extended from his chest.

"Can you feel it, Thomas?" The words dripped from its lipless chasm. "I'm eating you alive."

Strength melted as he flailed beneath the monster's grip—the monster that looked like his father. The misery, the helplessness, dragged Thomas's eyes shut. Dauðr was taking its time, savoring every speck. Dear God, don't let me die.

Thomas pulled harder at the fingers, but his arms were lead. He hung loosely in Dauðr's grasp. A woman's scream came from behind him, from somewhere far away. He opened his mouth to call to Jillian, but words wouldn't form. Threads snaked through the air as the dark entity drew life from his world.

Then the memory of the night he died attacked his fading consciousness. The smell of wet coyote and musty cornstalks filled his nostrils, dry heat beating back the freezing wind and snow, dirt clods digging into his unclad feet, and the terror of the thing that looked like his father but wasn't.

He couldn't charge it. He couldn't attack. It was too big, too full of teeth—teeth like needles. Then the little girl took his hand, and strength flowed into him. So much strength he knew he could do anything.

The polished black stone painted with the history of Jillian's world. They were there, he and Jillian. They were both in the picture, and the little girl had taken his hand.

And Bobby. Bobby was there, Bobby the coyote. But Bobby was gone now.

"Jillian," he managed, but only a whisper, watching as the thread attaching him to Dauðr grew thicker, and his strength ebbed further.

She stepped beside him and Dauðr's surface changed; a tinge of lavender grew in the farmer's cheeks.

"Alfhild," it said. "Dóttir."

Jillian crossed her arms. "Hello, Mother."

A cough shot from Thomas.

The monster leaned forward, its hideous face brimming with needle-sharp teeth barely a foot away from Jillian's

"Why do you keep trying to end me?" it asked.

"Because," Jillian said, "you have something I want."

A deep Jabba-the-Hutt chuckle rolled from the monster that looked like his father, the form dissolving into an enormous black shadow. "And yet another champion has failed you."

"Has he?" Jillian asked, then her hand was there. Small, soft. Jillian grabbed Thomas's hand from behind and squeezed. Energy rushed into him.

Your talisman.

A look of ecstasy grew over Dauðr's dark face. Bushes across another parking lot divider burst into flames.

It's doing it, Thomas thought. It's eating the world.

His left hand shook as he pushed it into his pocket, wrapping his fingers around the six-inch piece of gold plastic.

Your talisman, Thomas.

"I kept it with me. Always," his mouth said, but the words were silent.

He pulled; the broken toy caught sideways in his pocket.

No. He pulled and pulled, but it wouldn't come free.

Another surge of energy swept through him as Jillian squeezed his hand tighter. The piece of plastic shifted in his grip and slipped out easily. The world swam before Thomas; he pulled back his hand and swung it toward the monster, the jagged tip where the toy had broken free of Snake Mountain sliced the monster's shadowy skin as it passed. Black ichor oozed from the wound.

Blood. I've drawn blood.

The monster growled and squeezed Thomas tighter. Black spots swam in his eyes as he swung his arm toward Dauðr again; the broken end of the snake struck the glaring red eye of the monster, its screech a sound that never came from a human throat. Thomas slid his palm over Skeletor's snake, wedged firmly in the monster's eye socket, and shoved. The snake burst through the eye, and hot, dark liquid squirted over his hand, his skin sizzling at its touch but he felt nothing.

The black shadow twisted to become his father, the face of a coyote oozing from the side of its head, melting into the dark, twisting flesh. More strength flowed into his arms and he pushed harder, the plastic snake disappeared into the black beast. The body grew beneath his dad's clothes, then it exploded. Dauðr shattered and Thomas collapsed onto the ash-and-snow-covered asphalt.

Jillian half-caught Thomas as he fell, easing him to the pavement, his body drained, his head a skull covered in too-tight skin.

"Thomas," she whispered.

He tried to move but couldn't. She held him, cradling his head in her lap.

[6]

Thomas's eyes fluttered as Jillian stood. A scorpion monster took two gangly steps and collapsed. The vortex overhead flickered, the death of an old TV screen, the blue and indigo swirls drained of color. The whirlpool collapsed upon itself, and the wind died. The body of Dauðr lay in a heap of blackened ash that the winter wind pushed across the snow. What remained of the tornado of souls dissipated into the night. The giant creature above struggled for breath; already rotting sections of its exoskeleton peeled away and crashed onto the pavement, the putrid stench of decay filled the air.

Lights and sirens flashed into the parking lot, the straggling remains of police and fire-response vehicles from departments spread too thin by the night's horrors.

Then a woman's voice said, "Hello?" nearly too softly to hear. "I need help."

"Who's that?" Thomas whispered. My mouth's dry. So dry.

Jillian held up a hand and his eyelids became heavy.

Dear God. Jillian. Daughter? She's, she's—

The thought grew faint as Thomas tried to stay conscious. Jillian stepped over him, walking around the smoldering remains of the monster. A woman, the pregnant woman, once the home of Dauðr, lay on the ground, conscious. Fear and confusion stained her face.

Thomas watched through slits as Jillian walked to her and knelt. Tears ran freely down the pregnant woman's face, and Jillian wrapped an arm around her shoulder. "It's going to be okay," she said. "Help is coming. Rest now."

Jillian waved a hand over the woman's face. A slight lavender glow remained over her features for only a moment before she dropped into sleep. Jillian stood and ran to the stain that was Dauðr as emergency vehicles swarmed toward them.

What are you looking for? Thomas wondered as the elf woman with the teeth bent and sifted through the blackened ash.

"Where is it?" she shouted. "Where is your—"

Her eyes flashed red, and he heard no more. Unconsciousness dropped him into an abyss.

Savannah, Missouri—2017

Thomas didn't see Marguerite Jenkins at the funeral for Boyd and Emily; didn't expect to, really. It was just that she was part of all this whether she could remember it or not. Thomas and Jillian waited a few weeks and finally visited her at her parents' home near Savannah, Missouri.

"Yeah, I remember it all," Marguerite said. The three sat in lawn chairs behind the house, a wide expanse of brown grass ending at a hole that was once a country pond. Things like grass, trees, crops, and resting water disappeared from northwest Missouri after the Night of Explosions, but the state's agricultural people were working on bringing everything back.

"It was like watching a horror movie on a black-and-white TV," she continued. "I could hear my voice say words, and feel my body moving, but the words and the movements were out of my control. I was living a nightmare."

Thomas could relate. Part of his life had been a nightmare too. But all that was over. He and Jillian were living in Uncle Boyd's house. He worked at a local garage, was back at school finishing his teaching degree, helped his dad out on the farm when he could, and had given his mom a hand with heavy lifting when the city council commissioned her to paint a mural on a new building downtown. Jillian worked at a preschool. Her favorite thing was to teach the children finger painting; she was a natural at that. She also took care of the house.

Except the cooking. He did all the cooking.

Life was good, except that floating around Thomas's mind was a question Jillian would never answer, no matter how much he pushed for one. "What happened when Dauðr died?" He knew she had answered an important question for him that night, but couldn't dredge up her response. The last thing he remembered was Jillian pawing through the monster's remains, unable to find what she sought. Whatever it was, Thomas had a feeling she was still searching for it.

"Marguerite is in counseling," Marguerite's mother said as she served them iced tea made with the bottled water FEMA shipped in to the region. "And the doctor said she'll get through all this—eventually," she continued, before Marguerite shooed her back to the house.

"Mothers," she said to Thomas and Jillian, rubbing her swelling belly. She grimaced as she shifted in her chair. "Oh, man. I can do this. Just two more weeks until Jake comes. I hope I won't be that embarrassing to him."

"Jake?" Jillian sat forward in her chair.

A slight smile crawled over her face. "Yeah. He's going to be a boy. His father—" Marguerite's voice dropped at the word. "His father's name was Robert, so I'm naming my son Jacob. I want nothing about my baby to remind me of that sick bastard." She stared out over what was once the pond. "It's strange . . ." she said, her voice trailing.

"What's strange?" Jillian asked.

"Well." Marguerite sat her sweating glass on a lawn table. "It might be first-mom overprojecting, but I think Jakie's already communicating with me. I can hear what he wants. You know, inside my head. When he wants me to eat Nutter Butters because he's hungry. When he wants me to play music. When he wants me to read certain books, like *Peter Pan*. It's—yeah—it's strange. I—" She paused; her shoulders slumped. "I hope there's nothing wrong with him." She looked at Jillian, eyes wide. "Do you think that monster that was inside me could have done something bad to my baby?"

The smile that grew on Jillian's face was the most genuine smile Thomas had ever seen on her.

"No, Marguerite," she said. "I can honestly say your *sonr* will be the most perfect being I could ever imagine. You're a lucky girl."

Marguerite squinted at Jillian. "*Sonr?* What's that?"

"It means 'son' in ancient Norse," she said. "Sorry, it's a family thing."

<hr />

They didn't stay long. Jillian said she had a headache from too much sun. "Good-bye, Marguerite," she said. "Take care of little Jacob. I can't wait to babysit."

They walked across the lawn toward Thomas's car, holding hands. Jillian smiled again.

"What are you so happy about?" Thomas asked, kissing her hand as he opened the car door for her.

"Oh, nothing, really," she said, sliding into the passenger seat and clicking her seat belt. "I just have a feeling I'm going to be a great godmother."

Thomas stood outside the open driver's-side door. "Godmother? I don't remember her asking you that." He slid in and secured his own belt.

She leaned back and closed her eyes. "Not yet," she said. "But I think I'm going to make her an offer she can't refuse."

Thomas swallowed as he put the car in gear and drove into the afternoon, clouds beginning to gray over the horizon.

Acknowledgments

A WRITER AT WORK IS not glamorous. In my case, picture an unkempt introvert in his pajamas at a desk in a dark room, keyed up on coffee and pounding words into a computer, many of which won't make it into the finished product. It's enough to make you shiver. And, when a writer's not writing, they're grumpy. At least I am.

Thank you, my patient family, for giving me the time and space to write and be grumpy.

Although writing a book is a lonely task (I guess I do have The Beat Farmers, AC/DC and a mix of '80s music to keep me company), publishing a book never is.

Thank you, my first readers—my wife Kimberly, my high school friend David Kanoy, and my fellow D&D nerd Chris Komorech—for giving me input on *The Girl in the Corn*, most of which was that the manuscript needed more work, which I ignored. That came back to bite me later. If you're thinking about writing a book, folks, please listen to those people you trusted enough to read your unpublished manuscript. Sorry, Kim, Dave, and Chris. I'll listen next time.

And, thanks to everyone on the CamCat team who helped me so much.

I'd also like to thank podcaster and loveable rascal Tim Binnall who wanted a mention in each one of my novels so he'd be part of the "Offuttverse" (his word). Here you go, Tim. In this novel, your car gets stolen.

I hope you all enjoyed *The Girl in the Corn*.

Jason Offutt
September 22, 2021
Maryville, Missouri

For Further Discussion

1. Which character did you relate to most, and why?

2. How seriously would you take a six-year-old convinced they've seen something unbelievable, and why?

3. What role does the rural location play in the story?

4. Jillian tells Thomas fae inhabit his world. How would you react to this, and would you wonder if anyone you knew were fae?

5. How would you react to the paranormal aspects of this story if you were Boyd?

6. Characters in *The Girl in the Corn* fall on the "good" side, or the "bad" side, but is everything as simple as that? Is anyone completely good or completely bad? And, honestly, sometimes how can you tell the difference?

7. What would Thomas's life have been like if he'd simply walked away from Jillian?

8. At any point of this story, was Bobby capable of redemption? Why or why not?

9. Is this simply a tale of good vs. evil, or something else?

10. Considering the story's ending, what does the future hold for Thomas, Jillian, Marguerite, Jake, and the world?

Author Q&A

Q: What inspired this book?

A: My six-year-old's love of fairies and the fact that I suspect from lore world-round that fairies are NOT as kindly as the Disney corporation lets on.

Q: What was the greatest challenge when writing this book?

A: The greatest challenge when writing any book is finishing it. There comes a point during the process when (and I think most writers would agree) you get stuck and consider that maybe tossing the laptop against the nearest wall is a viable option of where to take the story next. Getting over that impasse is tough, but I've written long enough that I've, thankfully, found ways around it.

Q: Are there real-life models to your characters?

A: Thomas is a bit me in the early part of my life. No focus, no goals, no ambition. Simply going from job to job, not sure what I wanted to do until life thrust it upon me. Kyle was partly my dad (who was, surprise, surprise, a farmer who never pursued a teaching job even though he had the degree). And Boyd was a compilation of the various rural sheriff's I covered as a reporter early in my journalism career. Cops like Boyd exist, or at least they did back in the day.

Q: What would you consider to be your main characters' strength/ weakness?

A: Thomas's main strength is he's, at heart, a moral guy. His weakness is the fact that he has no real goal to work toward until Jillian comes along.

Q: How do you research your book(s)?

A: For *The Girl in the Corn*, a lot was experience. I live in the area I set the novel in, I grew up on a farm, and I worked as a journalist and spent a lot of time around rural sheriffs and their deputies to know what they're like and how they operate. The parts I wasn't so familiar with (how to make ricin and cascading C-4 bombs with homemade timers), I looked up. I'd hate for the FBI to ever dig into my internet search history. Oh, yeah, and the fae. I wrote five non-fiction books on the paranormal, as well as a paranormal-themed newspaper column "From the Shadows" that ran four years. Although no one can be 100 percent accurate when it comes to the paranormal, I based Jillian on interviews I conducted with people who had relationships with people who claimed to be fae.

Q: What would you consider the key theme of this book?

A: Not just that people should take a stand against evil (pretty obvious, I think. Shouldn't we be doing that already?), but that sometimes it's hard to tell the good from the bad.

Q: What do you want your readers to take away from this story? A thought? Hope? Idea?

A: Two, really. First, always do what's right. Second, not everything is as it seems.

Q: What was most fun about writing this book?

A: The fun part of writing any novel is creating characters who do things you would in no way do in real life.

Q: Do you have a favorite quote/book/writer?

A: Favorite quote: "No great mind has ever existed without a touch of madness," Aristotle.

Favorite book: This is a tough one. In my opinion, *In Cold Blood*, by Truman Capote, is the best book I've ever read, but I've also read *The Hobbit*, by J.R.R. Tolkien, at least thirty times since I was 12, so there is that.

Favorite writer: Rod Serling.

Q: What would you consider your super power?

A: To find humor in everything. For example, years ago when my mother was in the hospital recovering from surgery to remove part of her colon (cancer—a nasty thing), I informed her she now had a semi-colon. She didn't think it was very funny, even with all the morphine. I thought it hilarious.

Q: What about that quote/book/writer attracts you?

A: These people saw reality differently than the rest of us do, which makes their reality more real than ours.

About the Author

JASON OFFUTT WRITES BOOKS. He is best known for science fiction, such as his humorous *So You Had to Build a Time Machine* and his end-of-the-world zombie novel *Bad Day for the Apocalypse* (a curious work that doesn't include zombies), his paranormal non-fiction like *Chasing American Monsters* (that does), and his book of humor *How to Kill Monsters Using Common Household Objects*.

He teaches university journalism, cooks for his family, and wastes much of his writing time checking Twitter. You can find more about Jason at his website, www.jasonoffutt.com.

Twitter: @TheJasonOffutt • Instagram: thejasonoffutt

If you enjoyed Jason Offutt's

The Girl in the Corn,

you will enjoy his

So You Had to Build a Time Machine.

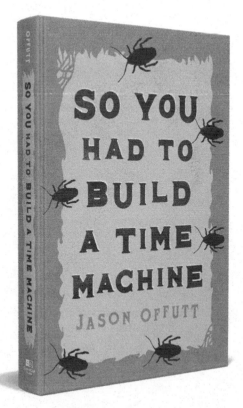

Chapter One   September 1

IT WAS A WARM, PLEASANT Kansas City evening, the sun dropping below the skyline as Skid walked home from work. A drink in a friendly quiet place to unwind, she thought, would be nice. Slap Happy's Dance Club was not that place. It was crowded, loud, and for whatever reason Skid liked it. Sitting at the bar, she ordered a vodka tonic, smiling at the people on the dance floor. People she had no interest in talking to. That was a headache she could do without, not that anyone would bother her tonight. She hadn't washed her hair in two days, and she was sporting a sweat-stained T-shirt.

Then some moron sat next to her.

"Hey," he said, startling Skid. That barstool had been empty a second ago. The guy was about forty and dressed in Dockers. A whiff of ozone hung in the air around him. *I hope that's not his cologne.*

Skid nodded. "Hey."

He looked nice enough, but lots of people looked nice. Her father Randall wouldn't approve of him, but Randall didn't approve of anyone.

"I'm Dave," Dockers guy said. "Let me buy you a drink."

Skid froze. *Let me buy you a drink* wouldn't fly tonight. No, sir.

Her plans were: Drink. Relax. Go home. Do not repeat. *I shouldn't have come in here.*

"I'm Skid and thanks, but no th—" The bartender set a Bud Light in front of her. "—anks."

"You're welcome," Dave said through the neck of his bottle, and Skid knew this conversation wasn't going to end well.

A frown pulled on the corners of her mouth as she turned away from Dave and looked across the dance floor. A big hairy guy in red flannel stood next to the bathrooms. He could have stepped off the side of a Brawny Paper Towel package. Yikes.

"Is Skid your Christian name?" Dave asked, laughing, "The Book of Marks, right?"

Don't do it. Don't talk to him. Her last relationship ended two months ago when a thirty-two-year-old fool who acted like a teenager thought dating a nineteen-year-old behind Skid's back was a good idea. Spoiler alert, it wasn't. She'd successfully avoided men in her life since that one (*Guy? Jerk? Loser?*) and planned to keep it that way. She wanted a quiet life of watering plants, reading, and sitting in coffee shops ignoring everyone, especially those pretentious types who thought they were poets. She also wanted to find a couple of women who liked to binge watch online baking shows and didn't make her want to jump out a window. Of course, that would mean getting close to someone.

Now there was this guy.

She turned to him. Dave who drank Bud Light grinned at her like he'd just won twenty bucks on a scratchers ticket. Skid never bought scratchers tickets.

"I had a wreck when I was a kid," she said, pausing for a drink.

"Russian dancing bear, clown car, motorcycle, and tire skids. The usual. Now, if you—"

"Your last name's Roe, isn't it?" Bud Light Dave said.

"Maybe." Skid cut him a side look then elaborately looked around the bar for someone, anyone else, to talk to besides Bud Light Dave. There were no good prospects, so she decided to finish her drink, leave, and pick up Thai food on the way home. Stopping at Slap Happy's Dance Club was looking like a bad idea. Her eyes briefly met those of Brawny Man, who quickly turned away. The giant stood scanning the room with his back to the wall.

She sucked the last bit of vodka tonic from her highball glass, slurping around the ice. The bartender set down his lemon-cutting knife (absolutely the wrong knife for the job, Skid noted) and motioned to her empty glass. She shook her head.

"I'm a doctor," Bud Light Dave suddenly said, which seemed as likely as him being Mr. Spock from *Star Trek*.

She squinted at him. "Sorry. I don't have any pain. Unless I count you."

Bud Light Dave took a long suck off his bottle. "I'm not that kind of doctor. I'm a theoretical physicist. I spend most of my day postulating space-time."

Maybe, she considered, he actually thought he was Spock. She'd dated worse.

"Where?" Skid asked.

Bud Light Dave gazed at a beer poster, the guy holding a can of cheap brew and way too old for the bikini model next to him. "A little place south of town. Probably never heard of it."

"Try me."

"Lemaître Labs," he said, turning to face her. "But I probably shouldn't have mentioned that," his voice suddenly a whisper lost in the music.

She had heard of the place, a government weapons lab. Skid lifted her empty glass and swirled, ice clanking the sides. *Leave. Leave, Skid. Go home.*

But Skid couldn't resist two things: one, knee-jerk self-defense, and, two, proving someone wrong.

"Okay, science boy," she said, setting down the glass. "What's the underlying problem with the Schrödinger's cat scenario nobody talks about?"

A smile broke across Bud Light Dave's face. He smiled a lot. "I knew there was a reason I sat by you." He leaned back on his bar stool. "It's not so much of a problem as it is an ethical dilemma. We don't know if the cat inside the box is alive or dead, but we do know looking inside will kill it if it still is alive. At this point, the cat isn't alive, and it isn't dead. It's alive *and* dead. The would-be observer has to ask himself a question: should I, or should I not open the box, therefore preventing, or perhaps causing, the zombie catpocalypse?"

For a moment, just a moment, Skid considered she may have misjudged this guy. "Yes, but I was going more for chastising Erwin Schrödinger for being a bad pet owner."

This brought out a laugh, and Skid realized Bud Light Dave's smile was kind of nice, and, maybe the way his eyes looked in the dim bar light was kind of nice, too.

She shook her head. *No. Go home, now.*

"What about you?" he said. "What was all that about the Russian dancing bear and the clown car? You don't look like the type."

"Excuse me?" Her eyes flashed. She'd dealt with this kind of bullshit all her life and hated it. "What do you mean by 'type'?"

He took a drink and shrugged. "If I may perpetuate a probably unrealistic stereotype: four teeth, gang tattoos, rap sheet, the usual. You seem too well-educated to be a carney."

Standing, she jammed her glass onto the bar coaster. "My father had a master's degree in chemical engineering and worked at Los Alamos National Laboratory before he ran the family business."

Bud Light Dave nodded. "Los Alamos? Daddy was not a light-weight. What's the family business?"

Skid stretched over the bar and plucked the knife from its citrus-stained cutting board. "Hey," the bartender barked. She ignored him.

"A circus," she said. "I grew up in a fucking circus." Skid took a deep breath and drew the knife behind her ear, holding it by the tip of the blade.

Bud Light Dave was motionless. Someone behind Skid shouted, and Brawny Man took a step toward her but stopped. Skid lined up the too-attractive fake-boob model in the Dos Equis poster at the end of the bar.

"Skid," someone said. Bud Light Dave probably, but she couldn't be distracted. *Why are you doing this, idiot? Just walk away.*

But it was too late, she'd put herself in The Zone. Skid's arm shot forward and the knife flew from her fingertips. A blink later the knife was buried an inch into the wood paneling behind the poster, the blade pinned between Fake-Boob's baby blues.

Skid uncurled her hands toward Bud Light Dave and wiggled her fingers. "Ta-da."

A couple nearby clapped, but she didn't notice. She was proving some kind of point.

"So, you were raised in a circus, huh?" Bud Light Dave said, still grinning. "What's your rap sheet look like?"

Good people worked in the circus. Nice people. Sometimes even honest people. Family worked in the circus. Randall's mantra ran through her head—*If something needs done, do it*—and before Skid knew what was happening, she'd pulled her right hand back in a fist and let it fly at Bud Light Dave's stupid face.

The connection was solid. He fell backward in slow motion, the best way to fall, like Dumbledore from the Astronomy Tower, or Martin Riggs from the freeway. Blood splattered from Bud Light Dave's nose as if he'd caught a red cold. A smell, like a doctor's office, flooded Skid's nostrils as he dropped. She twisted her shoulders for a follow-through with her left if she needed it, just like Carlito the strongman had taught her, but she didn't need it. Bud Light Dave was there, on his way down, falling through air that suddenly felt thick and heavy.

He was right there.

But he never hit the floor; he simply vanished.

MORE SPINE TINGLING READS FROM CAMCAT BOOKS

CamCat
Books

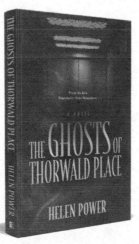

Available now, wherever books are sold.

CamCat Books

VISIT US ONLINE FOR
MORE BOOKS TO LIVE IN:
CAMCATBOOKS.COM

FOLLOW US

CamCatBooks   @CamCatBooks   @CamCat_Books